THE SISTERS OF HOPE SQUARE

Also by Faith Hogan

My Husband's Wives
Secrets We Keep
The Girl I Used To Know
The Place We Call Home
What Happened To Us?
The Ladies' Midnight Swimming Club
The Gin Sisters' Promise
On The First Day Of Christmas
The Guest House By The Sea
The Bookshop Ladies
The Women at Ocean's End

THE SISTERS OF HOPE SQUARE

FAITH HOGAN

An Aria Book

First published in the UK in 2026 by Head of Zeus,
part of Bloomsbury Publishing Plc

Copyright © Faith Hogan, 2026

The moral right of Faith Hogan to be identified as the author of this work has been asserted in accordance with the Copyright, Designs and Patents Act of 1988.

All rights reserved. No part of this publication may be: i) reproduced or transmitted in any form, electronic or mechanical, including photocopying, recording or by means of any information storage or retrieval system without prior permission in writing from the publishers; or ii) used or reproduced in any way for the training, development or operation of artificial intelligence (AI) technologies, including generative AI technologies. The rights holders expressly reserve this publication from the text and data mining exception as per Article 4(3) of the Digital Single Market Directive (EU) 2019/790.

This is a work of fiction. All characters, organizations, and events portrayed in this novel are either products of the author's imagination or are used fictitiously.

9 7 5 3 1 2 4 6 8

A catalogue record for this book is available from the British Library.

ISBN (HB): 9781035906574; ISBN (XTPB): 9781035906567
ISBN (Ebook): 9781035906550

Cover design: Gemma Gorton
Typeset by Lumina Datamatics Ltd

Printed and bound in Great Britain by Clays Ltd, Elcograf S.p.A.

Bloomsbury Publishing Plc
50 Bedford Square, London, WC1B 3DP, UK
Bloomsbury Publishing Ireland Limited,
29 Earlsfort Terrace, Dublin 2, D02 AY28, Ireland

HEAD OF ZEUS LTD
5–8 Hardwick Street
London, EC1R 4RG

To find out more about our authors and books
visit www.headofzeus.com
For product safety related questions contact productsafety@bloomsbury.com

For Bernadine Barrett and sisters everywhere,
I'm lucky to have the very best.

For there is no friend like a sister
In calm or stormy weather;
To cheer one on the tedious way,
To fetch one if one goes astray,
To lift one if one totters down,
To strengthen whilst one stands

— Christina Rossetti, *Goblin Market and Other Poems* (1862)

1

Blythe

Thirty-Four Years Ago

It was probably not Blythe's earliest memory, but it was her most vivid of all from childhood. It wasn't even a good memory, not really and perhaps that's why it stuck with her. They were in the old tree house at the bottom of Pappy's garden in Hope Square. She and Rae; of course, they were always together. Mrs Macken, the lady novelist who came into the hotel every Thursday afternoon to drink coffee with Pappy, said they were peas in a pod. Except of course, she was wrong, and Blythe had told her so, too. They were not peas, they were sisters.

'The sisters of Hope Square,' the old woman laughed.

'The Sisters of Hope Square.' Rae repeated it now when Blythe told her about them both being no better than Pappy's runner beans. It was one of those long summer days. Their parents had travelled over to the mainland on some business that meant they had to go alone. It was no hardship on Blythe to be left at the hotel for the day. Mrs Daly, the cook, would make them lunch and Blythe had the run of the place, so long as they stayed out of the way of paying guests.

Today, because the weather was fine and Mrs Daly had a funeral lunch, she'd handed them old blankets and a box of chalk and told Blythe, they could make their own fun in the old tree house until she called them for lunch.

It was a novelty for Rae to climb up what felt like a great height to the top of the wooden ladder. When you were at the top, you were taller than Pappy, not so tall as their father, but still, if you stayed near the back, you were hidden from view. Blythe was eight years old this summer, she'd been climbing up here since she was Rae's age. She'd lost interest in it, for a while, but now her sister was allowed to come up too, it was fun again.

They were prasticing their numbers. Rae was due to start school in September and even though everyone knew Miss Macken was the loveliest teacher in the whole world, Blythe didn't want the other kids calling out her sister for not knowing her numbers.

They were cuddled up in the blankets when she heard a man's voice, singing loudly somewhere near Pappy's borders. Rae looked at her with wide eyes, there was something unsettling about the voice. They crept to the edge of the tree house, peered down to where Pappy's roses were a backdrop of pink and fuchsia and red.

The man was in the middle of them. Pulling out whole bushes with his bare hands and shouting. Everything about him seemed a bit mad. He moved with a manic looseness, as if someone had slightly loosened the hinges on his arms, waist and neck. His roars were growing louder with every plant he pulled. His words, terrible words, cursing Pappy and the hotel and all their family.

Rae, next to her, began to cry. Blythe fearing the man would spot them and come up and pull them from their roots next, dragged her as quickly and quietly as she could to the back of the tree house. She pulled her close, huddled down into the blankets. Still, they could hear the howling, becoming louder, filthier. Blythe tried to hush her sister, but Rae was terrified, shaking and crying and sucking her thumb, a habit she'd promised to give up before she went to school.

'Hey!' it was Mrs Daly. She must have heard the racket from the kitchen. 'What on earth are you doing there, Charlie Carney?'

'Hah! I'm saying goodbye to this dump and Jack Scott can go do what he likes, but he's never seeing another penny of my money.'

'You won't be much of a loss. I'm sure Mr Scott will get on just fine without you hanging around the bar like a bitter breeze.'

'What on earth?' That was her grandfather's voice. Next to Blythe, Rae struggled to get out from beneath her hold and the blankets wrapped around them. 'Off with you, Charlie, you're not content with wrecking your own home, you think you'll do the same to everyone else's.' Blythe had followed Rae to the edge of the tree house. It was like watching a horror movie, or what she imagined it would feel like to watch one, because her heart was racing. Next to her, she held on to Rae for fear she'd fall off the edge, she was so transfixed by the macabre sight before them.

'It's the last time you'll go and collect my wages before I do…' the man said, and he pulled one more plant with a flourish. Now, Blythe could see, he was bleeding. All down his arms, probably cut open by the thorns.

'If you don't want to pay your debts, keep away from my hotel.'

'That won't be a problem anymore. I'm out of here on the next ferry,' the man said now, and he thumped the air with such ferocity, he almost lost his balance.

'Well, may the wind be at your back,' Pappy said then and Blythe wasn't sure what that meant, but whatever it meant, the man made a grunting noise before looking around the garden and she thought for a moment, he might strike out at the hydrangeas next. She held her breath, but then he turned and suddenly, it seemed as if he had stiffened up.

It was almost an anticlimax really, when he walked out the back gate.

'It's his poor family I feel sorry for, those lovely boys, you couldn't get a better kid than Kip Carney,' Mrs Daly said. They had moved down to inspect the damage.

'Well, the mother is a decent enough sort, I suppose.'

'Aye, she's too good, that was half the problem. Those boys will take after her, with a bit of luck.' Mrs Daly picked up a beautiful rose; it was a miracle it had managed to survive the culling and crushing.

'Still, the apple never falls far from the tree, I wouldn't be having too much to do with any of Charlie Carney's lot. They're coming from bad stock, no fault of their own. But you can't change what's in the blood, can you?' Her grandfather picked up his precious plants one at a time and laid them on the path, as if they might be about to be put to bed.

'Will they be alright, Pappy?' Rae called down to him now.

'They'll be fine.' He smiled up at his two grandchildren.

'Lucky it wasn't apples, so…' Blythe said, thinking of that thing he said that she didn't understand.

'I suppose it is,' her grandfather laughed. 'Do you girls want to help me save them?' He didn't have to ask them twice. They scampered down the ladder and were stuck to him for the afternoon, replanting the roses that stood a chance of survival.

'Ah, how Gisela loved these flowers.' Her grandfather spoke softly now. 'Nature was her refuge when she came to the island first. She lived in Still Water House, you know that? She was so happy here, she set her heart on the place for her grandchildren. That's why we bought it for your parents.' Pappy smiled down at them now.

That day, it seemed to Blythe everywhere fizzed with a brilliance that held the air with a strange mixture of significance and anticipation. She felt it in the hotel too when they returned to it for lunch, the brasses gleaming, huge bouquets of fresh flowers crushed to attention in vases on every surface. The windows shone, smelling of fresh lemon and vinegar and glinting in the afternoon sun. In the reception the long sideboard was heavy with plates of mixed sandwiches and a huge bowl of jelly trifle. The boiler bubbled up behind the bar, on hand to fill the fat tea pot warming above it.

'Der Liebling,' Pappy said softly, as they tucked into lunch. 'Your old granny would be proud; two lovely Enkelin…' He still spoke smatterings of his wife's German when he was emotional. Blythe looked up to see tears in his eyes and maybe young as she was, she understood the difference between tears that are sad and those that are grateful. It was important to him; the idea of his legacy being carried on. He'd told her about how her grandmother came to this place without a relative to call her own, only to find herself blamed for a war she had nothing to do with. Gisela was one of the lucky ones, sent off to boarding school in Sussex just weeks before her family was blown up in a bombing raid that took out not just their home and factory, but half the village too.

The Bäcker family certainly had no appetite for war. Gisela Bäcker had found herself as a young girl, in a country where she wasn't welcome, without a living relative in the world to call her own. Her best friend, another outsider, Wendy Johnson, from an Anglo-Irish family insisted that she spend her holidays with her family at Still Water House, on Pin Hill Island. It was as far away as one could get from a world that seemed to be intent on turning itself inside out. One fateful summer, the German orphan girl had fallen in love with an islander called Jack Scott and that was that.

Jack Scott, a young ambitious farm boy had little more to recommend him than good looks and a capacity for hard work. When he had clapped his eyes on Gisela, he knew, immediately, she was the one for him, even if his parents and his friends tried to talk him out of having anything to do with the German girl. He set his cap at Gisela and within the year, they were married.

There was a trust, money her father had squirrelled away in American bonds. Although it took two years for it to be released, and when it was, it was certainly much shrunken from the vast fortune that her family had built up through their small but lucrative engineering works.

When it came, it took them both by surprise. They'd been living modestly in a small room above the local haberdashery where Gisela had managed to get a job as a shop assistant. An inheritance from Germany went a long way on island property prices, as islanders left in droves for jobs and what they believed would be a better life on the mainland.

If Gisela was treated with some suspicion, thanks to her German background, her money was welcomed warily. Behind closed doors, some of her neighbours harboured jealousy and bitterness against the striking young couple who seemed to be setting out on a path that no one else was brave enough to take nor had the money to join them on. The idea of a hotel was far beyond what anyone ever expected on a place like Pin Hill Island. But, the big old Georgian houses on the square were being abandoned one after the other, buying one and then another proved well within their means as prices plummeted and confidence in island living shrank.

Jack and Gisela opened the Hope Square Hotel with a lot more optimism than business savvy, but somehow, they pulled it off.

Blythe begged her grandfather repeatedly to tell her the story of how he'd fallen in love with her grandmother and how the hotel had come about, just one more time. She was fascinated by the photograph of Gisela, a thin blond woman, with eyes the colour of lilacs – although there was no way of knowing that from the sepia print on her grandfather's sideboard. There was something about her, haunting, as if her early experiences of life were never quite forgotten. Although her smile was wide – there was no missing how she held onto her husband's arm as if it was the last raft in an angry ocean.

'Now, there's tea and biscuits,' Pappy said, and he ruffled Rae's dark curls affectionately. Blythe loved coming to the hotel and not just for the biscuits. When she was here, Blythe felt as if she had uncles and aunts all through the village. Every time she went out the door someone stopped her, knew her name, asked after her parents and Pappy.

'Aye, that's Muffeen Mòr for you, die Herzhen.' Her grandfather smiled as if he was as proud of Blythe as he was of the island and this hotel he loved so dearly. And Blythe's heart was swollen with love for him and for the hotel and for the island, too.

2

Blythe

Present

Already, the apple trees were abundant, the branches pulled low to the ground with heavy cookers nesting between the leaves. Blythe knew, even from the look of the first buds at the start of the season, it was going to be a bumper crop. It helped that the trees had shelter at the front of the house from the strong winds and sea spray from the Atlantic that roared in winter at the back of Still Water House. Last year was disappointing, so the trees had rested and this year, with a little extra care, they were coming up trumps. Blythe took great satisfaction in the thought that her hard work, pruning and fertilising, had paid off.

Today, she would make apple crumble. It was early, yes, but there was no point leaving fruit on the trees for the crows to come along and peck at them. She was looking forward to packing up the old Aga with her mother's trays and filling the house with the aroma of cooked apples and baked crusty sugar. Her home cooking was part of the reason Still Water House had maintained a high four-star rating on all the best accommodation sites. Of course, the house itself was charming, a vast white Georgian, sitting on its own mature grounds with twelve bedrooms currently to let out and original features she'd been careful to retain and restore. It wasn't just the house that people loved. They had, she knew, the perfect location, a sweeping drive at the front and to the rear, a still water pool fed from the dramatic Atlantic Ocean beyond. She had invested a lot of time and energy over the years in making it into something very special. She had a feeling that this year, after twenty years in business, was going to be its crowning glory.

This year was going to be her year. The Still Water's year. She was sorry that Marcus Johnson had not lived to see it. And Pappy, too. She had a feeling that Pappy would have been happy and proud, despite everything that had happened. And Marcus? Marcus would have hated it; the idea that she somehow passed him out – the Hope Square Hotel would never be a White Diary property.

She was certain, that this year Still Water House would finally take its place among the cream of Ireland's country house crop. Obviously, she had applied before; every year for the past five years in fact, to be included in the Irish Country House White Diary. It was the most prestigious listing in the country; inclusion was reserved for only a very select number of properties. It had been Blythe's dream to see the house feature in it since she had set out on the path of opening the house to guests. Until this year, there had always been some impediment to her acceptance. She suspected the biggest obstacle was that they were stuck out here on an island. The house had to be reviewed by an undercover inspector and from what she could make out, that evaluation was carried out by a woman in her late seventies with severe gout and mobility issues.

Late yesterday evening, she received a booking online with queries around dietary options and accessibility for an elderly female guest, who hoped to come and stay in a few weeks' time. There was a series of questions around travel and most importantly, amenities available to a single, immobile woman of a certain age. The potential guest called herself Morwenna Whythe. Blythe had known instantly, it had to be Maura Whither, the publisher of the White Diary.

She knew she shouldn't count her chickens before they'd even become eggs, but she had a good feeling about this. She would wow Morwenna Whythe, with Siggy at her side and even Kip. All the little old ladies adored her husband, Kip.

Blythe smiled now thinking of the apples, full and ripe in the garden. Siggy loved apple tart too, like mother like daughter. They could have some later, and the rest she would allow to cool before storing them in the trunk freezer at the back of the pantry. She looked at her watch, it was almost eleven. No point hanging about. She used the long bread knife to ease out, dislodge and then pull down an old shopping basket from its resting place at the top of the kitchen dresser. Blythe knew she was the only one of her friends who still enjoyed nothing more than settling down to a morning of baking. Most of the other women she knew had proper jobs. They did things like nursing or teaching or project management. Blythe had no idea what project management was – she'd left college before she'd finished her degree. It had all happened so quickly, Pappy calling her home because her parents had been in the most awful accident. At the time, it hadn't felt like a sacrifice at all. That had been her life, she'd never worked outside the family home and business. There had been no need. Their family owned a huge hotel. They were known as the Hope Square Sisters, it meant something then, she and

Rae, young, pretty, their futures mapped out before them – or so they thought.

Funny how things turn out, no one would ever have imagined she'd end up with Kip Carney. Least of all, Blythe or Kip, probably. Although, she'd fancied him like mad when she was at school, but Kip was one of those guys – everyone fancied him. Of course, he was older than Blythe, back then, he hardly knew she existed, probably. He was that rare blend of being as good natured as he was good looking. He was far too busy playing rugby and keeping up various part-time jobs around the village to have much time for anything else.

Pappy had set his heart on Robbie Hall for her. Robbie's family owned a huge hotel on the mainland. Water under the bridge now, all that felt like a million years ago. She still thanked her lucky stars – or maybe her mother, for steering her in the right direction all those years earlier. Even now, seventeen years after they got married, it still pulled her up short, this love she felt for him. He was her rock, even if it sounded too hackneyed to say aloud. Kip wouldn't believe it anyway, because he absolutely believed it was the other way round. And he certainly didn't mind if it was too corny to admit it. They'd been together through thick and thin. She'd never have made it without him. While the general population thought it was a cosseted life, living in the big house, being from the hotel people on Hope Square; the truth was, from an early age, it was hard work. Blythe had been turning out apple crumbles and sherry trifles with ease since she was twelve.

As the years passed by, she found the whole process of baking and cooking for her family and the guests they kept all year round had developed into an almost meditative practice. Nothing could possibly go wrong in the world when you were elbow deep in a doughy mixture.

She set her basket on the ground beneath the first apple tree and reached up, taking a moment to admire the firm cooking apple in her hand. The birds had not yet begun to wreak their worst upon them. Hah! She smiled; glad to have beaten them to it. In her pocket, she heard her phone beep, that annoying sound that was always followed by six more alerts. WhatsApp. She was in so many groups at this point; the damn thing drove her bonkers sometimes. Between her charity work, the school governing committee, the grower's market of which she was a founding member and the various groups her friends had set up for book club and general gossip, very often Blythe found herself wishing technology had never progressed beyond the landline. She slipped her hand into her pocket, pressed the little button at the side of her phone. That would either switch it off or silence it for a while.

Later. She would sit down, when the Aga was full, have a cup of tea and check her messages.

The morning flew by; it always did when she was busy. Kip had managed to get a few days' work, repairing some garden furniture at a retirement village on the other side of town. Her daughter, Siggy, was at school, she'd be home just in time to dig into warm apple crumble. Blythe sighed contentedly, there was no great hurry with having lunch or indeed doing much more than pottering about for the day. Her work in the guest house was mostly done for the day, the rooms were made up and ready, the garden looked splendid, and the pantry was full. She'd learned from a young age, that the secret to running a successful business was being prepared, and there was no better feeling than knowing every job on her checklist was ticked off.

By the time she'd finished clearing up, the kitchen began to sweat with the warm heat of the Aga and the aroma of stewing apples, spicy cloves and fresh baked pastry.

'Something smells good.' Siggy slipped around the door, sniffing the air appreciatively.

'I baked your favourite,' Blythe smiled, her daughter always made her heart feel a little lighter. Motherhood had surprised her in how much she'd delighted in it, especially when Siggy was smaller. Even if pregnancy had taken her by storm (well, maybe hurricane was more accurate), once she laid eyes on Siggy, that was it, she dived headlong into a whole new baby powder scented world of finger painting, Play-Doh making, bark tracing, and rock pooling. Whatever else life had thrown her way, or not thrown her way, as it turned out, the gift of Siggy was one she would always be grateful for. Blythe had called her after her own grandmother. It was a family name, passed through generations that had been obliterated in the second World War, leaving only Gisela Sigried Bäcker – a woman she'd known only through the handed down tales from her grandfather. As Siggy had grown, she'd become an equal mix of both her parents – inheriting the Bäcker lilac-coloured eyes and Kip's easy-going way. Siggy was striking, more than beautiful, with height from both Rae and Kip, she was almost six foot and these days, thankfully, she walked tall. She smiled easily and she chose her words carefully – a trait she hadn't inherited from her mother! Her daughter was a young woman Blythe felt justified in being proud of, more with every passing day. If she had one wish for her daughter, it was that she would be content to stay forever on Pin Hill Island. Siggy was only seventeen, too young to settle down, but she wanted more than anything something to anchor her daughter to this place. She was the only Scott of her generation, the last Hope Square girl left. Well, technically, she was a Scott-Carney, but she would inherit everything, this place and the hotel, one day it would all be Siggy's, Blythe was adamant about that. She was a great kid, but Blythe knew, better than most, how easily life could swap out what you wanted for what it felt like giving you. She was absolutely determined; her daughter would not be short-changed in life. She would keep her safe, keep her close, help her to avoid making the same mistakes that had cost her so dearly. 'It'll be ready soon, I was going to have some with coffee and sit outside, will you join me?'

'You don't have to ask me twice.' Siggy shared her mother's sweet tooth; she could sniff out sugar from rooms away. Blythe listened as Siggy chatted away about everything and nothing, as daughters do if you're lucky. While Siggy set about making a pot of coffee, Blythe placed the five apple crumbles on the drainer to cool. They would be safe here so long as she dragged the dogs outside, away from temptation. She cut two generous slices from the smallest tray.

They were just sitting comfortably when there was another flurry of notifications on her phone. Siggy pushed the phone towards her mother.

'You had it switched off again.' She shook her head in disbelief, she was always doing that, picking up Blythe's phone and switching it back on again.

'Oh, later…' Blythe said, she really didn't want to spoil her afternoon just because Fiona Dixon had decided it would be a good idea for them all to fundraise for some new cause.

'How can you leave it to later? I couldn't do that in a million years,' Siggy laughed, and Blythe knew; Siggy never missed a call or a message. She checked religiously, constantly swiping her screen over and back, she had the dedication of an addict to it. 'It could be important, it could be Dad.'

'It definitely won't be your father.' Blythe laughed, Kip's only interest in the phone was following the rugby results.

'Fine.' She picked up the phone, clicked open the app. There were dozens of messages, across several groups. It was as if everyone she knew had gone message crazy. All those thumbs up, they made her feel dizzy. They weren't just in the groups either. She scrolled down through the names until she came to a message from one of her closest friends.

'Well?' Siggy's voice intruded softly.

'Hang on...' Blythe said, scanning quickly through the messages. 'Good news,' she looked up at Siggy. 'A new family are moving into the McDaid cottage.'

'Oh, that is good news,' Siggy said as she pressed the plunger on the coffee pot.

'Apparently, they're moving in next week.'

'Are they related to old Henry?' Siggy asked.

'They must be, I mean...' That cottage had been tied up in a legal wrangle for over a year at this point. Henry McDaid had died without making a will and it seemed that suddenly he had more relatives than you could count.

'Well, if not, new people in the village will be a good thing,' Siggy said softly. And of course, she meant it, her daughter was sweet like that, expecting the best in everyone, it was another reason to worry about her. The world beyond Pin Hill was not as rosy as her daughter believed, Blythe had learned that the hard way. She hoped more than anything, that life would not throw her darling girl in the way of things to spoil that about her.

'Hmm,' Blythe said, because you never knew exactly who was going to show up on the ferry and decide to put down roots; although that wasn't a conversation she wanted to get into with Siggy – they'd had too many disagreements about it recently. Too often, Blythe found herself biting down words to avoid another long debate with her increasingly liberal daughter.

3

Rae

Present

Rae peered at her reflection in the half-light of her bedroom mirror. She sighed. She'd have to do. She patted down her hair, probably she could do with a visit to the hairdresser, but really, for years she'd just made do, clipping it when it annoyed her, so it never really looked as if it grew at all. Other women her age coloured their hair. She knew several of her school chums who'd easily pass for a decade younger than their true age. Rae's hair had turned pewter grey when she was still in her twenties. She'd gotten out of the habit of having it properly done. Marcus had convinced her, of course. They couldn't be seen to favour one business on the island over the other. It was literally, Duffy's or Doherty's – Nell Duffy had a small salon above the local credit union. At the other end of the village, Dawn Doherty operated a very brisk trade in the front room of her Victorian redbrick. At first, it didn't seem such a big thing. After all, back then, all she had to do was run some shampoo through it in the shower and she was 'done'.

Later of course, Rae recognised what she had given up; without even realising it. It was not just about safeguarding bookings for the hotel by remaining neutral in the ongoing cold war between the two hairdressers. It wasn't even about saving money, which was always top of Marcus's mind. Now she could look back and really reflect, she realised, it was not just her hair that had suffered. That one decision had so many other consequences. Most of all, she missed the gossip and the camaraderie of those monthly visits to Dawn's. Would she have told one of those women what her life was really like? Maybe and maybe not, but Marcus made sure that opportunity never arose. More than that, she knew now, as she looked at her reflection in the mirror, not taking care of herself properly had made her smaller. She'd actually shrunk into a smaller version of herself. For a long time, she couldn't bear to look at her reflection in the mirror. She had once been a striking, vital girl – but living a small life all these years had taken from her, not so much her looks (true what they say, wasted on the young). It also chipped away her confidence, or maybe her very essence.

Marcus was gone almost eighteen months at this stage. And still, it felt as if he was here, watching her and judging her if she boiled one drop more water than she needed for her cup of tea. She had changed nothing of her life since he'd died. Had she dreamed of something better without him? How on earth could she start to propel her life forward at what felt like this late stage? The truth was, she couldn't possibly make an appointment with Dawn Doherty now, fearing it would, as Marcus had fully convinced her, cause ripples of gossip around the island.

She might as well face it, she was turning into an old woman, long before her time. Maybe that was the price of fifteen years of being at the very bottom of your own list of priorities.

That afternoon, instead of a few hours much needed pampering, she kept their annual appointment, with the accountant. Still, she had to make some small effort, there was no good turning up there looking like she'd just lost all interest in life, when in fact that had occurred many years earlier.

Phil O'Connor had been doing the hotel books for years. Marcus liked her because she was cheap. Her rates were much lower than you'd get on the mainland, that's for sure, even if he disliked the idea of anyone knowing the ins and outs of their business. Probably, at some point, Rae knew, she could have taken on the job herself, but Phil didn't have very many clients. They'd been at school together, so she stayed, it felt like a small act of defiance.

'We're ticking over?' It wasn't so much a question as it was an optimistic presumption. She said it as she placed a cup of coffee down on Phil's desk. She'd bought them two lattes from the coffee shack that had opened a few years earlier down at the sea front.

'You don't need me to tell you that your income is down a lot this year,' Phil said, her voice as neutral as if they were talking about the price of sand in Arabia. 'I know, it must be hard, but...' of course, she meant, since Marcus had died. Rae had noticed it since her husband passed away, this habit people had of avoiding mentioning it, while still alluding to it. As if it was the beginning and end of all her problems, the excuse for all things beyond her control and yet, no one was brave enough to put a name on it.

She wanted to tell them they had it all backwards; but there was no room in pleasant conversation for that.

'I've stopped doing weddings,' Rae said softly.

'But aren't they rather...'

'They were our biggest income stream.' Rae looked towards the window. Phil had an amazing view of the sea from here. Honestly, Rae thought, she could sit here all day long and watch the foamy waves break out in the bay.

'And you've just…' Phil looked as if she wanted to ask a thousand questions, obviously flummoxed, she had no idea where to begin. Hope Square was the only proper hotel on the island, but they'd never made a profit on just offering hotel accommodation.

Marcus was the one who came up with the idea of boutique island weddings. It really took off after the marriage equality referendum. Suddenly, there was a surge in weddings and couples who'd been dreaming of getting married forever wanting to tie the knot immediately. DINKY's – double income, no kids yet – couples were happy to pay over the odds for somewhere charming, somewhere different, away from their daily lives.

Marcus had tapped into the market, pricing well above the going rate for a product that he sold as unique. An island wedding, in a boutique hotel, the Georgian grandeur of the Hope Square Hotel, where guests could flood out onto the town square where for a little extra, they could pitch a marquee and feel as if the village mall was thrown in to the package. At this point, there must be thousands of wedding photographs sitting on office desks taken beneath the great old horse chestnuts on the square. To be sure, it was a lucrative business, but Rae just didn't have the stomach for it. In Rae's opinion, binding yourself to someone for all eternity was far too long to be stuck in limbo if your marriage was not happy.

'Weddings?' Rae said and she knew that Phil, like everyone else, would assume she was too heartbroken to carry on with events that reminded her of her own loss. She had settled into an uncomfortable chair opposite Phil, and she looked around the office now. It was spruced up, just a bit; there were new shelves, a fresh coat of paint and the addition of a print of a huge salmon leaping from water that looked so vibrant it made Rae shiver. 'That's…' she pointed to the print.

'Jarlaith's,' Phil said and she turned to gaze on it as if it was painted by Michelangelo himself. 'A birthday present, sure where else would I hang it?'

'It's very striking.' Of course, Rae had heard that Phil's son had been shortlisted for a photography award a few years earlier. 'You must be very proud.' She felt that familiar taste of envy, although, the idea of children of her own had long ago been abandoned. And since Marcus died, she had Siggy, who really, she loved as much as she could any child of her own.

'Ah, you know,' Phil said then, because she'd never been a woman to wear her heart on her sleeve, even if it was obvious she was as proud as punch. She shuffled the papers on the desk before her. 'The thing is, Rae, from what you've given me, I don't think you have enough to pay both your tax and the mortgage on the place.'

'Of course I have enough to pay my…'

'The bank payment hasn't gone through in six months…' Phil held up a sheaf of statements as if she needed to prove it to her.

'No, no. Of course they've been paid, there must be some mistake, it transfers automatically from the hotel account… we've never missed a payment.' She leaned closer, took the pages in her hand, the only thought in her mind that perhaps she'd sent over the wrong statements. She looked down through them, there were payments here and there and everywhere, but when she looked back to the previous month, there was no payment to the bank. These were the correct statements; she looked up at the top of the page to check. 'I don't understand how...'

'You simply haven't had the funds to cover them when they were due,' Phil said but she had lowered her voice as if to keep the news from the salmon leaping from the water.

'They haven't been in touch to ask for a meeting or... not even a letter in the post. I can't believe it.'

'They might not have spotted it yet, but they will and by the time they do, between penalties and everything else, you could be looking at up on twenty thousand euro just to set things straight and then, there's the rates...'

'Oh, God, I forgot about that...' The previous year, she'd managed to cut a deal with the council. They'd halved her rates because for almost six months they'd torn up the path in front of the hotel and ripped apart her car park while they sorted out the village water system. This year, they'd be looking for the full amount and there was no cutting a deal with them a second time round.

'There's also the tax bill.'

'Well, that one I have to pay.'

'The good news, if I can call it that, is that it's a lot less than other years, because...'

'Because business is down?'

'I'm afraid so. By my reckoning, it's down by a lot. I mean, I don't know how you're still open, never mind buying me lattes.' Phil smiled at her now and they both laughed. They'd known each other for years and maybe, if you couldn't laugh when things were bad well, then, what was life anyway?

'So, what next?' Rae asked, because surely, there was something they could do.

'Easy enough to solve if you have a couple of suitcases of money stashed under some of those hotel beds,' Phil said. 'Or else, you need to go to the bank, see if they'll negotiate, lengthening out the loan, bringing down the monthly repayments, they might, you know, you've banked with them for years...' She stopped because they both knew, that meant nothing these days. The bank that Rae had always been a customer of had closed the local branch and now, the nearest branch was on the mainland. She didn't know anyone there and they certainly didn't know her or have any great fondness for her business. 'Sorry, it's been a tough run for you, I can't imagine how you're even still opening your doors, much less managing to keep the place looking as good as it does in spite of everything else around you.'

'Ah, you'd do the same.' It was terrible, but Rae heard herself say these things, even though the very mention of Marcus's death filled her with complex emotions of which grief was only one. A year and a half later, and she was still floored with the intensity of her feelings. They say it gets easier; she couldn't imagine that happening any time soon. So far as Rae could see, it just got easier to hide it from others if not from herself.

'Let's sort out the tax bill first,' Rae said because they had to start somewhere, and it seemed as good as anywhere to begin.

Later as she sat in her little flat at the back of the hotel reception, Rae thought about this place that had been her home and work for two decades now. God, there was so much family history in it. Four generations of Scotts had lived here. Her grandfather had invested its future in her, well in Marcus mostly, convinced that he would have the business acumen to carry it on for generations to come. Pappy had believed she would leave it to her children, and to her children's children, so the Hope Square Hotel would carry on long after she was gone. Her sister, Blythe, thought the same. And sometimes, it felt as if it was far more important to Blythe at this point than it had been to her grandfather way back then.

Funny.

Rae had worked her whole life here, or near enough it, but maybe it was because of Marcus's sudden death, somehow it just wasn't the centre of the world to her anymore. If it ever was? Her plans had been scuppered before she'd ever had a chance to make them. What did she know when she was seventeen years old? When she was a kid, she wanted to be Joy Adamson with a lion called Elsa and to spend her life helping animals. Later, she lapped up every episode of *All Creatures Great and Small* and longed to train to be a vet. What had happened to that? Life. Her parents' death when she was too young to handle it had sent her off the rails when she'd most needed to feel the ground firm beneath her feet. Marcus had come along, and he had wrapped her up in a security blanket that had made her feel safe. Somehow, without her realising, his ambition became her life's work. Marcus had charmed her grandfather, whispered in his ear those things Pappy most needed to hear; Blythe probably still couldn't see that he'd been the one to come between them as sisters. Dreams of being a vet had faded, and this place had taken over. Rae had stepped up to the plate, she'd done her duty, but now, as she sat here looking around the tiny sitting room, it felt as if it was all empty promises. Her life was hollow, and she was losing heart. It had never meant to her what it had to Marcus and to Blythe. Now, it felt as if it was slipping away from her even as she sat here.

4

Kip

Thirty-Four Years Ago

It had been an ace day, until the moment Kip Carney had swung open the door into the tiny kitchen expecting his mother to be standing as she usually was at their kitchen sink.

He was rushing home to tell her his news. Mr Flaherty, the school principal, had got word he'd been picked for the junior Connaught rugby team. He'd called him from class, no bad thing as Mrs Murphy was trying to beat a bit of Irish into them. Kip liked Mrs Murphy. Alright, so she told him he was as thick as an ass and wondered aloud daily what his mother was thinking sending him to school at all. Kip couldn't understand how other kids seemed to be able to string all the letters together that just jumbled up on the page before his eyes. He couldn't explain to his annoyed teacher that he was cleverer than any of them on the football field. But once the spring shot daffodils through the hedgerows, he occasionally brought a small bunch for her desk because he knew she liked them, and she often slipped him an extra banana from her lunch box if she spotted his own was thinly filled.

'Mammy, Mammy, you'll never guess what,' he'd come rushing in from the front hallway, full of his news to share with her – when you're twelve years old, the whole world revolves around you. Or at least it did for Kip Carney until he pushed through the door that day.

The weird thing was that the kitchen was exactly the same. Quieter, somehow, emptier, his mother instead of standing at the kitchen sink was slumped to the floor in front of it. Her nose bloody, her gaze strangely unseeing – even when he drew up close and fell to his knees next to her, she hardly blinked, never mind looking at him.

'What happened? What is it? Did someone do this to you?' His mother never answered him. But somehow, he gathered her up, she was a tiny thing. Already, he was taller than her, broader than her, strong enough to carry her probably, if she'd trust him to. He bundled her across the floor into the rocking chair that his father often said was older than all of them put together.

Now, Kip wasn't sure what to do, once his mother was safely in the chair. He looked around the kitchen. Then he walked to the cupboard where his mother kept what little medicines were needed in the house. There were plasters, TCP, cotton buds and paracetamol – surely some of these could help to patch his mother up.

He grabbed the lot, brought them to the table next to his mother. 'I'll get Dad, he'll know what to do.'

'No, Kip, no,' she murmured. 'Your father is gone.' She reached up her sleeve and pulled down a tissue, began dabbing it at her bloody nose.

'Gone where?' His father never went anywhere, well not during the day anyway. You could set your watch by him. On dole days – he was up and spruce to go and collect his money, then, six nights of drinking in the local pub and a seventh night of darkened mood when everyone knew to keep clear of him.

'Gone gone.' She shrugged and then she began to cry again, as if her heart would break and somehow, Kip understood. His father had left them.

'It's alright Mammy, everything will be alright.' He put his arm around her shoulder, although it was uncomfortable – theirs wasn't really a family for hugs and the likes.

'Will it?' she looked at him now.

'It will,' he said with a lot more conviction than he felt.

'How will we live? I mean...' She looked around the kitchen, their needs were simple, but even so, they were just about scraping by.

'We'll be fine,' Kip said, although he had no idea how.

As it turned out, without his father in the house, they were better than fine. Once his mother's sadness faded and his brother's anger subsided, their home became something it had never been when their father lived with them – peaceful.

Oh, the kids in school had a field day, of course, jibing and jeering at them, but Constance Macken, his favourite teacher in the school, told Kip not to be minding them, instead to show them all that he was better than any of them at the one thing he was good at.

Kip lost himself on the rugby pitch. He was fearless, relentless and always sportsmanlike; a clean and honest player who relied on talent and hard work. Everyone thought Kip was all about the rugby – but Kip knew, to be a good man, you had to have a lot more to you than that. And he wanted more than anything to be a good man, to be a much, much better man than his old man had ever been.

5

Siggy

Present

Siggy Carney had learned early in life that it was easier to go along with things than to strike out on your own, especially where her mother was concerned. She knew her friends had regular screaming matches with their parents about everything from the length of their school uniform skirt, to being allowed to go to the youth club disco on the mainland.

For her part, Siggy had no interest in wearing anything but school trousers, and even they had to be especially ordered because she was taller than the other girls at school. Skirts were a disaster. She had her father's legs – great if you're a rugby full back but best kept covered if you don't want to be called thunder thighs. Thankfully, they hadn't called her that in a while, she hoped if she stuck to pants, they might forget about it. As to the idea of going to the mainland for what seemed to her like a sort of prolonged cattle mart, well, it was an easy pass. Crowded places made her feel panicky and music that was too loud loosened something in her brain, so her balance veered off on a course that made her feel trippy –

and not in a good way. Her mother truly believed that Siggy was simply pliable. Blythe Carney had no time for things like being overcome in crowded places. She could barely abide friends who had gluten intolerances. Vegans were a pet hate. She called them faddy eaters. Her friends, girls she hung out with at school at least, had no idea that Siggy was relieved not to be joining them on nights out. Not that she'd admit it to her mother or to the other girls, but in some ways, it was a relief to be molly coddled when it came to avoiding the monthly club nights the other girls seemed to live for.

She told Rae, though, because she knew her aunt would not judge.

'You could stay here, if you wanted, you know, for a sleep over?' Rae said. She had overheard some of the other girls in the corner shop, discussing what they would wear to Girls Night.

'I suspect even that would be a red flag to my mother.' Siggy laughed.

'She's just afraid for you...' Rae said then and she switched on the coffee machine. The hotel, as usual, was empty, just the two of them. It was hard to believe that they'd lived on the small island for seventeen years, but it was only in the last eighteen months she'd begun to really get to know her aunt.

'It's crazy, you know she basically picked out all my friends for me in primary school.' It was true. Her mother had set about designing a circle around Siggy that consisted of only *the right sort of girls*. Daughters of shopkeepers, well-to-do farmers and the local school principal were in. Anyone who lived in a council house or whose parents claimed a social welfare payment was frozen out with cool distance and tidy remarks that somehow always contained a 'but' at the end.

The fact that the 'chosen few' were level one bitches seemed to be completely lost on her mother. 'You know, she still warns me about the mainland kids on a weekly basis.' Siggy rolled her eyes. The mainland kids were a bunch of girls and boys sent across to attend school on the island. On school nights, they stayed with local Irish speaking families – because their parents wanted them to get extra Irish language tuition in classrooms with a third of the numbers of any school on the mainland. 'Seriously though, how far astray does she think I could go? Pin Hill is hardly a "den of iniquity".' She put that into air quotes. It was one of those phrases her mother had used when she was talking about some scandal she'd read in the Sunday paper. 'It's not like she can stop me growing up, even if it feels like that's what she wants; to keep me as this perfect little girl forever.'

'You can probably blame me for that.' Rae shook her head and handed Siggy a cup of steaming black coffee. This was their secret guilty pleasure. Her mother certainly wouldn't approve. Double shot espressos with biscotti on the side – more than two and Siggy got the jitters. Rae confessed that if they drank them after five, she wouldn't sleep for the night.

'I don't see how it's your fault,' Siggy said, sipping the coffee. Rae was the mildest, kindest, most non-judgemental person she knew.

'Oh, you think I'm chilled now, but when I was your age, I was the handful.' Rae laughed now and so did Siggy. Nothing seemed less likely than her sensible, ugly-shoe-wearing aunt being a wild teenager. 'Still, though, it's good to get out and have friends, you know, shoot the breeze,' she said this as if she was trying out the phrase. Maybe she was right, but Siggy would far prefer to come here than hang out with a bunch of girls who spoke non-stop about things that made Siggy feel like an outsider. 'I bet if you talked to them both – I mean, your dad isn't like that, is he?'

'No, my dad isn't like that, but he agrees with her on everything. I think if it was left to my dad, I could do just about anything. He'd been off playing in South Africa when he was my age – imagine, South Africa back then – how cool was that?'

'Your dad was always the coolest,' Rae giggled as if remembering something that brought her right back to being seventeen as well. And Siggy wondered, why on earth they hadn't spent more time together over the years, why it was only now they were really beginning to bond.

'Yeah, but that was like a gazillion years ago.' Siggy rolled her eyes, she couldn't imagine her dad ever being cool. These days, he lived in Snickers pants and the mullet hair he'd had in his heyday was cut within a millimetre of a buzz. 'He's like a properly old man now, in his fifties. Urgh,' she said distractedly, because out on the square, she noticed a boy she'd never seen on the island before and there was something about him, she found it hard to take her gaze away.

'Well, no matter, I'm sure they'll come to terms with you getting a bit of independence before you collect your old age pension,' Rae joked, following her gaze, and they both laughed, because sometimes, it felt as if they were on the same page, without a single word being spoken. The boy was hot, good looking in a way that you couldn't miss, no matter what your age. Rae was so different to Siggy's mother. God, they were two opposite sides of the coin and yet, somehow, she looked at them and she envied them each other. They should be close, fused together tighter than Siggy was to any of her so-called friends, and yet, here they were – sisters divided in some strangely unspoken way over something

Siggy couldn't fully understand. It was something to do with the hotel and her mother's decision to turn their home into a guest house. Still Water House was way busier than the hotel these days, although, Siggy had a feeling that Rae didn't give a hoot about things like that.

In fact, sometimes Siggy wondered, if Rae cared about anything much at all, apart from the legion of cats she fed at the back door of the hotel and of course, she cared about Siggy. There was no question about that. And in return, Siggy adored Rae, there was something about her aunt, a connection that ran deep. A few months earlier, Rae had offered her a part-time job. Just a few evenings a week after school. Blythe had agreed, through slightly gritted teeth, that she could take up the offer. The fact was, there was little or nothing to be done when she arrived in for her shift in the afternoons. Instead of changing beds and cleaning showers, as she would have had to do if she was working under her mother, they sat with coffee and biscuits and chatted happily about everything under the sun. There were no limits with Rae, she felt as if she could say anything and it would be okay. Instead of going back home tired, Siggy felt almost relieved – she could talk without a filter, laugh at things only the pair of them found funny and for those few hours, she felt as if the pressure was off. For a brief respite, there was no end of year exams, no book that her mother expected her to read, no guests in room nine that she needed to think of when she craved a long hot bath but instead had to ration the water, just in case.

'Everything alright? You look worn out.' Because she did, she looked positively worn out today. Siggy only noticed it now that the boy had moved away and she really looked at her aunt.

'Ara, I'm grand, don't heed me. I'm just tired, that's all, I didn't sleep very well, must have drunk too much coffee yesterday,' she smiled, but Siggy had a feeling that there was something more worrying her.

'So, no more coffee today.' Siggy flicked on the kettle for a refill. 'Green tea?'

'I know, I know, I'm a glutton for punishment, but I need coffee.'

'On your head be it,' Siggy said, and she rinsed their two darling old china cups and set about grinding up the beans for fresh coffee. 'It's quiet here.'

'I'm sort of glad of it, if I'm honest. I think I need to do a reset.'

'Okay,' Siggy said, and she hunted around the coffee machine to find the stash of biscotti that usually sat on the saucer if she was serving a customer.

'There's a packet of ginger nuts there somewhere; we've had the last of the others,' Rae said, reading her mind. She took a gaily patterned spiral notebook from the sideboard and sat again at the table with large banquet chairs around it, just a little away from the window.

Of course, Siggy knew why she always chose this spot. As sure as they sat in the window seat, there would be people coming in for coffee. For some reason, if the place looked empty, they tended to walk on by. It was a pity, because Siggy loved the elegant window seat which looked out across the village square, with the great old chestnut trees almost crouched down with heavy branches of huge leaves. It was the perfect spot to people watch from, or just to sit and look out at the world – or the tiny patch of it that was Muffeen Mòr, pass by.

This place. Sometimes, it felt as if time had stood still. Except of course, it hadn't. Nothing ever truly stays the same. Look at Marcus, so much a part of this place and then when no one was expecting it, all that vitality just gone out like a light. She thought about him often. Funny, because in real terms, she hadn't been close to him, but when she stood still in the hotel, it felt as if he was still here, lingering close by, keeping an eye on all of them.

Her father's van parked up just a little way along the square caught her eye. She hadn't realised he was meant to be working in town today. Siggy could have sworn he was meant to be helping at the retirement home, clearing winter away from the grounds so the residents could make the most of the good weather ahead. Perhaps he had stopped off to run some errands in the village. Then, she spotted him standing a little way over on the green, almost hidden amidst the thick tree trunks. He was talking to someone and Siggy peered a little closer. Rae was right, her dad was a legend on Pin Hill Island back in the day. Capped for Ireland – it was a great honour to have someone from such a small place on the Irish rugby team. Even still, people – especially older people – loved to stop him to chat about the latest match and what he thought were the chances for this year's Triple Crown. She realised some time ago that he never complained if he had to have the same conversation ten times over in the one week. He just stood there and chatted and smiled and tapped people's backs and said, *well, you never know, maybe this year*, as if they all had some part in how things would turn out. People loved her father, no doubt about it. Siggy caught herself smiling as she watched him, kneeling now on the banquet chair to get a look at who he was chatting to this time.

Fiona Dixon. Her mother's friend? She was an unlikely woman to want to talk about rugby, perhaps she was offering him a job? But then, as Siggy watched, she saw Fiona move forward as if in slow motion, put her hand up to Kip's face, as if she was about to kiss him.

No.

No way.

She must have been imagining it. She moved closer to the window, changed her angle slightly. From here, it seemed as if they were much further away from each other. No. No. It must have been her eyes playing tricks on her, surely Fiona Dixon would not have set her cap at her dad?

That would just be ridiculous.

And yet, as Siggy continued to watch them, even as they went their separate ways, she couldn't quite shake the feeling that she'd seen something completely out of kilter with what she wanted to believe to be true.

Her father and Fiona Dixon – even the vague notion of it knotted her up uncomfortably, drying her mouth and making her feel as if the ground had somehow lost traction beneath her feet.

'There was a time when you could come in here and order a dinner fit for a king on a Wednesday afternoon. Now, all I have to offer are a few shop-bought biscuits.' Rae intruded into her thoughts and laughed as she said this, but Siggy had a feeling that it wasn't really a joke.

'You know the village has moved on from dinners in the middle of the day like cabbage and bacon or a lamb stew?' Siggy said. 'It's all wraps and paninis these days, you could do those here, if you wanted…'

'I have a feeling that the wraps and paninis will have their day too,' Rae said.

'So, what then?'

'That's the question, isn't it… authentic Italian pizza or ethnic street food – do you think the island is ready for that?'

'Hmm.' Siggy wasn't sure what to say to that. Ethnic street food was a million miles away from anything her mother was likely to serve up for dinner.

'Wishful thinking, I'm letting my imagination run away with me,' she said a little sadly then, it seemed to Siggy.

'So, what's really on your mind?' Siggy placed the coffees down before them and took two ginger nut biscuits because she couldn't resist an open packet of biscuits if she tried. 'Don't say, *nothing*.'

'No, you're right, but I'm not sure anyone can help with what's on my mind now.' She smiled at Siggy and maybe, that was part of why Siggy liked coming here, because when Rae said things like that, it felt as if they were equals. 'The truth is, I need to drum up more business...'

'With lunches?' She made a face, because surely Rae knew, that there just wasn't the foot traffic for lunches on the island – not unless she wanted to take on a contract for meals on wheels, and that was hardly a money spinner.

'God no. Too much work, not enough return, and let's face it, there's only me here now.'

'So, conferences? Events?' There was a huge market for these apparently, she'd heard her mother talking about it recently. She didn't dare mention weddings, although she'd heard her mother saying often enough that the hotel must have made an absolute fortune on those over the years. Rae had cancelled as many as she could after Marcus's death. Siggy could understand that. After all, they'd been such a happy couple, obviously completely devoted to each other, seeing other people starting out on their happy ever after – well, it was probably just too hard for Rae at this point.

'Maybe between us, we'll come up with our new USP?'

'It sounds like you're all business today.' Siggy laughed and tucked into her first biscuit.

'Okay!' Rae laughed too, held up her hands. 'I might have borrowed a management and marketing book from the library van yesterday.' She pointed towards the sideboard where a huge white hardback sat next to the condiments stored there. 'Between ourselves,' she lowered her voice.

'Of course, Aunty Rae.'

'I don't want your mother worrying, but the place is not faring well this last year.'

'It's probably been the worst eighteen months ever.' Siggy reached out and took her aunt's hand in hers. 'I mean, come on, give yourself a break.' If there was such a thing as an annus horribilis, then that's what the last year was for the Hope Square Hotel and for Rae in particular. First Marcus died – which was enough to knock anyone sidewards – and just as the funeral was driving towards the cemetery, the council began to rip up the whole square and most of the hotel car park to fix water pipes that so far as anyone knew never needed fixing to begin with.

'Unfortunately, the bank doesn't really care about that and neither does the tax man, and both have to be paid.'

'Oh, Rae.' So that was it, the hotel was in financial trouble. Of course, she should have seen that from a mile off.

'Ah come now, it's not that bad. There's no good crying over spilt milk, but I must do something about it. And as of now, I'm promoting you to the role of marketing manager.' She held up her coffee cup in mock salute.

'Fancy title.'

'Yes, sorry it doesn't mean a pay rise, kid, but you know, you've got to roll with the punches.'

'You know I don't expect payment for my consultancy work.' Siggy made a face. 'Anyway, with the family legacy at stake, the least I can do is roll up my sleeves when I can.' She'd do anything to help Rae out. 'Actually,' Siggy said then. 'You know, Mum wanted me to train as a cook...'

'Yes.'

'I've always preferred the trade fairs, getting out and meeting people, selling the place, I mean, I'm not sure how good I am at it, but I've been going to them since I was yay high...' Rae would be terrible at it, they both knew that. She had as much killer instinct for sales and business as a goldfish in a piranha bowl.

'I'm sure you'd be brilliant at it, but before we go packing our bags for the tourist fairs, we need to think about our...'

'USP?'

'Exactly,' Rae said, and she took up her cup and raised it to Siggy and they toasted a new beginning for the hotel. 'To better days ahead. With a bit of luck, we might even earn enough to have cream in our coffees next year!'

Later, as Siggy was making her way home, she thought about her new title. Of course, Rae was only ribbing her, but if she could help in any way at all, well, she'd be happy with that.

She must have been daydreaming as she rounded the corner off the town square, because she managed to walk straight into the boy she'd been watching earlier.

'Oh, I'm so sorry...' she stuttered. God, she nearly gasped, he was even better looking up close. She felt her stomach cartwheel, the strong coffee suddenly feeling too heavy for this warm day. Then, remembering herself, stepped back, embarrassed, knowing full well that she'd managed to stand on his feet as well as almost coming close enough to kiss him.

'My fault,' he said and he too took a step back, and almost bowed as if saying sorry to royalty. 'I'm new here, I should watch where I'm going, rather than look all round me as I walk...' He was young, maybe her age, maybe a year older, dark-skinned, eyes that creased up in the sort of smile that made not smiling with him utterly impossible for Siggy.

'Let's agree it was both our faults.' She laughed. 'I'm Siggy by the way.'

'Danial. Danial Val. I've moved into a cottage,' he nodded back towards the pier, 'with my grandmother. The McDaid place?'

'I know it well. We all wondered who would take it up, as soon as the sign came down from outside, the island grapevine has been alive with speculation.' She laughed again, she couldn't help it, something about him made her feel lighter, happier.

'I'm not sure we are what you were expecting.' He looked towards the path.

'I hope people have been welcoming,' she said then, because she knew well enough, some of the islanders could be a bit off with newcomers. Her mother was not alone in her intense suspicion of anyone who had not been born and bred on Pin Hill.

'Mostly, but you know, it's a small place, we're... different,' he said, and he smiled at her.

'Well, I'm appointing myself your official welcoming committee, right now,' she said and they both laughed at this. 'You are very, very welcome to Pin Hill Island.'

'Why thank you, madam of the welcoming committee.' His voice was smooth, his accent sitting somewhere between

Oxford and European, he made another bow, deeper this time, as if he might almost genuflect before her. He was making fun of her and the sight of him prompted a fit of giggles. 'Look, I don't know if it's okay to say this,' he stood now to his full height before her. Unlike most of the other boys on the island, he was taller than her. Probably, she'd guess, six-three, six-four, it was nice, he made her feel almost delicately feminine by comparison. 'Maybe, we could go for coffee or a coke or something... if you're free...' He was watching her now, but she could see, he was endearingly self-conscious.

'I'd like that.' She stopped herself from adding – very much – knowing that even if it was true, it would make her sound too available.

'Okay,' his smile was infectious, so they stood there, gawping and smiling at each other for rather too long, until Siggy remembered, her mother was due to pick her up on her way home. Her mother would not like Danial Val. Siggy knew this without even having to think about it.

'So, I better get going,' she spotted her mother pull in on the square opposite.

'Tomorrow at the coffee shack?' he called after her.

'Say around twelve?' That would give her time to get the breakfast rush over at home with her mother.

'Okay, that's a date.' His smile was amazing. It felt like pulling herself away from a magnet as she made her way across the square to her mother's parked Volvo, all the while trying to keep her expression as neutral as possible. This was a secret she wanted to keep to herself for now, and it felt as if she was hugging something wonderful close to her for the rest of the evening.

6

Blythe

Twenty-Two Years Ago

There was never a question in Blythe's mind that one day she would run her grandfather's hotel.

It was in her blood.

Rae might be carried away on the idea of becoming the next Dr Doolittle, with every stray cat and dog in the village traipsing about after her, but Blythe wanted the hotel.

She was there at every opportunity.

She called in on her way to school, after school, every weekend, over the summer holidays, there was forever something to do, Pappy always managed to keep her occupied.

'I swear, I think your father must have added something to your tea when we weren't looking,' he often joked, and she could see how proud he was when she took on some job and made a success of it.

Blythe could make a bed with hospital corners quicker and better than any of the local women he employed to come in on busy mornings. By the age of ten, she could turn out an apple tart better than her mother, by twelve, she was turning them out by the half dozen in no time.

'Oh, if only there were grandsons,' he'd say sometimes and then he'd laugh, because he must know, there was no boy who'd be as good at running the hotel as Blythe. Pappy was like that, thinking that the hard jobs were for men, women belonged in the home – but from the start, Blythe set out to show him that she was far better than any grandson could have been. They'd have the Scott name, to be sure, but that was all.

'Urgh, boys,' Rae shivered in a grand mock fashion and then she pulled Blythe to her, winding her arm around her sister's. 'Imagine if there were boys instead of one of us,' she sounded truly disgusted. She'd always trailed around after Blythe and as they grew, hung off her every word. 'Pappy, you're so silly, no boy would ever be as good as Blythe.' She said it with blind devotion and Blythe had looked at her and loved her even more – if that was possible.

When Blythe told Pappy she intended to go to catering college and study hotel management, she thought he'd burst with pride. He told every old codger who came in that day for lunch that his granddaughter was going to be a big wig running her own hotel one day.

Of course, Blythe only wanted the Hope Square Hotel, but who knew, maybe she'd own a chain of them – she wouldn't say no to that.

'I can't imagine anything worse,' Rae said as they snuggled down on the sofa to watch *The O.C.* that night.

'Yeah, but that's because all you want is to have a house full of cats and dogs and an endless supply of time to care for them.' Blythe rolled her eyes, they were opposites, in every way. Blythe had always been a Scott, whereas Rae was much more like her mother's side of the family – quiet, submissive, happy to stay in the shadow of her older, more ambitious sister. Maybe this was one of the reasons why the sisters were so close.

'Not entirely true, I wouldn't say no to working on...'

'I know, I know, a wildlife reserve,' Blythe laughed. Rae had more posters of lions and elephants hanging up in her bedroom than she had popstars – which made her a bit of a square among her friends, most of whom could see no further than Britney Spears and Maroon 5. She'd done her school project on David Attenborough, when all the other girls were obsessed with Harry Potter. Blythe imagined her, one day, running her own rescue shelter, with all sorts of animals under her roof, hopefully not elephants, though. 'Here, you can start practising right now.' She threw a cuddly toy dog at her sister's head and of course, they almost missed the beginning of their favourite show thanks to the ensuing horseplay.

It was Rae who made sure that Shane McPherson knew that Blythe would be expecting him to ask her to the summer fair dance. Blythe knew well that Fiona McLaverty had already set her hat at Shane, but that was only because he was like the only decent-looking boy in their class. Not that he had a lot of competition, after all, half the boys in her school were related to each other one way or another. There's no getting away from it, if you didn't fancy red hair, big teeth and freckles, Shane was a mile ahead of any of them. He was nice too, you could chat to him, like a normal human being, which was more than you could say for the rest of the savage boys their age.

A few of the other girls would want to go to the dance as his date too, but Blythe knew, well enough, the one she had to watch out for was Fiona.

Fiona was everything that Blythe was not. She dressed like Christina Aguilera and managed not to look like a haystack with crucifixes. And she was funny. People listened to her because she always said the first thing that popped into her head, which was cute – if not always kind.

She was exactly who Blythe imagined all the boys would fancy.

'What's wrong with you?' Rae said when Blythe said this aloud. 'Sure of course, Shane would pick you over horrid, obvious Fiona any day.' Rae was like that, she thought no one could hold a candle to Blythe, but then, Rae was just a kid, what did she know?

Perhaps she knew more than Blythe gave her credit for, because a few days later, Rae pretended to trip as she was walking back from school, so Shane had to link her home and of course, Blythe just happened to be home early that same day. She'd nearly fainted when she saw her sister being half carried up the drive, but years later, they'd laughed about it, because somehow, it had worked.

Shane did ask her out. Although, he saw clear through Rae's obvious trick – she couldn't lie to save her life. Blythe almost died of mortification. Still, she had to hand it to her sister when it came to loyalty, no one had her back like Rae. They went on six or seven dates, it might have gotten serious, but they lacked a chemistry that even then, Blythe knew was crucial if she was really going to fall for someone. So, when September came, she set off for the mainland without a backwards glance at Shane McPherson.

Rae for her part missed Blythe more than anything. She wrote to her sister every single week. Without fail there would be a small blue envelope waiting in the post when Blythe arrived home from college each Monday afternoon. The letters were a mix of news from the island and small drawings of dogs or cats. Rae still collected stray animals everywhere she went, it seemed like there was always some flea-bitten animal trotting behind her.

Blythe found herself looking forward to these letters each week. Of course, there were phone calls home and occasionally, her mother would make the trip to Dublin, just to check that her daughter was taking care of herself properly. Once, they went for lunch at the Shelbourne Hotel and Blythe thought she'd die with the glamour of it all.

One day, she would make the Hope Square Hotel into something bigger and better than any other hotel in the country. Already she was on course to graduate at the very top of her class.

It felt, in her final year, as if everything was coming together.

It was at the Christmas party that Marcus Johnson finally asked her to dance. Marcus was the only other serious student in the year, of course he was older. He had worked in hotels since he was a kid. Rumour had it that his place on the course was sponsored by one of the big hotel groups, but no one had the nerve to ask him straight out. He was like that, a little intimidating, serious about the work. Some of the others called him a bore, but Blythe had been drawn to him, maybe because he was older, mature, brilliant. They'd been neck and neck all the way through their course, each of them sharing top marks at an even pace from the beginning.

At the start, she disliked him, but then, somewhere along the way, she could see – he was hungry to get on, he was driven, maybe just as much or more than Blythe.

And he was good looking. Charming, when he wanted to be, with it. She had watched as he held doors open for the female lecturers and she'd wondered cynically if he thought it would affect his year-end grade.

But then, one afternoon, they'd started to talk.

Properly talk.

She'd told him about the Hope Square Hotel and how she'd always dreamed of taking it over.

'And it's all going to be yours? No brothers or sisters?' he asked. He came from a big family.

'I've one sister. Rae. No, she's not interested in the hotel at all. Happy to be a silent partner at most, I think as soon as she's finished school she's going to train to work with animals.' It was strange, talking about Rae here, all these people she'd spent the last four years with and she had no idea if they had siblings or anything else much about them beyond this bubble life they lived in college, the jumping off point to their glittering future selves.

'Our very own Paris Hilton.' He was making fun of her.

'Hardly, but we do alright.'

'I'll bet, the only hotel on the island? It must be a licence to print money.' He looked at her now and she wasn't sure if he was serious or still joking.

'Let me tell you, we work very hard. Even if we are the only hotel on the island, we offer a top-class experience. My family has been in the business for generations; nothing is ever allowed to slip.' She held his eye.

'I believe that.' He sat back a little, as if appraising her from a new distance.

'Oh?'

'Well, everything you do, here in class, you work harder than everyone else, you have…' he stopped, looked around as if he was going to say something shocking. 'Standards.'

'Standards.' She repeated the word, not entirely sure if she liked it or not, but then coming from Marcus Johnson, she knew, it meant something. 'I suppose, I have,' she said and yes, she knew, there were plenty here who only came because they couldn't get into a straight business degree. 'But so have you...'

'Ah, but the difference is, I'm driven by lack as much as by ambition.'

'Hah!' she thought he was joking.

'I'm serious. I don't have a hotel in my back pocket to fall back on.'

'Hold on, neither do I... I'm just as...'

'I didn't mean it as an insult.' He held up his hand to stop her arguing with him. 'I just meant that I'm going to have to make my way in the world and I intend to make a good job of it. I don't want to end up like my parents.'

'Would that be such a bad thing?'

'No, in some ways, maybe not. They are good people, but we haven't a bean, that's the reality. I left school at sixteen for a part-time job and I managed to make something of it, but the lives they've settled for, well, I want more. I've always wanted the sort of security my parents never had the guts to go out and get for themselves.' As he spoke, she could hear the thinnest slice of bitterness cut through his voice.

He told her about his family, their twenty-acre, mostly bogland farm in the midlands and the fact that after his leaving cert, he could not wait to get away.

He spoke plainly, but there was a vulnerability about him that he'd hidden so well before this. Blythe felt her heart soften towards him just a bit. She noticed his eyes, brown with tiny flecks of gold that flashed when the light caught them – and how they creased when he smiled at her. He was, she decided that day, the fittest of all the boys in their year. His lithe body was a result of a lifetime of hard work, working on the bog and fencing for weeks on end seemed to produce a certain sort of physique. Marcus had a body like an Adonis, it probably helped that he did very little in the way of high living.

He was good looking, too. Very good looking, in fact, now that she really studied him. And she found herself looking at him, increasingly, catching his eye and then her insides buzzed with a desire for him that caught her by surprise. Soon, she no longer saw him as a competitor, was she falling in love with him? Maybe, she liked the fact that he was ambitious; the idea that here was someone who fully intended to make something out of nothing. That day, sitting there, she absolutely believed that he would be the most successful of their class.

This was a million miles away from wanting to go to the village dance with Shane McPherson. It had all been so childish. In hindsight, it had been as much about getting what Fiona wanted – because it was like that between them; their friendship was a constant competition to see who'd win.

Shane was just a challenge – the one boy every girl wanted to go out with, because of his good looks. It didn't hurt either that he could string a sentence together which didn't involve you feeling like he was guessing your bra size at the same time. Now for the first time, she'd fallen hook, line and sinker for someone. Marcus Johnson was in a completely different league to any other boy she'd known. He had, she suspected, hidden depths and that was damned sexy, maybe more so, when her whole life had been spent on Pin Hill Island where everyone knew your business and there was no room to keep a secret for much longer than it took the tide to turn.

Blythe realised this, as she watched Marcus walking along the path towards the college, early, their first class was not due to take place for at least an hour. They were in their last semester, and it was only now she was beginning to see how gorgeous he was; how come it had taken so long? She'd been so busy competing against him that she hadn't properly noticed him.

'I need Rae here,' she thought to herself one day. 'I need Rae to fall in front of Marcus Johnson and make him walk her home, so he is ambushed into asking me out.' She laughed then, thinking of her sister's antics on her behalf. She hadn't told Rae about Marcus, mainly because there was nothing to tell. It was new ground for her. The only fella Blythe had ever really fancied on the island was Kip Carney. That was years ago, when she was a kid and everyone looked up to Kip. He was a celebrity on Pin Hill – but of course, he was way older than Blythe or any of the other girls who had his official rugby photo pinned to their bedroom wall. Kip Carney was in a whole other league.

The problem was, Marcus never went to any of the college social events. Blythe had always believed he thought himself above them. Now, she wondered if maybe he couldn't afford to socialise, not on a regular basis at any rate. There was only one way to get him on his own and that was by asking him for help on her end of year project.

'Hey Marcus,' she said a lot more breezily than she felt.

'Blythe, hey,' he said. He was putting his bag in his locker, organising his books for the day ahead. She peeked inside, couldn't help it. Oh my God, was it alphabetised?

'I wondered if I could ask you a favour...' she took a deep breath to regain her composure.

'Sure, you can ask,' he laughed at this, but when he pinned her with those brown eyes for just a fleeting second, she thought she'd melt.

'The end of year project? I'm doing it on the Hope Square Hotel – you know, I told you about...' They were meant to be doing a complete overhaul, making something more of something already existing. Most of the other students were doing their project on a nearby hotel, who'd offered the college access to its workings. 'I'm struggling with it, maybe I'm too close to it, would you take a look...' She put her head to one side coquettishly.

'I don't know, I'm quite busy with my own, I'm...' he broke off, closing his locker and turning to look at her. She found herself batting her eyelashes, even though, she was never that sort of girl. Marcus was having a strange effect on her, it was unnerving. Obviously, she liked him a lot more than she realised.

'What if I bought us both dinner, or I could make it, at my flat – you could come over one evening, have a read through and there'd be a free dinner and dessert too...' she laughed, but inwardly loathed the ring of desperation in her voice.

'Uh, okay, that sounds like a fair deal.' He flashed her one of those killer smiles again and she wanted to turn herself inside out for him, right there, standing at the lockers in the main corridor.

A little part of Blythe felt slightly guilty.

She knew, her grandfather would have a conniption if he realised that she was sharing the contents of his end of year accounts with some stranger to score a date with him. But it was all she could think of doing to get Marcus to notice her.

They'd agreed that he'd pop across the following Thursday evening, and Blythe had scrubbed and cleaned the flat until it almost shone. She reckoned anyone who kept their ring binders in alphabetical order would definitely knock points off her for a dusty lampshade, never mind the ten-year build-up of grease under the cooker hood. She'd made spaghetti Bolognese with crispy bread and splashed out on a few bottles of semi-decent plonk. It was a simple, studenty meal. She didn't want to look as if she was trying to impress him, although she had made ice cream for afters. Well, she couldn't bear to walk past the freshest of strawberries she'd spotted in Moore Street on the way home from college that day.

'Sorry, I'm late,' he said, looking at his watch and smelling the garlicky, basil infused air appreciatively as he made his way into her empty sitting room. She'd bribed her flatmates to stay away for a few uninterrupted hours.

'By about two minutes!' Blythe laughed. It was another thing she admired about him, he was always on time for class. He never forgot things either, not like some of the other boys who spent more time borrowing pages or pencils and most of them looked as if they'd never seen a hairbrush. Marcus on the other hand was always turned out like a man who was going places. He reminded her of one of those guys you see on billboards advertising designer reading glasses; smart, but there's no covering over the smouldering sexiness beneath, unlike the other boys who dressed like extras from a Nirvana video.

They pored over the project for about three-quarters of an hour. He asked all the right questions, too many of them probably. Blythe felt a crease of guilt at the amount of information she gave glibly away about the annual takings and the breakdown of where they were making the largest profits and what wasn't working. Her grandfather would faint, if he realised. But she rationalised, there was no harm in it, Marcus was not the competition, it was all in the name of love.

'You've done a terrific job, top marks!' Marcus said when he came to the final page. 'After all that, I'd love to go and see the place…' He laughed as they tucked into dinner.

'Anytime, you'd be very welcome,' she said then, buoyed up on the way the evening was going. The way he was looking at her now, it felt different to how he had seen her before, as if he was finally noticing her.

They quickly made their way through the first bottle of wine. It turned out wooing and chatting about their future dreams was thirsty work. She brought out the homemade ice cream just as it felt as if he might be about to leave.

'Oh my God, Blythe, this is delicious,' he said as he finished the first spoonful. His eyes travelled from the ice cream to her face, to the project and back to her eyes, again. When he looked at her, it felt as if he wasn't just seeing her, he was properly seeing her, maybe even undressing her, and she shivered with eager desire.

'Ah, it's nothing. Sure, I've been making desserts since I was a kid,' she said, but she had only really perfected this recipe since she arrived in Dublin. She took down the second bottle of wine and poured them both generous glasses.

'I never realised you were so…' he said, and he left the words hanging there for her to fill in, which was probably both wise and dangerous.

'I think we're both…' She leaned towards him, forgetting what she was going to say. The wine finally taking hold of her and then, somehow, he was kissing her. Short, innocent kisses at first, then something longer, deeper, probing, promising, and her whole body felt as if it was being coaxed into a net of taut expectation. The more they kissed, and his hands moved across her back, then to her face, then down and towards her breasts, she thought she'd explode with longing for him. Their breathing, heavy, their kisses more urgent – he shifted his weight next to her and she could feel the longing in him, which made her crave him even more.

Ding dong.

Oh, God. No.

Her flatmates had arrived back.

'Saved by the bell.' He laughed, pulling away from her and straightening himself up, while she tried to regain some sort of composure as she heard Diana and Chloe make their way into the flat.

The moment was broken. But still, she was filled up with this urgent need for more of him.

'I should be off,' he said then, strangely embarrassed as if they'd been caught out by her parents, rather than her flatmates.

'Don't leave on our account.' Diana laughed.

'No. No. Early morning. I'll…' he looked at Blythe for a moment and she felt as if the whole world was waiting on his next words. 'I'll see you tomorrow, yeah?' he said then and she nodded at him, because she wasn't sure she could formulate any words properly just yet, she was still so caught up in what had just happened.

'Tomorrow,' she said softly as she heard the front door close behind him and then she looked at her flatmates and they all burst out laughing together.

7

Rae

Present

Rae woke early the following Saturday morning. Still unburdened by any great idea that might save the hotel from the financial ruin it very much looked like it was facing. Perhaps she shouldn't have mentioned anything to Siggy, but she'd kept it light, purposefully so her niece would not worry. There was only one person she truly wanted to tell, but of course, Blythe was also the one person she couldn't imagine facing with the news that things were as bleak as they seemed.

Missing Blythe had become a dull ache in her a long time ago, but even then, it was already too late, now that Marcus was gone, she couldn't go crawling back to her sister, there was far too much water under the bridge for that. Their relationship had broken, in a way that while there were no obvious cracks, Rae could not fathom how to mend it. For fifteen years, it had withered slowly, it was still dying from the roots up.

Blythe had always been the hotelier among them.

Well, she and Marcus.

But of course, Marcus wasn't here now and look what had happened without him. How many times had she wondered, what might have happened if he hadn't strolled into her life all those years ago – would she have made a better life for herself? Well, if the last year had shown her anything, it was – probably not.

In the eighteen months since he'd died, she had allowed – no, more like she had fostered the drying up of the business. It should be no surprise that she was deep in debt with no real way out, not in time to make payments to the bank, the council and the tax man at any rate, and yet, somehow it all felt unreal. Honestly, maybe it wouldn't come as such a huge surprise to Blythe when she eventually told her, and Rae wondered, which was worse, the distance between them or the inevitable disappointment she would see in Blythe's eyes. She had to do something. She couldn't go crying to Blythe, not after all that had happened over the years, she just couldn't face the humiliation of it.

Instead of twisting her thoughts in a spiral that was getting her nowhere, and because the sun was up and a light breeze was whipping creamy froth on the waves, she decided to take a good bracing walk along the beach. Again, as always, she felt sad as she set out that she didn't have a dog to take along with her. She'd always wanted one. She sighed now, felt that familiar longing as she watched a russet spaniel break free from his owner a few yards ahead. Marcus was always adamant, you can't have cats or dogs in a hotel. That's what Marcus said at any rate, and she knew, there was no room for discussion about it.

As she strolled through the still sleeping village, she felt that familiar ache for company – is it possible to mourn for the four-legged companions you've never had? Rae had felt these pangs regularly over the years. It was just another thing she'd sacrificed for the Hope Square Hotel.

She was resigned to the fact that she would be remembered by the kids on the island as that slightly potty lady who knelt and spoke to every cat and dog she met on her travels.

Today the wind was heavy with the odour of bracken and seaweed. Its salty flavour rested on her lips, so by the time she turned at the end of the beach, she felt ravenous for her breakfast and a good cup of coffee. The walk back was punctuated with calling seagulls, watching herons and a group of black guillemots who were busily working the shoreline.

As she neared the pier, she spotted an unfamiliar figure, standing and looking out to sea. It was, she could see as she got closer, a woman, dressed in what looked like a cloak made of gold and rusty red.

'Hello,' Rae said as she walked up the steps.

'You had a good walk,' the woman said, her accent was thick, but her English was perfect.

'I had an early one.' Rae laughed. The coffee shack was just opening for business. 'I'm hoping that Surfer Dude will make me a strong hot coffee, do you fancy one?'

'Sure, thanks,' the woman said and when their coffees were ready, they turned back to look at the vastness of the ocean once more. 'I'm Melissa Val, by the way, I've moved into the old McDaid cottage.' She said the name as if she was trying it on for size.

'Oh, you're our newest resident, how marvellous,' Rae said then, thrilled to have someone new living in the village. Rae loved all the newcomers. They brought much needed vibrancy. They tended to be hippies mostly, or at least, they didn't strike Rae as typical nine to fivers. They wore colourful clothes that were the opposite of fast fashion and most of them had some craft business on the go. None of them spent much time or money in the hotel and Marcus had detested them for that – among other things he never fully named. Secretly, Rae envied them a lifestyle that did not run by a rigid timetable. She loved browsing their homemade art, jewellery and pottery stalls on market days. They were, as far as Rae was concerned, a healthy dose of vitality on the island – and here now, Melissa Val in her wonderfully colourful robes, with all the trappings about her of a place that Rae would never get the chance to see, well it was simply marvellous. 'What on earth brought you to Pin Hill?' she asked after they had chatted for a while.

'Basically, it's a long way from Mauritania.' The woman laughed, but there was no humour in the sound.

'I'm sorry. I shouldn't have asked.'

'It's okay. Things are just a bit raw for me still. I came with my grandson; we left everything behind…'

'Your children are…'

'My only son was… well, he died a year ago. It's just the two of us now.' She smiled sadly and Rae was struck by the quiet dignity of the woman, her sadness was palpable and yet, here she was, still standing, still gracious. This was genuine grief, beautiful, despite its unsettling rawness.

'Well, I hope you're settling in well,' Rae held up her cup in cheers.

'I'm not sure everyone is as glad to see us as you are…' Melissa said thoughtfully.

'Oh, don't worry, some of the locals can be a bit funny about newcomers, but they'll get over it. Mostly, when people come here, they settle outside the village, so you're going to be a bit of a novelty, for a while.'

Of course, there had always been newcomers. Her own grandmother had been a blow-in. Gisela Bäcker had been on the point of leaving when she had fallen in love with Pappy. No one wanted a German girl in 1946 – but Pappy adored her and somehow, against the wishes of everyone around them, they'd made it through. When Pappy had been dying, Rae had a feeling it was his darling Gisela's name he had on his lips in those final breaths.

It was strange then that Blythe had never liked the idea of newcomers to the island. Far from holding out a hand of welcome, as the descendants of an immigrant, Blythe was harsh in her judgement of any outsiders who decided to settle on the island.

By the time she returned to the hotel, Siggy had already opened for the day. It wasn't her job, of course, she still had another year in the local secondary school and Blythe normally kept her busy at their guest house, but it seemed more often, Siggy liked to escape to the hotel. Rae was always glad to see her. It was one of her biggest regrets, that Marcus had scuppered her relationship with her niece for so many years. Now, they were revelling in a connection that was as much friendship as kinship. Of course, it helped that the hotel was in the centre of the village. Still Water House, on the other hand, was literally in the middle of nowhere, at least here you were likely to bump into villagers occasionally.

'Aren't you a sight for sore eyes,' she said as Siggy switched on the espresso machine and pulled out two large pastries she'd bought in the nearby bakery.

'I've been trying to think up ideas to save your bacon,' Siggy really didn't understand the full extent of danger that the hotel was actually in.

'All saving is gratefully received.' Rae sat down, unwinding the long scarf from around her neck and hanging it across one of the high stools. They had the place to themselves, the next rush might come after morning mass – or it might not, of course.

'I'm here to serve.' She swung around to the outside of the counter but as they ate their pastries, she was uncharacteristically silent and Rae found herself wondering, if perhaps she'd come here for some other reason.

She knew better than to ask if there had been a row with Blythe. The last thing she wanted was to get in the middle of that, but at the same time, she couldn't help but feel something was amiss.

The hotel foyer ran the full length of the front of the building, so it included the reception desk and the bar, which was also the dining/breakfast room as well as the coffee shop. It was large enough to be multipurpose, small enough to be cosy and easy to manage unless there was an unexpected crowd – which didn't happen often anymore.

'Siggy, what on earth are you doing here? I thought you were off to meet some of your friends to study?' Blythe seemed to appear from nowhere these days. When Marcus was alive, she had a knack of turning up when he was at his Knights of Saint Columbanus meetings, or when he went out with the local rambling group. She hardly ever called when he was likely to be here. This morning, Blythe was carrying a huge bunch of flowers. 'The peonies are gone mad at home, far too many for me to use in the guest house and I thought, why waste them…' She put the massive bouquet down on the bar counter. Looked at Siggy, 'Well, since you're here, make yourself useful, go get a vase – actually, you might need a few vases.' Then she smiled at

Rae, 'Sorry, honestly, I'm not trying to dump them on you; I remembered those amazing flower displays you used to do.' She dropped into the stool next to Rae. 'Do you remember them, people would come in from all over the island, just to see them...' she laughed now, for once she was light-hearted, back to being the Blythe that Rae had adored when they were kids.

'That was so long ago,' Rae said dully. Then she looked at the bouquet, 'These are amazing, Blythe, thank you, they'll really cheer the place up.' She bent over them to sniff their scent. 'Heaven,' she said then. 'The gardens in Still Water must be beautiful these days.' It was funny how the tables had turned. There was a time, they couldn't keep on top of the grounds at the house, but Pappy had kept the large garden at the back of the hotel in perfect order. Now, the hotel garden had been dug up and put back together badly. It looked like that movie, where kids dug all day long, except she had the council to thank for the damage.

'I'm sure Kip wouldn't mind popping over to give you a hand, you know, out there,' Blythe nodded towards the back of the hotel.

'Ah, that's really sweet, but even if it was perfectly landscaped, what with running this place on my own, I'd never have the time to properly maintain it,' Rae said.

'Will these do?' Siggy was back with two large cut glass vases. They were as old as Blythe, probably, but they'd do the job.

'Perfect, darling,' Blythe said and they watched as Siggy arranged the flowers into the two jars.

'Where do you want them, Rae?'

'One on the bar and one on the reception desk,' Blythe said before Rae had a chance to answer. She blushed slightly,

'Sorry, old habits die hard. I'm usually directing things in the guest house.'

'Your mother is right, the bar and the reception desk,' Rae said softly.

'You were meant to go and get your hair cut, young lady,' Blythe flicked out Siggy's hair as she passed.

'I know, I know, but I just didn't have time.' Siggy made a face.

'Well, if you and Rae want to go together, that might be nice,' Blythe said and Rae had a feeling that it was more about her hair than it was about Siggy's.

'Actually, I'm thinking of getting a colour,' Rae said then, because she would not rise to whatever bait Blythe had unconsciously laid for her.

'Oh, that would be a nice lift. I've often wondered if you'd think of covering over the grey,' Blythe said, touching her own regularly coloured hair.

'Would you go some mad colour? I mean, green or blue or really pink-pink?' Siggy had her own sense of humour.

'I might,' Rae said, keeping a poker face.

'Oh, please don't. Don't become one of those women with cookie monster hair and no bra, we have enough of that type already running about the island.' Blythe rolled her eyes.

'I was thinking royal blue,' Rae made a play at admiring herself in the mirror behind the bar opposite.

'I'm sorry I mentioned it now.' Blythe was starting to seethe.

'I'm only joking.' Rae pushed against her. 'Do you really think I have the time to spend sitting in a hairdressers getting colour topped up every few weeks?'

'Thank goodness for that,' Blythe muttered. 'Still though, a nice mahogany colour would soften you out, you're much too young to be grizzled.'

'Thanks so much, I didn't realise I was...' Rae smiled. Her sister had never been a woman to hold back.

'You know what I mean... you're still pretty, you should be making something of yourself.' Blythe harrumphed and when Siggy caught Rae's eye, they both burst out laughing.

8

Blythe

Present

By the time Kip arrived home for dinner, Blythe was deep in concentration over the guest book. Should she give her mystery guest the ground-floor room with the four-poster bed, or the less palatial rose bedroom? The first had splendid views across the island, while the slightly more modest second room had French doors leading out into the small sunken garden with a terrace Kip had levelled off, so it was easily accessible for the less mobile.

She heard Kip, mooching about in the hall, probably taking off his work shoes before coming in – the habit of a lifetime, she couldn't have muck walked across every washed floor and cleaned carpet in the house. When he tracked her down he reeked of wood stain and filler.

'What do you think, darling? Which one is going to be the one to bag our place in the White Diary?' she asked absently when he kissed her cheek.

'Really?' He laughed, 'you're really asking me?'

'Of course,' she glanced at him now, he looked... different, as if she'd spotted him across the room and it took a moment to recognise him. Silly, she was just so distracted with this White Book business, it really was driving her nuts. 'I just can't decide, perhaps I should just keep both aside and let the woman choose for herself when she arrives?' She walked to the cast iron fireplace – Kip had put it in years earlier. It was one of the many finds they had come across together, as they'd scoured every house clearance sale and auction when they were putting the whole place together. There was no chimney of course, this room had been sliced off to make space for the ensuite. The original fireplace, a drab old grey slate had cracked when they'd knocked through the wall next to it. She'd been devastated at the time, but now, she was pleased, because she'd painted the cast iron a pastel pink and it gave her an inordinate sense of joy to fill the hearth with fresh flowers in summertime and pinecones in winter. It was far nicer than the drab old thing that was there to begin with. 'Surely, that would be worth at least one gold star? Although, it's hardly practical, I can't very well turn away paying guests for the want of making up my mind.'

'It's a good complaint.' He sounded tired.

'What's that, darling?'

'Well, each room is as perfect as the next...'

'Oh, yes, I see, of course, I suppose, it's what Siggy would call a first world problem.'

'Isn't it just.' He muttered under his breath, and she looked down at his feet. His big toe was showing through his sock again.

'Ah Kip, look at that sock, you didn't walk around like that all day, did you?' He was forever pushing out through his socks, that was the price of big feet – that and extra expensive shoes.

'Course not, I was wearing my work boots.'

'Duh, I know you were wearing boots, but that can't be comfortable, come on, take it off.' She put out her hand for the sock, because she knew otherwise it would just continue to go through the cycle of washing, drying and folding away and Kip would never complain, never throw it away or do anything to replace it.

'Okay old mother hen.' He was making fun of her now. She'd started darning his socks early in their marriage. Honestly, otherwise she'd have been buying him new socks every other week. She knew her friends would think she was bonkers. It was a matter of principle as much as anything for Blythe. She couldn't bear the idea of aiding and abetting those sweat shops on the other side of the world. 'Never mind your obsession with my toes, what's for dinner, I'm absolutely famished.' And he made a point of sniffing the air appreciatively before she pushed him away playfully.

'Go have a shower, dinner is in the oven, we can eat when Siggy gets home,' she called to him as he took the stairs, two steps at a time. She'd thrown on a casserole earlier in the day. It was funny, but these days she had to make a thing of keeping the routine of family mealtimes. She knew a lot of Siggy's friends went home and never left their bedrooms. From what she could gather breakfast, dinner and tea was consumed while they were immersed in some online game or scrolling endlessly on their phone. It was downright unhygienic. Blythe believed that carry-on like that could never lead anywhere good. No wonder every other woman she knew was going around the place with finicky children and eating habits of their own that were nothing less than distorted. It was far from vegan or keto or Mediterranean diets any of them were raised here on Pin Hill. Blythe had made it very clear to her, when she'd heard about the carry-on in other people's houses, that it wasn't good enough. She'd heard her own friends talking about how their kids slipped away once they became teenagers, so stealthily, that you hardly noticed until they had gone completely. Well, she was holding onto Siggy for as long as possible, in every way she could.

'I was talking to Ros Stokes today,' Kip said when he arrived at the kitchen after his shower.

'Oh, how is she?' Ros was one of the few outsiders that Blythe really liked, but she was more like a local than anything else. She'd worked as a ranger for a while before taking up a position as the island goat herder a year earlier.

'She's good, you know, Ros, always up to something.'

'She and Jonah Ashe will be making things official one of these days, I'm sure.'

'Hmm, probably,' Kip said, because he had no interest in island gossip, most of it passed him by, even when Blythe made a point of sharing the latest juiciest bits with him. 'Anyway, she's running a camp for some of the older kids on the long weekend. It'll be a hike up the mountain and then, camping out for the night, a bonfire, caring for the goats, that sort of thing.'

'That'd be good for a lot of them, get them off their phones for a while, make them move about a bit,' Blythe said. She took down a bottle of red wine, poured out a glass for each of them.

'Yeah, that's what I said. Ros wondered if Siggy would like to join in.' He took his glass from her, but his eyes didn't meet hers.

'Ah, now, sure what would she want to be going out and climbing up a hill for? You know as well as I do that the place will be full of horse flies and midges and all sorts. Siggy isn't like those other kids, she is busy, here and in the hotel.'

'I know that, Blythe, but it's not just about getting air in the lungs, it's about the social side of it too.'

'She can invite people over here, I'm always telling her, she's welcome to invite any of her friends.'

'I told Ros she could go.'

'You didn't?' Blythe felt the blood rush from her head. 'Why on earth would you do that?'

'Because it'd be good for her.'

'Good for her?' She was gawping at him now, the wine that she'd just sipped felt as if it was acid making its way slowly into her stomach. She closed her mouth then, because no words were coming.

'Yes, Blythe, good for her. You know fine and well she's the only one never allowed to go anywhere.'

'That's absolutely not true.'

'The discos on the mainland?' He placed his glass deliberately on the drainer next to the sink and Blythe felt something stir in her. Kip never, well, hardly ever lost his temper, and on those rare occasions when he had over the years, he'd walked out the door, disappeared for a few hours, come back and mulled for days over whatever was bothering him.

'She never wanted to go to those bloody discos.'

'She knew there was no point asking.'

'What do you think she's missing out on? You know well what goes on at them, haven't we both watched *Normal People*? Dear God, Kip, is that the carry-on you want for your teenage daughter?'

'Siggy isn't like that,' he said in a low voice that sent a chill through Blythe.

'Don't be so naïve, they're all like that, when they get together – one egging the other on, that's how it works, you should know that better than anyone. I'm sure that the rugby scene isn't immune to groupthink. I mean, I know that you sporty types aren't always the brightest, but surely, the basics of herd mentality aren't too much of a stretch even for you.' She said it in a scathing way. Maybe she wanted to win the argument, but she never wanted to hurt him.

'Anyway, I've told Ros she's going now.'

'She's absolutely not.'

'Blythe, everything about our daughter is not up to you. She's seventeen, for heaven's sake, it's time to start letting her go.' He ran his hand across his head, a habit that always signalled he was under pressure.

'Go? Up a mountain? Can you hear yourself? I'm not letting our daughter up a mountain with a crowd of ne'er-do-goods to be eaten alive by every sort of insect under the sun, I'm just not.'

'Come on,' his tone had turned softer, as if maybe, he might persuade her. 'She's going to be finishing school next year, Blythe, like it or not, she'll be old enough to leave here. What are you going to do then? Tie a ball and chain to her leg so she can't get past the avenue? There are a whole lot of skills she's going to need before she goes out into the world and you're not going to teach them to her by simply showing her how to make a tiramisu.'

'I know all this,' Blythe said, but suddenly she felt winded. She dropped into the chair. She did know her daughter was seventeen years old. She knew, that in a year's time, school would be over and probably, Siggy would want to go to college. They hadn't even talked about that, Blythe couldn't face it. But it was there, all the time, looming at the back of her mind. After all, that's what kids did, wasn't it? She felt lightheaded even thinking of it.

'I seem to have lost my appetite,' he said so softly that she felt a chill run through her, a ghost shiver, as if something inevitable, grim and merciless had just brushed past her. It made her stop breathing for one long moment. He sounded... different. Blythe felt that familiar pang of worry turning over in her stomach. When she looked up, he was gone. She heard the back door slam, the engine of his van turning over. The clock ticked slowly on the wall. And then, that unrelenting silence that unnerved her when she didn't fill it in with chores or gossip but allowed the clawing fingers of the past to reach forward and hook into her present contentment.

She would not permit it. Siggy most certainly was not going scurrying up a mountain just because Kip thought it would be character building for her, or some other nonsense of that variety. She made up her mind, she would not give in on this, she would hold firm, as she had always done, as she intended always to do, it was for Siggy's own good – even if Kip didn't see that yet. Given time, he'd agree with her, he always did, she was sure of it.

She took a large gulp of red wine. The shock of the alcohol to her system was just what she needed. Something to throw this jittery feeling off her nervous system, something to calm her down. She walked out to the hall, picked up the register. She'd always found it soothing to run her fingers down along the bookings. Double check that everything was as it should be. She took it and her glass of wine into the drawing room. Dropped into one of the deep sofas that she'd had refurbished a few years earlier. She pushed her reading glasses further up her nose and began to study the entries on the page in front of her. At least they weren't going to find themselves double booked – it had happened once before, and it was a complete nightmare.

Hah, it wasn't something that was likely to happen at the hotel any time soon, she thought meanly. Of course, Marcus had been the dynamo keeping that place going for years, her sister Rae, well, she hadn't a clue really. Rae slyly slid into running the hotel when Blythe always believed all she'd ever wanted was to spend her life surrounded by animals. It still made her blood boil to think of the pair of them plotting behind her back with Pappy all those years earlier. Rae's denials had only widened the wedge between them, even now Blythe found herself wishing she'd at least been honest enough to admit to their treachery.

Well, Blythe reminded herself for the umpteenth time over the years, the hotel's business was not her concern anymore. Marcus had made that perfectly clear on many occasions.

It had driven her on though, however much she might have declared them not to be in competition with each other. She couldn't deny, making a success of the Still Water Guest House had been fuelled by a desire to outshine them – to show Marcus she could beat him at his own game. He might have taken her hotel from her, but that didn't mean she couldn't come out on top.

With that her phone pinged. She lunged for it, fully expecting a voice message from Kip. An apology, perhaps. But no, not Kip. It was weird, but that argument had completely thrown her. They never argued – she and Kip. Never. And she had been cruel. She knew where his tender spots were, that was the trouble, when you were married for eighteen years, you know exactly how to wound the other person.

Then, she remembered the phone in her hand. Perhaps it was a slew of congratulations because surely by now, word would have gotten out. Her committee had been successful in lobbying the council for a zebra crossing outside the local primary school. It had taken a bit of work to swing it, not that Blythe minded hard work. She was quite proud of herself, really. The committee had been in place for years, under the control of the school council, and in the vice-like grip of the old parish priest. Nobody listened to priests anymore. Once she'd taken it over, they'd done trojan work. Within the space of the last two years, there were refinished playing grounds for the kids, a defibrillator installed in the old telephone box and upgraded street lighting all along the footpath. Now, this, the safe crossing, was the final piece she'd set out to do.

Instead of the gratification of congratulations, it was one of the WhatsApp groups, but not the school committee. Instead, it was their book club group. Someone had shared a photograph of a dark-skinned woman, standing on the pier, wearing long robes and a turban in the style of one of those impossibly glamorous women in the 1970s. She could be a silver screen goddess, who had stepped into middle age and retained that dazzling magnetism of youth and vitality that Blythe felt she herself had allowed to slip away so she only noticed it after it was already too late. Wow. Blythe felt a wave of admiration at the sheer elegance of her. Then, a new notification broke her concentration. What on earth? Her eyes blinked, pushing her reading glasses high over the bridge of her nose, she peered at the phone screen to read the caption. 'Our Newest Resident!!!!' All those exclamation marks, it had to be Lorna Duffy. At almost seventy, she was as excitable on text as she was in real life.

There was no need for it, in Blythe's opinion. Honestly, Lorna would probably insist on emojis to punctuate her tombstone. Then there was a flurry of comments. Blythe watched as each of her friends waded in, commenting on the woman's appearance and a slew of questions about what she was doing on Pin Hill. Apparently, she had moved into the McDaid cottage, right in the middle of the village. Well, it was bad enough to have the island overrun with eco warriors, bohemians and hippies, but at least they had the good grace to take over cottages that were long abandoned, usually with the worst of the island land around them. But this woman, an outsider, would be living in the village, it was too much. Blythe felt that souring sensation of fear rise in her stomach. Outsiders. Nothing good could come of them living here. All she wanted to know was – how long this woman intended to stay and if there was any way she could be persuaded to leave?

It was not Kip's key in the door an hour later, instead, it was Siggy, making her way back from the village.

'Hi darling, perfect timing, you must be ravenous?' She looked at her watch, just two minutes to six. 'Where were you until this hour?' It was small talk. Siggy had a small band of friends, carefully chosen by Blythe many years earlier. In Blythe's opinion, you had to be selective. Each year, the local secondary school filled up with kids from the mainland who were sent to board in houses around the island – you didn't know what you were dealing with there. As far as Blythe could see, no good came of mixing yourself up with them.

'Something smells good, casserole?' Siggy bent down and kissed the top of Blythe's head. 'I was at the hotel, with Rae...' She sighed as she flopped into the chair opposite.

'Lovely,' Blythe said, although she'd be lying if she didn't admit to herself that sometimes, she felt a prick of envy at the way their relationship had so quickly grown. Still, you had to be charitable. No matter the divide between them, Blythe knew, life for Rae must be hollow now that Marcus had passed away. 'How are things in the hotel?'

'Ah, you know... Quiet.'

'I'm sure. Well, she'll be pulling herself together, probably at this point. It is a year and a half, after all...' Blythe was sick and tired of everyone making a special case of Rae. Anyone would think she was a bloody saint, the first widow in the history of the island, which she was neither. Oh, of course, everyone believed that Rae and Marcus were the perfect couple. The John and Jackie of Pin Hill, if you could believe that after everything that happened between them all.

'I don't know, I'm not sure you can put a timer on getting over the loss of the love of your life – look at the way you always spoke about my great grandparents. Pappy never really got over losing his wife, did he?'

'It's really not the same thing at all...' Blythe said, annoyed that anyone would compare Marcus to Pappy.

'Of course it's the same thing. Marcus and Rae were devoted to each other,' Siggy said with the earnestness of one whose age and naïveté have not yet robbed her of the notion of one true love being the same thing as blind devotion.

'Yes, of course,' Blythe said, because she had to keep up the pretence, otherwise, who knew what would come out if the walls began to fall. 'But I mean, there were no children. Children bond a couple together in a way that well... it's not the same thing at all,' she said and she looked down to the crossword puzzle that had put her to sleep earlier, and tried to pretend that she had some interest in finishing it.

She suddenly felt uneasy – hadn't she just rowed with Kip over their one shared child – maybe not so uniting after all.

'For the love of God, Mum, don't go saying that to anyone else, will you...'

'Why on earth not, if it's the truth.'

'*As you see it*. But it could be hurtful to anyone who can't actually...' She stopped, cocked her ear, looked towards the window. 'Where's Dad?' she said and then, something in her expression changed. She made a show of checking her watch. 'I thought he'd be here before me...'

'He was, but he had to go again.' Blythe folded up her paper, plumped up the cushions on the sofa.

'Oh?'

'Yes, he had to go back into the nursing home,' there was no way she was telling Siggy that he'd walked out because they'd had an argument about her.

'That's...' she dropped into the seat then, as if she had somehow tuned into Blythe's upset. 'Is there something up?'

'Of course not, unless you count an extra coat of weather stain for the garden furniture an emergency.' Blythe laughed now, but it sounded hollow. 'Right, let's get our dinner, shall we?' she said, holding out her hand to make a thing of pulling Siggy from the chair. 'You're on washing up tonight,' she said to change the conversation.

'Ah Mum...' Siggy said, because usually she shared the job with Kip, but then suddenly she brightened, as if she'd just thought of something else. 'So, just the two of us?' she said, linking her arm through Blythe's.

It was only later, as Blythe lay in bed, that she wondered if Siggy was relieved that Kip was not there. But of course, that was ridiculous, Siggy adored her father, didn't she?

9

Siggy

Present

Siggy had given it a lot of thought – the idea of a unique selling point for the Hope Square Hotel.

'I'm so sorry, I haven't come up with anything new, but...' She really wanted to help. The idea that Rae would confide in her, ask for her advice, well, it made her feel suddenly important. Her mother never asked for her opinion. To Siggy's mind, her mother had all the answers.

'Stop making excuses before you even start.' Rae pulled across two of the dining chairs against the table, so they could sit next to each other, shoulders touching, equals. The hotel wasn't open yet. Siggy's mother said there was a time when it seemed as if it never closed. These days, Rae had changed her opening time to ten o'clock most mornings. It meant she still catered to the few regulars who filed out of mass and liked to come and gossip or read the daily paper with their morning cup of coffee. 'So, start again, big smile, what have we got...' Rae prompted her.

'Okay, well,' Siggy cleared her throat and sat just a little straighter, 'the Hope Square Hotel is a charming, family owned and run, boutique hotel. The location is a big plus; it's bang smack in the middle of one of the most picturesque villages on the wild Atlantic way. And we have the sea, just a short walk away.' Siggy was warming up. 'Of course that means, it's the perfect destination for families, for couples' getaways, for fishermen and for surfers.'

'Are we spreading our net too far?' Rae said lightly. Full rooms meant full staff and while that would be great for revenue, it meant that Rae could never manage the place single-handed.

'Okay, well, how's this… instead of going for the holiday makers, can we revisit the idea of small quirky weddings?' Siggy knew Rae had cancelled as many as she could redirect elsewhere after Marcus died. Now, her expression darkened. 'Please, hear me out, it's the perfect location, the hotel is beautiful and original and it's homely. It can accommodate a good-sized wedding party, but it still feels like a very intimate place – so say, give it a maximum capacity. We market to out-of-town couples wanting a relaxed elegance about their wedding. We can do up new photographs, put together a full package. Price it reasonably, but not too reasonably, so they know they are getting quality and…'

'I'm sorry, Siggy,' Rae held up her hands. 'I don't think I have another wedding in me, not now.'

'No, you're right. I'm sorry. I should have seen that for myself.'

'I think you're onto something with the whole "boutique" thing though, I mean, I really liked that.'

'Yeah, I liked it too and you know, I think with a bit of embellishment we could definitely market the hotel as boutique.' The problem was, when she said embellishment, what she meant was a Michelin-starred restaurant or a world-renowned piano player in the lobby, or at the very least a cocktail bar that some influencer had made famous for having a drink named after them.

'Okay, so we've narrowed it down,' Rae said in her brightest voice. 'We know what we don't want?'

'So, no to weddings?'

'Emphatically,' Rae said.

'Okay, let's start again from what we have, shall we?'

'Right. We have location.'

'Agreed,' Rae said except she knew, location was not enough to save them. All the old streams of business that had always kept the place afloat were being dried up. The lunch time trade had moved across to garage delis or the small artisan coffee shop on the main street. As to the bar, well, that market was on its knees now thanks to crippling taxes, a shifting social scene and much more fiercely enforced drink driving laws.

'Coffee?' Siggy said finally to break the silence.

'Sure, why not?' Rae looked at her watch. It was time to open the doors. Their regular crowd would be arriving soon. She gathered up the bits and pieces they had scattered on the table. Siggy set about grinding beans and heating up the machine. Behind her, she heard Rae open the front doors, felt a light breeze of fresh air waft around the reception behind her. Then voices, unfamiliar voices in the doorway and moving through the reception area that she had not expected. 'Come in, come in, of course, you're very welcome.' Siggy looked around to see Rae leading in Ros Stokes with another woman – a striking out-of-towner, tall, thin, skin the colour of hazel wood, her hair piled high in a turban, made of fabric that looked as soft as water, wrapped around her narrow pretty face. 'Siggy, any chance you could magic up another two cups of coffee for Ros and Melissa?' Siggy knew immediately, this had to be Danial's grandmother – she was as beautiful as he was handsome, the same eyes, warm and friendly, even with complete strangers.

'Of course, just give me a minute.' Siggy smiled at the two women and set about making four coffees in the fine bone china cups that had been here probably since before her own mother had been born. She grabbed a plate and scattered some ginger nut biscuits on it. She carried three coffees over on one of the old silver trays, set prettily with the dainty cups, saucers, milk jug and sugar bowl.

'Siggy, join us, won't you?' Rae said as she put down the tray. Siggy didn't wait to be asked a second time, she was intrigued by Melissa Val.

'So, it's just you and your grandson?' Ros asked.

'Yes, Danial will stay here with me, too. There are only both of us left now.' And she told them about her family, back in Nouakchott. A city in the desert of Mauritania. 'My son was a professor in the university, his wife a lecturer in women's studies. They spoke out, said things that powerful people do not like to hear.'

'What sort of things?' Siggy couldn't help it.

'Oh, it might take only two flights to get to Muffeen Mòr, but Mauritania is a lifetime away. It is very beautiful, but life there can be cruel if you are poor and uneducated. There is a rampant slave trade and anyone speaking up against it… well, they either end up in prison or…' she stopped. Her voice had begun to shake, she took a deep breath and Siggy noticed that her hands folded together gently in her lap before, tightened now. 'Worse.'

'I'm so sorry.' Rae placed her hand on Melissa's arm for a moment. 'And your son and his wife?'

'My daughter-in-law disappeared, he went to look for her. They swore they had not taken her, but witnesses said she was arrested as she flew back from a fundraising lecture in London. My son couldn't rest until he knew what had become of her and—' she stopped, looked out towards the village green, closed her eyes then for a moment, as if remembering a terrible nightmare. 'Well, they came and arrested him at the university. They told me he died in prison, they tried to make out it was appendicitis, but of course it couldn't have been that. He'd had his appendix out years earlier. The police – they are not very bright, but they are very dangerous. I feared for Danial, if we stayed there so...'

'You will be safe here,' Ros said softly. 'Danial will be safe here too, if he can settle, I mean, it must be very different from Nouakchott.'

'It is certainly colder.' Melissa smiled and she pulled her cape up closer around her shoulders.

'Wait until the winter comes,' Siggy said then, pushing the plate of biscuits towards Ros and Melissa.

'Will your grandson go to school here?' Rae asked.

'Oh, dear, Danial? No. Danial had just finished his final exams before we left, he's going to be eighteen in a few weeks' time. He was hoping to go to university until... well, after his mother. He took it all very badly. And then, when his father was arrested... I knew we had to leave. Already, it felt as if the police were watching our house, you never know what they'll lay at your door once they feel that you might be some sort of threat to them and Danial, he's a good boy, he'd never get into trouble. He just... well, he needed to start again.'

'He could attend university here, I mean, next year, if...' Ros said.

'Maybe, but for now, I think we both need to catch our breath.'

'Of course,' Rae said softly. 'It's a good place for a fresh beginning...'

'The thing is, he needs work, I'm not sure there are any jobs here for a young man.'

'Yes, of course, he'll need to be busy, get to know people, make friends his own age, quite aside from making some money...' Ros said then.

'The island isn't exactly teeming with opportunities,' Siggy said. 'Most kids leave for college as soon as they finish school, then they either travel or settle into jobs on the mainland.'

'It's all farming, fishing and tiny family businesses here, I'm afraid.' Ros looked from Rae to Siggy. 'I know that well enough. A year ago, I was in a similar situation.'

'It's not easy,' Rae agreed.

'The thing is, even if he could help out without pay, somewhere, anywhere, I think if he had a reference, someone to vouch for him if an opportunity arose, then...' She looked at Rae again.

'And you hoped he might work here?' Rae said softly. She looked across at Siggy only briefly catching her eye. 'Let me think about it,' she said then, because of course, Rae, just like her mother but in very different ways, always wanted to do the right thing. She would try her best to make a place to help Danial, except they both knew, there was no place to make for him at the hotel.

'What did you say he was going to study at university?' Siggy asked then.

'Computer Science, but he is very bright, very...' Melissa stopped for a second. 'Very sharp, he picks things up quickly and he's always had part-time jobs. He's a hard worker, if you give him a chance.'

'I would love to give him a chance,' Rae said, then she held up her hand. 'But you see, we're not busy. Actually, we are trying to figure out ways of making more business in the hotel, because this last year has been—' She stopped and smiled sadly. 'Well, it hasn't been easy.'

'Of course, I understand.' Melissa Val looked at Rae and nodded as if she understood absolutely everything in that moment. 'Maybe, until he finds a proper job, he can come here and help you make your plans?'

'Oh, I couldn't let him do that, not without offering some sort of payment.' Rae shook her head.

'I'm sure Danial will pick up a proper job in no time, but coming here, it would give him a purpose. He'd meet some of the locals, make some friends and maybe it would be good for other people in the village to see that newcomers are welcome here,' Ros said softly.

'I'd be very grateful. A young man in a strange country with no friends and only his memories to keep him company – apart from his grandmother, he needs something more.'

'Of course, of course,' Rae said then and it felt as if they all exhaled a sigh of relief. 'I'd love to have him here, but only for as long as he wants to come, and I will see if there is any work going, so he can get a proper job as quickly as he can.' She smiled and Siggy thought, Danial Val might be just what this place needs – a breath of fresh air, she for one was really looking forward to seeing more of him.

10

Blythe

Twenty-Two Years Ago

Blythe was so excited. She'd spent all morning getting ready. A full two hours in the bath, she'd even shaved her legs – which she'd never usually bother doing unless the sun was splitting the rocks. She'd spent the best part of an hour getting herself together.

'It's only a jobs fair,' Chloe kept telling her. Still, she'd been kind enough to lend Blythe her lovely new leather jacket.

'Yes, but I'm going with Marcus.' Blythe had no interest in the actual fair. When she graduated, she planned to go back to Pin Hill, and work in the Hope Square Hotel with her grandfather. Her parents kept dropping hints about travel and getting a job on the mainland, just for a few years, before settling for island life, but Blythe was set on what she wanted to do and where she wanted to do it.

She was just applying her mascara when she heard a crash coming from the kitchen at the back of the flat.

'Chloe?' She wondered for a moment if her flatmate had returned. But the silence that followed her calling out, convinced her that no. There was no way Chloe had come back. She was already running late.

'Chloe?' she tried again, her voice barely audible. Oh, no, she'd left the kitchen window open. Could it be that stray cat that was always hanging around the narrow alley at the back of the flats? It could be. She wouldn't put it past him to jump up on the shed roof opposite and then make his way along the border wall. 'If that's you,' she began to give out. She'd have to catch him and give him his marching orders. He was feral, so far as she could tell. She fed him, of course, but there was no way he was coming inside. A cat like that, even if she had a litter tray, he'd probably relieve himself on beds and in laundry baskets, anywhere he could burrow.

Then, the sound of a foot on the door saddle sent a shiver of fear along her spine.

Blythe's heart froze.

That was no cat.

Shit.

She looked at the door of her bedroom. Should she lock herself in, hope that Marcus called for her earlier than they'd arranged? Her phone was still charging out in the sitting room. She tiptoed towards the bedroom door. Hardly daring to breathe, sweat breaking loose beneath her blouse now, undoing all that lovely pampering of earlier.

She was at the door.

Then she remembered there was no lock.

There had been a key here, when she moved in first, a big old black thing. It looked like something out of Harry Potter. Hers was the only original door in the flat. The others all had silver yale locks. Now, as her hand hovered over the door handle, she remembered, Chloe had asked if she could borrow it to use as part of a costume she was wearing to a fancy dress party. Had she returned it? Blythe's mind ran a blank.

She couldn't think. In the room opposite, she could hear voices, two at least. Irish? Or maybe foreign. Two male voices. Or was there three? It was impossible to make out, because the blood was pounding through her veins at such a rate, she could hardly hear herself think. She slipped behind the bedroom door. If she moved it even slightly, it would creak. It had been like that since they moved in. Usually, it didn't bother her, although, it had woken her flatmates a few times if she came in late.

It would definitely alert the two men opposite that she was here if she moved it so much as an inch. She peered round the door again. They were going through Chloe's room, pulling out the drawers, flinging clothes across the room. The bed, she could see had already been turned over. The place was a mess. They were moving fast, she could see hands, arms, bodies – practised at pulling a place apart to find what they wanted.

'Goran, look.' One of the men called to the other. Blythe assumed he had come across the rent money that Chloe was meant to drop in to their landlord the following Monday. Oh, God, her whole body had begun to shake. She couldn't stop shivering, it felt as if she was so cold and yet, sweat drained down her neck, along her spine, her palms were wet and sticky. She felt like getting sick, right here, except, she wasn't sure she could even do that, such was the paralysing fear within her.

'Ha, students, I told you they would be a good bet.' The other man laughed then. He sounded foreign. They both did, definitely not Irish. Blythe closed her eyes, prayed they would leave, become distracted by something, anything.

'Sergei, look,' this voice was different again. Were there more than two? Oh, God. She felt weak, as if she could faint at any moment, and there was no way out of here. Her bedroom window looked down on a sheer two-storey drop. There was no wall, or garden shed outside here, just a hard, concrete busy road beneath. Blythe felt as if she hadn't breathed in hours. She badly wanted to inhale deeply, but she was trying to breathe as gently as a rabbit, it was making her lightheaded.

'Hah, so, this is what you heard, Goran.' One of the men had walked into her bedroom. He was huge. Filling up the doorway. As broad as he was long, her grandfather would say, and Blythe found herself thinking of Pappy now.

'So, student girl, I suppose you think you are very clever, on a big adventure, hiding here and listening to us.'

'I told you we should have worn our masks.' The other man had joined him now, he was smaller, beady-eyed, he stared at Blythe like a falcon eyeing up his prey. 'Now look...'

'Oh, Goran. This one's not going to be telling anyone, anything.'

'We're meant to be stealing, not...'

'She's seen us now. What else do you know? You've heard our names probably,' the bigger one was in her face now. She could smell food: chips, fried, something else on his breath. Weed?

'I... I... I'm not going to tell anyone. If you let me go, I won't come back here. I'll tell you where everything of value is, I'll even take you to my bank and withdraw all my money for you, but please, don't hurt me.' She was crying now. Sobbing, like a pathetic child. She could smell her own sweat – how could that be – she'd spent the whole morning cleaning and pampering herself and now, she reeked of heavy, unwashed sweat.

'That sounds like an offer we can't refuse,' the smaller of the two men said.

'Give me the bank card. And your wallet and any other money,' the larger one said then. 'Quick. This isn't window shopping, hurry.'

Blythe went to the other side of the room. Picked up her bag. In it was almost every penny she had. She took out her wallet, handed it to them. Her mother had given her a hundred-euro note two years earlier. It was for emergencies. Blythe had tucked it into the lining of her bag. She ripped the lining now, pulled out the hundred-euro note. 'Here. It's everything.' She handed it all to the smaller one; waited a beat, while his accomplice snatched it from his hands.

'Bank card number?' he smiled through yellow crooked teeth, tucked the cash into his jeans pocket. 'Now.' He shouted, almost making her jump.

'It's two five, two five,' she said and immediately regretted it. That was her only bargaining tool. They could kill her now. She'd be another statistic. Just a robbery gone wrong.

Ding dong. The front door bell. It took the two men by surprise.

'Marcus. Marcus. I'm in here. Call the police. There are two men, they won't let me go.' She was hysterical. Screaming. Jumping up and down. She could see the two men opposite her look at each other, unspoken words passing between them. Then, the smaller one turned away and he was gone, out through the door, towards the back of the flat. The larger one stood there, eyeing her for a second. She was still screaming. Calling out to Marcus. Praying he heard her through the door. 'There's a spare key. It's in the...' The man opposite her turned. She was certain he was going to follow his accomplice to the kitchen, out through the low window, and out onto the back alleyway. She was almost ready to breathe. Almost. Perhaps they would not kill her after all. Then, in the most violent pivot she'd ever seen, he turned, bounded across the bed and had his hands around her neck.

'Listen to me, if you say one word, just one word to the police, so help me, I'll come back here some night and when you're sleeping soundly, I'll wrap my hands around your neck, just like this... tighter, tighter. So tight you won't be able to call for help, do you understand?' He was whispering into her ear. She couldn't breathe. She couldn't answer. 'Do you understand me?' he said again.

'I won't tell. I swear,' she whispered then, because even getting the words out was a torture. She could hardly breathe, could hardly stand. She just needed to get away from him.

'Good. I'm glad we understand each other,' he said then and moved away from her, but as he raced out the bedroom door, his jacket caught on the handle and she spotted a thin, long gleam. He was carrying a knife, sharp and deadly-looking tucked into the back of his trousers.

Dear God.

She began to cry now. Not the soft sobbing of earlier. This time, it was gulping wails. Deep and loud, so she could hardly catch her breath. She wondered if Marcus was still outside. Had he heard her at all?

And then, she saw the door move ever so slightly and there he was, and honestly, she'd never been so happy to see anyone in her whole life. She wanted to throw herself into his arms, but she couldn't stand. She couldn't breathe. He looked at her, ran to her side.

'Are you okay, Blythe? Did they attack you, are you... oh, God, you can't breathe?' and he dug around the inside pocket of his jacket. Somewhere outside, in the sitting room, she heard her phone ring out. It was one of those sounds, so very disconnected from her at this moment, she only barely registered it after it had finished ringing. 'Here,' he said, whipping out a blue inhaler as if it was the answer to all her problems. 'Open your mouth and breathe in deeply when I press it.' Within two short puffs, she began to feel as if her breathing was going to be okay. She'd have taken a third, but he put the inhaler back in his pocket again. He lifted her from the floor, guided her to the side of the bed. They sat there for a long time, she sobbed and clung to him. He murmured things like, 'There, there, it's alright now. They're gone now. You're safe.' Except Blythe didn't feel safe. Instead, she felt as if the shadow of that guy who'd almost strangled her would always be at her side.

'You're okay, Blythe, nothing happened. Do you want to report it to the guards?' Marcus asked her and she had a feeling that he wanted to get going. The careers fair was a big deal for him after all.

'No.' She tried to steady her voice. 'There's no point, is there? I mean, the guards have enough to be doing, they won't want to deal with something that isn't even a thing.' And she stood up then, trying not to tremble or to fall over because it honestly felt as if her knees might buckle beneath her. The last thing she wanted was to make a complete fool of herself.

God, she thought, as they sat next to each other on the bus that day, Marcus is amazing. She'd never known what it was to need a hero, but today, it felt like Marcus had been a hero to her, if he hadn't been there, well, she didn't want to think about what might have happened.

It was later, much later, that she remembered the missed call on her phone. At the jobs fair, she searched her bag, but of course, in the panic of getting out of the flat, she'd left it behind. She didn't want to make a big thing of it at the fair, but as they travelled back into the city again, she asked Marcus if he'd come back to the flat, just to check things out – of course, she was hoping for much more.

'Sure,' he said, but he looked at his watch, and she had a feeling that he would rather be somewhere else.

'I'm sure it'll be fine, but...'

'In that case,' he said, and he left her at the door, standing there with her key in the lock and was at the end of the road before she had a chance to tell him about the wine in the fridge.

She didn't have time to think about what it meant that he could just saunter off like that, leave her standing there, what if those two guys had come back? They could be waiting in the flat for her to return. What if she was walking into a flat filled with crazed knife carrying psychopaths who'd made their way back in just to finish her off? Despite all these thoughts, she turned the key in the door, fear in her chest, but also, intent on finding her phone to return whatever call she'd missed earlier.

The missed call was from the hotel. Her grandfather never rang her mobile, he always stuck to landline numbers, fearing the cost of speaking for too long on those 'yokes' as he still called them. She knew it must be important so she called as she moved through the flat, switching on one light after another, checking beneath beds and in wardrobes, although maybe the rational part of her brain knew that those thugs would not be back again.

'Oh, der Schatz,' he sounded as if he was crying.

'Pappy, what is it? Is everything alright?' Instantly, she assumed he'd fallen in the hotel, made it to the telephone and needed help. 'Are you okay?'

'Me? No, not me, I'm...' He was fine, she could hear that much in his voice. 'I'm sorry, liebstes Mädchen. It's your parents. They've been in an accident.' He was sobbing now.

'I don't understand, Pappy, what's happened?' Then she heard a commotion at the other end of the line, her grandfather's heartbroken sobs moving into the distance.

'Blythe?' This voice was not readily familiar, it was thick, gruff, business-like. 'It's sergeant Byrne here, I haven't met you, but I've been stationed on the island for a few months now...' A cold shiver moved along her spine.

'Okay?' she wanted to tell the stranger on the phone she didn't care who he was, she just wanted to know that everything was alright. For a moment, it felt as if she stood, tippy-toed on the edge of a wave, one wrong move and she was going under, if she could just stay here – not allow the water to suck her into the depths. 'My parents?'

'Yes. I'm so sorry to have to tell you. There's been an accident. They were driving back from Muffeen Beag – it seems that they lost control of the car – you know those old cliffs at Widow's Cove? There's been some subsidence... and well...' He stopped, perhaps allowing her to fill in the blanks. She knew that road well, there was a sheer drop into the ocean. It was over six hundred metres in places.

'Are they alright? Have they been brought to the mainland – where are they?' She heard her voice rising, as if it was far beyond her control, a tiny knot of panic had slipped into it, but it was growing with every passing nanosecond. Now, it was erupting inside her – so she could hardly breathe. It felt as if everything was coming in on top of her, the day, the break-in, Marcus and now this – this was horrifying.

'They went over the cliff...'

'They're not...' Dead – she couldn't say it, but it was the word that dangled there, unspeakable. Unthinkable.

'I'm so sorry. Your father died instantly. By some miracle the passenger door of your parents' car seems to have opened, your mother was flung against the cliffs. Sea and air rescue managed to lift her and take her to the mainland. It's not looking good for her, I really can't tell you how sorry we all are here, Blythe.'

'And my father is...' Oh God, words had deserted her. Later she couldn't remember hanging up the phone.

And then, nothing.

She must have gone back to her room, packed a bag, filled it with God alone knew what, but then, by seven in the morning, she was on a bus, back to the west, no thought of her final exams – which were due to start the following week, no thought to the rent on her flat or the milk, just about to turn in the fridge. For most of the journey she cried. Cried for her father, for her mother and for Rae. But she cried for herself also. Fear bubbled up in her. She kept seeing that face, heavy dark eyebrows, a thin scar running across the lip and hearing his heavy accent. Sergei. That was his name. And even saying it in her head made her feel nauseous. She tried to force it all from her brain; from her thoughts. At about the halfway home point, she realised he wasn't in her thoughts, somehow, he had travelled with her. He was sitting next to her. Standing over her. She had been so scared, his presence had never really left her at all. Now, here she was, on her way back to Pin Hill Island, her safest place in the world and she wasn't escaping the fear. And now, instead of crying, she closed her eyes. She had to be strong. She had to pull herself together. Pappy had enough to deal with, she couldn't go to pieces, so she vowed she would stamp down on the terror of what had happened and push it to the back of her mind. That was the only thing she could do now.

Everything of the next week somehow blended into itself. There was a funeral for her father. Later she would remember it only in isolated snapshots – as if some paparazzi had documented the whole thing with a long lens in twenty-second breaches.

They stayed, she and Rae and Pappy in the hotel.

She couldn't possibly think of going back to Dublin. Everything about it made her stomach churn. She couldn't even face Still Water House, which was meant to be home. Even in the hotel, an unexpected shadow could make her jump, a voice from the next room or the scent of aftershave, sickly, sweet and cheap turned her stomach and filled her with terror. The idea of going back to Still Water House terrified her. It was huge. She'd spend her whole time checking and double-checking doors and windows, seeing shadows and threats where there were none. She wasn't sure Rae could face going back there yet, either. Instead, she took over one of the large family rooms in the hotel. The sisters slept, or more accurately, spent each night not sleeping, but lying curled up together in a double bed, while four other beds lay empty around them.

Pappy organised the funeral.

Later, when she had Siggy, a daughter of her own, she would think, how unthinkably heartbreaking it must have been for him, organising his own son's funeral.

Her mother couldn't do it. She might have avoided being plunged to her death in the sea – but nobody could say she survived to the point of living again. Instead, she spent weeks that felt like forever, in a high-end nursing unit. There were broken bones – fifteen of them in total, there was a punctured lung, a suspected spinal injury and most worryingly of all – her mother didn't speak for almost two months after the accident. Shock, they said.

Blythe thought it was more than shock, it was grief too and maybe guilt, however misplaced, remaining a stumbling block to her ever really being the same person again.

By the time the funeral was over, Blythe had already missed her final exams. And a lot more too, that she couldn't even begin to process, much less tell anyone about. Marcus Johnson was like a dream she'd had, but not real. In her mind, he became her Sir Galahad, a point of safety when she felt so close to danger, it had almost paralysed her senses. Nothing had happened, she tried to tell herself that, but even that day, coming home on the bus, when she heard a foreign accent in the seat behind her, it made her shiver. Her fear was compounded with shocked grief, so her whole body trembled at the proximity of an accent she couldn't place. The woman opposite her made the bus driver stop so she could gather herself with a cup of tea from a garage on the side of the road. Her life before that phone call from Pappy, all of it felt as if it had happened to someone else.

'I'm not going back to Dublin,' about that she was adamant. In the days and weeks that followed that terrible night, she'd only just managed to cover over a rising sense of panic at the thought of being in the vicinity of strangers. She needed to be surrounded by the people she loved. Occasionally, she thought about Marcus Johnson. He never called to see what had happened to her. She covered over the fact that he'd just walked off that night, hadn't made sure she was okay. At this distance, it was easier to remember how it felt when she'd run into his arms and suddenly the world felt safe. She sometimes wondered what her fellow students had said when she didn't turn up for her exams. Did they care? Did they even notice? She figured someone would have told them, but it didn't matter then, only later when her head began to clear.

It was afterward, too, that she realised Marcus hadn't cared very much for her at all, which was a shame, she had really liked him, maybe even thought that they might end up together. Silly stuff, she pushed him firmly from her mind. Maybe she was better off without him. That thought had somehow lodged inside her. It stopped her from going slightly mad, from calling or texting him. It was perhaps the punctuation mark she needed; a small pause in falling head over heels for someone when there was that doubt that he might not be everything she'd built him up to be in her fantasies.

In the confusion of everything, she hadn't applied to do resits, so it felt as if she'd thrown away her years in college. 'Anyway, what more do I need to know?' she asked her grandfather late one evening after she had returned from another long day at her mother's side in the hospital.

'Nothing, meine Kleine, you were already a better hotelier than any of us before you left for college.' He said it so plainly, as if it must be true.

'So, you'd trust me with this place one day?' She smiled at him now.

'Let's just say, I hope to be around for a long time yet,' he said softly. Oh, how he'd aged since the accident that had whipped away his only son. The last few weeks had changed everything Blythe held close.

'Then I don't have to go back and sit those exams next year?'

'I don't see how you could, even if you wanted to.' He shook his head sadly. 'Your mother will need a lot of care when she eventually comes home and Rae, well...'

'I know.' Since their father's death, Rae had completely altered. For the first few days, they'd hardly said a word – either of them. They were, of course, in deep shock, in mourning. Blythe felt as if beneath the grief, she had turned into something as arid as the desert. That first night, curled up beneath the faded counterpane, Blythe had put her arms around her sobbing sister. Rae had cried all night through, there was no stop, only an occasional hiccup where she'd run out of tears but turned instead to swallowing down her grief. It had been like that for days. For her part, Blythe could make no sound – she had passed to a place beyond grief.

The day of their father's burial something shifted.

Blythe wasn't sure exactly what, but Rae disappeared for hours, so much so, that Blythe worried that she wouldn't be back in time for the mass which was due to start at midday.

'Oh, my God, Rae, where were you?' she said when she spotted Rae sashay through the front doors of the hotel. Her hair looked as if she'd been crawling through the boglands, the knees of her pants, mud covered. 'Is that...' She stared at the dark red love bite on her sister's neck.

'Can I not go out for five minutes without someone on my case, seriously Blythe?'

'We're due at the church in fifteen minutes.' Blythe tried to keep her voice even, but she felt as if she was standing on a ledge, beneath her was a yawning emptiness that scared her with its capacity to swallow what was left to them. She had to get a grip. She was meant to do a reading; she didn't want to be one of those girls who went to pieces on the altar, making everyone feel uncomfortable. Pappy would hate that.

'The funeral isn't going to start for half an hour.'

'Yes, but we have to be there early, people will want to give their condolences, and Pappy doesn't want us traipsing in the door at the last moment.'

'Oh, for God's sake. I'll be ready in plenty of time.' She pounded up the stairs. It was only then that Blythe realised, for the last few weeks in Dublin, she'd had hardly any letters from Rae – what was going on with her, exactly?

Later, at the funeral, Blythe put her arm around Rae. She could hardly process that right there, in that honey-coloured coffin, her father was being taken away from them. Suddenly, it washed over her like an icy tide that almost sent her off balance – she'd never see her father again. Rae shrugged her off unexpectedly, making her stumble. Blythe felt ten times more alone than she had before. It was confirmed, even if she could talk about what she felt she'd left behind in Marcus Johnson, she couldn't tell the only person she would have confided in.

The next few weeks, felt to Blythe as if they were living on a roundabout of hospital visits, hotel duties and trying to keep what remained of their family and her sanity together.

Pappy was great – although nearing his ninth decade, he made his way into the belly of the hotel daily. From his vantage point midway between reception and the bar, he looked after locals and guests, with a welcoming word for everyone and a good finger on the pulse of village goings-on thanks to the morning mass brigade and the evening crew, dropping in for a quiet pint to finish off their day.

Rae on the other hand was a completely different story.

'She's acting out,' her grandfather said when Rae snapped at Blythe and then slammed the kitchen door behind her.

'I know, she adored Dad, but we all loved him, and we have to stick together, it's not going to be easy when Mum comes home.'

'I've been thinking about that...' her grandfather said softly. 'You know I've loved having you both here? But a hotel isn't the place for a convalescent woman, who's trying to heal not just physical scars but emotional ones too...'

'I know, Pappy, don't worry. We'll go back to Still Water House when she's discharged...' It was the only solution. Blythe was dreading it. There was a silence in their great old Georgian home that no radio could wash out; it would not be so easy to push unwelcome thoughts from her mind there. The hotel was at its busiest now; it made it easier to convince herself that everything would be okay than facing up to the reality that was panning out before her. 'It'll be good to get back, maybe that's what Rae needs, to get back to some sort of normal?'

'Maybe,' her grandfather said, although he didn't sound too convinced.

The problem with Rae, it transpired, was not that she was unsettled, but rather a long-haired heavy metal biker called Danno who had more attitude than horsepower and a temporary hold over Rae that Blythe hoped would lessen as soon as someone new came along.

It turned out that it was also about Marcus.

Yes.

Marcus Johnson above all people.

The truth came out one evening when they were in the middle of a screaming row over something so small, Blythe couldn't remember halfway through the argument what had started it.

'You stopped answering my letters,' Rae spat at her.

'I what?'

'My letters. You met some dude – you didn't even tell me his name. You made him dinner and drank wine with him and that's the last letter you sent me.'

'Rae? I...' Blythe was gobsmacked. Had she really forgotten to return Rae's letters once Marcus came on the scene? True, she'd fallen crazily head over heels for him – obscenely so, maybe as much because of his restraint and his detachment – he remained unavailable to her to a large extent. Oh, they met for study and went to college events together, she sat next to him in the college canteen, but they hadn't slept together; obviously. There was no formal girlfriend–boyfriend arrangement. Somehow, without seeming to try, he managed to keep her on tenterhooks – not on purpose, she was certain it wasn't intentional – wasn't she?

Now, in hindsight, with everything so undiluted and raw, Blythe wondered if she'd ever have been able to take things further with him. Had he loved her? Or even liked her? Or had he just been interested in her because one day, she would own a hotel, the one thing he seemed to want more than anything else. Maybe, if he just reached out...

These days, so far as she could gather from others in their class, he was working in a hotel on the continent, improving his languages, building up his CV – probably, still working to some internal plan to make a great success of his life.

'Anyway, none of that matters now,' she said then, seeing Rae on the verge of tears. 'This Danno – what's he done?'

'It's not what he's done... it's what I've done for him...'

'Oh, no, Rae, you're not...' Pregnant. That was the one thing she wasn't equipped to cope with now, not with the prospect of caring full time for their mother as well as everything else.'

'Of course not, but it's...' She started to cry, sob as if her heart might break. 'He needed money and... No one is going to notice, but I just feel so badly about it now...'

'What did you do?'

'I...' Rae and Blythe might have been sisters, but they were completely different people. Rae wore her heart on her sleeve. Instead of a poker face, she had a window to her soul.

'Did you steal money?' Dear God, please let her not have done something completely stupid.

'No. No, of course not, but I promised Danno I'd get him two hundred pounds from the hotel to fix his bike.' It came out in interrupted blurts, but at least, if that was the worst of it, well, maybe it wasn't so bad. 'And today I saw him with Adele O'Regan and if I don't get him the money, I know he's going to choose her over me and I simply can't bear it...' And she was off in heartbroken sobs again.

'Oh, Rae...' Blythe pulled her close. 'Sweet, sweet Rae, he's not worth it.'

'You don't know him, he's... he's...' She stopped, wiped the tears from her cheeks with a force that was almost like a slap. 'I'm in love with him.'

'You're *not* in love with him.'

'How do you know? What would you know about love anyway, all you ever loved was the hotel – you've never once fallen madly, truly in love with anyone apart from the hotel.' She spat the words out.

'That's not true.' Blythe tried to keep her voice level, but she wanted to cry. She'd thought she was in love with Marcus, she'd been utterly infatuated with him, that was true, but had she ever loved anyone blindly enough to want to go out and steal to hold onto them? She wasn't sure that was in her DNA – maybe Rae was right, the thing she loved most was the Hope Square Hotel, maybe it would always be the love of her life.

What did any of that matter now? All that mattered was that Rae was hurt – she'd bloody well put that Danno boyo in his box first thing tomorrow morning and that would be an end to it.

'Listen to me now, Rae Scott – you're worth a thousand of that old Adele O'Regan and if Danno Kelly can't see that, well then, he's not worth the spikes on his biker jacket.'

'Oh, Blythe,' Rae sobbed, and she threw herself against Blythe, holding onto her as if she was life itself and Blythe prayed hard that everything was going to be okay.

11

Kip

Present

Kip was seething.

He hadn't realised how angry he was until he spotted Ros walking with a bunch of kids across the bog at the back of the nursing home.

Blythe had gotten her way again.

It wasn't just that. As far as Kip could see, it was worse that Siggy just accepted it. Not that he'd been much of a rebel himself back in the day. God knows, he'd have stood on his head in the freezing snow if that made his mother happy.

But his mother was not like Blythe.

God love her, but his mother asked for nothing in life. The one thing that drove her was to see her two sons settled down and happy. She'd never made a demand on them, beyond a promise not to turn out like their father.

'Ah, Kip, come on, if you keep walking round here like that, people will think that someone has cancelled the World Cup this year.' Shane McPherson was dropping flowers into the nursing home.

'There's no end to your generosity.' He was joking with him. The flowers had come from the Church of Ireland ladies who'd put on a great display the previous day for a visit from the archbishop. 'I thought you were working for the other side?' Shane was the administrator in the local Catholic church.

'My job as warden in one church seems to mean I'm responsible for all of them,' he laughed.

'Always good to be in demand, I suppose.'

'So, what's up?'

'Nothing.' He liked Shane, but he couldn't even begin to put into words what was bugging him. 'Just got out of the wrong side of the bed I guess today.'

Wrong side of the bed, indeed.

He'd have to have it out with Blythe. They couldn't go on like this, it was stressing him out – the idea that in a matter of months, Siggy would be finished school and heading for college.

She hadn't even told Blythe where she wanted to go.

Of course, she'd told Kip. It had taken quite a bit of cajoling to get it out of her. They'd been in the garden, Siggy sitting at the still water pool, her feet hanging over the side, while Kip filled cement in between the crazy paving which the frost had cracked in places over winter.

She was hoping to study art history in Galway.

'That's nothing to keep secret, surely?' He'd patted her head.

'But what about Mum?'

'What about her?' And that's when he realised. Siggy's forehead had furrowed into a thousand lines, far too many for a kid with her whole life ahead of her. She was genuinely afraid to tell Blythe that she hoped to leave the island.

She had a dream. Maybe just like Blythe.

'I'd like to be working in one of those big auction houses, you know, buying and selling antiques and art and...' Siggy's whole expression changed when she spoke about it.

'Well then, that's what you have to go after.'

'Easier said than done.'

'Do you not think you'll get the points?' It was all about points, apparently. It was like a foreign currency to Kip. He'd lost interest in school long before the leaving cert. You didn't need points or university education to score a try – and he'd scored plenty of them.

'Dad!' She laughed. 'It's an arts degree – it's not rocket science, I'll definitely have the points.'

'I had to ask.' He shook his head. 'Anyway, your mother will be fine. It's good to know you have a plan, I mean, I bet there's plenty of others who have no idea what they want to do.'

'Probably.' She shrugged. 'Although it doesn't feel like it. Damian O'Brien wants to study Chinese in Austria.' She laughed at that, because maybe she had only just realised how crazy that sounded – so far as Kip knew, the lad had never gone further than Dublin in his life.

'I think you'd make a great...' He stopped. 'Auctioneer?'

'Art Dealer – I think.' She smiled at him.

'Do you want me to tell your mother?'

'No. I'll do it, but close to the time, I think, because I really can't face the next year of...' She stopped. They were kindred spirits, he knew that. Maybe he spoiled her, a little, behind Blythe's back. Only with small things, like a fiver here or picking up a bar of chocolate or a magazine for her if he was on the mainland.

He tried to be a good father. Some things were beyond

him, he'd never read Siggy a bedtime story, but he'd made her laugh, told her tall tales about comical creatures that lived in the still water pool at the end of the garden and he'd never once lost patience with her, even on those days when he had run out of it for everything else in the world. There wasn't a thing he wouldn't do for her and for Blythe. But surely, it was time to start letting Siggy make her own way a little more in the world. Surely, it was time for her to get a chance to stand on her own two feet, to have enough freedom so if she was going to fall, it was close enough to pick her up.

The other kids her age were regularly going to the mainland to pubs and clubs and getting up to all sorts. It was enough to scare him witless, he didn't want to think of his daughter getting drunk any more than Blythe did, but at the same time, it was part of growing up. Of figuring out limits, boundaries; Kip remembered fondly it was the scrapes and shenanigans from his youth that bonded him with friends who had been as good as brothers when he was miles away from home.

Of course, Blythe had none of that. She'd always been the sensible one. Everyone on the island knew, the weight of a whole family – a dynasty really, had fallen on her shoulders before she'd even had a chance to finish college. Kip suspected, she'd probably never really, truly cut loose. Not in the way that kids did now, not in the way that they did twenty or thirty years ago. Blythe had somehow moved from childhood to adulthood without pausing in between.

It was no good. It was making him sick with worry. He tossed and turned most nights, thinking of what awaited Siggy when she finally flew the nest. How on earth would she survive when she'd hardly been out of Blythe's sight for more than a school day?

Kip stopped. That little voice rose up in him again – Blythe always gets her own way. He hadn't even had a say in the child's name. He'd always planned to call his first daughter after his mother – Rose. It was a lovely name. But somehow, it had fallen down the list of baby names from first to second and then, *if she looked like a Rose, well, maybe...* In the end, Blythe had decided – Gisela Sigried, after her grandmother. Kip had stood there, at the altar, staring wet-eyed at this beautiful baby, still hardly daring to believe that she was his, that they were a family. It was later, when he realised it – his mother's name had been forgotten. There were no more daughters.

And all these years later, it made him angry, but he knew it only made him angry because of everything else. All those other arguments that they'd never had over the years, quite simply because it was easier to give in than to disagree.

Well, Blythe, he thought to himself then. *One day soon, you won't be getting your own way, because I'll be damned if you'll make a prisoner of your own daughter the way Rae was made a prisoner of for that old mausoleum on Hope Square.*

12

Rae

Present

Danial Val turned out to be every bit as lovely as his grandmother. He arrived bright and early the following morning and he proved to be the perfect distraction from her restless night.

'I am so thankful to you for saying I can come and work here.' He had the most perfect manners, but with that, there was no missing, a slightly mischievous glint in his eye. Rae had a feeling, once he gained a little confidence, he could be marvellous fun to have around. Of course, he probably wouldn't be around for very long, young people willing to work tended to be snapped up quickly by businesses who were a lot busier than the hotel.

In Danial's honour (Rae suspected), Ros Stokes organised an unofficial meeting of her walking group for coffee that day too – so it felt for once as if the hotel really was open for business and things had fallen back into something like a normal rhythm.

'Come sit with us for a while, Rae,' Ros invited her over. 'We're thinking of starting a swimming club...' Ros had worked as the island ranger for a while, but these days, she was the official Pin Hill goat herder, more than that though, she'd set up a walking group for locals and visitors. Finbar Lavin reckoned she'd single-handedly increased foot traffic onto the island since she'd started by about two hundred percent. Everyone adored Ros, she was one of those newcomers who had managed, somehow, to make the island their own.

'I'm afraid I haven't been in the water in more years than I care to admit,' Rae said. The truth was, as a kid, Billy Purcell had pushed her in off the pier and she had completely panicked. Of course, they'd fished her out. No harm done, apart from to her pride and Billy Purcell's backside, which Blythe had given a solid kick afterwards. It had been enough to put Rae off the water. She didn't like heights. She didn't like being out of her depth in water or otherwise, ever since. If she was honest, she wasn't all that keen on Billy Purcell either.

'Well, it's not really a Swimming Club meeting, I mean, it started out that way, but now, well, we're just having a chat.' Jay, who was once the local postman on the island, pulled out a chair next to him and patted it.

'We're just talking about this spate of break-ins over the last week on the island.' One of the other ladies leant forward and whispered not too quietly.

'Break-ins?' And inwardly, Rae felt her heart race a little faster.

'Yes, apparently, it's everywhere, but here in the village, there's been four in just the last few days alone,' old Mrs Seager said carefully.

'And of course, they seem to know exactly what they're doing…' Fiona Dixon sounded as if she was as disgusted as she was cross. 'They are targeting older people, well, people living alone at any rate…'

'Have they gotten anything of value…' Rae began, because most people here on the island had little worth taking. This was the west of Ireland – not Martha's Vineyard.

'Of course, there are one or two new blow-ins.' This from Mae English whose family prided itself on being island residents for over three hundred years. Marcus had cruelly called the Englishes 'the batch family' – his sneaky way of calling them inbred.

'I'm sure it's not just…' Rae began and then a cup of perfect frothy coffee was placed before her, and she looked up to see Danial had made it and now he was clearing away the used cups and taking orders for fresh coffees and teas all round. Rae smiled. At this rate of going, he'd have taken in enough money to pay himself a wage in tips alone.

'Well,' Mae said, making a show of watching Danial's retreating back before adding, 'it's funny how there wasn't a thing amiss until we started seeing all sorts walking the streets of Muffeen Mòr.'

'I just can't help but think of dear old Constance Macken…' Jay Larkin looked across at Ros, because of course Constance had been her great friend also. 'Back in the day, Constance would have been out there organising a welcome committee for newcomers and putting us all to shame.' He smiled sadly.

'Probably, she would.' Rae giggled at the memory of Constance, who was, by any standards a total legend when it came to looking out for people – she collected waifs and strays better than any lint roller.

'It doesn't really help anyone, pointing fingers when we have no idea who's to blame. Surely, we want a united community. We need to hold onto the essence of what Pin Hill Island has always been, a place that looks after her own and welcomes people who come here for whatever reason. I mean, look at us – half of us are blow-ins,' Ros said.

'Well, isn't that the truth,' Heather Banks said with conviction. 'I mean, I never intended to stay here and if it wasn't for Constance and Ros and the way they made me feel as if I belonged, I'd probably be living a very different life, heaven knows where.'

'Maybe we should set up our own little community policing group, instead of a swimming group.' Jay said then.

'Isn't that a little like vigilantism?'

'I'm hardly talking about buying a batmobile!' He laughed. 'No, I mean, a WhatsApp group, you know, those of us taking a walk about in the evenings, we can log in that we've been along a certain route, keep an eye out for things that look suspicious.'

'That doesn't sound like a half bad idea at all.' Ros said softly. 'Although, to be fair, now most of my walking isn't around the village, it's across hills and coastline, but I can keep my eyes open for more than just roaming goats, too.'

'It might help some of the older people sleep a little easier.' Heather said and she looked at Rae. They were in similar positions; both in big empty buildings, alone and probably, giving off a similar vibe. A possible promise of thousands buried in a mattress somewhere, if only you could find the right one.

'Okay, this is getting us nowhere, I say we run those foreigners out.' May barked from behind her too-sweet tea. 'They have no business here, I mean, who invited them anyway,' she cocked her eye towards the bar where Danial was emptying the glasses and rinsing them in the sink.

'If it's Danial that you're referring to, I simply couldn't do without him here.' It was the truth. Rae had been hard pushed to find things to keep him busy, but now, he was unearthing all sorts of jobs himself. The place hadn't looked so spruce in ages, and she was enjoying his company. 'He's been invaluable, and I really can't sit by while you direct comments like that about a member of staff in my hotel.'

'Hmph, well pardon me for breathing my own fresh air. I'm sure, if that's what a lifetime of business means to you,' May grumbled. 'It's not how your grandfather would have done things, mark my words, if right was right, it's not how your sister would do things either.'

'Anyway, back to the matter at hand,' Jay said. 'What about this WhatsApp group?'

'It's a good idea – I'm definitely in,' Ros said and then she crossed over the bar to Danial and tried to slip a five-euro note into his hand as a tip. Later, Rae spotted the five euro slotted into a small glass with a neatly written note taped to the side – *staff tips to be shared equally.*

A loud crash at four o'clock in the morning woke Rae with a start.

It was strange, because for so long now, it felt as if she'd had the place to herself. Winter had been exceedingly quiet, which she was thankful for, she had too much to process, too much to deal with. She could never have faced up to a hotel full of guests asking after Marcus and worse, feeling their looks of pity when they didn't think she noticed.

Again.

Another crash.

What on earth? It was definitely in the hotel. For a moment, Rae was frozen – unsure whether she should check the bolt lock on the outside door of the flat or grab her dressing gown and the first makeshift weapon she could lay her hands on and go investigate. But no. She wasn't Blythe. Her sister would be out of her bed in short time and marching towards whatever trouble dared turn up on her doorstep. Blythe had always stood up for her, she'd protected her like a mother wolf before Marcus had come along.

Silence.

She wanted to believe she had just imagined those crashes, but she knew she hadn't. Someone was in the hotel. Not close by and unless they knew the place, it was a warren of rooms and corridors and steps up and down in unexpected places.

There wasn't a sound. The whole place felt as if it was just resting on an inhale, waiting for what would come next. For the first time since he'd died, she almost wished Marcus was still here. She spotted her phone, still charging on the nightstand. She picked it up with shaking hands. Dialled the local garda station. By some miracle her call was answered. She whispered into the darkness. *The Hope Square Hotel. Intruder. She was here alone. No. There was no burglar alarm. No. There was nothing worth stealing.* They promised to have someone outside the front door in ten minutes. For her part, she promised not to move, apart from checking that the front door of the flat was locked.

She waited there, for what felt like hours, but when she checked the time on her phone again, she knew the guard on the phone had been true to his word. Outside, she heard the loud knock on the front door. It echoed right through the hotel. She must have slid into the mules she'd been wearing earlier – not that she remembered putting them on, or the dressing gown, or where she had picked up the trophy Marcus had won in a table quiz a few years into their marriage.

She crept quietly towards the front door. Afraid to make a sound, just in case she'd bump into someone on the stairs. The hotel, so familiar, felt completely alien to her now, bathed in the blue flashing light of the garda car parked outside.

'Thank goodness you're here.' She almost collapsed with relief against the two guards standing on her doorstep.

'You're alright now, Rae,' Hugh Gilmore said. She was glad he had come because he was as gentle as a labrador, but he looked ferocious thanks to a lifelong dedication to the gym. 'We'll take a look, but we need you to come with us, if that's alright.'

'Of course.' They'd be walking about in circles for the night if she didn't lead the way. Honestly, it wasn't so much that the hotel was huge, it certainly wasn't all that big. Rather it was maze-like, thanks to the fact that her grandfather had joined three buildings into one without ever consulting an architect or a planner.

They walked the length of the hotel. Four floors, every corridor, every room and ensuite. On the way, they double-checked every window and every door. Rae had even pulled open wardrobes and looked under beds, just in case. It was when they wound around a little-used back stairway that she spotted the open window. On the floor beside it, an ancient vase had been pushed off to the floor.

'Oh!' Rae breathed and she bent down to touch the vase. 'It was just this,' she said then, but really it was so much more. She remembered the day Marcus had placed it here.

How often had she dusted beneath it, careful to leave it back exactly in that original spot. And it struck her again, nothing had changed here, she had not even had the courage to move this ugly vase.

'Unlikely anyone came through here...' Serena McGourty, a young Ban garda who occasionally dropped in for a cup of coffee on her rounds, peered out the open window. They were three floors up.

'It was so loud, I really thought,' Rae's voice wobbled with far more emotion than she could ever explain.

'It's okay. I mean, you know, staying here alone, well, it's a lot less...' Hugh stopped. 'I'm sure when summer comes and you have a full house; it's a completely different place.' He had known Marcus well. For a few years, they'd played winter five-a-side at the local community centre. And then, they didn't, and Rae had known whatever falling out there was between them, it had annoyed Marcus.

'Let's just go through the rest of the hotel and if you'd fancy it, we can sit down and have a cup of tea. Not long until it gets light now,' Serena said, picking up pieces of the vase as if it was something that Rae would ever want to put back together again.

13

Blythe

Present

They'd been in school together, Blythe and Mae English. Oh, they'd never been friends, Mae had always been one of those girls who scowled too much, sloped everywhere and slouched against walls outside of the main groups of girls that made up their year. Blythe might have completely forgotten her, except for the fact that she'd left a year before Blythe, to have a baby. Mae had married a man who was at least ten years older than her and never had a good word said about him, not even after he'd died of liver disease. He left Mae with four kids and a mountain of money owed she had no way of paying back.

Blythe knew all of this, only because she'd been a lifelong member of the St Vincent de Paul charity on the island. Mae was one of their most truly deserving cases while her kids were growing up. So far as Blythe was concerned, Muffeen Mòr had not let her down, but Mae somehow always believed she was still owed.

Blythe was surprised when she stopped her to chat on her way to the post office.

'Have you heard about these break-ins?' Mae wasn't a woman for small talk.

'Break-ins? On Pin Hill?' She checked that she'd heard the woman properly, after all, this was Pin Hill. Blythe couldn't remember the last time they'd had a serious crime on the island.

'It's them bloody foreigners, I tell you, your sister is worse for encouraging them. Next thing you know, we'll be overrun with them.'

'I'm not sure I follow...' Blythe said.

'I told her, *Blythe* wouldn't have them near the place, nor the old man, he'd have given them short shrift, I'm sure.' Mae crossed her arms over her sizeable breasts and exhaled as if she'd just completed a particularly arduous task.

'Rae has taken on new staff in the hotel, and they aren't locals?' Blythe was just about catching up, what with the vigorous head nods back towards the hotel, the dramatic eye rolls, and huffing and puffing. Mae had a habit of saying more between her words than with them.

'You didn't know?' Mae laughed then, a cruel sound, because she loved having one up on other people. 'Ah, well, probably she knew you wouldn't stand for it, giving jobs to blow-ins instead of local hardworking lads.'

'Ah...' Blythe smiled. She'd had no idea. Business in the hotel must be better than she'd thought, if Rae could afford to take on a full-time employee. Still, she felt uneasy, she'd never been keen on outsiders. She didn't trust them. Never had. 'And you're worried because...'

'Are you not listening? Because of the break-ins. All over the village at this stage, four houses over the last week alone.' Mae shook her head crossly, her anger was palpable. 'Oh, it's alright for the likes of you, out there, buried at the end of your fancy avenue, with security systems and all sorts probably, but the rest of us aren't so lucky.'

'I wouldn't wish a break-in on you for all the world, Mae, or anyone else for that matter,' Blythe said, although, from the side-eyes Mae was giving her, she wasn't sure that the same could be said in reverse.

'And as for them taking over that cottage...' Mae said, and Blythe had a feeling she was only warming up.

'The new family?'

'The Vals, that's what they call themselves. Here we are and there aren't enough houses for ourselves, and these strangers that haven't any connection to the island at all are falling into the lap of luxury.' Mae was still complaining.

'Ah...' Blythe said and of course, the whole country was up in arms because there simply weren't enough houses to go around. The immigration crisis had only added to the problem. 'The old McDaid cottage is hardly the lap of luxury...'

'Hah, easy for you to say.' Mae blew a long ribbon of cigarette smoke into the air. 'But, compared to my little house, you should know it well, you called to it to poke your nose in often enough over the years...'

'I never poked my nose in, I asked if I could help.' Blythe was quick to correct her, because it was true. When Mae had four snotty kids, Blythe had arrived with food baskets and gifts that were meant to come from Santa Claus.

'Anyway, I'm still there, only now I have two sons and one of their partners if you can believe it, and three grandchildren all bunking in with me. Can you imagine what that's like in a three-bedroom house that you can't swing a cat in at the best of times? How could any woman be sane, I ask you?'

'That can't be easy,' Blythe said and she knew it was all she could afford to say, because Still Water House, after all her hard work, would probably be akin to Buckingham Palace to Mae's eyes.

'Don't get me started,' Mae said crossly and maybe, when Blythe thought about it, she could see why Mae always seemed to be so angry with life. 'But there's plenty of money to put people from the other side of the world into the best of accommodation, everything laid on probably too – food in their bellies and money in their pockets and my sons can't even get a council flat on the mainland, never mind a house for my grandchildren.'

'You're probably not the only one feeling like that,' Blythe said, because of course, there were plenty of other people across the country in similar predicaments. Hadn't she seen it often enough on the evening news?

'Course I'm not. Plenty of people on the mainland are in the same boat, between these foreigners from God knows where and then all those crowds running away from war on the edge of Europe. Sure, we'll all be living in tents before we know it. It's time to put the foot down, let them know we're not having it.'

'Well, I'll call into the hotel and see what Rae has to say about it all.' Blythe smiled. The sun had come out and they had moved to the shade of a huge old sycamore. Occasionally, warm light dappled through the canopy of leaves overhead and Blythe felt it trickle across her nose and eyelids. She had closed her eyes, turned to face upwards.

'And, it's not just the houses that are the problem,' Mae cut into her thoughts again.

'What's that?'

'It's the jobs. There's no jobs for my boys in Muffeen Mòr. I mean, they've asked around, but no one wants to give them a job. But they'll bend over backwards for these strangers.'

'I'm quite sure that's not the case,' Blythe said.

'Oh, are you now.' Mae poked her in the side with a sharp elbow. 'What do you call that then?'

'Huh?' Blythe managed, because for a moment, she couldn't quite believe her eyes. In front of the hotel, a young – quite obviously foreign – man was shining up the brasses on the front door. Blythe felt that familiar feeling of terror rise in her. She couldn't help it. Even all these years later, it was there, just under her skin, that suspicion of strangers.

'See what I mean? Your uppity sister won't give my Jason a job, but she has one if some blow-in arrives knocking on her door.' With that, Mae threw down her still-lit cigarette butt on the ground, stubbed it angrily with her foot and marched away like a woman on a personal mission. Blythe couldn't blame her for being angry, it was a disgrace to think that Rae would give a job to an outsider over a local and she'd damn well let her know it, too.

14

Siggy

Present

Rae was out, of course, but Siggy decided to call into the hotel anyway. Danial would be there. Siggy picked up her pace once her friends had veered off towards the coffee shack on the sea front. He'd been on her mind occasionally since that day they'd bumped into each other. Actually, that wasn't true, the truth was, she couldn't stop thinking about him. Every time she opened a book to read, when she sat in classes that might have once interested her, her attention skipped away from her, remembering things he said or the way he'd looked at her that day on the square. They'd gone for coffee as agreed a few days earlier, but Siggy found that only made more room for him in her thoughts.

'Hah, I timed that perfectly,' she said when she walked into the bar and saw him wiping down the coffee machine ready for the next customer.

'I suppose you did,' he said then, taking down a cup and holding it up to check that he was right in thinking she would like an espresso. She nodded and smiled, funny, but around Danial Val, she couldn't help smiling. There was something about him – different to anyone else she'd met, not just in the obvious way either, there was no question, he was the best-looking boy around here, that was for sure. It turned out that despite the miles between them growing up, they'd read the same books, liked the same music and now, they laughed at the same jokes. Somehow, she had more in common with him than the other island kids who were divided into two groups, those obsessed with staying put on the island and those who couldn't wait to leave.

'I finished it,' she placed the book she'd been reading on the counter. 'Here you go, knock yourself out,' she said because he had told her it was his favourite book and he'd left his copy back in Mauritania. She'd read it over the last two days, consumed it so quickly that she knew she'd have to read it again. 'You were right,' she said pushing it towards him.

'I know, right? I've read it so many times,' he shook his head, looked a little embarrassed at himself.

'No, no, I can see why you loved it.' Usually, she read fantasy, she gobbled them up – this was a change. Her mother had been over the moon to see her with a book in her hand that didn't involve dragons or elves or alternate dimensions.

'I can't take your copy.'

'Of course you can, it turns out we had a second one. My mother has a selection of books in each of the rooms.' She stopped. Her mother would have a thing or two to say if she knew that Siggy had met up with Danial for coffee or that he filled up her thoughts far more than her schoolwork or any of those other things her mother liked to imagine kept her occupied.

'Rae said there's a library here, in a van?'

'Yes, the mobile library, it comes over on Thursdays, you can just join, Marisa will be delighted to have a new member. If you tell her what you like to read, she'll make sure to have a selection for you the following week.' Siggy had grown up looking forward to going to the library van, in terms of social life as a young kid, it was the highlight of her week on the island.

'I'll definitely join that,' he said, placing her cup before her. 'We've been in the bookshop in Ballycove, the woman there promised to put aside a box of books for each of us to collect next time we're on the mainland.' He was smiling now.

'Joy? Yeah, they're great too,' Siggy said. 'So, do you have days off here? I mean, are you planning on exploring the island or…'

'I would, but you know, I'd need a guide and…' He was making fun of her.

'Ha ha, well, just so you know, there's plenty to see here, if you know where to look.'

'Maybe you'll show me?' He was serious now.

'I might…' She tossed her hair, as if she was one of those popular girls in school with impossibly shiny hair.

'Whoa, I thought you were my official welcoming committee.'

'I forgot about that.' She laughed. 'Of course I'll show you the sights.' And she fell back into the default crazy smile that she couldn't stop when she was around him. 'If you're free this Saturday and the weather stays fine, I'll bring you to the best places to swim,' she said, thinking of the old tidal pool at the other side of the island. Of course, the best place to swim was the still water pool at the back of her own house, but her mother would have a fit if she knew that Siggy was hanging out with Danial. Siggy often wondered if perhaps her mother had some valid reason for her suspicion of strangers; but she couldn't think back to one thing that might have happened to make her mother so full of misgiving. They'd fought about it, when Siggy was too young to realise that some battles were never going to be won. She'd been invited to a birthday party of a girl who'd just arrived on the island. All the other girls in her class were looking forward to it. Of course, her mother refused to let her go, her father just rolled his eyes, shrugged his shoulders and she knew eventually, changing her mother's opinion was a waste of her own time and energy. There was as much chance of undoing her mother's firm opinions than there was of turning the ocean backwards.

'Another cup?' he asked, noticing she had finished her coffee.

'I shouldn't...' She smiled, but he took her cup and rinsed it out, began to measure out the beans for a refill. Her mother assumed she was here to help Rae, so she set about tidying up around the reception area. It was a default operation, taking Rae's scarf from the chair and leaving it in the flat. It was as she was coming back to chat with Danial that she spotted the open letter on the floor where it had slipped from the sideboard.

She hadn't meant to read it, not really. But it had drifted to the floor as she passed and when she picked it up, she spotted the deeply highlighted red notice at the top.

Warning Notice.

It was from the bank. Siggy scanned the letter quickly. Reread it again, because somehow the meaning hadn't quite sunk in. She felt her hands shake. Rae owed the bank a lot of money and she hadn't been keeping up the repayments. For months. How could this happen? They were threatening to take things further. Rae could lose the hotel.

Siggy felt winded, as if someone had come along and punched her in the guts.

'Hey,' Danial had appeared at her side. 'Coffee made, come on, before it gets cold.' He was smiling at her now and despite the cold fear rising in her, she felt her stomach tumble over in a frenzy of butterflies at his proximity.

'Thanks,' she said, keeping her voice even, despite the confusion in her heart.

They sat next to each other, at the bar counter that only served beer at funeral parties these days, and even then, it was mainly tea and coffee, soft drinks and the occasional bottle of wine.

'So, your family own a guest house – it's like here?' he asked then.

'Still Water House? Well, yes, I suppose so…' And she looked around, seeing the hotel differently now, somehow that letter had made it all seem a little less substantial than before.

'They will expect you to take it over, one day?' Somehow, he put into words that thing that Siggy tried to push from her mind when she thought about her future.

'Probably, but…'

'It's not what you want?'

'I'm not sure, maybe someday, but I want to see a bit of the world first, you know? I don't just want to slip into old age. I think…' She stopped, because it felt a betrayal to say that she felt that was what had happened to Rae. Somehow, she knew, that even if her mother believed Rae had stolen the hotel from her, the fact was that Rae didn't belong here. She wasn't happy in the hotel, maybe she'd never been happy here. They might be sisters, but her aunt and her mother were chalk and cheese. Her mother was the hotelier, for sure, but Rae, no, Rae should have been set free years ago.

'See the world?'

'Maybe.' Although, she had a feeling her mother would do everything in her power to keep her here.

'I'd like to see New York,' he said a little wistfully. 'Of course, it's no good going like this.' He held out his hands.

'Oh, God, yes, me too,' it slipped out like a relief, despite herself.

'Well, maybe one day.' He looked her in the eye and for a moment, it felt as if much more lay between his words – her heart missed a beat, and she felt her cheeks flush. Silence that was as awkward as it was delicious lingered between them. She thought he might lean forward and kiss her, but then, he smiled and looked away and she realised, she was disappointed that he had not.

'So? New York, when?'

'Well, right now, I have nothing to offer – unless I go as a translator, but I'm not sure that's what I'd want to spend my life doing.'

'So, what will you do?'

'I don't know. Well, I know what I'd like to do. I'd like to finish my studies, properly qualify in a university, a good university. Maybe get a scholarship to one of the big east coast universities in the US for postgraduate work and then who knows, go where the wind blows, but make a difference.' He sipped his coffee thoughtfully. 'Yes, I'd like to make a difference.'

'You could, you know...' she said softly.

'I think for now, I must earn some money. I need to get a proper job, one that pays. My grandmother has left everything she knows and loves to keep me safe. I want to repay that sacrifice in any way I can.' He smiled at her now and there it was, that something she couldn't quite name. Electricity? And she realised, the scariest thing about Danial Val was that he had no idea of the effect he had on her – or what it would mean if something happened between them. He was, she knew, the very last person on the island her mother could bear to see her being friends with, much less anything beyond that.

When she arrived home later that evening, her mind was full of him. Her thoughts stitching over and back across the conversation they'd had earlier in the day. Somehow, he'd made her feel energised, as if the inertia of going through the motions had melted away from her. She didn't have to keep on pretending that she would live exactly the life her mother expected of her for the rest of her days. Indeed, if the letter she'd come across in the hotel earlier was anything to go by, Rae wouldn't be able to keep doing the same thing for much longer either.

The hotel. That was it. She'd start off by helping Rae to save the hotel. If she could help Rae to secure the hotel and her mother to have Still Water House included in the White Book, then maybe her mother would see, she was well fit to choose what she wanted for her own future.

After dinner, she raced upstairs to her bedroom where she set to making her plans.

The following morning, Siggy had what her mother would call, a spring in her step. She had maybe not a strategy, but at the very least, a few new suggestions for Rae.

'Well, look who's all enthusiastic.' She smiled when she arrived at the hotel to see Danial polishing the old brasses on the front door.

'Hello to you, too.'

'How long have you been here?' she asked then.

'For two or three hours before you even thought of getting out of bed, probably.' He laughed and so did she, because the truth was quite the opposite.

She went immediately to find Rae to show her the work she'd done the previous evening. There were four options. The first one wasn't really an option; it was a pathway to whatever they might do next.

'We ask Danial if he'll redesign the website – since he knows all about SEO – maybe we market things from right there at the front desk.' She pointed out towards reception. They were in Rae's flat. Sitting next to each other on the lumpy old sofa that had been here for as long as Siggy could remember.

'That's a great idea. Now, all we must decide is what we're going to market...' Rae looked around the little sitting room. It was meagre, compared to the rest of the hotel. There was such a faded, empty air to the place. No window to speak of, well, there was a tiny square with old-fashioned opaque glass that might have once opened out against a brick wall opposite, but had for too long been painted shut. Now, the main source of fresh air came either from the reception outside or by leaving the bedroom door open, because in there, a huge window looked out across the car park. 'Actually, I've been thinking...'

'Okay.'

'This is radical, but I thought, the building is too big. I mean, it's three huge houses into one, right?'

'Technically, yes.' Rae sat a little straighter on the sofa next to her, obviously piqued. The hotel as it stood today operated as one huge Georgian building, but the façade still had three front doors. There were three staircases – although two of them were hardly ever used – and three rear exits, each leading out to the same car park at the rear.

'What if you sold number three?' There, that was it. The Hope Square Hotel was a huge building, far bigger than they could ever fill in today's terms. Siggy's grandparents had purchased the original houses one after another and knocked them into one big building. Number one was an end property, while number three was closest to the old bank building.

'Who on earth would want to buy it? I mean, I don't think I could just sell it, could I? Surely, there's planning laws or...' Her voice trailed off.

'I can think of lots of people who'd want to buy it,' Siggy said. 'These properties are probably the most desirable on the island. Number three could easily be turned into anything from four luxury apartments to eight normal sized one- or two-bedroom flats and I mean, it's all there – the ensuites, the original features for the most part, fireplaces and covings and with the price of property these days... I'd say it could really make it worth your while.'

'Then what?' Rae said quietly, but Siggy had a feeling that she was either shocked by the idea of something she wouldn't have considered in a million years or maybe her mind was whirring past that letter in the day diary and doing up the sums. Like it or not, this made good financial sense.

'Then you have a manageable size hotel. You can invest in upgrading it or you can decide to scale back, just make it into a guest house. You could even turn over a whole floor for yourself – make a proper home with a lovely sitting room and an open fire, with bookshelves and an actual window that looks out on the square.'

'Oh, I don't know about all that...' Rae said softly.

'Know about what?' Blythe was standing at the door watching them. Her voice so unexpected it gave them both a start, so the notebook went flying to the floor in the surprise.

'Mum, you gave us a fright.' Siggy laughed nervously, instantly feeling guilty, as if in even suggesting the sale of part of the hotel, she'd done something wrong.

'Nothing, nothing at all, we're just daydreaming,' Rae said and she got up and moved to the door.

'Hmph, well for some. It looks like rain out there today and you pair have the time for daydreaming.' Blythe looked around the flat as if it might yield some extra information she was not privy to. 'Any coffee left in that pot? I'm absolutely parched.' She flopped into the chair that had for years been Marcus's favourite.

'I'll make some fresh for you, hang on,' Siggy said, jumping up.

'So, what about these break-ins...' Blythe was saying as Siggy headed for the foyer to get fresh coffee.

15

Kip

Twenty-One Years Ago

It was midway through May; off-season, when Kip's mother told him to go up to Still Water House and see if he could help there for a few weeks.

That was his mother all over.

Although, as he cycled up the avenue, Kip felt a bit of a fraud.

It wasn't as if he had any actual qualifications to help, but by the same token, there was no denying the avenue alone could provide a team of men with enough work to keep them going for the summer. It was badly overgrown, with a thick ridge of grass cutting from the start to end up the centre of it. Of course, the trouble was, there were no men available on the island at this time of year to take on jobs in a place like this.

Every available man was either running his own farm or out on a trawler from well before dawn with little appetite for much more than a good night's sleep before the following day began.

So, maybe his mother was right. After all, there wasn't much more to keep him busy up at their little cottage.

The garden didn't even pose an afternoon's worth of exercise for him and over the years, on weekends and holidays, he'd painted and updated the inside of the cottage, exactly to his mother's specifications.

He doted on his mother even though, still, he had to work hard for so much as a spoonful of praise, but that was just her way. The last thing she wanted was for him to lose the run of himself.

'I'm here to see your mother,' he told the younger of the two sisters when she opened the front door.

'Mum?' she looked at him blankly.

'Aye, don't ask.' He rolled his eyes and they both laughed. She, Rae, showed him into a grand hall, that smelled slightly musty, and had surely seen better days, but there was no escaping the fact that with a little attention, it could be truly knockout.

'Hang on,' Rae said and she poked her head around the door of what he assumed was a sitting room. 'Mum, there's someone to see you.' He heard her whisper, before opening back the door and letting him in.

'Mrs Scott, I'm...' He held out his hand to the tiny woman who was lying on an ancient-looking day bed. He'd hardly have recognised her as the striking woman he remembered from childhood. Mrs Scott and her family were the big wigs on the island – everyone expected their two daughters to go off and marry lords or princes one day. Of course, things had changed with the death of their father.

'Ah, Kip, how lovely.' Mrs Scott murmured as she tried to raise herself slightly to greet him. It looked as if every movement caused her some pain and he sat close to her, just opposite, to save her having to move any more on his account. 'Tell me what you are up to these days? We're all so proud of you on Pin Hill.' She smiled and he could still see traces of the great beauty she had once been.

'That's very kind, but...' He always felt embarrassed when people praised him, it felt undeserved, after all, what did he do apart from kick a ball around a pitch for a few months a year and he got well paid for doing it. 'It's off-season now, so, I'm at a loose end and my Mam, she thought you could do with some help around here...'

'What kind of help?' Blythe, the oldest daughter had appeared as if from nowhere and was standing in the doorway at his back.

'Hey,' he said turning to look at her. He hadn't laid eyes on the kid in four years, but now, looking at her, she wasn't a kid anymore. Somehow, the scrappy girl that she had once been had disappeared and, in her place, a striking young woman had emerged. Kip suddenly found himself lost for words.

'So, you're looking for a job?'

'No, no, not at all,' he said because he already had a job, just not a day's work to do for the next two months. He was lucky. He was injury free, many of the other players would spend their down time getting physio or resting up damages from the gruelling season they'd just put in.

'So, charity?' Blythe walked over to stand next to where her mother was resting on the sofa.

'Not at all.' His voice had risen, but suddenly he wasn't sure why he'd come. A mixture of deep embarrassment and sudden shyness overtook him in the face of this intense girl. 'No, that's not it at all,' he said then.

'Oh, Kip, don't mind Blythe, her bark is worse than her bite.' Mrs Scott laughed then. 'Blythe, bring us in a nice pot of coffee and some of that shortbread you made earlier, tell

Rae she's welcome to join us, too.' She shook her head, her face still lit up with amusement.

'Sure,' Blythe said and the way she looked down at her mother almost made Kip's heart break. Suddenly, he knew, they needed help a lot more than they realised.

'I'm sorry Mrs Scott if I've overstepped the mark, it's just I've driven my mother round the twist doing jobs she doesn't need to have done and she thought, with the size of this place, I could at least help keep the grass down or make myself useful in some way about the place for the few weeks I'm home.'

'Don't be sorry, I'd be glad to have you. As you can see, the grounds are about to overtake the house if we don't do something about them, but there's literally no one available. Every man on the island is up to ninety with the good weather – I can't blame them, they have families to feed and by comparison, what's this place other than a folly to times past.'

'It's a beautiful place,' Kip said and he realised he'd lowered his voice, but the fact was, from the moment he walked onto the avenue he had the strangest feeling as if he was exactly where he was meant to be today. 'I'm no expert gardener, but I can keep the grass down for the summer and maybe clear up that driveway for you.'

'That's so kind of you. I'll pay you, of course.'

'I didn't come for the money,' he said, but then he felt, rather than saw, Blythe behind him and he realised that it might soften her towards him in some small way if she didn't feel as if he saw their family as some sort of crazy reverse charity case. 'I'm happy to work for my dinner, does that sound fair?'

'Breakfast, dinner and tea, if you'd like them,' Rae said then as she dropped into one of the fat chesterfield chairs next to the huge empty fire grate.

'We can help you, you know, between our other chores,' Blythe said then, leaving a tray filled with three large mugs, a delicate cup, cafetiere and enough shortbread biscuits to feed a large family.

'You have enough to be getting on with,' her mother said and she smiled with such pride at Blythe. 'Honestly, I don't know how you already fit so much into the days.' She shook her head then.

'I can definitely help,' Rae said, picking up a piece of shortbread and leaving the coffee pouring to her sister. 'I mean, I'd like to, you know, maybe take on one area outside,' She said then and Kip thought, yes, he'd enjoy working alongside Rae. There was an endearing innocence to her and a twinkle in her eye that spoke to him of a sense of fun that would shorten any job.

The next few weeks raced by. Soon, he settled into a routine of sorts. A run along the beach first thing in the morning and then a quick shower before heading up to Still Water House on his bicycle. Mostly, he was tinkering about in one of the many sheds and outhouses by the time Rae – or sometimes Blythe – would find him and insist on feeding him something to start the day.

The days themselves were long but satisfying. There was something about the peace of the place, getting to grips with the overgrown garden and grounds when the weather was fine. When the rain poured down for three days on end in the middle of July, he organised one of the sheds so it was easy to put his hand on any tool he needed in a matter of moments.

Most days Rae helped for an hour or two. She was good company, a little lost perhaps in her own way, flailing beneath the death of her father, the weakened state of her mother and trying to find purchase for her own identity in the shadow of her older, much more accomplished, confident and, in Kip's opinion, more striking sister.

Whoa. When Kip realised that he did indeed feel that Blythe was the more beautiful of the sisters it pulled him up short. Falling for one of the Hope Square sisters was not on his game plan this year. Even less so, because she was younger than him, impossibly strong-minded and more disconcertingly, she didn't even seem to register his existence. Well, not beyond being perfectly polite and gracious because he was doing such trojan work around the house. It was her ambivalence to him that drove his desire on even more, probably. He'd become used to women and girls fawning over him, not that he'd taken advantage of it. There was too much to unpack about his own parents and how things had ended up there for Kip not to realise that he had to tread softly and very carefully when it came to falling in love.

'Hey.' Blythe almost made him jump when she came up behind him silently one afternoon in the garden. It was midway through August, and it felt as if they'd hardly gotten to know each other, despite the fact that she seemed to dominate his thoughts more and more with every passing day. 'Thought you might like to try some homemade lemonade.' She handed him an ice-cold glass, a pitcher in her other hand. It was one of those intensely hot days, when even the shade was too warm to sit in. He drank the glass down in about three gulps. 'So, it's good, yeah?' Blythe laughed then and he thought, she doesn't laugh half often enough. Right there, he decided that there was nothing he wanted more if he was to ever settle down with anyone, than to make them laugh like Blythe Scott did just now.

'Sorry, I shouldn't have gulped it down, but yes, it's very good, and...'

'I know, it's a scorcher. Why don't you take a break? You know, you're not tied to the job here,' she said softly, and he watched as she put the pitcher down and sat at the edge of the still water pool. 'Come on,' she called back to him tossing off her shoes and submerging her feet and legs into the still water. It seemed to Kip as if to join her might be to take a slice of heaven.

'You're right. It's too hot to work in this sun.' And he dropped to the ledge next to her and pulled off his old work boots and thick socks, plunging his feet into the pool, and it felt divine. The freshness of it shimmied up his legs, sending pleasant cool shivers along his spine. He bent forward, submerged his hand and arms up to his elbows. The relief was like a thousand small arrows of balm flying up through him.

'So?' She looked at him now from under her fringe that had bleached blonder in the bright sun.

'So,' he said then, and he held her eyes for longer than he'd meant to, but what the hell, he'd never felt like this before. Blythe, the more time he spent here, he thought was amazing. She never stopped giving. She looked after her mother, she took care of Rae, she seemed to keep the whole place running and when she wasn't doing that, she was racing to the hotel and keeping that show on the road as well. And she was damned sexy. Even sitting here next to her filled him with a yearning to move closer to her. He wanted to put his arms around her, pull her to him, feel the softness and strength of her body next to his. Stop it. He had to talk to her, stop thinking like this. He wanted to tell her she was amazing, but he couldn't do that, not without sounding a bit weird.

'Kip.' She said his name softly. 'I...' she turned to look at him and for another long moment, no words passed between them, but maybe something else was said in the silence. 'I wanted to thank you, you know, for all you've done for us. I mean, it feels wrong, that we haven't paid you, that you don't want anything and yet, you've done so much.'

'I'm happy to do it, Blythe, that's the truth,' he said then and he was being honest. 'I'm not great at sitting home with time on my hands, I needed something to fill my days and honestly...' he stopped. 'You know, I'm not always going to be able to play rugby, someday, I'm going to have to retire and working here, well, it's given me a sense of what I'd like to do.'

'Become a gardener?'

'Maybe,' he laughed. But he meant so much more than that. He'd tackled lots of odd jobs about the place, too. Every time Mrs Scott invited him to have tea with her, he found some little task to take on in the house as well as outside. 'And I've loved this place, it's very...' he looked down at the pool where his feet were dangling next to Blythe's, 'special.'

'I suppose it is.' She laughed then. 'When my dad was... well, before the accident, Rae and I used to spend every summer day down here at the pool.' She laughed then and he felt her gaze across at him, assessing him. 'Come on.' She said, pulling off her T-shirt so she was sitting next to him for a second with just her bra and shorts on. Then, suddenly she was in the pool. Screaming with delight at the cold. 'What's stopping you?' She held up her hand and he grabbed it and then she was pulling him and suddenly, the cold welled up around him and he felt more alive than he'd ever felt in his whole life.

'It's amazing.' He spluttered, 'this is amazing!' He shouted above her shrieking for joy. He felt like a boy, filled with that childish happiness that was so fleeting, you hardly recognised it was gone, until one-off moments like this, if you were lucky enough to experience them.

'Kip,' she said again and later, he marvelled at how he'd heard her, because it was little more than a whisper, but when he turned, she was right up next to him, her face tilted towards his and he knew, or maybe he didn't know, but this was right. He pulled her close, felt the length of her against him. He kissed her long and slow right there in the centre of the still water pool and far off in the distance, his whole world melted into insignificance at that moment.

For all the glory on the rugby pitch. All the prizes, the travel and even the wins, Kip knew, he'd never felt as content as he did that year in Still Water House. Quite aside from him and Blythe, he felt as if he belonged there. It wasn't just the place either, he was growing fond of Rae and absolutely adored Mrs Scott. On those afternoons, when she was able, she called for him to come and join her for tea in the afternoon. Kip knew she always tried to make it for the hottest part of the day, in the hope that it was some little break for him out of the sun. Some days Blythe would have baked, other days, it was shop-bought biscuits on a tray set out by Rae served up in the grand, faded drawing room. Even on the warmest days, Mrs Scott was settled under a heavy woollen rug from the mills over in Ballycove. She was frail and he hated to admit it, but he thought she was growing weaker each time he saw her, but even so, her spirit was like a flame. When she smiled, it felt as if the whole room brightened up, she had the most amazing eyes, you knew, when you spoke, she was really listening to you.

It was on one of those afternoons that she asked him to open a card she'd received in the post and read it to her. Kip had self-consciously stumbled across the letters. Mrs Scott smiled indulgently.

'You should have said,' she murmured when he'd finished. And he looked at her, that familiar emotion of shame and inadequacy roiling up in him. 'It's nothing to be ashamed of, it's dyslexia, as common as the hydrangeas in the garden, I'd say,' she said then. 'I read about it, in *The Times* a few months ago. Some study, carried out by one of the top universities, do you know what it said?'

'That people who can't read feel as thick as two short planks?' He was aiming for humour; it had long become his only weapon of deflection.

'No, you must never say that. They said that in research, they'd found that people with dyslexia who spent their whole lives compensating, tended to be much brighter in other ways.' She smiled then, held his eye until it felt uncomfortable for him. 'I'm paraphrasing, but you understand, Kip?'

'Aye, Mrs Macken was always saying the same thing to me in school.'

'Constance is such a gift to this island, isn't she?'

'She's lovely, everyone's favourite teacher.'

'Anyway, Constance is right, especially when it comes to you. Do you know how many intellectual derelicts there are in this world? People who can read and write and yet, can't support themselves, can't make their own beds in the morning or stick by a wife for longer than it takes to break her heart?'

'I know that well enough.'

'Hmm. Well, you're not like that, Kip. I've watched you out there, in the garden, here in the house, you're a very clever man, I don't believe there's a single thing you couldn't do if you set your mind to it.' She said this with such conviction, that Kip felt a knot of unexpected emotion rise up in him.

'You are a very special person, Mrs Scott. I've never met anyone like you, it's been an honour not just to spend time here, but to get to know you all.'

'It's a joy for us. I'd like to think that when I'm...' She smiled sadly now, 'well, when I'm gone, you'd still be here.'

'Oh, don't be talking like that.'

'Listen to me,' she said, her expression suddenly serious. 'I have two daughters, and I worry about them both. But I look at you and Blythe together and...' She stopped, because so far as Kip knew, Blythe had never told anyone about that kiss in the pond or the fact that when they were alone, sometimes they held hands and once, she'd thrown her arms about him and clung to him so hard, it felt as if she needed him more than the air itself. 'You're right together.'

'Ah, Mrs Scott.' He wasn't sure now if she was just ribbing him.

'I know, I know, I shouldn't be saying these things, but there might not be the chance again. You'll go back to that other world. It could be a year before you're properly back here on Pin Hill again and by then...' She looked out the window. 'Well, I don't think I'll be here to admire the garden and the fine work you've done next summer.'

'Don't say that,' he said hoarsely, but maybe he knew it was true as well as she did.

'Well, just remember what I said, Blythe is the most caring daughter a mother could ask for, but these days, she doesn't let too many people in – I think it might be her father's death.' She shook her head sadly. 'She's cut herself off, as if she's afraid that people will set out to hurt her. But she's pure gold underneath. True, she can be a stubborn piece of work sometimes, she knows her own mind so well, there's no talking sense into her, but if you love her, all I'm asking is that you persevere, she will make you very happy one day.' She stopped, there were footsteps in the hall and then as the door opened, she whispered, 'promise me.'

'I promise.' The words slipped out, by accident or in surprise, but once he'd said them, he knew, a promise is a promise and this one he fully intended to keep.

16

Blythe

Nineteen Years Ago

Their mother was dying. Blythe realised it long before anyone else seemed to notice. Rae was oblivious, drifting from Blythe, drifting from everything. She was too young to fully grasp exactly what was going on and their grandfather was in denial. Who could blame him, he'd lost so much already.

Blythe had taken over.

It wasn't that she'd meant to, but she was the oldest, and it was in her nature. She got up each morning an hour before everyone else, put on a saucepan of porridge, made sure that the fridge was stocked for whatever was needed for the dinner later. She trundled up and down to the clothesline in the garden, and made sure that their lives were as straightened out as she left the kitchen each night before she went to bed. First thing in the mornings, she brought a cup of tea to her mother; she sat there while it was drunk and then tried to cajole her into some breakfast. Mostly, they would chat, other times, she would sit by the window and watch the sun come up and trace across the fields. She loved those moments, sitting there in the silence, just the two of them. Even before she realised her mother was slipping away, she knew it was precious, more so now, because it was confirmed in her mind, those mornings were in short supply.

For what felt like a long time, Blythe just kept on going, putting one foot in front of the other, keeping all the plates balanced, she was a Scott, and that meant something.

It was a funny thing, because for all she did, she had a feeling that the only person who really saw her was Kip Carney and even he wasn't around all that much most of the time. Certainly, every time he came back to the island, he made his way up to Still Water House or tracked her down in the hotel. She wasn't sure if she was his girlfriend exactly, but when they were together, she felt somehow as if some vital part of her had slipped into place. Then, of course, he left again and she was never courageous enough to ask him straight out, if there were other girls, or if they were, God, she hated even saying, but exclusive.

He could have other girls, she wouldn't be surprised if he did, she wasn't even sure she'd blame him. They never slept together, oh, they came close, now and then, but Kip was always the one to pull back, as if in the crossing of some invisible line, he might crack something valuable between them.

But he was devoted to her. She knew this, underneath it all, she knew it. Her mother and Rae both adored him. Pappy? She wasn't sure why, he hadn't said anything exactly, but it was there on the atmosphere between them, like a note, hanging on the end of a bar – slightly out of tune, out of place, as if it was something that would have to be sorted out at some point, but Pappy did not have the will to do it just yet.

Kip was still the closest thing to a celebrity in the village. But, you'd never think it, because there was no big ego there with Kip. He might well be one of the best rugby players from west of the Shannon ever, but he didn't lose sight of who he truly was beyond the playing field. Their start in life was so different, she in this huge house, bought with her grandmother's fortune, and the lingering distrust of the locals for German money they still felt did not belong on the island. He, on the other hand, was reared in a tiny council house, his mother beloved by the islanders, even if that love was tinged with pity.

It made his success even more amazing, really, having been called up to the panel to play for the national rugby team. In off-season, it seemed as if everywhere Blythe went, he popped up before her. He'd even been on the television after he scored a try that didn't quite save the day, but might have if only it wasn't against the All-Blacks.

Blythe almost didn't realise it until the end of the previous summer. She had fallen in love with Kip Carney, it came as a surprise as much as an awareness. This was not the way she had felt when she was a kid, when every girl in school had lusted after him. This was different. She'd come to admire, not just his good looks, although, it didn't hurt that he was a bloody good-looking man; but more than that, she loved the way he made her mother howl with laughter. It seemed to Blythe, there was nothing he could not do. He'd turned the garden round completely, with hard work and a vision that was unexpected. Even inside their home, he'd tackled jobs that had been on her father's to-do list for years. Little things at first, like patching wallpaper and filling cracks around the window frames to keep the draughts at bay. The strangest thing about him was he had no idea how accomplished he really was and that only made him more attractive in Blythe's eyes.

And Kip was decent – for all the adulation, it never went to his head. He made time for everyone. It didn't matter if you were the Archbishop of Ireland or a dog in the street – he'd stop and say hello and the word was, he'd be the first to hand you a fiver if you needed it.

Sometimes, she wondered if he knew she was head over heels in love with him.

In the back of her mind, she sensed his reluctance to take things further or make their relationship somehow more official had more to do with the age difference between them, than it had her grandfather's disapproval.

At least Rae had settled down, even if, Blythe worried constantly that she'd go off the rails again. She was Rae after all, far too trusting for her own good. You never knew if she'd arrive home with a cat or a dog or some no-good boyfriend who'd never done a hand's turn and saw the Scott girls as a ticket to a free lunch.

The notion that the hotel was the most stable thing she could count on, occurred to her when she was in that drowsy state between slumber and awareness. It was almost dawn, and she was waiting for Rae to return from some date she'd breezed out the door to earlier. Blythe had woken at two o'clock, checked Rae's room to find she had not yet returned and immediately her mind raced to the worst scenarios possible. At every turn, she imagined her sister being set upon by some masked stranger. In her gut, she felt that familiar crazed fear well up in her. Since that day in the flat when those intruders had assailed her, her thoughts had raced in all the worst directions when she became stressed. God, she scrunched her eyes closed remembering it again. She'd been sure she would be murdered there or die of complete and utter terror that she couldn't get away.

She sat now at the kitchen table, trying to steady her nerves, trying not to think of the worst thing that could have happened to her sister, but every second felt like an eternity. Sometimes, she thought she might go mad, worrying about Rae and their mother and Pappy; honestly, if it wasn't for the hotel. At least she had the hotel, she knew where she was with the hotel. It felt like a calling, as if she was doing what she was always meant to do, and even if life beyond it was skimming past her in some ways, at least she had the satisfaction of that.

It was pneumonia in the end.

One long weekend where her mother wheezed and hacked and slept fitfully through it. The night before she died, she called Blythe to her room.

'Promise me.' She breathed and her voice was so low, Blythe had to lean across her just to hear.

'Anything, just ask,' Blythe said because she adored her mother.

'Promise me you'll take care of Rae and this place, when I'm...'

'Of course I'll take care of everything, Mum, of course, you don't need to worry about anything...'

'You're such a good girl. I can see it. You've got a good heart and I'm sorry. I'm so sorry, that I'm...' She began to cry, and Blythe thought that the tears would split her in two because she could hardly breathe as it was.

'Please Mum, don't be upset, really, we're going to be fine. You need to rest, everything will be fine and by Monday, the antibiotics will have kicked in and this summer, we'll get you outside in the garden again and...' It was a lie. Maybe they both knew it, but her mother smiled, that serene smile that made Blythe feel as if it could be true and everything just might turn out okay in the end.

'Of course, everything will be fine. I can depend on you. But I'm asking so much of you ...'

'You have never asked for too much.' Blythe breathed and she kissed her mother on her forehead and was glad to see the worried creases disappear from her mother's mouth with that. She fell asleep then for a few hours and Blythe hoped that maybe that was the worst of it over.

In some ways, it was; her mother passed away peacefully in her sleep a few hours later.

This time round, Blythe knew, the funeral was in her hands. Her grandfather was slowing down, to the point that these days, he walked with a stick that he joked made him look distinguished.

She planned it with great care – her mother had been a woman of taste, but valued simplicity. There would be a church service, with flowers and hymns and a funeral lunch afterwards in the hotel. She couldn't face a long three-day event in their home as was the custom on the island. *Let them talk*, she thought to herself, *let them talk*.

Perhaps because the funeral had been condensed so much, she'd been taken aback by the turnout after the mass and burial. The hotel, when she arrived back from the graveyard, was thronged, walking through the front door alone took almost ten minutes as she negotiated handshakes and condolences from familiar faces from across the island and many who had travelled over from the mainland.

Strangely, Blythe found herself searching the crowd for Kip. Although it was completely pointless, he'd already rung her from South Africa. There was no way he could make it back in time, but they'd spent so long on the phone, the operator had cut them off twice – fearing the Irish team would not cover the charges. If he was here now, she knew he'd stand head and shoulders higher than anyone else in the foyer. She took a long deep breath, just thinking about him calmed her in some weird way.

It was when she reached the bar that she spotted the one familiar face she never imagined she'd see again.

Marcus Johnson.

He was standing next to the staircase, holding a cup of tea and chatting to her grandfather as if they'd known each other their whole lives. Blythe found herself doing a double take, rubbing her eyes to make sure it was not some cruel mirage – an oasis of familiarity in this desert of grief.

'Hey,' he reached towards her, pulled her close and kissed her cheek when she approached them. She breathed in the taste of cologne from his body, noticed that his suit looked expensive, his tie was pinned with what looked like a French rotary tie clip. He was every bit the successful hotel manager she'd always known he'd become once he got his degree. She felt that familiar stab of regret, that she'd never had the chance to finish up properly.

'What on earth are you doing here?' All the basic conversational skills had deserted her. She put her hand to her hair, regretted not having taken the time to get it done before the funeral. She felt acutely the fact that she was bedraggled and washed out, having stood in the wind and watched as her mother's grave was covered over with earth, until at last, she could tear herself away. At some level, she knew she must be still standing there with an awestruck expression on her face. She only just remembered to close her mouth and not fire a dozen hot and heavy questions at him, by some miraculous surge of personal reserve.

'Well, that's a nice how do you do, indeed,' her grandfather laughed at her surprise.

'I was just telling Jack.' He stopped, smiled at the old man and Blythe wondered at the familiarity that seemed to have sprung up between them so quickly. 'I've just returned from overseas and taken a job in that new five-star hotel in Galway. One of the chefs there told me about your mother. I'm so sorry, Blythe, truly sorry.' He shook her hand again and she realised that his appearance had made her forget for those few moments exactly why they were all gathered here.

'She hadn't been well, you know, since…' There was no point going into it all now, so much had happened since that last time she'd seen him, when he left her standing there to go back into the flat on her own. And then, he'd never called her. She'd disappeared from her life in Dublin, and there had been nothing. Not a card or a call when her father died, not so much as a whisper from him after that day. She'd forgotten that, as the years had passed, only thinking of how crazy she had been for him, once.

'I was telling Marcus about the accident and how things were here, with all of us and the great job you've been doing, helping out here in the hotel,' her grandfather said, and somehow the words stung, because she didn't see herself as helping out – she saw herself as running the place.

'It's been busy, alright.' She brushed it off as if it meant nothing.

'You should think about maybe taking on more help. Blythe told me all about the hotel, of course, but I didn't imagine it would be quite so charming.' Marcus turned his full attention to Jack now.

'You'd be surprised how many youngsters can't wait to get away from the island, it's damn near impossible to take on staff who'll stick with it for any length of time.' Jack shook his head ruefully. 'Thankfully, Blythe seems content to stick around.'

'Ah well, she has the place in her bones at this stage, I suppose.' Marcus smiled at her and there it was, still that effect he'd always had on her. Back then, she thought it was love, maybe she'd always been out of her depth with him.

'I love it, that's the truth of it. And I have great plans for the place.'

'Ah hush now,' Jack put his hand on her arm. 'Sure, today's not the day to be thinking of plans,' he said in that way he always did when he didn't want to entertain any changes she might suggest. For all he praised her and depended on her, she knew he still saw her as just a girl. She hadn't fully grown up in his eyes. When would he trust her to take over the hotel? He shook his head, sharing a look with Marcus, as if they understood each other. Then, he picked up two glasses of brandy from a passing tray, handed one to Marcus and took one for himself, turning his back on her as he did so. Suddenly, Blythe felt as if they had dismissed her. She stood stock still for a moment, utterly alone in a room full of people there to support her. Ridiculous. She was just upset, sensitive to every little thing, she raised her head and tried to fix something close to a smile to her lips before moving to thank the many other people who'd come to pay their condolences.

17

Rae

Present

'There's something different here, I can't quite put my finger on it,' Blythe said, as she looked around the flat. 'Did you get new curtains or...'

'No,' Rae said softly, enjoying watching her sister's discombobulation. The fact was that she'd changed things round slightly. Oh, it wasn't so much, just swapping out tired chairs for ones that had been hidden away in unused rooms for years. She'd changed the rug too. The old one was fit for nothing more than the bin. She'd taken a rust-coloured circular one from one of the best rooms in the hotel.

It was the strangest thing. After that vase broke in the night, Rae had felt compelled to shift the kitchen table, just six inches to the left. The room was so small that it blocked up the doorway slightly, but it had a liberating effect on her. It was heady; as if it released something locked up inside her for far too long. Just six inches and it felt as if she'd crossed a threshold, eased herself from the grip that had held her for so long. It calmed her, as if with each inch a little more of Marcus's power was fading. So, then, she moved the cushions around on the chair. Gingerly at first, gripped by the irrational fear that he might burst through the door and make her put them back. He'd had that curious, terrible capacity, where he knew exactly how to make her shrivel up within. It was not that he called her names as such, but he had a way of looking at her, his presence alone when he was displeased, those long, drawn-out days of silence – it was oppressive. It made her feel smaller each time.

'The place feels different, as if it's...' Blythe stopped, looked at Rae, maybe she felt what Rae was too ashamed to put into words. The place felt better with each day that passed.

'It's...' Rae looked around, trying to put it down to something more than it was, 'it's probably just that I've had a bit of a spring clean.' This was her chance. Rae thought, now was the time to mention Siggy's suggestion about the hotel. It had tossed around in her mind for days, but the arrival of a second, strongly worded letter from a man purporting to be her bank manager was the final straw. She had woken this morning, with the intention of calling up the local estate agent and getting his advice.

'Hmm.' Blythe ran her finger along the bookcase, checking for dust and Rae shrank back. How could she possibly tell her sister about the mess she was in now?

Rae wished she could just pour her heart out to Blythe. They had been as close as it was possible to be, once. Rae remembered as clearly as if it was yesterday, how Blythe looked out for her when they were younger. Probably, Rae was responsible for more of Blythe's frown lines with her teenage shenanigans than Siggy ever managed to etch across her mother's face.

There was no trace of that closeness left between them today. Rae hadn't felt it in years and it saddened her, because when she'd needed Blythe the most, the gulf between them was so wide, Rae felt they'd never bridge it again.

'How on earth can you afford to pay staff when the place is like a morgue?' Blythe looked around now, as if to confirm her first impression was on the money.

'Well, I'm not actually...' Rae began to explain.

'And these robberies? Did you ever? I can't remember the last time there was a break-in on the island, can you?' she said then and rolled her eyes, because they both knew, the last break-in had been down to an old boyfriend of Rae's which gave both Blythe and Marcus plenty to crow about.

'Hmm, it's terrible, yes...' Rae said softly, because it was only yesterday, she'd overheard some of the old dears talking about it in the supermarket. Apparently, there had been two more, this time in Muffeen Beag, targeting elderly people, living alone.

'Oh, yes, it's just a blessing that it wasn't worse. Mrs Deere was staying at her daughter's house, because she's just had her hip done and old Jim Kelleher is as deaf as a post. Apparently, they ransacked his cottage while he slept soundly through the whole thing. They even managed to send his cutlery drawer crashing to the floor and it didn't wake him.' Blythe was looking towards Rae's bedroom door as she said it. 'You're not nervous here, are you? On your own? I mean, it's a huge building and...' She stopped. 'Sorry, I mean...' And for a moment, there it was, Rae could see it, she was worried about her living here on her own, despite everything that had passed between them, she still cared for Rae.

'No. No. To be honest, I hadn't even thought of it.' Rae smiled as winningly as she could manage, but she'd never had much of a poker face. Of course, Blythe would put her discomfort down to losing Marcus and the idea of being alone here without him. 'Anyway, I have Danial here, so… you know, it doesn't feel as if I'm completely on my own.'

'You know there's been talk around the village…'

'No.' Rae put her hand out to stop Blythe, 'please don't tell me, the Christmas choir think I've taken a young lover.'

'Don't be disgusting, Rae, he's young enough to be your son,' Blythe exhaled loudly. They didn't talk about the fact that Rae and Marcus had not produced a family. Marcus wasn't one for having his business bandied about the place. It became yet another taboo subject between the sisters, although Rae had many times wished she had someone to confide in.

'Well, thank goodness for that much,' Rae said, and she picked up her coffee cup, put it to her lips, sipped the dregs.

'They're saying that the break-ins only began after *that* family moved to the island.'

'*That family?*'

'Oh, Rae,' Blythe rolled her eyes as if she despaired of all that was rational. 'Don't be obtuse, it doesn't suit you.'

' "That family", as you call them, are a grandmother and her grandson. They've travelled thousands of miles to live ordinary peaceful lives; they have every right to call this place home and live their days out like the rest of us.'

'Pah! That's never what these people want… surely, you're not naïve enough to believe that.'

'Blythe,' she had to stop her sister there, *these people*, she wasn't going down this road again, her sister had been the same for years, distrusting outsiders. 'Have you met Melissa Val?'

'No, but I know her sort.'

'Ah, Blythe, really, I thought we were better than this...'

'What's that supposed to mean?'

'Our own grandmother was treated with suspicion just because she was a German emigrant. Pappy told us this often, the way the older people looked at you sometimes, because you resembled her, thinking you were above yourself. The sly comments, always hinting at the same thing; the idea that Gisela's money was somehow tainted by the Schutzstaffel.'

'That's a completely different thing. Our grandmother's arrival didn't coincide with a spate of break-ins,' Blythe said, and in her hand, the cup and saucer that she was holding rattled, so she placed them on the table.

'No, only the downfall of the Axis powers.'

'Oh, Rae, stop being so annoying. You're the one living here in this huge place, smack in the centre of town, you're a sitting duck if that guy decides to break in one evening, you've probably even given him the key.'

'Oh, for goodness' sake, Blythe, he's a lovely kid, he's not trouble.'

'And you'd know, I suppose.' Blythe's colour had drained.

'Really, Blythe?' Again, she was throwing up a reminder that for a short while, Rae went off the rails. 'That's all so long ago.'

'You can't have him here.'

'You're the very one who has headed up every island welcome committee and given a céad míle fáilte to any Tom, Dick or Harry who washed up here over the years.'

'That was different, that was tourism – they were adding to the value of the island for everyone...'

'Oh, yes, and what about that lovely group of five that booked into the stables a couple of years ago...' Rae couldn't not mention it. It had tickled her for years afterwards, that Blythe had booked in a bunch of very respectable-looking guests to Still Water House. They weren't in the property five minutes when they were dancing naked around an open fire in the back yard, baptising each other in the still water pool and chanting to some freaky deity they were convinced talked to them through the white thorn bushes that bordered much of the property.

'Of course, you would bring that up...' Blythe sighed dramatically at the terrible memories being dredged up.

'Anyway, if you make your way down to their cottage, knock on the front door and introduce yourself, you'll see what I mean. She's a lovely woman, cultured and dynamic, she is a great addition to the island.'

'Do you hear yourself, Rae? She's a grandmother and she's here for one reason and one reason only; to lay all her troubles on our health service's door and her son is having rich pickings across the island when old people are asleep in their beds.'

'You've gone too far, Blythe, Danial is just outside, I can't have you speaking like that about him. You're wrong. I know you're wrong and if you can't say something nice, then I'd rather if you said nothing at all.'

'Hmph. So, that's how it is, is it? Even a five-minute blow-in means more to you than your own sister.'

'It's just good manners,' Rae said under her breath.

'Yes, well, it might be considered good manners too, if you let a local try out for a job before you go handing it out to the first ne'er-do-good that darkens your door.'

'No one else came looking for a job,' Rae was beginning to lose patience now. She found herself grinding her teeth in that way she'd done for years in her sleep. The dentist said it was stress. If it was, at least it was the sort that bubbled away beneath her skin, the sort that mostly, she'd become so accustomed to, she hardly noticed it anymore.

'Mae English told me that when her son came looking for a job here, not six weeks ago, you sent him packing with his tail between his legs.'

'I wouldn't say I sent him packing, but there wasn't any job for him.' Rae looked at Siggy now, who had come through the door, perhaps to offer coffee refills; they both knew what was coming.

'Mum, even if Rae had a job vacancy, do you really think one of the English boys would be right for it?' Siggy said. 'You know as well as anyone, they've caused more trouble around here than the Pope has spent in prayer groups. Seriously, Paulie would swipe the eye out of your head and come back five minutes later for the eyelashes.'

'I see.' Blythe rounded on Siggy. 'So, she has you in on it too?'

'No, Mum, not at all, but I could hear you from outside. We're lucky if the whole island hasn't heard you.'

'Oh, right, so when was I going to hear about *him*?' She jerked her thumb towards Danial – who was in the bar keeping the show on the road.

'That's different, he's not...' Rae began to speak, but already, Blythe was making her way out of the sitting room, stalking towards the front door, leaving in her wake a shocked Siggy and an almost-tearful Rae.

18

Blythe

Present

'Blythe,' Fiona Dixon stopped her as she made her way from the travelling library that afternoon. Honestly, she'd been so riled up, she'd have walked right past her old school friend. 'Oh my God, are you alright?' Fiona stood in front of her, examining her through oversized, most likely obscenely expensive, sunglasses.

'I'm fine, why wouldn't I be?' Blythe snapped. But she was not fine. She was far from fine. She'd fallen out with everyone at this point, Rae, Kip and even Siggy who hadn't done anything wrong, but she'd snapped at earlier for no good reason. Maybe it *was* the peri-menopause – she'd never been an overly emotional person before. And as to Rae, it wasn't even because of that boy she'd employed. Well, okay, it had started out as that. Blythe had seen them on the square together: Siggy and Danial. It felt as if something in the crust of the earth beneath her feet had broken. Then, just like that, it was confirmed; everything that had been niggling her about that boy had fallen into place.

To top all of that, she had an uneasy feeling that there was something going on with Kip, something that frayed deliberately at her nerve endings. She'd hardly closed her eyes the previous night, her mind racing with the worst-case scenarios. Next to her, Kip slept peacefully, but it felt as if there was a chasm between them, even though they were separated by little more than inches in their king-size bed. 'Oh, don't take any notice of me, my mind is a complete muddle.' That's the only way she could describe it.

'Come on, I've known you since we were kids and you can't fool me, you look like a woman who bought a jar of honey and opened it to find a nest of wasps.' Fiona had always been quick, she'd never been one to open a book, but when it came to people, she was the quickest study Blythe had ever known.

'Okay, you got me, I'm just a bit browned off.'

'Well, that won't do... we can't have our premier guest house owner looking glum.' Fiona laughed, then she looked up and down the street, before checking her watch. 'Listen, have you time to come for a coffee...'

'Sure.' Further along the street, she spotted a small, belligerent woman making a beeline towards them. Saved by the bell – or by Fiona at least. She didn't think she could take another moment of Mae English passive-aggressively blowing her cigarette smoke into her face.

'So, what's up?' Fiona's eyes were ready to pop when they finally sat at a table at the side of the little coffee shack. She took sweetener from her bag and stirred in two small tablets. Fiona had been on a diet since they were in school. It paid off, probably. She was thin as a rake, compared to Blythe at any rate.

'Nothing, it's probably just the menopause. I've fallen out with Rae.'

'Well, that's hardly new – what is it this time? Tell me she isn't back to jumping out windows to meet up with no-good boys!' Fiona laughed and despite herself, Blythe found the image funny. Rae's teenage wildness and the stress it had caused Blythe, was a lifetime away now. No one was less likely to lose her head than Rae these days. She had become a different person when she married Marcus.

'It was stupid, an argument over nothing if you want to know the truth of it.' She felt even worse, because she knew it was entirely her fault. They should be close, after all, Marcus was gone and even if Rae didn't realise it, Blythe had always known that he'd inserted himself like a spanner in the works of their relationship as tenaciously as he'd stolen the hotel that should have been hers, if right was right. She hated when they argued. Even now, as old as they were, Blythe was emptied out by it. They were grown women; it was absurd to be still walking on eggshells around each other. She shared the edited highlights with Fiona.

'And so, you see, Mae English does have a point. It is our duty to look after our own, before we go looking after people who've blown in from the far corners of the world.'

'Hardly blown in, Blythe, she's a friend of one of the McDaids, you know the niece that had that fancy gallery in London? Don't you remember, old McDaid always talked about her as if she was the cat's pyjamas,' Fiona sipped her coffee coolly. 'I've met Melissa, you couldn't find a nicer woman, actually I was thinking of inviting her to our next book club.'

'The grandmother?' Blythe was shocked. She couldn't imagine discussing the latest Jilly Cooper with a woman like that. Melissa Val looked far too worldly to be content with anything less than reading their way through the Booker Prize lists – when they spent more time gossiping than discussing books. 'Really Fiona, I don't think you can just bring someone along, I mean, you'd have to check it was okay with everyone else for a start and...' What she meant of course was, that they held their meetings on strict rotation in their own, all well-to-do homes.

'I'm hosting the next meeting, so surely it's entirely up to me who I invite?' Fiona smiled now and Blythe hoped that she was only saying this to annoy her.

'Anyway, that's completely beside the point. The book club is a whole other thing,' she was too upset to have it out with Fiona right now. After all, the book club had been Blythe's idea, she had set it up, invited everyone to join. How could Fiona just hijack it from under her as if it were *her* book club all along?

'It's not just the newcomers, or the fact that Mae English has gotten under your skin though, is it?' Fiona cut to the quick of things, sensing that Blythe wasn't up for a sparring match today.

'No,' Blythe said. 'But she has a point. After all, there were plenty around the village who'd have loved that cottage. If it had gone up for sale on the open market, I'm sure there would have been lots of offers.'

'The Vals are renting,' Fiona said dully.

'Of course they are.' Because people like that would get all the state help to line some faceless landlord's pockets, while the house was allowed to go to rack and ruin.

'They are renting, because the house is still tied up in legal details, apparently, it can't be sold until the deeds are sorted out. Melissa told me, if they've settled here by then, she may put in an offer, but Pin Hill is so different to where they've always lived, she is reluctant to put down roots until she's sure.'

'So, she could end up buying it and living here permanently?' This was the last thing she wanted to hear.

'Apparently, yes. Blythe, I know you think that people who...' God, she was so careful not to call a spade a spade, 'were not born and bred on the island, are all here to lap up state payments, but Melissa Val and her son are certainly not that.'

'So you say.'

'I do.' Fiona's voice was firm, in that way it always was when she refused to see anyone else's point of view.

'And so, I suppose, you approve of Rae giving a job to that woman's grandson, just because she's *not* poor.'

'Ah, Danial, yes, I've met him. I suspect he'll be very good for business, good-looking lad like that, the girls will be lining up for coffee once word gets out that he's there.'

'Hmm, do you think?' Of course, she was right, hadn't Blythe seen as much with her own eyes? It was why Blythe felt as if a crater had cracked open beneath her feet. While she'd been waiting for some of the old dears to finish selecting their books in the library van, Blythe had spotted Siggy and the kid sitting in the square outside the hotel. Whatever they were talking about their heads were touching, there was no missing the intimacy in the way they were sitting next to each other on the park bench. And then, Blythe had watched, horrified as Siggy met his eyes, and even if no one else realised it, maybe not even Siggy or Danial, Blythe could see it from yards away. Siggy was in love with him. And Blythe felt as if her heart had crashed down through her body and split wide open on the footpath at her feet.

'Anyway, I don't suppose he'll be here long,' Fiona smiled.

'Oh?'

'Well, he's a bright lad. He won't want to hang around on Pin Hill. His parents were university lecturers in Mauritania. Danial's hardly going to settle for clearing tables for the rest of his days.'

'Mauritania,' Blythe said dully. The fact was, she'd had to look it up on a map. She'd had no idea where it was, but then, she'd landed on a Wikipedia page and she'd fallen down a rabbit hole for the best part of an hour reading about the people and the turmoil and the rich traditions of a place that felt like it might as well be on a different planet, not just a different continent to Pin Hill Island.

'You're miles away.' Fiona laughed. 'You really are gone off on one. Has anything else happened...' She stopped. 'Actually, no, hang on, I know what it is, of course, we're at that age, it's all going downhill from here, apparently.' She tossed her head back and laughed and Blythe looked at her dully. 'The peri-menopause? I was chatting to Joy, you know in the bookshop over in Ballycove, and she said, yes, it gets worse before it gets better.'

'It's not that.'

'I told you, at the start, I'm getting the HRT, why be a martyr?' Fiona always lowered her voice when she talked about the menopause, as if people wouldn't know she was no longer twenty-five.

'Seriously, Fiona, I'm just down in the dumps. Maybe I'm low on iron.' Because she certainly wasn't going to tell Fiona Dixon what was really bothering her. The less air that fire got, the better. Hopefully, it would blow itself out. Maybe they'd have whatever they'd have and then, Danial would move on to the next girl to come his way. He was certainly good looking enough.

'Well, if there's anything I can do...' Fiona sat back, peered along the road and then down towards the beach. 'Did I tell you, I had my colours done?'

'Didn't that go out with the Ark – they were talking about that nonsense thirty years ago...'

'Say what you want,' Fiona laughed. 'It has literally changed my life. Maybe you should have it done. It'd take that washed-out look from you...' Still catty beneath it all. People didn't change, Blythe thought, and that didn't do much to cheer her up either.

'I'm not washed out,' Blythe snapped, but of course, next to Fiona, everyone was washed out – her whole life revolved around maintaining her good looks. Well, that and a full social calendar with occasional dabbling in extra-marital affairs that her husband was either too blind to see or had given up trying to stop. 'Am I washed-out looking?' Blythe asked now, more a question of herself than Fiona. Her friend could be brutal, once the words slipped out, she was already sorry.

'You just look tired, nothing a good night's sleep and leaving your worries to one side wouldn't sort out.'

'I don't have any worries.'

'Well, that's what I would have thought.'

'Oh, you're impossible,' Blythe said, and she pulled her jacket more tightly around her. She needed to get a grip. The fact was, she had a lot to be thankful for. She was in good health; she had a daughter that she adored. Her marriage was rock solid, wasn't it? That question lingered in her mind more often than she cared to admit these days. Once again, she pushed it aside. She and Kip may not be exactly Romeo and Juliet, but they were still going strong, a team, united. God knows, there were plenty, like Mae English who'd give their remaining teeth to have even a tenth of the blessings Blythe took for granted.

'You've never changed Blythe.' Fiona laughed.

'What's that supposed to mean?'

'Well, if there was something bothering you, something I could help you with, you wouldn't tell me anyway, you've always been a one-woman team, fixing your own problems or stewing in them until you have no choice but to do something about them.'

'I'm not sure that's a compliment.' Blythe knew it was bang on the money.

'It's not.' Fiona laughed now. 'And it sort of is, I mean, I admire you. I couldn't have made the success of my life that you've made of yours. You got up and made something of what you had, you did it on your own terms.' She stopped, lowered her voice and pinned Blythe with a look that she knew meant more than anything else Fiona had said already. 'And you, my dear, you didn't marry into your money,' she rolled her eyes, because that was exactly what Fiona had done. 'And when your grandfather and that awful Marcus did the dirt on you, you bore it with dignity; you damn well wiped his eye.'

'He wasn't awful.' Blythe, as always, was quick to jump to Marcus's defence. The strange thing was, she didn't know why she did that, because while he might have been Rae's prince charming – he was a downright snake in the grass to Blythe.

'Whatever, you keep telling yourself that,' Fiona said. 'Anyway, look where it got the pair of them. I don't suppose that she's selling ten cups of coffee a day and there you are, with all your stars and on the verge of being included in the White Diary guide,' Fiona said and Blythe could see it now. *Admiration.* It was the first time she realised it. Fiona rated what she'd done with Still Water House, even more so, because Fiona was one of the few people who knew exactly what had driven her all these years.

'Hmph.' Blythe sighed then. 'But I still look like crap and Rae is over there and even if her roots are grey and she hasn't worn a scrap of make-up in fifteen years, she looks like Twiggy's younger sister.'

'I never liked her as much as you, anyway,' Fiona said impishly, and she passed her extra biscotti across to her friend and they sat in contented silence for a while, looking out at the waves.

'Oh dear, what time is it?' Fiona bent down to search in her large designer bag. She pulled out a small compact mirror and patted her nose with a thin veil of powder. She looked at her watch then as if there was somewhere she needed to be, but they both knew, Fiona was as free as a bird with no one to answer to except herself. 'Oh, look at the time, I'm meant to be at the retirement home dropping off a sponsorship cheque for their new gazebo.'

'Oh, the retirement home? Kip is out there this week, working away,' Blythe said.

'Really?' Fiona said, but she was already draining her espresso, closing her enormous bag over. 'That's nice, darling,' she said, getting up quickly and it felt as if suddenly, she'd remembered something that was far more pressing than any sponsorship cheque. It would be a man, of course, some man who belonged to some other poor trusting wife. 'Must dash,' she said after air-kissing Blythe on both cheeks. Blythe watched as she tottered on her ridiculously high heels towards her Mercedes, and she couldn't shake the feeling that she'd missed a step somewhere in their conversation.

What would she do if Siggy fell in love with someone

and decided to leave Pin Hill one day? The idea of the Val boy? So much worse than just an outsider she couldn't trust, from what Fiona said, he was even worse than she thought. Exactly the sort of person Blythe had always carefully steered Siggy away from. Oh, God. She didn't want to think of him dangling the carrot of travel and adventure before her daughter – that wasn't at all what she wanted for Siggy. What had she wanted? To keep her safe. To keep her close. To keep her here. Siggy running the guest house and the hotel – that had always been the dream. A relationship with the Val boy was out of the question.

19

Siggy

Present

There was only so much Siggy could take. Usually, she managed not to get angry, not to rise to the bait, but that morning, her mother had spent half an hour saying the vilest things about Danial and his grandmother and Siggy had just snapped.

'You don't even know them, much less who's behind those break-ins.' If the words had to come out, ideally, it might have been at a normal volume, but Siggy was so upset, that she screamed at her mother.

'What on earth?' Her father had just come through the door.

'It's alright, we're just...' Blythe gave Siggy a look, it wasn't an apology, but maybe, she knew she'd crossed a line.

'You do know that the Sweeneys are in the dining room expecting breakfast in a five-star environment, they haven't paid the guts of a thousand euros to spend their holidays listening to a pair of fish wives,' he said, dropping into his usual chair at the kitchen table. 'As for Maria, she'll think we've lost the run of ourselves.'

'I'm sure Maria has heard a lot worse.' Maria Stapleton had six lumbering sons and none of them seemed able to finish a sentence without including at least one swear word as punctuation.

'Aye, well, maybe,' her father said and reached out to pour some tea from the pot. 'Are we alright?'

'Humph,' Siggy said.

'I was just saying about that family in the McDaid house…' Her mother put four boiled eggs on the table.

'Ah, the Vals,' her father's face lit up. He'd really liked Danial when they'd met a few days earlier, walking the dogs along the beach. 'Lovely people.'

'No, Kip, they are not lovely people.' Her mother sighed and rolled her eyes. 'We know nothing about them, and everyone in the village is saying that he's a real ne'er-do-good. Apparently, back in… wherever they came from, he was a…'

'Now, now, Blythe, we all know what the gossip mongrels are like in Muffeen Mòr, let's just take them as we find them and from what I've seen of that lad, he's a good bloke.'

'Oh, I might as well be talking to the wall. You can't know a person, just because he's handed you a cup of coffee…'

'Speaking of coffee…' He buried his head in the pages, suddenly lost in whatever sports drama was taking up the news.

'Hmph, well the less we have to do with them, the better.'

'I work with Danial, Mum, I'm not going to ignore him or avoid him.'

'Yes, well, I'm sure Rae will see sense soon enough there, too. In the meantime, keep your distance, if he's involved in anything illegal, I don't want you near him.'

'Are you for real?' Siggy wanted to cry.

'Tell her, Kip.'

'Really, Blythe, don't you think...'

'Dear God, am I the only adult in the building?' Her mother placed her fingers on her forehead as if to ward off an impending migraine. 'It's my final word, you're to have nothing to do with him and if I see you knocking about with him, you can say goodbye to that job in the hotel until he's well clear of it, do we understand each other?'

'Mum, I'm seventeen – when are you going to understand, you can't just make decisions like this for me... I'm...' But of course, there was no point. Her mother was well capable of going to the hotel and telling Rae she didn't want Siggy anywhere near the place. Siggy didn't want that to happen, not because she'd lose her job, but because she loved spending time with Rae and yes, now, she looked forward to it even more, because dishy Danial Val was there too! 'There's no point talking to you, is there? Other people can say things to their mothers, but here, it's like living in North Korea,' she couldn't take any more of this nonsense. 'I'm not hungry,' she said then, pushing her plate away and stalking out of the kitchen as she fought back her tears of frustration with her mother.

She decided there was nothing for it but to head to school, so she set off walking. She hadn't made it to the end of the drive when her father's van pulled up next to her.

'Want a lift?' He had the soppy look about him, where she knew, all he wanted was to make things right with her.

'I'm sorry Dad, for back there, but, come on, what's her problem?'

'Look, your mother is the best woman in the world, but she's always been suspicious of newcomers, once they settle in, she'll be fine, just let it wash over you, for now.' He patted the passenger seat for her to sit in.

'I don't know how you...' She was going to say, put up with her, but then, of course, she thought about that day in the square, so she said no more and threw her bag into the van before her. 'Oh, my God, Dad, what's that smell?'

'Alright?' Her father looked across at her.

'I... that smell, it's...' She stopped. She knew what it was, Fiona Dixon's perfume, but as soon as she put the name on it, well that was it, wasn't it? The game was up. Did she want to be responsible for ending her parents' marriage? And for what? For what couldn't be anything more than a fling with horrid old Fiona Dixon.

'STOP THE CAR.' She hadn't meant to scream, but she needed to get out, to breathe fresh air – to think.

'Okay, okay, pet, I'm stopping, it's alright,' her father said, and he sounded just like he had when she was five years old and she didn't want to go to school because Shakira English threatened to stuff her head in the girls toilet if she didn't hand over her treasured Barbie pencil case.

'Oh, God.' She flung open the door of the van and jumped out to get away from it.

'Are you alright, what is it? Do you feel sick?' He was hovering about her now, solicitous and loving as always, but she couldn't look at him. All she could think was – how could you? How could you do this to Mum? To sleep with her best friend, especially now? Now, after all these years, they must have known each other forever, why not have a fling back when everyone was single? Siggy couldn't breathe – it felt as if the sky was closing in on her, as if everything around her had moved just a little too close, the trees on the avenue, the gravel under her feet, the sheep in the field, the van door opened next to her with the aroma of very expensive perfume leaking onto the road.

Her mother never wore perfume. She couldn't bear to smell anything even vaguely synthetic, as she called it. When Siggy was thirteen, she had to hide a precious bottle that her friends had bought her for her birthday. Funny, but after the first few wears, she felt the same as her mother. To her mind, there was something false about it. Of course, she knew this was completely her own view, that women the world over adored perfume. Millions were spent on the stuff every year, probably, but there was one perfume she could pick out at a hundred paces above all others and that was Fiona Dixon's. Not because it smelled so good, or elegant or any of those other things it probably purported to endow on its wearer, but rather because everything about it was too much. Too sweet. Too cloying. If a perfume could smell like leopard print, leather and rhinestones, then that was how Siggy would describe Fiona Dixon's signature scent.

And her father's van reeked of it.

'That smell?' she said then, catching her breath and immediately regretting she said it. She needed to think this through.

'What smell?' Of course her father wouldn't notice. The dogs could blow off a week of onions, garlic and vinegar and he honestly wouldn't complain. He put it down to a damaged septum after a particularly unfortunate tackle with an Italian full back early in his professional career. *Nobody's fault* – that was what he always said, *nobody's fault*.

Siggy tried to pull herself together. She had to think. There could be a completely innocent explanation for this – even for what she thought she saw in the village square that day – her father may have done nothing wrong.

Still, if he was having an affair with Fiona Dixon, it would not turn out well for her parents. Of course, Fiona was rumoured to have had several affairs, but her husband either didn't mind or didn't notice and they'd stuck together despite any gossip.

Her mother was made of completely different stuff. Blythe Carney, for all her faults, abhorred any sort of deceitfulness. Alright, so she was far from perfect. She tended to take things over, barge her way through and she could be a bit of a bully when it came to getting things done. But she was decent and true. She had standards and that was more than Fiona had – strangely, Blythe was one of the few people in Muffeen Mòr who never listened to the wagging tongues when it came to Fiona's affairs.

'Siggy?' Her father's face hovered before hers – she winced at the concern there. If her parents separated, what would become of him? He would have to leave Still Water House – where would he live? What would he do without her mother? Would he go and live with Fiona? She shuddered at the thought of that – it would kill her mother. And not just because they would be the talk of the whole village, but rather because she had a feeling it would break her mother's heart.

'I'm fine. I'm fine. Really, it's just the van. It's…' She stopped. She needed to think about this before she said another word.

'Stuffy? I know, I must get that window sorted out.' He leant back into the van, took out a half-drunk bottle of water. 'Here…'

'I'm okay, if you don't mind, I might walk the rest of the way.'

'Are you sure you're fit for it? I mean, you're white as a ghost.'

'Well, unless you want to walk with me?' She smiled at him, managing somehow to keep her lips from wobbling, the tears somehow held back in her eyes.

'I can.' He looked at his watch. They both knew, it was the one morning he couldn't be late, he'd promised to bring one of the residents in the nearby retirement home to get his hair done first thing. 'No problem, I can ring them.'

'Ah, Dad, I'm alright, really, already I'm beginning to feel a lot better,' she said, keeping her gaze firmly away from the van because she had this irrational fear that if she looked again, Fiona Dixon might be sitting there, perched in the passenger seat smirking back at her.

'Let's just sit here for a few minutes together. It'd be good to have a little rest after...' He leaned against the van's bonnet, tapping the space next to him for her to rest too.

'Really, I'm fine. Go on. You're going to be late. If I feel unwell – which I won't, I can always ring Mum or Rae, either of them will come and pick me up.'

'Promise me you will ring them?'

'I promise,' she said, and she felt his light kiss to the top of her head after he took one last look at her before heading off to work in his van.

It was typical, of course, just as soon as one part of life seemed to be taking off, another tumbled away from her, and she fully expected it to crash into a thousand smithereens.

Well, like for like, and if she was weighing up the way she felt for Danial against something to balance it out on the other side of the scales – it would take something humongous to tip things over evenly.

Danial.

She was in love with Danial. Or at least she thought it must be love, certainly she'd never felt such an overwhelming attraction for anyone in her life before this. Oh, there had been boyfriends, of course, she'd gone out with Jason

Commerford for a whole three months last year. But it was nothing like this.

Not that she could tell anyone.

She might have told Rae. But, what with losing Marcus and all the other worries Rae had now, well, it seemed almost disloyal to feel so happy by comparison. She definitely couldn't tell her mother either, not after this morning's showdown. Danial Val was everything her mother did not want for Siggy.

So, Danial was her secret and she held it to her like a prized treasure she couldn't quite believe was hers. It was such early days, they'd only just met, really, well, they'd only kissed a week ago.

It was magic. Better than she could have dreamed, and she had dreamed of it, constantly, waking and sleeping, Danial Val had filled up her thoughts since that first day they'd met. She hadn't for a moment expected anything more than friendship to come of it, she was just helping him to settle into a new life in a new place.

And then, last week, he'd asked her if she'd like to join him on a run along the beach after he'd finished in the hotel. Siggy was no runner, but she'd have offered to swim with sharks just to be near him for a while.

It was the most perfect evening. They'd met at the coffee shack which was just closing for the day.

'I haven't been running in years.' She'd laughed, but she'd pulled out her best shorts, they were short enough to make her legs look as if they went on forever, but at the same time, they fanned out perfectly to accentuate her bottom. She'd tied her hair up in a ponytail and pulled it through an old baseball cap – knowing it would sway gently as she moved.

'I won't go too hard on you, don't worry.' His running gear looked as if it had been worn for years and when she saw his lithe body glisten in the evening sun, she had a wobble of worry – did she really want him to see her collapsing in a sweaty heap on the sand?

'Good, I've been meaning to get back into it, but you know, somehow...' Until this moment, she'd never been bitten by the running bug, but here now, with Danial, she'd run to the moon if it was next to him.

They didn't make it as far as that, but they did manage a slow jog to the end of the beach where the three sisters, a formation of enormous rocks, stood against the cliff face. They sat for a while, in the shade of the rocks, looking out to the horizon in the distance. It was one of those evenings when the shore was dotted with sea birds, prancing along and pecking in the sand. Occasional walkers passed them by, hardly noticing them, lost in the sounds of podcasts or music, missing out, in Siggy's opinion, on the gently foaming roll of the waves and calls of the birds in the distance.

'I can see why people come here and never leave,' Danial said.

'You've only seen the summer yet.' Siggy laughed. 'It's maybe the best season.' Although she wasn't sure about that, either, because she for one loved the winter on Pin Hill. She could sit and watch the clouds, a thousand shades of grey spool in from the sea and there was nothing like tramping across the land with mist shrouding you and cleansing you of every worry.

'Maybe, but I think I will love every season just as much.' He stopped, took in a lungful of salty sea air. 'It's the peace I love, not the climate, remember, I've already had a lifetime of sun.'

'I really think you should experience forty days of rain, or more likely, forty weeks of grey skies, before you make any great declarations.'

'Perhaps, but I won't change my mind about the peace,' he said, and she wondered what his home place was like. She imagined that the sunlight painted everything a continuous orange tint, the air was dry and sandy against the skin, maybe one day, she'd see it for herself. She smiled then because somehow, just being near Danial Val made her feel like experiencing a bigger world was a real possibility.

'It was warm enough to last me a lifetime.'

'I hope it's not just the weather you like.'

'The people are lovely too... some of them are really lovely...' He turned to look at her then and she felt as if the air had suddenly shifted around them.

'Mostly, I suppose, except my mother, the things she said in the hotel...' She was babbling, because she was nervous. The tension between them was electrifying, it threw her off balance, so somehow, what she most wanted to happen, she managed to fracture, and her heart sank as he looked towards the water then.

'Not your fault. Actually, she's one of the reasons I love this place so much.'

'Oh?' She looked at him as steadily as she could muster, but her heart was beating so rapidly it felt like thunder; she was sure he would hear it above the ocean roar.

'Because without her, there would be no you...' he laughed then, looked down at the sand beneath their feet, as if he was suddenly too shy to say any more. And they sat there for a while, wordlessly, but with a lifetime's worth of words flanking them, it felt as if everything of value in the universe was hanging on a thin thread between them.

'I feel it too.' She whispered, and she wasn't sure if he heard her, so she turned to look at him. He was already watching her, and then he pulled her towards him, took her face between his long slender hands and kissed her mouth with a tenderness so real, it made her want to cry with a relief she never knew she needed. Those first kisses turned quickly to something much more urgent, seeking, hungry. And Siggy, for the first time in her life, was completely consumed by it all. They stayed there for ages, until darkness drew in and the sea swept up too close to be ignored.

Later, they raced back up the beach, holding onto each other, laughing, drunk on this connection that had simmered since the first day they'd met.

It was, indeed, she thought then and since – love.

Had her parents once felt the same about each other? It was hard to imagine it. They were so different. Her mother so driven to make the guest house the very best in the country. Her father, content to live a life where enough was enough, and more concerned with doing for others than he was with getting paid or making anything for himself.

But her father having an affair? No, she didn't want to believe it. Surely, he'd never do that. And yet, the evidence was stacking up against him and Siggy had no idea what she should do about it.

As she walked into Muffeen Mòr that morning, she thought about Danial and the fact that before he came, all she'd wanted to do was to get away. Now, it wasn't so simple. And yet, when she thought of her parents and the idea that her life might be planned out to run along the same tracks as her mother's or Rae's, she wanted to run as far away from Pin Hill Island as she could get.

20

Kip

Present

Kip knew he shouldn't have just left the kitchen like that. He should have stayed, stood up to Blythe, told her exactly how he felt. But there were so many reasons not to, chief among them the fact that the Sweeneys had always had such keen hearing. He'd occasionally wondered over the years (oh, yes, they were regular visitors) if they permanently stood with their ears pinned to an overturned glass against the wall.

This was the one thing he'd always hated about the guest house.

For all the grandeur surrounding them, the ultimate price was that sometimes, their house didn't feel like it was actually their home. They couldn't have a good old air-clearing, blazing row because there always seemed to be someone else to think of in a nearby room. The guest house was opened fifty weeks of the year, what were they supposed to do? Keep track of every argument until the last week in December and then have it out, all the way through until January? Families didn't work like that, well, healthy families didn't work like that in his opinion.

Instead of telling Blythe exactly what he thought, that she couldn't be more wrong about the Vals – he had gotten up from the table in silence, walked out the door and followed Siggy down the driveway to put things right with her before she went to school.

Siggy and Danial.

Oh, boy, but Blythe would blow a gasket if she realised that those two were crazy about each other already. It was a shame, because a first love is such a big thing. Siggy and Blythe should have been chatting about it. Blythe could be enjoying her daughter's happiness and yes, waiting to pick up the pieces after the inevitable first fight or break-up. In Kip's opinion, those were the moments that were far more important than learning how to make brown bread scones.

He so badly wanted to be the person in Siggy's confidence, but the problem was, that putting him between mother and daughter created a wedge between himself and Blythe that was unthinkable as far as he was concerned.

For all her faults, he still adored the ground she walked on. Didn't he?

It was as he was driving away from Siggy that day, when she'd come over a little funny – time of the month, probably, that something started to niggle him. He'd watched her, in the rear view mirror and he couldn't get it out of his head.

It was wrong.

This overprotective relationship that Blythe had created around their daughter.

And more than that, suddenly, watching her walking along, so miserable-looking, when she should be on top of the world, well, it did something to Kip, it felt as if it unlocked something in him.

It wasn't just that Blythe was wrong, they were both wrong. He was every bit as at fault as she was, he needed to go back and have it out with her. Not now, he couldn't go now, because he'd promised old Charlie Coggins that he'd take him to the barbers. Actually, they both knew, Charlie really only wanted to get into the bookies, but what harm. When Kip was a kid, Charlie had owned a travelling butcher shop. Kip knew only too well that if it wasn't for Charlie's big heart, there would have been a lot less meat on their plates most weeks. He owed Charlie, even if the old man didn't know it, Kip knew it, and that was enough.

'Blythe.' He called out when he arrived back in the house a few hours later. There was no sign of her at first, which was a pity, because the Sweeneys were obviously out and it was the perfect opportunity to get things out in the open.

'What are you doing back?' She made him jump when she came through the front door behind him.

'We need to talk.'

'Oh?' she said, but there was no missing the fact that she knew it was something serious. He waited until she hung her jacket on the coat stand and then followed her into the kitchen. 'Lunch?'

'No,' he said, because he knew that making lunch and eating it, would push aside what he needed to get into the open.

'Okay,' she said warily.

'It's Siggy.'

'Siggy? What's wrong with her, has something happened?' Suddenly, she was panicked.

'No, she's fine, nothing like that, it's just this thing, the way you are with her, I can't take it anymore...'

'What do you mean, *the way I am with her*?'

'You know very well what I mean...' he said, because surely she wasn't completely blind to it.

'Is this about that bloody trek up the mountain?' She sighed. 'For heaven's sake, Kip, it was just a walk and they got soaked anyway, they'll all be lucky if they don't catch pneumonia out of it.'

'It's not about the trek.'

'Well then... what?' she held up her hands, rolled her eyes. 'I don't have time for this, honestly, I have to straighten out those rooms before the Sweeneys get back and...'

'It's the Vals, it's the fact that you hardly let her breathe, Blythe. You can't keep her at home wrapped up in cotton wool for the rest of her days. She's seventeen years old, can you not see that this...' He stopped, because he wasn't sure he had the words for it, or at least, words that would not inflame things further. 'She needs more freedom, to choose her friends and to...'

'Hang on one second, what's this about those Vals?'

'It's about...'

'You can NOT be serious?' She jumped up from the kitchen chair. 'Dear Lord, tell me that you're not suggesting that the likes of those blow-ins are good enough for our daughter...'

'There's nothing wrong with them, Blythe, they are as good as anyone else on this island, maybe better than some.'

'So, we're arguing about two people that we hardly know and...' She pivoted on the spot, then bent down so she was eye level with him where he sat at the table. 'Listen to me, Kip Carney, she's my daughter, and no matter what kind of silly notions other people might have, I'm keeping her safe. I've worked my whole life to make sure she has the best chances possible and I'm not going to stand by and watch her throw them away on some... some outsider that could up and leave here in the morning, with our daughter in tow – can't you see that?'

'Blythe, she's going to end up wherever she wants to, the question is, will she ever want to come back?'

'What's that supposed to mean?' She was white now, livid with rage.

'It means that sometimes you have to let people go, so they'll want to come home again.'

'That's such a lot of nonsense – you know that, don't you? The last thing our daughter needs is notions about leaving the island – she's much better off here, where it's safe and there's a good roof over her head and a business she'll inherit one day. Tell me, is there anyone else on the island with that sort of future ahead of them?'

'You just don't want to listen, do you?'

'It seems to me that you're the one not listening here.' She folded her arms in that way she always did when she'd already made up her mind.

'It's no good, is it? We'll never be on the same page with this, it makes me wonder…' He shook his head sadly.

'We're on the same page if you begin to open your eyes and see sense about it.' Her voice was thick with sarcasm.

'That's right Blythe, because you always know everything, things have to be your way or no way.'

'That's not true.'

'That's exactly true and Blythe, it's no way to have a marriage,' he said sadly, and with that, he got up from the table with a heavy heart and headed out to his van.

It was as he was driving in the road, his head filled with counter arguments, that it dawned on him – Blythe's attitude towards Danial was no different to Pappy Scott's attitude towards him all those years ago. It was never put into words, but they all knew, the old man never thought he was good enough for Blythe – and now history was repeating itself it seemed. 'Bugger.' He banged the steering wheel. 'Damn it all anyway.'

21

Blythe

Nineteen Years Ago

Everyone knew, Rae never enjoyed the hotel. She liked the camaraderie of working with the village girls; the guests adored her; she was such a sweet thing. But she had no interest in running the hotel. Blythe could see it, Rae didn't have that same passion for the hotel or the island that had been fused to her own bones for as long as she could remember.

Sometimes, when she wasn't pulling her hair out with worry about her, she pitied her sister – how awful not to know where you truly belonged – Blythe couldn't think of anything worse in life. There was some comfort to knowing who you were, where you belonged and that a predictable path lay before you. Poor Rae.

Not that she hadn't broken Blythe's heart since their father died. She fully expected her to go completely off the rails now their mother had passed away. She was acting out, of course, it was nothing more or less than that. But it wasn't fair, how could she not see that, Blythe was doing her best to keep the show on the road and Rae didn't seem to give a damn about any of it.

Blythe had lost count of the mornings she'd come down to the kitchen to make breakfast for their mother, only to notice the back door left on the latch, which meant of course, that Rae had slipped out while they all slept to meet up with her gang of friends, who spent their time racing motorbikes along the dangerous bends that wound up the north side of the island and drinking cheap beer until the light crept up from the mainland.

These days, there were times when Blythe looked at her and it felt as if she hardly knew her. Not that she wasn't the same lovely Rae she'd always been, but rather, she'd blossomed into something far more striking than any other young woman in the village in Blythe's opinion. Underneath the eye liner and the perfect pout, she was still dear Rae. Still innocent beneath it all and happy to give a hand anywhere help was needed, but with that, there was no missing the fact that when they went to mass on a Sunday morning, every eye turned to catch a look at her.

It was strange. Blythe felt a mixture of deep pride and deeper protectiveness. She hated the idea that her sister was being taken in by some smooth waster, but also, she wanted her to have the very best life she could possibly have. Even though when she looked around the village, probably the best of the fellas left was Kip. Any decent fella had hightailed it off to college and there was no sign of them returning in the current jobs market. Dublin was booming these days, they were calling it the Celtic Tiger, but it hadn't reached Pin Hill in any real way. As to Kip Carney, well, he was on the other side of the world at the moment, his career winding down – who knew where he'd end up at the end of it all. Blythe hoped with all her heart it would be here.

And now, amid the awfulness and grief of losing her mother, Marcus Johnson had unexpectedly arrived on the island. He was nothing like Kip. Kip was good looking and straightforward, she knew where she stood with him, which was more than she could ever say about Marcus. But? They had hardly anything in common, not like she and Marcus. She knew, in her heart, Marcus would give his right eye for a place like the Hope Square Hotel – he'd settle down here on Pin Hill Island and think he was made up to run the place with her.

Marcus had booked into the hotel on the night of her mother's funeral. He told Pappy that he had holiday time owed, and if they needed a hand in the hotel, he'd be more than happy to help out. Blythe should have been over the moon, but something about him, about him being here and the way he and Pappy spoke niggled her. She couldn't say what it was exactly, but an irrational fear twisted in her gut when she thought about him in the hotel. She tried to convince herself that it was because he reminded her of that horrendous moment when she was in the flat with the intruders – yes, that had to be it, hadn't it? Just a crazy association, her mind playing tricks on her, but it meant nothing.

Two days after the funeral, she bumped into him as he was coming back from his morning run. Blythe and Rae were both walking towards the hotel from visiting their mother's grave.

'Good morning,' she said stopping when she saw him approach. She hadn't mentioned Marcus to Rae, because why would she? They had only just buried their mother – Blythe's falling in love or lust or whatever it was, a few years earlier wasn't up for discussion.

'Hey,' he said, coming to a stop at the hotel entrance. 'Actually, I was going to find you today.' He shaded his eyes from the morning sun. She could smell the faint aroma of fresh sweat mixed with soap from him, his skin glistened and she couldn't not notice his strong arms as his hands rested on his hips while he caught his breath.

'Really.' This is it, she thought, he's finally going to ask me out and she felt a buzz of tension shoot through her. Her ego needed this, even if at the back of her mind, there was Kip. Her darling Kip – who should be here now, rather than off chasing footballs like some outsized kid.

'Yes, you see.' And then his eyes slid off to the side and for a moment, Blythe had the strangest feeling that something terrible was happening behind her back and her head shot round, half-expecting a car to come speeding into them or a low-flying crow to land on her shoulder. 'Ahem,' he said and she followed his eyes, because his voice had become a distracted mumble. Rae. He was looking at Rae.

'Hiya,' she said, gathering up the old planters they'd taken from the family plot earlier when they'd replaced it with fresh flowers. She was wearing shorts, short shorts – the sort she only ever really wore around the house, and no one noticed much about them. Here, Blythe saw Rae with fresh eyes. She was striking, a beauty – the legs, the eyes, the skin, the hair – she was built like a thoroughbred, and Marcus Johnson was obviously dazzled. Her dark hair, loose, fell over one eye and of course, she was so tall – almost as tall as Marcus and he was well over six foot. Between them, Blythe felt tiny. Inconsequential.

'Hello.' He held out his hand, then pulled it back, probably realising that he glistened with sweat. For once the shoe was on the other foot. He looked as nervous and out of kilter as Blythe always felt when they ran into each other – except he felt this way about Rae, not about Blythe. 'I haven't met you before,' he said and suddenly it felt as if Blythe was no longer standing there on the footpath between them. And even if they didn't notice her, even if they had eyes only for each other, Blythe felt as if everyone could see the ball of disappointment rising in her throat and hear the soft sound of all their relationships suddenly tilting in an unexpected direction.

She'd never forget that day.

That was the start of it all going wrong.

Alright, so she reminded herself often in the days and weeks that followed. She was grieving her mother. Her father too, probably, because when he'd died, everything had been so wound up around keeping her mother alive that she wasn't sure she'd ever had a chance to fully grieve his loss.

'Marcus has invited me out to dinner.' Rae almost sung out the news when she arrived back the following day. She stopped. Perhaps she picked up on the devastation in Blythe's expression. Maybe she put it down to the fact that their house was in mourning; it felt almost obscene that anyone could be so happy to Blythe. 'Sorry, I know, I should be...' she said.

'What?'

'Well, I am sad, of course that Mummy has passed away, but Pappy said it was probably an ease to her and now, she's with Daddy and really, you know they were completely devoted to each other so...'

'He said that to make you feel better,' Blythe said flatly, cruelly probably.

'I *do know* that.' Rae said a little sulkily. 'But she'd want us to keep going. She told me so, herself, before she...' Rae's lower lip wobbled, and Blythe felt a mean stroke of satisfaction. At least she was sad about their mother's passing. The fact was, every time Blythe thought about that day outside the hotel when Marcus's whole expression changed on meeting Rae, it felt like a knife turning in her guts. She wanted to scream until the windows rattled in their frames at the idea that Marcus would come all this way, after all this time, only to end up fancying her sister. And that was it, call it what you want, but from the moment they'd locked eyes, Blythe knew it was all over. It hurt like hell, digging down into her and churning up feelings she'd always believed she was much too good for, chief among them, a burning jealousy that felt as if it might consume her. Jealousy? She'd never been jealous of anyone in her life, and of Rae? She was suddenly out of her depth. The pain was crippling when she allowed the idea of Marcus falling in love with Rae to sit for any length of time in her mind. 'Anyway, he's collecting me here, at eight. We're going over to Ballycove with Jay Larkin and Finbar Lavin.'

'On that old boat of Finbar's? Are you serious? That thing is holier than the pope's prayerbook.' Blythe felt her blood pressure funnel up through her body, right up to her head. She was too young to suffer from high blood pressure, but bloody hell, this was too much.

'Ah, Blythe, you know well that no one is safer on the water than Finbar.' She laughed. 'I thought you'd be pleased, at least I'm not on the back of a motorbike.'

'Pleased?' She was ready to explode. 'How can you even think of...' She stopped, because she couldn't tell Rae that she'd loved Marcus Johnson once, she'd seen him first after all.

'What, Blythe?' Now, Rae was upset too. Her voice raised, her face flushed with an anger that was so uncharacteristic it stopped Blythe in her tracks. 'It seems to me that no matter who I choose to hang out with, it'll never be good enough for you. You've done nothing but judge every one of my friends for years and now...'

'I...' Blythe wanted to fight back, to say no, this was different. This was all about the fact that she had loved Marcus first, had secretly held onto the notion that he would come for her amid the trauma and grief of their father's death. But in her heart, Blythe knew she didn't love Marcus now – she wasn't jealous, not in that way that she wanted him for herself, that wasn't it. And yet, she had this sense of foreboding, the idea of him filled her with a gloomy dread. Because he'd been there that day. Maybe? But she had a feeling it wasn't in the rescuing of her that Blythe had this uneasy turn in her gut when she thought about Marcus. It was the idea that he'd just walked away, when if he really had anything about him, he'd have made sure that the flat was safe before she went back into it that night. He didn't even check the following day. That was what she hadn't put together at the time. Marcus Johnson was no knight in shining armour. He might just be the very opposite, but Blythe had no way of putting all of this into words for a sister who wouldn't want to listen even if she tried.

'I... I... I...' Rae mimicked her now. 'It's always about you, Blythe, or the hotel, or this house or the family name or...' She stopped. 'For once, let me have this. Let me have one good thing, amid all the sadness and loss and loneliness, let me have this one good thing.' She was on the threshold between pleading and screaming and Blythe knew it was no good. This was happening whether she liked it or not. She'd learned the hard way, that neither lectures nor locked doors could hold Rae back if she wanted something.

That evening, Blythe left the house before Marcus called to collect Rae. She walked to the end of the garden, sat in the shade of the old apple trees, watched as he strolled up the drive, stood for a while, as if surveying the house. Her breath caught for a moment between the sheer familiarity of him and the reality of why he was standing at Still Water House. She closed her eyes, prayed to her mother to help her to somehow find a way to keep her head, to save her from the pit of despair it felt like she was hanging over. When she opened her eyes, somehow, something ever so subtle had changed within her. Marcus was walking around the side of the house. Had Rae not heard the doorbell? But no, she came running out through the open French doors. Later, she realised what it was that had twisted around in her thoughts. He'd looked like an estate agent, as if he'd come to take stock of the house. He'd walked with an air of calculation, as though he was sizing up the place for potential that Blythe could not quite fathom.

She sat there and watched as he and Rae sashayed down the avenue, as if they hadn't a care in the world. And maybe they hadn't. But even then, a little voice in Blythe's mind wondered if she was watching the swagger of a man who had just landed squarely on his own two feet.

22

Rae

Present

Blythe would only try and talk her out of it. That was what Rae told herself while she waited for the auctioneer to arrive. Anyway, nothing was settled yet and it wasn't as if she hadn't tried to call her sister. She couldn't count the number of times she'd dialled Blythe's mobile, only to hear the call ring out on the other end.

And she'd checked with Siggy. There was no problem with Blythe's phone. It worked perfectly well when she wanted to call Siggy to ask her if she could pick up some groceries on the way home from the village the previous day.

She tried to calm her nerves. It wasn't set in stone. She wasn't putting the place up for sale, just looking at options to save the hotel. Cathal Regan arrived one minute ahead of schedule. They'd been in school together, well, she'd been a year or two ahead of him, but everyone knew Cathal. He'd always been the kid on lunch break buying and selling and trying to make a quick pound before the headmaster was any the wiser.

He'd moved from working in the local chippie when he left school to helping at old man Timmy Stenson's auctioneers. Luckily for Cathal, Timmy had a remarkably pretty daughter who apparently found Cathal irresistible and so, Cathal had taken over the auctioneering business and probably quadrupled the profits since he put his name over the door.

'Hello Rae, well, you were the last woman I ever thought would ring up looking for my services...' He smiled as he said it and then stopped, looking up and down the street before he came through the front door.

'You and me both,' she said and she meant it, because selling had never been something she'd thought about before now. Pappy would be turning over in his grave, and as for Marcus, but that wasn't something that was likely to sway her anyway.

'Of course, no one could blame you.'

'Excuse me?' She looked at him, not quite understanding.

'You know, with,' his eyes drifted to his feet in the way that most people's did when they spoke about her bereavement, 'well, losing Marcus, he was such a good businessman and you were both so devoted. And then, a woman on her own, I can imagine, what with all that's happening in the village, it's only natural to be a bit nervous. A place like this? It's only a matter of time before those gurriers set their sights on breaking into somewhere bigger and grander than the old people's cottages...' he said gently.

'Oh, no, it's not that at all,' she said quickly, because whatever about the break-ins, she was not missing Marcus, in fact, without him here, it felt as if finally, for the first time in years, she had peace, she could breathe. 'It's time to shake things up. The hotel is too big to manage on my own and...'

'Of course, of course,' he said and then his face changed to that familiar expression she'd seen so often since Marcus died.

It was pity mixed with something else, that uncomfortable feeling that they didn't know what to say for the best. 'So, tell me, you mentioned you wanted some advice on one part of the hotel.'

'That's right,' Rae said and she quickly closed out the front door of the hotel. It wasn't a busy time of day. They rarely had a customer at this hour if she was honest, but the last thing she wanted was word getting out around the island that she was thinking of selling, at least not until she told Blythe what her plans were at any rate. 'You see from the outside,' she waved a hand towards the front of the hotel and explained about how years earlier three buildings had been made into one. It was obvious from outside, they'd held onto the original façade, with doorways painted each year and original stonework and railings, too. 'But I've been thinking of downsizing, making the place more boutique and I'd like to free up some funds to do that, so what I wondered was, if it would be possible to sell off what was number three – this area over here and the floors above it.'

'I see.' He smiled, took a step back and surveyed the lobby area. 'So, you'd be doing this work yourself, before it goes up for sale?'

'I don't know. I mean, I suppose that's why I asked you here. I wondered if I needed to sell the ground floor – could I just sell the upper floors, there's access around here, it would be easy enough to make to...' There was a small anteroom with an emergency exit into the car park at the rear of the hotel. This anteroom was large enough to fit in a lift next to the original staircase that had been retained to comply with fire regulations.

'I see,' he said. 'Can we walk the four floors, just to get a better sense of what we're dealing with?'

'Sure, come on.' And so, she led the way. All the while, Cathal listened and took notes and occasionally, he pulled out a measuring tape. She noticed he recorded things like the slate fireplace in what had been a first-floor drawing room and the various cast iron fireplaces in the other rooms.

'The chimneys are all still...' He nodded towards the ceiling.

'They'd need to be cleaned out, checked properly, I mean, it's years since anyone lit a fire up here, but yes, I suppose, in theory they are all working fireplaces, with a bit of sorting out.' They'd re-roofed the whole building a decade earlier, that was the reason for the crippling loan on the place. Even so, Marcus had insisted on keeping the chimneys and the original slates.

They walked right up and into the attic rooms, although Rae hardly ever came up here now.

'You'd be surprised, people go mad for attic flats.' Cathal smiled.

'Hmm.' Rae was dubious. She couldn't imagine living in a place where she had to bend down every time she walked through a doorway.

'Ah, yes, but you must be what? Six feet?' He smiled at her. He by comparison was hardly five-five. 'No, there's a place for everyone and something like this – quirky, a one-off, I could really sell this for you.' He said it as if he feared she might ask some other auctioneer from the mainland to come and look the place over. Little did he realise; it had taken all her courage to ask him to pop in.

They walked back down to the lobby again, this time he asked if she would show him the car park at the rear, although it was easy enough to walk into it from the street. Most of the locals parked here all the time. Probably they didn't realise it was owned by the hotel, but it was a huge area – mostly marked out into spaces and bordered by a tall stone wall.

'Obviously, the original buildings had each a third of this area, but we can make a right of way to give access to the main street,' she said because she'd been thinking about this.

'Nobody expects a yard this size in the middle of a town. I say you give them the six or eight parking spaces closest to the property, get a wall built and allow them right of way to use the exit onto the existing car park and from there onto the main street.'

'Seriously, but that's tiny?'

'That's the secret to making this work. You give away the least you can for the biggest amount of cash. Then, if you want to come back and get a second bite of the cherry, there's always the option to do that. Do you realise how the holiday homers go crazy to think they're getting their own designated parking space – they LOVE that.' He shook his head as if it never failed to surprise him, because the one thing there was loads of in Muffeen Mòr was wide open spaces.

'I haven't made up my mind yet, though.' She turned to him now because it felt, the way he spoke, as if the whole place had already been carved and quartered.

'Of course. Even if you do, Rae, there's a lot to think about before you put up a for-sale sign.'

'I know, the lobby?'

'Mainly. And with these old properties, it's good to check that the deeds are in order, you know, wills and all that...' He smiled. What he meant of course, was that the property was in her name.

'It's all in order,' she said softly. Because if the whole village had ever been keen to know about anything it was how on earth Blythe had not ended up inheriting the hotel and Rae had.

'Okay, well, you sort out that paperwork, so we have it all clear if you want to go ahead with it and I'll go back to the office and see if I can't have a think about the best way to figure out the ground floor.'

'Really?' She felt a wave of relief bubble up inside her. 'Honestly, I've walked through the place a thousand times, trying to figure out what to do for the best with it and I really couldn't decide.'

'Whoa, I'm not going to be reconfiguring the hotel for you, but I'll give you an idea of the numbers – a rough guide to the costs and profits differences between dividing the place up and selling as a four-storey Georgian house or holding onto the ground floor and just letting the top floors go out to sale.'

'What's your gut feeling?'

'My gut feeling…' He stopped, bit his lip for a moment. 'The full house, original Georgian centre of town, would have gone for up on two million in its original state a few years ago – but…'

'It's been changed so much over the years?'

'Not so much that. I think anyone with the sort of money who'd want to buy it as a property in one, won't worry about putting it back to the way it was. There's no doubt selling it as three-storey over ground floor is not going to make you half of that. No, the thing really is nothing like this has come up on the market in years and you know, everything has exploded in terms of property – honestly, the sky is the limit at this point. A Georgian house, on an island? I can imagine the holiday home set would love this, now they're being roasted off the continent thanks to global warming.'

'Upwards of two million.' Rae repeated and she felt rather stupid for being shocked at the value of the place. She didn't need two million euros; she hadn't the first idea what she would do with that sort of money. If anything, it seemed preposterous, scary even. All she really wanted was to pay her bills and live a quiet life.

'Anyway, that's all pie in the sky, right? Only if you decide to go ahead with it?' Cathal smiled at her, but she felt he was a spider to her fly. Whatever about losing Marcus or not being able to run the place alone, you'd have to be stupid not to realise that the hotel wasn't making a bean these days.

She walked Cathal to the front door, hoped no one would spot him leaving the hotel. Strangely, when he left, she felt excited at the prospect of maybe selling the place. She wasn't sure, but the idea of the old attics at the top of the house being used again. Fires lighting in the grates and voices filling up the rooms, somehow brought a sense of hopefulness to her. It was too long since there was the sound of a happy family in these rooms, far, far too long.

23

Rae

Nineteen Years Earlier

Rae was nineteen years old before she knew what it was to fall madly, deeply in love. And that's what this was, she was certain of it. Love at first sight. Marcus Johnson was nothing like Johnno and the other boys she knew on the island. He was older for one thing. Ten years older, which should have been ick, but oddly, Rae thought that made him even more attractive. Worldly. He'd worked in Paris, for heaven's sake. The nearest Johnno would ever get to Paris was a soggy baguette filled with bacon, egg and cheese from the deli at the local petrol station.

It felt that they were inevitable from the moment they met, as if he saw her, really saw who she was, in a way that no one else ever did; and that was just with a few scattered words on the footpath outside the hotel. She'd had to force herself to look at him directly. Eye contact felt like an act of lustful rebellion; but when she did meet his gaze, she knew, there and then, there was a connection. Next to her, Blythe had continued to talk, blissfully unaware of what was wordlessly passing between them. Rae hadn't heard a word, instead she'd been filled up with a sort of buzzing energy that made everything but Marcus Johnson fade into obscurity.

It was later that afternoon, she'd made some excuse to call into the hotel, hoping to bump into him, of course. She'd changed into a pretty dress, one that Blythe had given her the previous year. The tags were still on it. It had always been far too flimsy to wear on a motorcycle with Johnno and it didn't really go with her look then anyway. But that day, after meeting Marcus Johnson for the first time, she tried it on. Then she brushed out her hair and pinned it up slightly, with loose tendrils falling to frame her face.

'Oh, hello, again,' he said to her when he ran into her in the hotel foyer. In truth, she'd been hanging about for almost half an hour, fiddling with the flower display in the hopes of casually running into him.

'Marcus?' she said, trying to be nonchalant, as if it was totally normal for her to mope around the hotel on a day when any normal person would be lying in the garden, watching the clouds drift across the sky. 'You're still here?' she said, as if she didn't know that he was booked in for another night. Suddenly she became aware of the silence between them. She desperately wanted to say something urbane, grown up, sophisticated.

'Of course, I wouldn't have left without saying goodbye,' he said then, holding her eye for a long moment.

'You are funny,' because they'd only just met. And yet, it felt as if he was serious.

'I'm tempted to stay a little longer, but only if you were available to show me the sights?' he said then, replacing one of the flowers she'd just moved to the front of the display. She studied it a moment. He was right, it belonged at the back.

'Of course, where would you like to see?'

'I hear there's a very nice place to eat over on the mainland, would you fancy going for dinner...?'

'I'd love to,' she said a little too quickly, then found herself blushing, 'of course, it's quite busy here at the moment.' The truth was, she had no idea if it was busy or not, she just turned up when Blythe needed her.

'Maybe they'll let you have a few hours off this evening?'

'This evening?' she blurted. God, there would be so much to do, she'd need to wash her hair, put on a face mask. 'Let me think...' She tossed things over in her mind, but there was no question she wouldn't say yes, not really.

Marcus pulled out all the stops. It wasn't just dinner. It was dinner at the Blue Door – only the most popular and expensive place for miles around once you arrived on the mainland. She'd heard Blythe telling Pappy a few weeks earlier that bookings were like hen's teeth; taken weeks in advance during the holiday season.

'Ah,' Marcus said softly when she mentioned this to him. 'It pays to have connections.' It was dinner for two, Finbar had taken himself to a nearby bar to meet up with some of his fishing buddies.

'You know the owner?'

'Hmm,' he murmured, and a little shard of doubt crept up in her, maybe he had an ex-girlfriend working here, or maybe even a current girlfriend, who... Stop it, she told herself. You are here and this is new and wonderful. Except, she knew nothing about Marcus, beyond his name and the fact that he'd been pally with Blythe in college.

'So... you were at college with Blythe,' she said, trying to elicit something from him, because he'd surely know all about her from Blythe.

'Oh, there's not much to tell. I've always loved the hospitality industry. When things are done right, you feel you're making a difference.' He smiled at her and for the thousandth time since she'd met him earlier that day, she felt herself go weak at the knees.

'That's how I feel about animals and maybe working with them, one day...'

'You'd be magnificent,' he was the first person to make her feel that she could do something worthwhile. 'Veterinary or rescue or...'

'I'm not sure, that'll be down to how the final exams fall,' she laughed nervously, because she was no Einstein, but she wanted to impress Marcus. 'I suppose, the world is my oyster.' She said this, because she knew he had travelled, she managed to squeeze that much out of Blythe on the journey back home after they ran into him that morning.

'So, you'd leave the island?' He stiffened.

'Maybe...' She desperately wanted to back track. 'I mean, my home is here, in Still Water House and...'

'What about the hotel?'

'Oh, that's Blythe's passion... she's much better at that side of things than I am...'

'Don't do yourself down, you would be brilliant at whatever you turn your hand to, I'm sure.' His eyes suddenly drawn to the menu.

'Hmm.' Rae couldn't think of anything more depressing than being stuck in the hotel for the rest of her days. She sat for a while, staring at the menu, not really seeing it, but instead thinking of what to say next. Something winning, something that would make him like her more.

'Can I take your order?' she looked up to see the waitress watching her.

'You first,' Rae smiled at Marcus because she quite fancied the pizza, but it was hardly the sophisticated choice, safer to be led by him.

'Steak,' he said without hesitation. 'Medium rare.'

'Same,' Rae said then, although the idea of anything rare turned her stomach slightly, it just felt too close to the animal that had so recently been walking about a field somewhere.

'And wine?' the waitress asked.

'The house red looks good,' Marcus ordered with an authority that made her feel he would always know the right thing to do and say, there was something very sexy about that.

'Perfect,' Rae said, although the waitress had already taken their menus and was walking away from their table.

Perfect. That's exactly what it was, and she couldn't wait to tell Blythe when she got home. Honestly, even the boat ride back, the moon full and silvery lit up the water like a thousand stars around them, it all felt so surreal. Marcus was a perfect gentleman – something Johnno could learn from him. He'd walked her to the front door, held her in his arms and when they kissed, it was long and lingering. As she watched him walk back down the avenue, she was filled with desire for more of him.

Of course, Blythe was in bed when she got in. Not asleep. Blythe needed less sleep than anyone Rae knew, but her light was off and that meant she didn't want to be disturbed. The following day it was the same, Rae wanted so badly for her sister to grill her on every possible thing about Marcus, she wanted to tell her all about their date, but Blythe hadn't time to sit for so much as a cup of tea with her.

The week – because that initial extra day or two that Marcus decided to stay on quickly turned into a full, delicious, perfect seven days – was like that. Full of Marcus. Blythe and Rae might as well be living in different houses. It was as if Blythe didn't like him at all. Although, how could she not? He was everything that Johnno was not, and so it was hardly a stretch to expect her sister to at least approve, even if she didn't have the energy to be enthusiastic in the days following their mother's funeral.

Marcus had come to the cemetery with Rae. They'd sat wordlessly, while Rae cried and he'd put his arm around her shoulders, pulled her in close and somehow, she didn't feel so bereft then.

'I'll be back, on my next day off...' He told her that evening as he reluctantly caught the last ferry. Rae stood on the pier, long after the boat went out of sight, feeling as if all the happiness in the world was sailing away from her.

The following day, he rang the hotel. First thing in the morning.

'Are you checking up on me?' She laughed, she was just so happy to hear his voice.

'Maybe...' He was joking, of course. 'I just needed to know that you were there, you know, sort of put my mind at rest that you weren't a dream or a mirage and...'

'I'm definitely not.' She laughed then, and her insides did a somersault when he promised to ring her before she turned in for the night.

The following day, a huge parcel arrived with her name on it. It was delivered to the hotel, although, of course, she only came here when she was needed.

'Someone's popular,' Mrs Daly said when Rae arrived in for her shift. They had moved the box into the small storage space at the back of the reception desk. 'Go on, you must open it. Curiosity is killing me, I've been dying to know what's in it since it arrived.' She picked up a pair of scissors from the desk outside.

'I don't believe it,' Rae said, and she began to laugh. It was a huge cuddly toy koala bear. 'It's from…'

'Marcus Johnson?' Mrs Daly shook her head.

'What?'

'I don't know about him at all,' she said darkly.

'Why? He's lovely and look…' Rae held up the toy, it was the size of a small washing machine, but so soft. 'This must have cost a fortune,' she said then.

'Just, take your time with him,' Mrs Daly said, and she touched Rae's arm as she walked back towards the kitchen.

The thing was, it wasn't just a koala bear. A few days later, it was flowers, then the daintiest silver earrings. Every week, some gift or thoughtful card arrived. He was the most attentive perfect man (because Marcus was definitely a man, compared to Johnno and his bunch of friends). Rae thought she must be the luckiest girl in the world.

24

Blythe

Eighteen Years Earlier

It seemed that it was all about Rae and Marcus these days. Oh, Blythe told herself, she was well over whatever little crush she had on him when they were at college. They would never have been suited, not really. She was far too stuck in her ways and Marcus was one of those men who wanted a woman who would meet him halfway and was committed first to him and then to everything else. He had found that in spades with Rae.

There was one good thing. It had changed Rae; for the better, in Blythe's opinion. She had, almost overnight, become like a different person. Within six months, she was unrecognisable, from her clothes to her hair, to her overall demeanour. She'd settled into herself, somehow. Plans for veterinary college were not spoken about so much these days, although, there was still a convention of stray cats gathered at the back door of Still Water House each morning. Marcus came to the island on his day off each week and stayed in the hotel where he made himself sickeningly indispensable to everyone, except Blythe. He was, it seemed, quite perfect in everyone's eyes. Rae was showered with gifts and grand gestures, each surpassing the last. He was a model of adoration and attentiveness – nothing was ever too much. Blythe felt churlish for the way it made her squirm inside. And still, she couldn't put it into words, it was the familiar feeling that something of the solicitude rang out of tune with the man she'd known at college. It was a courtship played out against the backdrop of the hotel and under the gaze of their approving Pappy.

'It's too much isn't it, all of the presents?' Fiona said one day when she saw the huge display of balloons that had been sent over on the ferry for Rae earlier.

'Is it?' Blythe had no idea what she was saying. Fiona was engaged to Willie Dixon these days. He was a good egg, Willie, they'd all been in school together, although back then, Fiona wouldn't look twice at him. Suddenly, he was God's gift because his plumbing business had taken off. Willie was everywhere and more importantly, when he wasn't haring around in his spanking new van, he was turning up at anything worth happening in a Land Cruiser that cost as much as a small cottage on the pier road.

'Don't you think it's slightly creepy?' Fiona shuddered.

'I hadn't really...' Blythe said then, but of course, that was it, something about Marcus Johnson just didn't ring true. Perhaps it never had.

'Well, I wouldn't go near him with a bargepole, not if he was the King of England – I swear, he's a bad one.'

'Maybe, but how do I tell Rae that?'

'Tell Rae?' She laughed at that. 'Good luck with that, have you learned nothing over the last few years? The only way Rae will change her mind about him is if she sees it for herself.'

'Well, let's hope that's sooner rather than later,' Blythe sighed.

'Let's hope for all your sakes it is, because if Marcus Johnson gets his feet under the table here, that's when you'll see his true colours.'

The other thing was, it was plain to see, Pappy adored Marcus. Very quickly, it felt as if he was the grandson the old man never had; on those nights when Marcus stayed in the hotel, he'd stay up late with Pappy, playing chess and talking long into the night. One evening, Blythe overheard Pappy telling him all about Gisela and somehow, it felt as if he was projecting his own happy marriage onto Rae and Marcus, as if he saw them somehow as the young and shiny version of his past self, although they were only dating. Blythe had been frozen to the spot. Those sentiments were so far removed from how he saw Blythe and Kip. His apathy towards Kip had not changed. She suspected it was born of a mixture of things. The apple never falls far from the tree. That was what he said once; he expected that Kip would become his father. There was that other unsaid thing too, that hung on the air between them. Her grandfather saw Kip as the muscle, good enough to straighten a garden, but he would never be good enough to run the hotel with Blythe. The savagery of hurt she felt as she overheard Pappy and Marcus together, cut through her. How could he be so blinkered? How could her sister be so utterly immune to Blythe's misery which felt as if it protracted in equal measure to Rae's contentment? She had Kip, of course, she adored Kip, but he was gone more often than he was on Pin Hill. Kip could never be accused of overpoweringly grand gestures. Usually, the first she'd know that he was back would be when she'd look out the drawing room window to see him tending her mother's beloved roses. He'd snipped the first rose of the season and handed it to Blythe again this year. But Blythe needed more than a groundsman or a sentimental rose. Her life had become stuck in an unfulfilling groove, a rotation of moving constantly in one place, while Marcus circled with intent around the future that Pappy seemed determined to withhold from her. *Hush now*, her grandfather told her when she'd begged him to formalise her position as owner–manager of the hotel, *sure, this place is far too big for one girl to manage on her own.*

She wanted to scream at him, that she would not be alone. She would have Kip by her side. But of course, she didn't know that for certain. Kip had made no mention of marriage or their future together. On the other hand, she knew that life without him was inconceivable. In her heart, she knew he felt the very same, even if he procrastinated around the finer details.

Blythe had to work really hard to bite down on the bitterness she felt when she heard Pappy praise Marcus. But what could she say, hadn't she fallen for his charm at one point too? How could she blame Pappy for falling under his spell?

It was late in the year when Kip learned that a knee ligament injury meant his career as a rugby player was coming to a close. He was surprisingly pragmatic about it, which Blythe found in equal parts bewildering and endearing. Only Kip could be so unaffected by his own success that he was happy to slip into a life far away from the spotlight.

There was to be a final game, a testimonial of sorts, although it was part of yet another championship that Blythe only half followed. Still, half the village were travelling to Dublin for the game. They had a bus organised on the mainland for his supporters. She really should go and cheer him on.

'Of course you have to go,' Rae said one morning as she crunched through a bowl of cornflakes. She was standing in the kitchen in the hotel. The busy breakfast rush over now, it was just the two of them, setting the place back to rights.

'How can I leave Pappy and...' Blythe hated leaving the hotel, hated leaving the island, if she was completely honest.

'Oh, for heaven's sake, this place will be still standing here when you get back. It's Kip's last game, he'll want you there.'

'He hasn't made a big thing of asking me.' Again, she was comparing him to Marcus who by recent standards would probably put on a horse-drawn carriage for Rae in the same situation.

'Of course he hasn't,' Rae burst out laughing.

'What?' Blythe swung round to check if Rae was making fun of her.

'It's Kip – he's never going to ask anything of *you*, Blythe. He adores the ground you walk on, it's only a pity you don't seem to be able to see it.' Rae shook her head.

'Of course I can...' She stopped, 'do you really think he adores the ground I walk on?' It slipped out and once it had, Blythe felt as if she had completely exposed herself in some way that she'd always managed to cover over.

'And you're the smart one?' Rae rolled her eyes. 'Blythe Scott, listen to me, Kip Carney would do anything for you, he's been head over heels in love with you since that first summer he came to help mama with the gardens.'

'Well, he's...'

'He's a man of few words, true. But the way he looks at you when you're not even aware that he's in the room. He's always thought you're too good for him, you know that, don't you?'

'Too good for him?' Blythe dropped down onto the stool that her grandfather sometimes sat in to break the journey from the hotel to his garden. 'Seriously? But he's the international sportsman, he's the one that has every man, woman and child on the island falling over him. What am I, beyond a skivvy with notions?' That was how she felt these days, as if the autonomy she'd once had in the hotel was slipping from her, as her grandfather tightened his hold on the place more with every passing day.

'A skivvy with notions! Oh, Blythe, you're so funny.' Rae was bent over now, spluttering cornflakes from her mouth as her laughter turned almost into convulsions of hilarity. Blythe waited until she regained some control.

'It's how I feel.' That familiar wave of misery inflamed her once again.

'Are you actually serious?' Rae stopped, placed her breakfast bowl on the steel worktop and walked over to Blythe. 'Listen to me now,' she put her hands on each of Blythe's shoulders. 'You are much more than this hotel, we might be the sisters of Hope Square, but you are better than this whole island put together, do you hear me? Kip Carney is dead right, no one is good enough for you as far as I'm concerned too, but if I had to pick anyone that came close, it would be Kip in a heartbeat. That man would give up everything for you, Blythe. Can't you see it for yourself?'

'But it's so different to you and Marcus, I mean, with the way he's always buying you gifts and...'

'Ah, that's completely different, sometimes, I wonder if he's trying to impress me or Pappy,' Rae laughed again at this.

'And Pappy doesn't like Kip either.'

'Don't worry about Pappy, he always thought you'd marry into some hotel dynasty like the Four Seasons or the Hiltons.'

'Oh God – and leave Pin Hill?' Blythe began to laugh, because suddenly she felt so much better.

'You need to go and support Kip, once this is over, you'll see, everything will fall into place, Pappy might even take him more seriously, if he isn't off playing *that foreign game*.' She was imitating their grandfather, and it made them both laugh.

So, she decided she'd go. Maybe getting away might be good for her, after all. Rae was right, there were plenty of people to look after the hotel if she took herself off for one night.

Then, she saw the list of people travelling up on the bus for Kip's final game. Apart from a few of the long-committed supporters, it was all young girls. Mainly from the convent, just out of leaving cert with an empty summer to pass until they headed off for the big world beyond the island. Looking down along the list of names, she realised that anything could happen on that trip.

It was Kip's final hurrah and she should be there. Blythe told herself, it was not so much marking out her territory as it was supporting him in what would be a very emotional game.

It reminded her, too, time was passing. They were all getting older. That idea came with a jolt of uneasiness. All her friends were already paired off or about to walk down the aisle. She was increasingly looking like the last woman standing.

So, she put her name down. Kip was even more delighted than she'd hoped for, but for far more reasons than she'd care to admit, she was determined to put legs into their relationship now his career was ending. Perhaps she would shake off this feeling of lethargy and impending doom, perhaps she might just get her happy ending yet.

The trip was everything and less than she expected. Kip was carted off with an injury to his shoulder within six minutes of setting foot on the field, and she'd ended up in

A&E with him watching the remainder of his final match on a television not much larger than a box of breakfast cereal.

It was the early hours when they made their way back to the hotel, Kip heavily drowsy because of medication probably administered to ensure he wouldn't go mad and hit the town and maybe do himself further injury. They settled into the hotel room, and she lay awake most of the night.

The following day, there was a meet-up with the team, so she organised herself into a summery dress, then folded Kip into a fresh white shirt and made his hair as presentable as it ever was. He was no James Bond, but in the rugby set, he was as close to smooth as you were likely to get.

'So, you're the famous Blythe?' One of the long-retired players grabbed her arm as she stood near the bar, while they took photographs of the team and made a bit of a thing of Kip. This wasn't anything near the booze-athon she had expected, because against all odds, the team had managed to win their match the previous evening. Now they were buoyed up with the hopes of maybe progressing to the next round, which meant another match in six days' time. Every player was on their best behaviour; it set the tone for the afternoon.

They had one more night in Dublin. A low-key drinks affair where one of the team managers hoped Kip might wrangle a job with a company that sponsored some of the matches.

Blythe had a feeling that at the end of it, the dry old stick who did the hiring and firing might have given *her* the job, but Kip would never fit in with the slick branding and fast sales-y speak that they valued. There would be no job.

'It doesn't matter. There'll be other opportunities.' She

tried to convince him when they got back to the hotel. It was all a huge comedown; Kip's career ended here in a room filled with gifts and mementoes from his rugby career. A seven-foot-tall rabbit wearing the Irish strip, stood in one corner watching them critically. He was part of an in-joke between the players. Blythe looked at it and wondered how on earth it would fit into the tiny cottage Kip still shared with his mother on the edge of Muffeen Mòr.

'We both know there won't be, Blythe. My professional rugby career is over. I'm all washed up. I have nothing to recommend me except that in years to come, people will remember that one time I was capped for Ireland and maybe I'll get invited back to sit in the stands for the less important games to watch younger players do the only thing I was ever good at.'

'Kip, come on, you're just feeling down. Alright, it's the end of one chapter in your life, but another will open soon. You'll have to go looking for it and...' She tried to convince him, but it was hard, because over the last few days, she felt every bit as used up as he did.

The fact was, she felt as if she was the oldest woman in the room, every time she dared to think about it this weekend. Suddenly, the lovely tea dress she'd worn earlier seemed primly Victorian compared to the skimpy tops and ripped pants the other girls favoured. She was wearing her mother's pearl earrings for heaven's sake while everyone else was wearing leather strings on their wrists and delicate name charms at their throats.

In that moment, she wasn't sure why, but she put her arms around him and pulled him close to her with a hunger that she'd never felt before. Even as they made love, she wasn't sure if she wanted him or just wanted *something*. Something to fill a void that she still wasn't brave enough to name.

It was her first time. Really. Because even though they'd been going out together for years, she'd always held back, waiting for the right moment, waiting for something, she didn't know what, and so it had never arrived. And later, as they lay in each other's arms (she moving to the other side of the bed, so she was on his uninjured side) they both wept, moved by the experience of it.

This was NOT sympathy sex.

She knew it as it was happening, in those moments, she wanted this to happen with Kip, wanted him more than anything. Whatever it was, somehow, it seemed to cement them. They arrived back in Muffeen Mòr, standing closer together, finishing each other's sentences, connected in a way they were not before.

There was no plan to meet up again. No asking her on a date or making any great declarations, but the following morning, Kip turned up at the hotel with two chocolate bars and the suggestion that they go for a walk on the pier during her tea break.

A fortnight later, when her period was late, Blythe knew she was pregnant before she even took the test.

25

Kip

Eighteen Years Earlier

If Kip had given even a moment of thought to what would happen when he had to retire from rugby, never in his wildest dreams could he have believed that somehow, things would work out with Blythe.

But that was exactly what had happened. Blythe Scott had finally fallen for him, just as he knew all those other girls who fell over themselves to try to win him over, were about to turn away.

That was Blythe all over. She was never one to follow the crowd, it was what he liked about her, well, that and a million other things. He still fancied the pants off her, he just had to catch her eye at mass on a Sunday morning, and it did something to his core that no priest would approve of, but then, there was more to her than just that.

Blythe had been beyond kind to his mother when she wasn't well a year earlier. Kip was touring with the team in the southern hemisphere, a world away from Pin Hill Island, when his mother called him from her hospital bed. In typical fashion, she hadn't wanted to worry him and as it turned out, she – or rather Blythe – had everything in hand. Somehow, for once, he didn't feel the need to drop everything and rush to her. Blythe had taken her to A&E and bullied their way into the best consulting surgeon's list in the hospital. According to his mother, by the time her gall bladder was removed and she was back home, Blythe had managed to fatten up every cat on their road, even though she'd only been charged with feeding his mother's one small tabby.

And there really was no onus on her to do any of that.

He'd spent so long keeping her at arm's length. With good reason. For a start, old man Scott never liked him. That distrust, of course, he could lay at his father's door. Charlie Carney had hightailed it off Pin Hill owing money to every shopkeeper, pub and bookie on the island, it was hardly a stretch to think he'd stuck the hotel for a few quid on his way. And for all the supposed glory of being capped for Ireland, Kip always knew who he was – the dumb kid, who had little to recommend him beyond being able to score a try. What good was all of that, when it came to making a future with someone? In real terms, Kip always believed he hadn't enough to offer someone as good as Blythe Scott.

And yet.

And yet, her mother, dear old Mrs Scott, disagreed.

And it was her voice, those words that last time they spoke that kept him hanging on, when he might have given up. He would have given her up, if a better man had come along. Old man Scott seemed to think that the sun and stars rose over Marcus Johnson's head – but Kip saw through that weasel from the start. He was glad that Blythe had not been stupid enough to fall for his false charm. He loved her far too much to give her up for the likes of Johnson.

Then, when he'd felt sure anyone with half a brain would leave him for someone with at the very least a fixed income and a not quite so bashed-in nose, Blythe had turned up trumps, supporting him all the way through his final days on the pitch. Things were never better between them.

There was no happier man than Kip Carney the day she'd come to him and told him she was pregnant with his child. Oh, of course, he knew he should feel badly. Some of the old fuddy-duddies in the village would talk behind their backs, but that hadn't killed him when he was a kid. Back then, they were *that family*; the one on everybody's lips because his father had run off with another woman.

There was no settling Blythe on the matter though, and maybe he could see it from her point of view. Isn't that what women want? A big white wedding, a grand gesture, all the frills that go with it and a respectable twelve months before a baby appears.

Kip couldn't give a hoot for any of that, and he'd told Jack Scott precisely so. The thing his future in-laws didn't understand was that nobody intimidated Kip now. He might feel inferior in terms of many things, but behind it all, he'd lay down everything for Blythe. Sure, he knew the Scotts could buy and sell his mother's little house ten times over, probably, if they wanted to, and he knew they were well connected and respected well beyond the island. All of Kip's respect came from being capped for Ireland – which, when all was said and done, was only fleeting anyway. For that reason alone, it would be stupid to let it go to his head and so he never had lost sight of who he was beneath it all.

The fact was, Kip had seen many a big man cry his eyes out over a ball falling on the wrong side of a white line – he'd long since given up being intimidated by other people's stations or situations.

'I won't apologise,' he said, levelling a clear-eyed gaze at his future grandfather-in-law, 'because I think it's the best thing that's ever happened to me.' And he meant it – there was no match or score or award that could top the joy he felt at the idea of this baby.

'I'm not asking you to,' Jack Scott said, when he'd called him into the hotel one afternoon while Blythe was on the mainland sorting out some hotel business.

'Good,' Kip said, taking the seat opposite him. They were in the snug, a small cut-off section of the bar that had fallen out of fashion these last few years. 'So, what can I do for you?'

'I want to be clear with you, this place…' The old man waved a hand about the hotel. 'This place isn't on the table for you, if that's…'

'I'd be happy with Blythe if we were living in a tent on the side of the road. I don't need your hotel to be happy,' he said and naïvely he assumed Blythe wouldn't either once the baby arrived.

'Is that so?' The old man smiled and then he sipped from one of the thimble-sized glasses of whiskey he'd poured them both. At the same time, Kip pushed his away, whiskey was his father's drink, he never touched the stuff. 'So, if I was to hand the place over to Rae, you'd be fine with that?'

'I know nothing about hotels; I'd be more worried if you wanted me to come in and run the place for you.' This had crossed his mind at one point, what if there was an expectation he would work here? The idea filled him with dread – he quite simply wouldn't know where to start.

'That was never on the cards, I can assure you.' The old man leant back and appraised him. They sat for what felt like a long time, both lost in thought. Kip felt his stomach churn at the aroma of the whiskey.

'Look, this place is yours, it will always be the Scott legacy. I've no interest in seeing the name Carney above any door, let me tell you,' Kip said then, to quell whatever worries the old man was still holding onto.

'Fine. That's that I suppose.' And he took up his drink, finished the contents in a final gulp and gasp. It looked as if he was no more a whiskey man than Kip was and he wondered then, if that too had been some kind of test.

'That's that,' Kip said and he pushed his glass further away again.

'There's only one thing.'

'Name it,' Kip said, and instantly regretted his automatic answer.

'I'd hope that you are going to be a better husband than your father.'

'I'm my mother's son,' Kip said.

'Yes, they say that the man that's good to his mother will be good to his wife.' Jack glanced across at him now. 'I'll need a promise.'

'You're asking me if I'll be a good husband?' Kip sat a little straighter in the chair. 'I have no intention of ever doing anything to hurt Blythe. I've loved her for as long as I can remember and if I was going to promise anyone what sort of husband I'd be, that promise was made a long time ago to my own mother.'

'That's enough,' Jack said, and he sighed deeply as if he was finally letting Blythe go, even if it was breaking his heart to do so.

26

Blythe

Present

Fiona's house – the Grayling, stood dramatically on a precipice overhanging one of the bendiest roads on the island, which also happened to have the most spectacular view of the ocean. You'd never get planning permission for the Barbie Dreamhouse-inspired creation these days, of course. Fiona had built and rebuilt around an old cottage that had probably been on the site since pre-famine times. The only sign of the original place at this stage was a remarkably preserved stone wall that ran the length of her kitchen. Beyond that, the cottage it belonged to had been greedily gobbled by Fiona's appetite for glass, chrome and bleached maple.

The first thing Blythe noticed when she arrived for book club at Fiona's house was the aroma of fresh baking. She sniffed the air appreciatively. Fiona never baked. The nearest Fiona got to home cooking was a selection of discreetly placed reed diffusers that purported to scent her home with cinnamon or lemon or some other sickly-sweet smell. Blythe had baked palmier cookies, her home bakes were always the most popular, *not that it was a competition*. She always said that, to make the others feel better, but secretly, she felt it really was. She'd looked up the recipe for the cookies because what else could you eat when you were discussing *The Paris Wife*. She was really looking forward to book club this month, she badly needed to relax, indulge in a good old gossip and forget about her worries for an hour or two. Fiona would have a good selection of French wines on hand, but Blythe needed more than a crisp crémant, so she had tucked a large bottle of gin into her bag. Already, just knowing it was there soothed her frayed nerves.

'Darling, I thought you forgot about us,' Fiona embraced her in a perfume-filled hug, air-kissing her cheeks loudly.

'Not a chance, I've been looking forward to this evening all week.' Blythe said as she handed over the tray of food. 'Actually, really looking forward to it,' she leant in and whispered conspiratorially while taking the bottle of gin from her shopping tote.

'Don't worry, there's plenty of that in the house.' Fiona laughed.

'Have you been baking?' Blythe knew nothing was less likely, but that smell, oh, my God, she could almost taste the butter and sugar melting together – it made her mouth water just thinking of what it might be.

'You are joking?'

'No, but...' And that's when Blythe saw them. Platters of cannelés, dainty cinnamon rolls, madeleines, and tiny pink macarons, enough to feed a small village, all spread out on the low coffee table where usually Blythe's offerings took pride of place. 'You didn't get caterers in?' It had been one of the rules she set down at the beginning of the group to stop the women trying to outdo each other. It was home baking or shop bought, but no expensive off-site catering company because she knew two things, first, down that road lay the sort of competitiveness that led to fall-outs. The second thing was, she was the best baker and home maker in this room by a country mile and was it so bad that she enjoyed the praise abundantly heaped on her each time they met?

'Ah,' Fiona said, as if some invisible penny was just dropping into a slot. 'What have we got here, ladies?' she said as she led the way, making a show of uncovering Blythe's platter of cookies.

'Mmm,' there was a general murmur from the other ladies gathered in the various sofas and single chairs around the feast. They all had their mouths stuffed with pastries already, so she didn't need to ask, the look in their eyes was enough to know that this time, her offerings were coming in a poor second place. Blythe looked around the group, trying to figure out who had spent the guts of a day putting together the gorgeous-looking spread laid out before them.

'We've kept your favourite seat for you,' Fiona said then, in an effort to let her see that her place had not really been usurped. She made a show of plumping up the cushions on the best chair in the house, an obscenely expensive wing chair, the only one that did anything to support your back, in Blythe's opinion.

'Apologies,' the door to the kitchen at the far end of the room opened then and Blythe was glad she was sitting, because otherwise she might have fallen over from unpleasant surprise.

'You!' she said as she watched Melissa Val approach. The woman was so... so colourful in a flowing bright orange kaftan, against the grey and white décor that ran right through Fiona's house.

'Yes, hello, I'm Melissa, you must be Blythe,' she was holding out her hand to Blythe now, to introduce herself.

'I know very well who you are,' Blythe said then.

'And of course, I've heard all about you, well, a little about you at any rate.' Melissa dropped elegantly into the vacant space on the end of the sofa next to her.

'Hmph.' It was all Blythe could manage, because suddenly she was aware of eight pairs of eyes watching her.

'Blythe,' Heather Banks was holding up a champagne glass, 'Fiona has broken out the good stuff,' she laughed.

'That'll do for now,' Blythe said, taking the glass from her and knocking back the contents in one go. 'Now, Fiona...' She nodded to her friend who was already pouring her a generous measure of gin.

'So, let's get started,' Fiona said as soon as she'd handed Blythe a generous G&T.

'I thought it was simply marvellous,' Ellen Mitchell said, because she thought every book they read was marvellous, even the truly horrendous ones. Ellen had worked on the mobile library for years; she was still their best supporter. 'I want to read everything there is to read now about Hadley Richardson.' She bent forward, her fingers hovering between the macarons and the cookies. She chose a macaron and Blythe sucked down her resentment.

'Well, for me, it was all about the scene – I mean, come on, was I the only person here who wanted to reincarnate in the 1920s and dance the Charleston and fall in love.' Mary Larkin clapped her hands together and looked as if she might start flapping on the spot.

Blythe quickly tuned out. The conversation about the book they'd read, which she had really enjoyed, seemed to be happening around her. All she could think about was Siggy and Danial and the fact that even here, in this one place where she hoped to get away from her worries; they had followed her, in the shape of Melissa Val.

And everyone seemed to think that woman was the bee's knees.

What couldn't she do, exactly?'

She had even managed to flog a monstrous-looking painting, that was more like a mural, to Fiona. Blythe had nodded when they all admired it, but she couldn't make head or tail out of the thing. It was just a riot of colours, honestly, Siggy would have done as well when she was five years old. There was nothing to it, to Blythe's eyes, it was a confusion of random paint splodges.

And as for the cakes, the women were hoovering them up. Blythe's tray just about cleared by the end of their meetings usually, but between the eight of them, they had managed to scoff back six times the amount of food that they normally would.

In fairness, Blythe had managed to do the same with the alcohol.

Now, as she sat there, wrapped up in a gin-hazed mantle, she could feel her patience levels depleting. She kept sipping her drink, willing herself not to explode.

'What about you?' Melissa turned to her now and honestly, Blythe could have sworn that her voice dripped of dislike.

'What about me?' The words came out with more anger than she'd expected.

'Sorry, I just meant, I'd be interested to hear what you thought about the book?' Melissa smiled then, as if everything was perfectly normal in the world.

'To be honest with you, Melissa, our book club has never been all about the book. Usually, we only spend a short time discussing it and by now, well, if it was just ourselves, we'd be having a good chat about everything and anything under the sun.'

'Blythe,' Fiona's voice held a note of warning. 'Can I offer everyone a cup of coffee, I've had that blend you all loved last time imported especially...' she said, but there was a note of panic in her voice, as if she was racing against a tidal wave that was about to break loose.

'I'm sorry, if I've...' Melissa began, and she looked at Blythe and then from there to each of the other women. 'Thanks so much for having me, I really enjoyed meeting you all,' she said then as she got up to leave.

'You're not going,' it was a chorus from the choir on the Bergamo sofa.

'I think it's late for me, I'm an early riser, so...' She smiled then, making her way towards the door.

'No, please, don't go like this, Melissa. Jay has offered to come and bring us all home; it's such a long walk at this hour of the evening.' Mary Larkin tried to cajole her into staying.

'Mary, if the woman wants to go home, you should let her go,' Blythe said with slightly less satisfaction than she expected at the idea of seeing the back of the woman.

'Really, it's fine. I like to walk,' Melissa said. 'I'll collect the trays during the week, thanks so much for having me.'

'You'll come again?' Ellen sounded hopeful, as she rubbed her hands together to shake the last of the sugary crumbs from them.

'Maybe, we'll see,' Melissa said and she shot a look at Blythe which might have held a note of sadness, but really, since Blythe was absolutely seething at how the tables had been so suddenly turned, it went completely over her head.

And with that, she was gone, off out in the dusky evening and Blythe was left sitting there, facing eight angry pairs of eyes.

'What?'

'That was so embarrassing.' Mary shook her head sadly and her eyes fell to her hands clasped rigidly in her lap.

'Really Blythe, did you have to be so horrendously rude to the woman?' Fiona came right out with it.

'I don't know what you mean?'

'Oh, please, don't play stupid. You've had a face on you like a pinched clothespin since you came in the door and saw Melissa's macarons on the table.' This from Ellen.

'Excuse me?' For Blythe, that was the worst, because Ellen Mitchell had never said boo to a goose in her life.

'I'm going after her,' Heather said then, getting up quickly. 'Sorry, Fiona, but she can't go walking back alone. Anyone else up for the walk?' She looked around the room and of course, the three sheep on the sofa nodded obediently and got up to follow her.

After they left, the atmosphere stung with hostility. Blythe stewed silently, hoping for she knew not what – for it to pass, perhaps? Across from her, Mary had the look of a woman working her way nervously through her novenas until her husband, Jay, came to collect her. Fiona made a show of clearing away the plates and glasses of the evening, although of course, her cleaner would be arriving promptly at nine in the morning to put the place to rights as she always did anyway.

'Here, let me,' Blythe said, gathering up some of the empty platters to take them through to the kitchen. They were heavy, extraordinarily beautiful, exceptionally unique; Blythe couldn't help but notice now, as she stacked up four of them.

'It's okay, really, I'd rather you didn't,' Fiona said, and she went to take the platters from Blythe, 'we must be careful with them, Melissa's husband made them, and they are very dear to her.'

Fiona's words were swirling around Blythe's mind, because suddenly she felt her head swim, her balance completely at odds with how it should be. The sand and sea-coloured bespoke rug felt like a flying carpet beneath her feet. She was not used to drinking so much gin. She was not used to drinking much of anything beyond half a glass of wine with Kip of an evening. She must have drunk three very large measures in the space of two hours. What was she thinking, now, the whole room began to sway around her. The platters she was carrying tipped, first one way, then the other, in dreadful slow motion. She moved, what she thought was only slightly, but it turned out her whole spatial awareness had shifted out of sync. Now she was spinning, away from the flying carpet at her feet and towards the huge oil painting that everyone had been so taken with earlier. And then she watched, horrified as they slid, one after the other to a resounding crash, first, scraping against the canvas and then, slowly, ever so agonisingly slowly to a resounding crash into a thousand smithereens on the maple floor. Blythe, too, ended up falling with them. Strangely she knew the dismayed expression on Fiona's face had nothing to do with any injury Blythe might have caused herself. Rather it was all about the damage to the irreplaceable platters and probably ruined canvas that was now dripping with dark chocolate and cream.

'I didn't mean it, I swear,' Blythe tried to pick herself up off the floor, but now, it seemed everywhere was chocolate and cream, her limbs had turned to soufflés, and the more she scrambled to get up, the more she slid back down.

'Oh, God, what will you say to Melissa?' Mary whispered, while her lips stayed in the shape of a circle. There was an expression of terrified wonder on her face, a mixture of dread and morbid excitement; like one of those people who laugh in the face of tragedy, her nervous system unable to undo the horror that had just unfolded and make sense of what was coming next.

'Oh, God, Mary, I don't know, let's just get this cleared up and see what can be salvaged.' Fiona ran her hands through her hair, but even in Blythe's inebriated state she knew the best you'd save out of this mess was a shard or two at most.

'Here, let me,' Blythe had finally managed to pull herself up to a standing position. Funny, how, once all the damage was done, she'd suddenly sobered up.

'I think you've done quite enough for one night.' Fiona stood, hands on hips, her eyes burning into Blythe with as much anger as any woman could manage to hold behind them.

'But I...' Blythe began.

'Really, just go, Blythe, you've done enough damage already.' Fiona marched towards the hall and took down Blythe's coat, holding open the front door so there was no question that she was unwelcome here now.

'I'm so sorry, you know about the...' She looked towards the painting on the wall and the mess on the floor.

'You know what, Blythe, all the damage...' She put her hand up to her forehead as if she couldn't even begin to count the cost of repairs to make even half of it right, 'none of it matters. What's really annoyed me tonight, is how you treated Melissa. She was a guest in my home. You had no right to do that, not here, not anywhere on Pin Hill Island. You are not the Queen Bee, no matter how much we've all been guilty of allowing you to think it over the years. Tonight you've gone too far.'

'I...' Blythe was shocked. Nobody had ever spoken to her like that before, but was she sorry? She stood there, for a moment, with her mouth opening and closing, but no words were making it out. 'What do we know about these people, really, Fiona? You and I – we've known each other for years, but now, don't you see, everything is changing, Melissa Val and her son, it's all very well for you. But I have Siggy to think of, a business, a...' A marriage, but she could hardly admit that to herself, much less Fiona. Tonight had been too much. Melissa Val coming to her book club, indeed. And it was more than that. She was completely out of her depth after the evening. Everything she'd begun to believe about the Vals had been thrown up in the air tonight. It was obvious that Melissa Val was a cut above, not below. Somehow that only made things worse. Danial Val would take her daughter far from Pin Hill Island, Blythe was surer of that now than ever.

'Good night, Blythe, I would say, don't come back, but since book club is at your place next month, I will say you won't be seeing me there – and I doubt any of the other women will want to go either, unless you make it up to Melissa.' With that, she closed the door and Blythe found herself standing on the driveway with a light wind blowing the tears from her eyes, but still not touching the fury in her heart.

Those bloody Vals were ruining everything. It felt as if, with their arrival on the island, Blythe's whole world had started to fall apart. She slept fitfully again that night, but by the morning, she knew there was only one thing for it. She dug around in her pockets and pulled out her phone, scrolled down through the list of contacts to Mae English. She'd never texted Mae in her life, she only had her phone number because she'd had to contact her years earlier when Mae had won a voucher for the local supermarket in the annual chamber draw.

It was a short text.

Mae need not even know who sent it.

Blythe went to the settings option on her phone and made her number private. She wasn't exactly Bill Gates when it came to these things, but anyone could manage the basics. Her fingers shook as she began to type. Quickly. Before she could change her mind.

> Has anyone else noticed that these break-ins only began with the Val family arriving on the island? Apparently, *he's* been seen hanging around some of the houses that were broken into. Just a warning message. Keep your doors and windows locked. From a friend.

It was wrong, she knew that as soon as she'd sent it. But she couldn't bring herself to feel regret. After all, it was just a text. Just a rumour. Hopefully, it would be enough to get tongues wagging and make Siggy see sense about that boy.

After seeing them together in the town square, Blythe knew, she had to tread carefully around the topic with Rae. After all, hadn't Rae been the very one who'd run around the island after the most unsuitable boy she could pick? Hadn't they had this conversation a million times over, twenty years earlier, and where had it gotten Blythe at the end of the day? Nowhere. Actually, worse than nowhere. Marcus Johnson had swooped in, on the tail end of those arguments. He had used them to his advantage, putting even more leverage on his side when Pappy saw the way Rae settled down, almost overnight, as soon as Marcus appeared on the scene.

She was not going to sit back and let the same thing happen again.

She wasn't the only one who felt uncomfortable with the newcomers, there were probably plenty more on the island feeling the same way. Mae English for one, albeit for different reasons.

The sound of her ring tone. Damn it. Rae again.

'Yes.' She snapped into the phone.

'Oh, Blythe, thank God, you picked up.' Rae breathed and there was no missing the relief in her voice. 'I'm so sorry that we've fallen out and that....'

'Have you had second thoughts?' Blythe said then, because she knew well enough, that Rae had bent to Marcus's will continually over the years, she might just do the same now.

'About what?' Rae sounded genuinely baffled.

'Oh, Rae,' Blythe said in that way she always had when she despaired of her younger sister. 'What is it you want?'

'Nothing,' Rae said slowly. 'Actually, I wanted to talk to you.'

'Well, you have my full attention.' Blythe was aware of the irritation in her voice, but how else was she supposed to feel?

'No. I mean, properly, it's important.' Rae pleaded and for a moment a wasp of fear buzzed across Blythe's thoughts – illness? Some other terrible event on the horizon? No. She pushed anything like that from her mind. This was Rae, the most terrible thing that could happen to her, already had – she'd lost Marcus.

'In case you haven't noticed Rae, I have a lot on my plate at the moment,' Quite aside from the hangover from hell.

'We all have, Blythe,' Rae said and there was something about how she said it, that made Blythe stop. 'Can you come to the hotel today?'

'Okay,' she said then, because suddenly she had a feeling that Rae was holding back something that might just push her own worries aside for once.

Blythe had a strange sense as she walked through the front door of the hotel. Something had changed here, she caught it, only vaguely on the air, a tremor in the atmosphere. She had a feeling that things had moved a little sidewards from her grasp, the place was somehow less familiar, less her family heritage, less her own possession. Which was of course ridiculous, she had to remind herself, it hadn't ever actually belonged to her at all. Her grandfather had left the place, lock, stock and barrel to Rae, with Still Water House going to Blythe.

It looked the same, of course it looked the same. The blousy floral dark green wallpaper faded gently every year, the paintwork, neatly touched up by Marcus over the years when the doors were closed for Christmas and New Year. Today, the brasses gleamed, the oak counters shone and a gentle mixture of aromas from wood polish and fresh wildflowers mingled when she walked into the place. It was welcoming in a way that big fancy hotels could never replicate. Blythe hated herself for loving it now, as much as she ever had.

'Blythe, I'm so glad you came.' Rae appeared from behind the antique reception desk as if she'd known as soon as her sister entered the building. 'Come on, I've made broccoli and stilton soup, will you join me?'

'Okay,' Blythe said, because suddenly she was famished, even though the last thing she wanted at this early stage of putting their relationship back on an even keel was to let Rae know that she was in any way the lesser party.

She followed Rae in through the small living area that her sister and Marcus had called home for fifteen years. The soup was set out in a tureen on the table, a crusty French roll broken up on a wooden board next to it and places set for both sisters, with fresh butter and a jug of iced water at the ready.

Still, the room was depressing. There was no getting away from that. It was a room of leftovers – the sofa too lumpy to offer to a guest, the sideboard an ugly antique that had been picked up at an auction years before either of them could remember and replaced with something far more elegant in the lobby now. There was a small television and side tables with pretty lamps from the nearby pottery studio and this tiny round table pushed into a corner where the view stretched no further than the hotel reception beyond. There wasn't even a window here, well, not a proper one at any rate. It was all so depressing compared to the beautiful kitchen Blythe had installed in Still Water House a few years earlier. Rae moved around the little flat with such grace, such elegance. She was the understated version of their mother. She ladled the soup out onto their bowls. The aroma, fresh and salty, made Blythe feel more ravenous than before.

'So?' Blythe waited patiently until Rae was finished and sat opposite her. She looked at her now, her interest piqued because instead of filling in any awkward silence with small talk as she normally would have, Rae was quiet, thoughtful, as if there was something of great importance on her mind. Blythe felt a sense of uneasiness rub against her pragmatic shell.

'Okay. Promise me you won't get angry? That you'll hear me out to the very end…' Rae said, leaving down the piece of bread that she hadn't even bitten into yet.

'Oh, Rae, whatever it is, out with it – how do I know what I'll feel until I hear what you have to say,' Blythe said, tasting her soup.

'Fine. It's the hotel.' Rae looked down at the food before her, pushed it slightly away. That was the difference between them, Blythe ate through her worries, she'd always have to coax Rae to eat if she was anxious about something.

'The hotel?' Suddenly that pinprick of worry grew a little wider.

'I'm in trouble. Big trouble, if you want to know the truth of it. Since Marcus died, well, you don't have to be an economist to work out that our business has been decimated.'

'That's to be expected, but once you get back to yourself, you know, after…' She'd stopped alluding to the fact that Rae was still grieving the loss of Marcus, because what was the point in calling out the elephant in the room – it didn't, in Blythe's experience, make it go away.

'No. I mean, I'm in real trouble.' Rae looked at her now and Blythe noticed once again how much her sister had aged over the last fifteen years, as if someone had come along and unplugged some vital valve in her. 'With the bank.'

'The bank?' Blythe repeated, she didn't understand.

'Yes, Blythe, the bank. There's a huge overdraft on this place, there has been for the last ten years.' She stopped, Blythe knew, the car park alone had cost thirty thousand to tarmacadam a few years earlier. There had been a new roof when Marcus took over at first and umpteen upgrades since. Blythe knew very well the cost associated with bringing a place up to scratch. She had been circumspect in her upgrading of Still Water House going at it one room at a time, with Kip at her side doing the heavy lifting and only as they could afford it.

'Don't be ridiculous, Scotts have banked with the same...' She paused, because the bank was no longer where it had always been. In fact, for the first time in her life, Blythe had no idea who the bank manager was – she couldn't put a name or a face to him or her if she was paid to do so.

'I'm going to lose the hotel unless I do something very radical...' Rae began to cry, and Blythe found herself frozen to her seat. She couldn't reach out and comfort her, she was still far too angry about Danial Val, and this? This was too much.

'Oh, Rae, pull yourself together, I'm sure it's not that bad. You read about businesses every day of the week, up to their necks in debt and they just keep on marching through, hard work, a commitment to keeping the place open, doing what you have to do, that's all you need. No banker in their right minds would want to call in a debt on this place,' she read an article about it recently in the *Independent*; the cost of repossession and there was no guarantee with a place on the islands that anyone else would touch it.

'Blythe, you're not listening to me. It's too far gone. I can't pull it back.'

'Dear God, Rae, I mean...' There was so much Blythe wanted to say, but Rae reached across and gripped her hand and for a moment, it felt as if she was trying to communicate a death, rather than a turn in business.

'It's too late, Blythe,' Rae said with words that were as hollow as they were heavy. Blythe felt each of them like a blow.

'It can't be too late...'

'It's not just the bank. It's revenue and council taxes and...' Rae shrugged, as if it was already out of her hands.

'How long have you known this?'

'That doesn't matter.'

'It bloody does.' Blythe felt her blood pressure rise as if she might boil over, right here and drain into the now slightly nauseating bowl of soup.

'There's only one option...' Rae stopped, as if waiting for Blythe to interrupt her again, but Blythe couldn't think of anything to say. 'I'm putting number three up for sale.'

'You're selling the hotel?' A dull pain alerted Blythe that a blinding migraine threatened to take hold.

'Not all of it,' Rae murmured and she seemed to have grown small in the chair opposite.

'You can't do that, Rae, you can't just chop the place in half and think that...'

'It's a third of the original building, Blythe, and...' A small tear ran down Rae's cheek. 'Look at the place. Even if by some miracle I had it in me to work every hour for the rest of my days, this place is beyond faded.'

'It's charming.' Blythe's hand shook as she brought it to her pounding forehead.

'Call it what you want, but the fact is, we're competing with hotels on the mainland that have indoor swimming pools and spas. It needs a complete overhaul, for goodness' sake, Blythe, the wallpaper in the foyer's been hanging since before we were born.'

'That wallpaper was Pappy's pride and joy, it's like an installation, you can't possibly be thinking of doing anything to it.' Blythe's voice had risen, she was trying to stay in control, but now, her whole body was shaking with a mixture of fear and rage. She wasn't sure if she was on the point of tears or completely losing her rag.

'Blythe, calm down, it's only…'

'It's only our family's legacy, it's only…' She was trembling, she wanted to storm out the door, but she really wasn't sure if her legs would carry her.

'Please.' Rae pleaded. Blythe closed her eyes for a moment, tried to breathe so she could steady herself. It felt as if everything was falling in on her, as if all the points that had been her anchors were shifting out of her reach. She took a deep breath. 'It's already done, Blythe, the auctioneers are advertising it this week.' The words only barely penetrated Blythe's understanding. She was numb. She couldn't do this. For once in her life, Blythe knew for certain, this wasn't something she could sort out by the sheer force of her personality or her will to make things right. This was out of her hands, it had been for the last fifteen years.

'I'm sorry,' she mumbled then, because she was, she was sorry for everything, for what they had become, for where they'd been, who they were and for the fact that now, everything was falling apart. 'I have to go,' she said and she tried to walk with purpose, but she knew, she barely staggered, lightheaded from the hotel to her car.

27

Rae

Eighteen Years Earlier

They were in the kitchen, breakfast just finished, when Blythe told her. She'd only just found out. Well, she'd known for a few days, in her heart apparently, and Rae wondered if, when *her* time came, she'd just *know*. Later, Rae thought, she'd never forget that moment, Weetabix packet on the kitchen table, crumbs on the floor, old Beanie, their black and white tom circling Rae's legs in the hopes that she might sit for a while and take him on her knees and scratch his belly while he fell asleep near the warmth of the Aga.

It was the song on the radio that she really remembered the most. Radio one. Her father's station. Abba. *Waterloo*. That radio station was a constant background to the goings-on in this kitchen for as long as Rae could remember, it felt as if their parents had gone off that night and no one ever thought to switch the radio off.

'Turn that blessed thing off,' Blythe said and Rae reached up to the shelf where the radio sat between bills to be paid, and old plates arranged that they never used either.

Pappy descended into a morose silence. He nodded or shook his head, more than spoke, since Blythe told him the news. Blythe, for her part, seemed to have almost lost the power of speech – well as much as she was capable of such a thing.

Rae couldn't see what the problem was – Blythe was pregnant, surely this was something to celebrate? Rae wanted to have lots of children, some day. With Marcus. Not that they were anywhere near getting married or starting a family. All that stuff was years away yet.

Pappy called Blythe's pregnancy, *putting the cart before the horse*. It was all too obvious that he felt Blythe had let herself down and more damning – had let the Scott good name down.

'I don't care what either of you think or say, I think it's the best thing that's happened to this family in as long as I can remember,' Rae said, as she dished out sherry trifle that it seemed no one had an appetite for this Sunday afternoon.

'I can't eat this,' her grandfather said, and he pushed his chair back from the table and headed for the door. His car on the gravel drive outside was enough to let them know he'd gone back to Hope Square, where he could ignore Blythe more easily.

'Oh, Rae, what am I going to do? He can't stand to look at me,' Blythe said, and if she was anyone but Blythe she might have crumpled then. Rae thought she cried, at night, just as they were all falling off to sleep. She'd heard the muffled sobs through Blythe's door, but when she'd poked her head into her sister's room it was in darkness. So dark it was hard to make her form out in the bed, much less figure out if she was crying in her sleep or crying while awake. Which was worse? Rae couldn't tell for sure, but either way, it tore her up to see her sister so upset.

'Look, we're not living in the times of Jane Austen – these are modern times. Pappy will get over it when the baby arrives. You're getting married, what more does he want?'

'Hmph, yes, but to Kip.'

'You do want to marry Kip, don't you? I mean, you don't have to, not if you don't love him. I'll help you take care of the baby if you don't want to go through with it.'

'Oh Rae,' Blythe reached out and squeezed her hand. 'You're so sweet, never, ever change,' she smiled sadly. 'I adore Kip, but it's hardly a secret that Pappy has never been keen on him, he told me himself that he hoped I'd do better.' She rolled her eyes.

'Don't be silly, it's not Pappy who's marrying him, the only thing that matters is that you love each other.'

There had not been a Scott Family wedding in the village since their parents, and even if Jack Scott was sullen and disappointed at home, as far as anyone outside his immediate family was concerned, there wasn't a prouder man on Pin Hill Island.

He set about throwing as much money as he could at Blythe's big day. His granddaughter might be pregnant – maybe not yet showing, but she would have the very best that money could buy. From knockout flowers to an expensive wedding dress – Pappy wanted a fairy tale wedding for Blythe.

'It seems like a lot of fuss over just one day,' Marcus said softly when Rae gushed excitedly over the arrangements. She was storing a wine order in the open dresser that stood in a closed-off nook in the dining area of the hotel. Marcus, of course, was helping her. He had begun by emptying out the stock already there and now, they were placing the bottles carefully by some system that made sense to him, but not to Rae, although, she wouldn't admit that to another living soul. Occasionally, Marcus studied a label, and she could tell immediately if he was impressed or if a bottle somehow didn't meet his standards.

'Well, you only do it once...' she said then, because she thought she caught something in his tone, but when she looked at him, he was smiling at her.

'Of course, don't mind me, it's just... you know Blythe...'

'She's not the sort of girl you could imagine having a big meringue dress and a string quartet during the wedding feast?' Rae spotted another bottle with a matching label, picked it up and handed it to Marcus.

'No, not that, but...' He took it from her, brushed her hand and caught her eye for a moment.

'But what?' she was waiting now, because she had a feeling, he had somehow put his foot in it.

'I just never imagined her to be someone who would be so laid-back about anything,' he stopped, looked towards the shelves and then back onto the floor, trying to figure out what should go next. 'In college, she was so sure of herself, so set on striking her own path. Blythe Scott was the last person I'd imagine taking a back seat and letting someone else make the decisions...' He shook his head and smiled, almost shyly. 'Well, nothing like you.'

'Is that a good thing or a bad thing?' She was shamelessly fishing for compliments, hated herself for it, but there was something about him, she needed his approval more than anything. She looked at him now, so serious in sorting out the wines, his long slender fingers wrapped around each bottle, handling each one so carefully. He was like no one else she'd ever met before.

'It's a good thing, of course it's a good thing, my darling,' he said.

'So, in what way was she nothing like me?' Because she knew they were chalk and cheese, but she loved it when Marcus complimented her – it was like oxygen to her these days.

'Well, put it this way, if she and I were here today, she'd be telling me how to do this job, even though I'm the one with the degree in hotel management,' he laughed then. 'I much prefer the way our relationship is even-handed, and you know…' He shrugged. 'I suppose, you're more feminine, you know pure, more…'

'Ah.' Rae wasn't sure what to make of that, but she desperately wanted to take it as a compliment. 'So, I'm more submissive.' She giggled at the notion of it. He wasn't serious, of course he wasn't, the days of gender inequality were coming to an end. Marcus knew that as well as anyone. Of course, he was right about the hotel – Rae never wanted to be the boss here, whereas Blythe enjoyed ordering people about, making sure everything was just so, exactly to her standards. Sometimes, it annoyed Marcus, and more than once, he'd told Rae she must stand up for herself. After all, she too was a Scott, she should have an equal share of everything, but Rae just smiled at him. He was so sweet, but she had no interest in the hotel.

'Blythe has been around more, trust me, a man likes to be a man, likes to be the one to take care of things,' he said then, a small smile playing around his lips and she felt her stomach tumble over for him. God, she fancied the pants off him, like she'd never fallen for anyone before.

'Blythe is no man-eater, if that's the subtext to what you're saying,' she laughed at the very idea of it. 'She's always been first and foremost about the hotel and the Scott family – even Kip has had to wait in line until she was good and ready.' Had she always known that about her sister? She must have, because that was the truth.

'How well do we really know anyone?' Marcus said giving her an uneasy feeling that he knew far more about who Blythe really was, than she did. But he couldn't be right, could he? The Hope Square sisters knew each other better than anyone. Didn't they?

'I think I know my own sister pretty well,' she said then, because she loved Blythe, this whole conversation was beginning to make her feel uncomfortable. She looked around the floor at the remaining bottles, decided Marcus could sort out the last of them and took up the box cutter to break down the cardboard that littered the dining area.

'And yet, you were surprised when she told you she was pregnant.' He moved closer to her now, whispered it in her ear.

'Well, of course, I mean, it's Blythe and...' she stopped, watched as his expression changed to one of kind forbearance.

'Exactly, Rae, that's exactly what I mean,' he said in his most soothing voice, and he placed his hand on her cheek, leaving it there for a long second before leaning forward and kissing her forehead. She never wanted anything more than she did now for him to fold her into his arms and tell her that her world was exactly as she'd always believed it to be. Instead, he inclined his head as if all he could do was feel a deep pity for her naïveté.

Maybe that was the start, but in the run up to the wedding, Rae began to notice other things about her sister, small things. She began to wonder if Marcus was right, did she really know her sister as well as she always thought she did? When he first whispered in her ear that she should step up to the table and take an equal seat, Rae didn't know what he meant. Rae had never thought about her relationship with her family in that way before, but now, Marcus made her question if she had always settled to be second best.

'Doesn't it bother you?' Marcus murmured one evening when she told him that Blythe had rostered her on in the hotel first thing in the morning because one of the other girls had come down with a cold.

'Not at all, why would it?'

'Oh, Rae, Rae, Rae,' he shook his head sadly as if she'd somehow fallen short of the mark he expected of her.

'What?'

'Can't you see it?'

'See what?' The way he was watching her made her feel as if she was being closely examined and somehow, she was being found lacking, and because she was madly in love with him, this frightened her. She couldn't lose him. Marcus was absolutely putting himself out each week to travel from Galway to the island, just for her. They were madly in love, but she knew, that could change in the blink of an eye. Hadn't her own parents gone out for a drive one day and nothing had ever been the same since? Nothing is guaranteed in life. Lots of girls would fancy Marcus on the mainland. She'd never imagined herself to be jealous before, but she knew in a busy Galway hotel, Marcus would be surrounded by pretty girls his age and far more worldly than Rae. The idea of him falling out of love with her was chilling. She had never been with anyone like him before, he made her feel safe, special. She couldn't lose him now.

'Come on, I mean, she completely controls your day, she doesn't even ask if it suits and she knows I'm only here for one day this week. As to how she throws her weight around in the hotel, honestly, it's like she's your boss and you're nothing more than a paid employee.'

'Ah, now, it's not really like that at all,' Rae said, but of course, she *was* just a paid employee. Although, now he said it, she wondered if from the outside, maybe that's exactly what it looked like to others. Is that really what she wanted Marcus to think?

'I thought when we met that...' He stopped.

'What?' A rivulet of cold fear oozed from her pores.

'Well, you were both the Hope Square Sisters, that first day, when I met you, you were so...'

'I'm still the same person.' But in her mind's eye, maybe she knew what he meant. They'd run into each other when she'd been tanned and oblivious to him. The only thing she felt was grief, her mother's passing still so raw, she was cast adrift with no sign of the shore. She hadn't invested in her relationship with Marcus at that point, instead, it was Johnno that was stressing her out. Perhaps she'd seemed somehow more glamorous, more sophisticated, more commanding than she really was – certainly, she knew many of the islanders saw the Scott girls as being on par with celebrity heiresses. Their lives appeared to be rather glamorous from the outside, greeting people as they arrived in the hotel, they could afford nice clothes, to have their hair done regularly and they lived in one of the most imposing houses on the island.

'Anyway, maybe I was wrong about you, maybe...' He looked a little crestfallen. In that moment, it felt as if he'd glimpsed beyond the curtain. Rae felt the glowing light of his approval slip away from her on the stage of their relationship. Suddenly, she was in obscurity, in the darkness.

'Blythe is certainly not my boss,' Rae said crossly then, and she made up her mind to show Marcus Johnson just how fabulous she was. The next time he came to the island, she would be transformed.

Marcus had hardly boarded the ferry that evening when Rae made an appointment with Dawn Doherty to jazz up her image, make her more sophisticated, exceed his expectations. She adored Marcus, the fact was, she'd turn herself inside out at that point just to make him love her back.

The ceremony was, of course, in the local church where generations of the Scott family had been christened, married and buried for as long as there were records to check. Rae knew the wedding was the talk of the whole village – everyone who was anyone was hoping to be invited. Rae had no say in the guestlist, but Blythe had promised that there would be a seat next to her for Marcus if he was free to make it on the day.

Rae would always look back on those days as golden, even if she didn't fully realise it at the time. She was crazy for Marcus and in the most divine stroke of luck, he seemed to be utterly smitten with her.

It's funny but somehow, while Blythe seemed determined to dive into the darkest moods, Rae's life felt as if she'd suddenly stepped into a dimension completely altered. The arrival of Marcus on the island had changed everything. She loved when they did nothing more than walk the strand, sit on rocks and talk for hours about everything and nothing. Marcus was amazing. It really felt as if he was interested in everything she had to say. He was different to the other boys she'd dated, older, of course, that was probably it, but thoughtful and probably sexily experienced with it. When he kissed her, it felt as if he was opening a volcano of desire within her. She supposed he'd probably had lots of girlfriends over the years, not like the boys she'd hung out with on the island.

Now she could see them for what they were – just boys. As Marcus said when Johnno passed them out on his new motorbike – *petrol heads*. And he said it in a way that dripped of disdain and somehow, Rae looked at Johnno differently now.

She had no interest in Johnno or any of that crowd these days, if anything she did her very best to distance herself from them in Marcus's eyes. She knew, somehow, that his estimation of her would plummet if he realised she'd been sitting on the back of Johnno's motorcycle for the last two years with nothing more to show for it than poor school grades and a fraught relationship with Blythe because of it.

No. Marcus made her feel as if she could be somehow better than she already was. She found herself picking out clothes from Blythe's wardrobe that she felt he would approve of, demure dresses and sandals in pastel shades. Her biker chick days were relegated to the very back of the cupboard.

It was the same with the hotel. Before Marcus came, she turned up, did as she was asked, but really, she had more interest in chatting to the other women who came in to help than she had in running the place. That had always been Blythe's domain.

These days, she found herself taking extra pride, especially when Pappy complimented her on a job well done. He'd put her in charge of arranging the hotel flowers every summer. She'd duly picked and plucked and filled up jars in the reception, small posies on each dining table and in the bedrooms. Since Marcus arrived, she found herself spending more time on the job. She'd borrowed a book from the library van all about flower arranging. With every passing week, her arrangements were becoming more elaborate, more of a testament to her talent. In her way, she knew she was making her own unique mark on the hotel. Constance Macken, who had taught her in primary school, said they were becoming 'the talk of the village – an art in themselves'. Rae had been over the moon with that. She knew Constance was lovely at the best of times, still, she found herself working even harder to make each display surpass the last.

Blythe was the only grey cloud on her horizon. These days her sister wouldn't notice a flower arrangement if it was the size of a bus, but Rae had to remind herself – that didn't matter, not really.

Rae worried about her. All the time. She couldn't help it. Rae had a growing feeling that there was something more than the cold war with Pappy upsetting her sister. She had hoped Blythe would tell her. If the shoe was on the other foot, she would absolutely spill the beans. She told Blythe almost everything about Marcus in those early days. One day she'd snapped and cut Rae off, 'Oh, for goodness' sake, Rae, give me a break, he's Mr Perfect, I know, I know.' After that, Rae had kept things back, small things at first, but then bigger things, like Marcus's hope to one day own his own hotel, that they would one day work together, have a shared dream. Rae hated the idea of being stuck in a hotel for the rest of their days, but she didn't tell Marcus that. Instead, she allowed his dreams to wrap her up in a warm feeling of safety and belonging. She wasn't going to worry too much about things that were years off yet, love would find a way, she was sure of that.

28

Siggy

Present

It seemed to Siggy, there was so much going on. Her mother was like a demon at home. She knew it was nerves, pure and simple. Her mother had been, like, totally obsessed with the White Book entry for so long, it was driving her to distraction. And she, in turn, was making everyone else as anxious as herself. Somehow, her father managed to do what was needed and then stay out of the way.

Now, Siggy wondered about what that truly meant.

Was he hiding a secret more shocking than her own? She wasn't sure which her mother would find hardest to forgive, her father carrying on with her best friend or Siggy falling in love with someone like Danial, someone they didn't know, someone who was not on the unspoken list of suitable friends for Siggy.

When she read the text that had been forwarded to her phone late last night, she suspected the latter. It had kept her awake for most of the night. Oh, she knew that there were plenty on the island who would not want the Vals to settle down here, but she hadn't expected anything so vile.

And there was no missing what the undercurrent was, someone, she had no idea who exactly, but someone was suggesting that Danial was behind the break-ins that had taken place across the island over the last few weeks.

She almost threw her phone at the wall in disgust, she'd had to reread it a second time, to try to make sense of it.

It was so unfair. Whoever had sent that vile text, wherever it had originated, it was anonymous, of course, because only a coward and a trouble maker would send such a thing. Well, if their intention was to upset Danial, Siggy decided, she would not be the person to satisfy them. Instead, she deleted it immediately.

'Hello Siggy, I don't think I've laid eyes on you since I retired.' Jay Larkin's familiar face settled her. How bad could things ever be in a world where Jay Larkin was still strolling around the village.

'Hi, Jay.' Her mother had almost cried when she heard old Jay was retiring. 'How are you enjoying retirement?'

'Even better than I could have dreamed of,' he held out the daily newspaper for her to see. 'And what about you, is your mother keeping you busy in the guest house these days?'

'Yeah, it's busy alright, but I'm helping Rae too, in the hotel,' she said then.

'Well, I hope you get to have some fun when the summer comes, no good hanging about until my age.' Then he smiled and lowered his voice, so they couldn't be overheard by any passers-by. 'A little birdie told me, that love might be in the air over at the hotel...' And he nodded over to Danial, making his way into the hotel.

'It's not...' She stopped. Her first thought, how on earth did Jay know about her and Danial? Her second, God help her, she had to make sure her mother didn't get wind of it.

'It's alright, it's not common knowledge, and I won't be volunteering it to anyone else.' Jay smiled kindly.

'Thanks Jay, it's just...'

'Well, I think it's sweet. I spotted you both sitting in the square one of the days, and I thought, history repeating itself. I'm one of the few around here that's old enough to remember your great grandparents and no matter what people said or how young they were, when old Jack Scott fell in love with Gisela, wild horses wouldn't have put him off track.'

'We're kids, Jay, it's not serious...' She laughed, but then she thought about her mother, and she knew, she was the one person who'd give any wild horse a run for its money if she put her mind to it.

Siggy assumed there was simply no one she could talk to about her worries for her parents' marriage. She couldn't lay this on Rae's door – God knows, her aunt had enough on her plate already and she certainly couldn't say a word to her mother. That would be like igniting a nuclear bomb.

As for her father, well, perhaps she should just say something – brave it out, ask him the question although she didn't want the answer she fully expected to get. 'Are you having an affair with Fiona Dixon?' Eugh. It was too gross for words.

The idea that her father would be having an affair was unthinkable, but with Fiona Dixon of any woman in the village? Quite aside from being one of her mother's oldest friends, she was – well, she was Fiona.

Fiona was everything that her own mother was not. Her whole wardrobe seemed to revolve around leopard print and statement jewellery, she drove a huge white car with blacked-out windows that anywhere else would be owned by a drug baron. She wore her nails too long and her skirts too short, yes, she was the opposite of Siggy's mother. If she was being unkind, Siggy would call her vulgar. And just as those thoughts entered her head, she felt mean again and once more had to fight the tears from flooding into her eyes.

Honestly, Siggy felt, she hadn't been right since that morning in the van with her father. She'd tried to pretend that everything was normal, but she couldn't look either of her parents in the eye.

Not that her mother even noticed it, she was so consumed with readying up Still Water House for its evaluation as a White Diary guest house.

Rae had dropped her bombshell about her plans for the hotel the previous day.

Her mother had come home ashen faced. She'd hardly spoken a word all evening and when Siggy asked if she'd like to watch the evening news while they ate (to crack open the frigid silence) her mother had just mumbled that she wasn't very hungry anyway and excused herself to go upstairs.

Her mother was never not hungry.

It was the following day at the hotel that it all flooded out of Siggy. It's funny how it can take just one small word to loosen the stopper on your emotions. Danial had done no more than ask if she was alright, and she had found herself smiling sadly and seconds later, trying hard to keep in tears that had been fighting at the bottom of her throat for days.

'So, you see, I don't know what to do for the best.'

'I'm so sorry. My parents were…' He sighed sadly.

'I know, I'm lucky to have two parents, I know, I shouldn't be laying this on you.' They were sitting at the back of the hotel, facing onto the car park. Siggy had to shade her eyes from the sun, coming in from the west. It was late in the evening, one of those perfect evenings when everything was bathed in a warm orange glow. In the distance, seagulls circled a small pleasure boat as it bobbed on the waves.

'No. No. It is not that. My parents, well, they were very different people, my father did not want my mother to make trouble, he warned her where it would lead, but she was very...'

'Strong-minded? Like my mother?'

'Perhaps.' He shrugged. 'But my father, he was quiet, serious, and they were a good balance for each other.'

'I'm not even sure if my parents love each other anymore, not the way I'd want to be in love if I decided to spend my life with someone.'

'Do you think this could split them up?' he asked softly. And she realised that he'd just said the unthinkable. She couldn't imagine a life where they weren't all together – it was just too awful.

'I don't know.' Somehow, saying that calmed her. The fact was, she couldn't see how they could financially afford to live apart. The guest house made a reasonable income, but her father hadn't enough to move out and rent somewhere on his own. And as for Fiona Dixon, well there was no way she'd want to slum it in some grotty rented flat. Siggy figured that for Fiona, how things looked, would be much more important than how things were – a fall from her self-created pedestal would not be in her game plan.

'What I mean is, if you do nothing are they likely to continue as they are, maybe as happy as they are already content to be? Or, if you do something, will it make things worse?'

'That's the thing, I really don't know what to do.'

'Look at it another way, by telling your mother or confronting your father – how much better do you think that will make things?'

'Not one bit, probably,' she said and she knew that was a fact. If her father was in love with another woman – a word from Siggy was not going to change that. She knew that now she'd met Danial. Other people's opinions couldn't put you off, not if you were in love. It might make him end it, but it wouldn't change how he felt. 'I suppose, the other thing that's bothering me, is the idea of Fiona pretending to be my mother's friend and then being so…'

'Yes. I can see how that would make you want to do something.' He stopped for a moment. 'This is easy for me, it doesn't affect me as it does you, but I think you need to weigh up either side of the scales of doing or not doing. It doesn't matter about this woman Fiona – all that should matter to you is that your parents are happy.'

'Thank you, Danial.'

'I have done nothing.'

'You've listened.' She looked into his eyes; they were the most beautiful eyes she'd ever seen.

'I am glad you told me.'

'Really?'

'Yes, really. It means we are…' He stopped. 'Well,' he gently pushed aside some stray ribs of hair that had fallen across her eyes. 'We are…' Then he leaned in to kiss her and he didn't need to say another word because she knew, this thing between them was growing deeper for him too.

29

Blythe

Eighteen Years Earlier

Blythe hated being pregnant. She couldn't for the life of her see why so many women delighted in waddling about, wearing oversized clothes and meeting up for coffee with women with whom on the surface, they had little more in common than being in the same reproductive boat. How could anyone spend an hour discussing the merits of terry cloth nappies over disposables? It seemed there was no end to this nightmare she found herself thrust into. It was as if she'd stepped into an alternative universe of pregnancy yoga, folic acid, Silver Cross prams and feeding pillows. She couldn't even begin to get started on the heated debate over whether breast is best and those sisters who failed by virtue of finding themselves having for whatever reason, to use formula feeds.

Of course, she'd known all this was going on in the village. After all, it had been her brainchild – the Expectant Mother's Day Afternoon Tea for all the pregnant women on the island. She'd started it three years earlier, a way of filling up the hotel on a quiet afternoon. They held it in the conservatory at the back of the hotel.

Oh, how blissfully unaware she'd been of what it felt like to be one of those women, when she'd been calculating how much extra income this brilliant idea could bring in on an annual basis once she got it up and running.

The women, of course had loved it. Sitting there, guzzling tea and stuffing themselves with cucumber sandwiches and cake while they looked out over the back of the hotel at her grandfather's garden. Blythe had taken the conservatory in hand herself. It was one of those places, she'd always loved it, but over the years, Pappy seemed to forget it was there. She had painted it up in a soft shade of lilac, laid down quarry tiles she'd ordered from the mainland and dug out a variety of old tables from the unused stables. It took almost a month of scrubbing, cleaning and painting after all her other work was done. There still wasn't an electric light bulb in the place, but in the evenings, she dotted candles on every surface. Sometimes, when it felt as if the hotel slept, she slipped in here and looked up at the stars. Those moments were heaven. Even now, sitting here, listening to the incessant babble of the other women, she felt a swell of pride when she surveyed the results of her hard work.

This year, when it had been her turn to join the group (it would be churlish to refuse and it would only be this one time, she had no intention of getting pregnant again) she took an attitude, as she did with everything else during her pregnancy, of 'grin like a vacant lunatic and bear it until it's over'.

She'd been sitting there; at the head of the captain's table, admiring the way Rae had set everything out for the afternoon, with gleaming crystal and silverware, baby pink and blue napkins and a massive garland of the freshest blossoms suspended from the ornate ironwork above the table. The scent of the flowers overtook any of the other aromas that might create a nausea among the guests. It seemed all of them were set off by something, if it wasn't the coffee, it was the food. Blythe wondered if in fact she'd got off lightly, once her morning sickness was behind her. It felt as if they were sitting in a summer garden, such was the cascade of hydrangeas, roses, gerberas and delphinium all plucked from Pappy's garden. She was almost enjoying herself, because she'd ended up sitting next to Allendra Simpson-South, whose husband had just built the most monstrous holiday home on the southern tip of the island. Fiona Dixon would be green with envy, she was hell-bent on making best friends with the affluent newcomers. Allendra was the only child of an Italian industrialist millionaire. The couple were working their way through her fortune, with indoor and outdoor swimming pools and a helipad so they could flit across to their summer home without recourse to the tidal times.

Allendra was admiring the ancient grape vine that had survived in the conservatory for decades, despite being all but ignored for many years, when Blythe looked up to see Marcus watching her through the open doors leading out into the garden.

The sight of him surprised her. He was supposed to be on the mainland. Heaven knows, Rae had kept Blythe and half the village, probably, informed of his comings and goings whether she wanted to know or not. But it was not the fact that he was standing in the garden watching her that made her start, rather it was the expression on his face; unreadable, ominous, almost. She instantly wondered if something had happened. But then, as if she'd imagined it, his whole countenance lightened, and he waved at her and walked down towards the stables at the end of the garden.

'Redundant.' Rae told her that evening. 'They just handed out notice to their top people and let them go, no advance warning, nothing. Apparently, they've got new staff to come in and...'

'But surely, they can't just...' Blythe wanted to say more, but Rae was so upset. Her mind still raced ahead, because she knew that people don't just get 'let go' – not without a good reason.

'Huh?' Rae shrugged, unaware of the warning bells suddenly going off in Blythe's head. 'Anyway, Pappy said if he wants to stay on here for now, he's welcome.'

'Here?' Blythe repeated, suddenly blindsided.

'Oh, don't worry. As soon as you're up and running after the baby is ready to let you out of its sight, I'm sure that everything will be as tip-top as you like it, but for now, I think Pappy is just glad to have an extra pair of hands around the place.'

'I'm pregnant, not dying, I can take on extra if we're under pressure,' Blythe snapped. It was driving her mad, this thing with Pappy. Each day, as Marcus grew closer, Pappy pushed her aside a little more, not allowing her to run the hotel as she had always done.

'Pappy wants you to take care of yourself for now, we all do...' Rae soothed her, which made Blythe feel an uneasy tremble of fury creep over her.

Later, Blythe would look back on that day, as truly, the beginning of the end. At the time, however, the shifting of familiar landmarks in her life were subtle. So, subtle, you'd hardly notice at all. To be fair, Blythe hadn't argued too strongly when her grandfather insisted she take the mornings off and rest while Marcus and Rae took over the breakfast rush. 'They're well-fit for it. Sure, hasn't Rae been your right-hand woman since she was able to carry a plate to the table.' He'd winked at her, when she made sounds, as if she didn't feel as though she was at hell's threshold every morning when she woke up. The truth was, even if she wouldn't admit it, the mornings had been horrendous. They still were, if she didn't take her time about them. In the hotel, the smell of morning fry-ups made her nauseated beyond anything she'd ever experienced. Honestly, by the end of her second trimester, she really thought if she saw another plate of bacon and eggs, there was a good chance she'd turn the whole place into a vegan-only hotel.

'Well, if you're sure…' she said demurely, and she'd honestly never felt so relieved.

'Absolutely, just take it easy for the next few weeks, we have a wedding to get through, after all.'

'Of course.' She had little energy for organising her own wedding, she'd be happy with something very simple. Hadn't she organised more weddings than anyone else on the island? The gloss had long worn off an expensive day and a lot of fuss. Kip was the same, he really didn't mind what happened, so long as they were together.

'At least Marcus will be here now,' Rae said one evening when she arrived back from the hotel. It was summer holidays, and she was still waiting for her leaving cert results. She was hoping for a place in college, so far as Blythe knew, although they hardly talked about that now. 'Oh, Pappy, says I should take a year out, just until everything settles down,' Rae said breezily when Blythe mentioned it. 'I think it was Marcus, really, who put the idea in his head,' she laughed at that, a funny nervous sound that made Blythe stop what she was doing and look at her sister.

'Is that what you want?'

'I suppose, I'm fine with it. I mean, it'll still be there next year and for now, the most important thing is you and the baby.'

'God, Rae, for once and for all, will you please get it into your head, I'm having a baby, not a lobotomy. I don't expect you to put your life on hold for me. I certainly don't intend to change my plans all that much for it.' Blythe wished everyone would stop behaving as if life as she knew it was coming to an end, just because she was pregnant.

'I'm not putting life on hold. I mean, I'm happy to take the year out, Marcus is still here and...' She had that dreamy look on her face again that Blythe wanted to swipe at with every unreasonable bone in her body. It was just her hormones, she adored Rae, this irritation with her happiness was not jealousy. Blythe was determined; she would not allow it to be that.

'You're eighteen Rae, there'll be plenty of time for getting serious about boys a few years from now, when you have your qualifications and...'

'I know, I know, but Marcus says...'

'Marcus says a bit too much, if you ask me.' Blythe muttered under her breath.

'Well, just as well I'm not asking you so, isn't it?' Rae said and she flounced out the door and banged it hard behind her.

Blythe was convinced that Rae wanted to go to college. She'd never forgive herself if she was part of the reason she was not going. The following day, she went to see their grandfather.

'Pappy, I've been thinking.' She had lost valuable sleeping

time with this turning over and back in her mind. 'When Kip and I get married, I think we should move in here, with you… it makes sense. We can close up the house, until the holidays when Rae comes back from college and…'

'We'll do no such thing,' her grandfather snapped.

'But surely it makes no sense to keep two places going, when…'

'Why would you want to move in here, when you have a perfectly good house there to raise a child in?' He looked at her now and she saw again that newly-etched expression on his face. Something had closed behind his eyes since she told him she was pregnant. The distance between them widened with each passing day. Surely, it was just her imagination. All the same, she couldn't help but feel it was growing with greater speed since Marcus arrived in the hotel, and he and Rae had taken up some of her old duties.

'Because this is my home, Pappy, you know that we always agreed, one day, I would live here, and Rae would live at Still Water.'

'That was childish talk, things change, Blythe, you can't imagine that you're going to move in here with Kip and a small baby. It's madness of the first order.'

'But no, Pappy, it'll be easier than living in Still Water, traipsing in and out at all hours, you're not fit for the long days here, I want to help out, I want to take over, one day.'

'Shh, now, less of this talk.' Her grandfather batted it away with his hand.

'Jack, I've just sorted out that double booking for tonight,' Marcus popped his head into the small sitting room in Pappy's flat where they'd been sitting over undrunk mugs of tea. He stopped then, looked down at Blythe and smiled at her as if he almost felt sorry for her.

'What double booking?' Blythe said, her hackles up immediately.

'Oh, it's nothing, no big deal.' Marcus shook his head sweetly.

'You managed to book in two couples for room six for the whole weekend, that's what...' her grandfather snapped.

'There's no way that I...'

'Never mind, I've sorted it all out now anyway, I'm sure it was just a silly mistake, I mean, baby brain, isn't that what they call it?' Marcus laughed then, as if they were all in on the same joke. Blythe wanted to throttle him.

'Good man, Marcus, honestly, I don't know what I'd do without you here to keep us on the straight and narrow.' Her grandfather nodded at him and it almost felt as if, once more, she was outside the conversation.

'I'm afraid I won't be here forever, I'll have to get a real job, once Blythe is ready to come back.'

'Of course, you must already be applying...' Blythe tried to smile sweetly.

'Hah, we'll see about that,' her grandfather said then and the two men laughed as if it was the funniest joke in the world.

A week later, after she'd had to take herself to bed for almost three days thanks to a small bout of dizziness and swollen ankles which the local GP insisted was a case of pre-eclampsia, Blythe arrived back to the hotel to find everything had changed.

Oh, it wasn't that there were huge changes, but the whole front desk had been moved around, pencils changed from left to right, telephone stretched to the furthest end of the desk from where it had always sat.

'What on earth?' She cursed under her breath.

'Everything alright, Blythe?' Marcus smirked at her.

'Who messed up the desk?'

'Oh, sorry, I should have warned you, I reorganised it.'

'You... you reorganised it?' Bloody hell, he had some nerve. 'Why on earth would you do that?'

'Well, because it was the wrong way round, didn't you realise?'

'It was NOT the wrong way round,' oh dear, she could feel her blood pressure rise again, with the stress of just a mixed-up desk. 'What do you mean, it's the wrong way round?'

'Well, it was obviously set up for someone who's left-handed.' He said smugly.

'It most certainly was not,' she stopped, dropped the pen from her left hand.

'Oh, Blythe,' he laughed. He was so bloody smug, how had she not seen that before? 'Oh, dear, you see, *I'm* right-handed, so it all felt in reverse to me.'

'Yes, but you're not...' She bit down on the words. He was not in charge; she was the real manager of the hotel. This was only temporary. She would not stand for it, once this baby was born and she felt well enough again. She was going to be back here, where she belonged and she'd see bloody Marcus Johnson out that door in double-quick time.

'Not?' He looked at her now. 'No, maybe, but your grandfather loves the new set-up, you see, he's right-handed too.' He turned away from her, as if he'd just settled a toddler and she wanted to sink the stapler in his back, but somehow, she managed to restrain herself.

The whole conversation unsettled her, far more than it should have, probably, but she was in foul humour by the time she drove back to Still Water House.

'What's up?' Rae's cheerfulness only added to her misery. Could her sister not see how bloody unhappy she was? She missed the hotel; more than that, it felt as if life as she knew it was not so much slipping away from her; it was being pulled from her hands.

'Nothing.'

'If you say so.' Rae had stopped trying to figure out what was annoying her at this point. In fairness, Blythe snapped at her more often than she smiled at her these days. She was just so bloody miserable, and she was uncomfortable, all the time. If it wasn't her legs, it was her back. She was exhausted too. Well, you try sleeping when you can't stop worrying about every little thing that's suddenly beyond your control.

'Look, I'm sorry if I've been a total cow…'

'It's okay, Blythe, I get it, I'm sorry if you think I've lost patience with you, I'm just afraid to say anything at all now, in case you bite my head off.' They both laughed at that.

'Truce?' Blythe put out her hand and Rae ignored it, instead she wrapped her arms around her sister and held her in a hug so tight, Blythe thought she'd suffocate, but she didn't care, for the first time in so long, she felt safe.

'Did I tell you the big news?' Rae stood back then, still holding onto her sister's hands. 'We're going to the Vintner's Bash…'

'You're going to the Vintner's Bash?' Blythe's blood pressure suddenly shot past boiling point, she would have smoke coming from her ears any moment, that was if she didn't completely combust.

'Here, sit down,' Rae guided her to the most comfortable chair in the kitchen. She had filled their mother's favourite carver with cushions over the last few weeks, which Blythe enjoyed complaining about, but really, she was glad to have the added comfort. 'Yes, isn't it exciting, Pappy said I could go along too.'

'Go along with who, exactly?' Blythe felt a cold chill sink into her bones.

'With Marcus, of course, who do you think? The King of Kathmandu? Silly.' Rae laughed, shaking her head. Dear God, did everyone think she was completely stupid now?

'But Marcus isn't even a member of the Vintners Association...'

'Oh, he is... Pappy paid up his membership, he said that...' She stopped as if she suddenly realised something that had not been obvious before. 'Oh, Blythe, I'm sorry, I'm the dummy here, it must be your...' Her voice trailed off, because she didn't need to finish that sentence. Their grandfather had terminated her membership in favour of Marcus; it was glaringly obvious now. All those little things over the last few weeks, all those niggly things like new menus and changing suppliers for the kitchen, all that undoing of her work as soon as her back was turned – it wasn't just change or improvement at all. Blythe could see it now. They'd let her think she was paranoid, baby-brained, silly – but in fact, these last few weeks, right under everyone's nose, it was obvious now, Marcus was making a play for her job. For her hotel. For her future.

30

Rae

Present

Telling Blythe about her decision to sell the hotel was not nearly as hard as she had expected it to be; Rae had been dreading it. Still, the fact was, she couldn't stick a for-sale sign up outside the front door without letting her sister know first.

Once that was done, the days rolled into each other very quickly. The following Wednesday, the local newspaper ran a full-page advertisement for Cathal, with the hotel taking up half the page. Cathal had taken the photographs himself and to give him his due, the place looked spectacular in them.

The knock-on effect, which Rae had not counted on, was the uptake in trade in the days following the advertisement. Suddenly, the hotel lobby was busy with locals coming in for tea and coffee, sometimes getting quite maudlin at the idea of the old place closing.

'No, of course we're not closing down.' She had to say so many times over and explain that it was just downsizing.

The most surprising thing – which Blythe would probably be shocked about – was that she was quite excited about the whole thing.

'You can finally put your stamp on the place, Rae,' Siggy said to her as they were closing one evening. Rae always closed out the front doors on nights when there were no bookings. She savoured the fact that she did not have to be on call for the evening, even if it meant there was no revenue coming in at the same time.

'I suppose, maybe...' She glanced up at the for-sale sign at the end of the hotel. It was strange seeing it there, but Siggy was right, this felt like her chance to finally make a mark. She'd never had the freedom to make a decision around anything in the hotel over the years, in the end, she was always the one to give in.

'It's going to be fantastic, a real boutique hotel.' Siggy was so carried away on what the hotel might be made into. Even Danial had come up with some brilliant ideas about launching them online and really reaching out to new guests.

'At the end of the day, I'll be happy if we can make it manageable and keep the original charm and warmth...' Rae believed, the spirit of what Hope Square had been all about had been lost over the years. Marcus had stamped it out with a ruthless eye on the bottom line. Rae just wanted to live out her life in peace. She'd settle for a few nice rooms and having the place tick over with a trade that meant they were still afloat and she could one day hand the place on to Siggy to make what she wanted of it.

Honestly, she was more excited at the idea of having a little more comfort in her own quarters than anything else. For a long time, she'd craved a decent-sized window to sit next to and a kitchen that was cosy, in exchange for being surrounded by stainless steel and strip lighting as she cooked her dinner and generally ate it alone in the otherwise empty hotel kitchen. In an ideal world, she'd like a bathroom she could kit out like a mini spa, mind you, anything would be an upgrade to the faded avocado suite that had mould on the ceiling and beauty board up against the bath. Marcus never saw the point in improving anything that wasn't going to make the place money. He'd decided at the start that they could manage in a cheap renovation of the storeroom behind the reception area as their living quarters. It was one large store, divvied out between a bedroom, living room and bathroom. The guests enjoyed a much higher standard of comfort than the owners permitted for themselves. Rae knew it was wrong to live like that. Pappy had always kept his private rooms comfortable – he and Gisela had lived in style across several grand rooms on the first floor before Marcus took over the hotel.

Rae smiled now. She had changed around her own bedroom the previous day. Another small step for mankind – an enormous leap in terms of taking some control back in her own life. Overtaken by a moment of what felt like delicious mutiny, she had dismantled the double bed she'd shared with Marcus and dragged it piece by piece up to the third floor, changing it out for an antique queen-sized bed that she'd always admired. Honestly, she'd never slept better, since she'd changed it. She felt lighter, somehow as if she'd shaken off another shackle when she woke up in her lovely 'new' bed.

'I meant to call in,' Jay Larkin said when he bumped into her the following day in the supermarket.

'Oh, don't worry, half the village has already been in.'

'No, I mean, I wanted to tell you about when we left the post house, you know and moved to our little cottage.' His wife had operated the post office from one of the Victorian houses on the main street, just as her father before her had run it and probably, his father before him. They'd moved out after they'd both hit pension age. These days Jay's son ran the place and lived in the flat above it. Jay grabbed Rae's arm, steered her away from any listening ears. 'The best thing we've ever done was move into our little cottage. When I wake up and look around me, I swear, every morning, it's like winning the lotto. A small back garden – that's the real secret to heaven on earth, I tell you; you won't know yourself.' He lowered his voice. 'Old houses, Mary was always hearing bumps in the night. She never slept properly any night the safe was filled with cash for double social welfare payments the following day. God alone knows what she'd be like with these burglaries...' He stopped, perhaps afraid he'd said too much. 'Although, of course nothing ever happened, nothing ever does,' he laughed at this then, to take any creases of fear out of the conversation that he might have put into it.

'Don't worry, no harm done.' Rae wasn't sure who knew that she'd had to call the guards out a few weeks earlier due to what turned out to be nothing worse than a broken latch on the second floor. 'I know what you mean. Once the decision was made, it felt like the best thing to do. I'm hoping to modernise the hotel afterwards.'

'Ah, you're moving with the times, good for you,' he said nodding. 'Now, the other thing I wanted to say to you was, when they're doing the work, you know, if there's dusty old construction work being done, you're always welcome to stay with me and Mary, in our cottage. I know Blythe will want you out at the big house, but... well, it's a bit of a trek and if you want to be that bit closer to keep an eye on things, there's a room there for you with us.'

'Oh, that's so kind. To be honest, I hadn't even thought of that.' She genuinely hadn't. Would Blythe even want her to cross the threshold of Still Water House for any longer than it took for them to argue about the smallest thing? She hadn't heard from her since she'd told her that she planned to put the end part of the hotel up for sale.

'How is Blythe anyway? I haven't seen her about the place for a while?'

'She's good. I think, I haven't seen very much of her either to be honest. Between ourselves, I don't think she's keen on my plans to overhaul the hotel.'

'No, she probably wouldn't be, and of course, she'll be up to ninety now with guests and getting her name into that White Diary she's always talking about?'

'Probably,' Rae said.

'Nice lad, that Danial,' Jay nodded as Danial walked along the path on the other side of the square. 'Good move, getting him to work in the hotel.'

'How's that?'

'Well, you must have heard the murmurings...'

'No?'

'Oh, the usual naysayers on the island, saying his arrival coincided a little too perfectly with the break-ins. Someone made a comment on our WhatsApp group.' He put his hand up quickly to stop her fretting. 'Oh, don't worry, I deleted it before the gossips got a hold of it. I wouldn't pay it any attention. It's good that he's getting a chance to show people what a grand fella he is in the hotel. My Mary says he's the highlight of the church choir's day, going in there after practice. He looks after them as if he was taking care of the choir of King's College, rather than the island sing-song group.'

'He is lovely. But he's on the lookout for a proper paying job, he's just helping me out for now,' she said because she'd miss him when he left, which he surely would, but she wanted him above all else to be able to make a good start in life for himself.

'And you're doing your bit to make sure he gets it; your grandmother would be proud of you,' he said then, because of course, he was old enough to remember Gisela.

'I suppose I'm only paying it forward?' Rae laughed.

'Well, it seems to me, we are both working for the same thing… to keep Muffeen Mòr just what it's always been, a place that welcomes people, but also a place that looks after its own.'

'You might remind my sister of that. I don't think she's too keen on the Vals.'

'Ara, she'll come round, I have great time and respect for Blythe. I mean, even if she's a bit prickly at times, over the years she's done more than her fair share. Remember when she organised that container of donations for the Syrians and then, we had the job in hell of getting everything over to the mainland and off to the other side of the world before half the contributions went out of date?'

'Oh, yes, indeed, that's Blythe at her best,' Rae laughed now. Marcus was livid at the idea of having a big ugly container down on the pier. He was certain it would put people off staying on the island if that was the first thing they saw when they landed. However much Marcus complained privately, he knew well enough that it would have been poor form to make a song and dance about it. Instead, he had to give as generously as the next person, which annoyed him even more. Rae had enjoyed the experience, probably added to by her husband's seething opposition.

'Your sister's got a good heart, sometimes you just have to look beyond the anxiousness in people,' Jay said and then, he was off, to call in on some other old dear probably. His words stayed with Rae for a long while after that. It was disconcerting to suddenly have a different view of Blythe held before her unexpectedly, but of course, he was right. Beneath it all, Blythe had a heart of gold. Rae had just never imagined her to be anxious about anything in her life.

31

Kip

Present

It came out of nowhere on the morning of their eighteenth wedding anniversary. A dull ache that eased across Kip's heart. At first, he wondered if perhaps his heart was finally going to give out – so many of his teammates had stents in and all sorts of things going on in the last few years. But no. It wasn't that. He turned over to look at Blythe, sleeping, unaware of him, of the day's significance on any level.

He was not sure he knew who she was anymore.

It was all about Siggy.

Well, it always had been, for both of them, all about Siggy. But, stupidly, he'd believed that they had something much stronger beyond sharing a daughter. He had worshipped Blythe for as long as he could remember. Alright, he'd never expected their relationship to be equal exactly, he'd been more than happy to let her make the big decisions around the guest house. Blythe knew everything there was to know about the hotel business, he was content to carry on taking care of the place.

The fact was, that whether she realised it or not, Blythe had done more for him over the years than he could ever put into words. He was no carpenter, painter, plumber or electrician. But, he'd become all four, thanks mainly to her absolute belief in the fact that he could do anything he set his mind to. And to live up to her expectations, he'd taught himself every skill needed to bring the guest house up to her very high standards.

Sometimes, he walked past the old staircase and rubbed his hand along the balustrade. No one would ever imagine that this was his work – he'd replaced the original badly-worn and flimsy rail with a beautifully carved and smoothed substitute that guests commented on over the years. Blythe never made them any the wiser and Kip never expected her to. It was the same in every bathroom in the house. He'd never tiled or grouted or put in strip lighting in his life, but then, he rose to the occasion; *magnificently*, Blythe said each time. Only he knew, it was because Blythe believed in him.

And this had changed everything for Kip.

At a time when he expected to end up on the scrap heap, suddenly he was immersed in a whole new world. It was a world with endless possibilities where, against all the odds, he seemed to be once more on the winning team. This time, instead of playing in the backs, he felt like the winger. They'd never have gotten off the ground if they had to pay to get the place up and running at the start and as time went on, they fell into their own roles, easily, comfortably.

And then, just as Blythe turned over and pulled the quilt higher around her shoulders, he had his second epiphany. Did she even love him anymore?

The fact was, he knew they were on different pages now. Whether they were on completely different roads, he knew how trajectories worked, less than a degree could make a million miles in the difference eventually. Somewhere, along the way, he hadn't noticed, they'd gone off course, in ever so slightly different directions, but now the gap was widening. Soon, she would be too far to reach.

He knew that Siggy had fallen in love.

Well, he knew that she had a boyfriend – Danial. And instead of being able to come home and tell Blythe, what had he done? He'd bitten down his excitement for his daughter and watched a game of rugby on repeat with a sullen expression. He'd sat there for a whole evening while Blythe scrolled through Facebook or Instagram or some other social media app and he'd festered in this growing awareness that he could not tell her.

He lay there, for a while, trying to put aside that niggling feeling. It frightened him, Kip couldn't imagine life without Blythe.

There were so many things keeping them together, habit, those vows, money, Siggy and maybe on his part, more than anything else, the promise he'd made to his own mother all those years ago. He would not be his father's son; he would be a good and steadfast husband. That, and the memory of the day he'd come back and found his mother, inconsolable, bloody-nosed and broken on their kitchen floor.

What had happened to them?

Instantly, he thought, Blythe had changed. But if Blythe changed, wasn't that completely and absolutely *his* fault? He should have known back then, when Jack Scott sat him down in the hotel snug – he should have known then, that just because *he* never needed the hotel, didn't mean the same went for Blythe. Did losing that hotel break her heart? Kip, for all his bravery, never had the courage to tell his wife about that conversation with Jack. Later, he could see, he should have fought for her. She was going to be his wife. He should have stood up to Jack Scott and told him he wouldn't stand for anything that would make Blythe unhappy. Had he read the whole situation wrong? Probably – too many knocks to the head as a rugby player, he was never quite sure that he was getting the full picture of anything. He thought – at the time, he thought that old Jack was testing the waters – trying to figure if Kip was marrying Blythe for her money or because he really loved her.

Bugger.

He had to get up – he couldn't lie here next to Blythe with these thoughts racing around his mind for a moment longer. He knew where they went, round and round until he wanted to kick himself for being so stupid back then. He would try and talk himself round. They'd had a good life, a great adventure building up the business. They had a beautiful daughter. He felt that twist of anger within him again. He couldn't stand aside and allow Blythe to steer their daughter's life as if it was her own, he just couldn't.

He shrugged into his clothes, as quietly as possible. He had things to do, Fiona Dixon was pressing down on him to help some other poor case who had arrived in the village a few weeks earlier.

He owed Fiona. Well, maybe not owed exactly, but they'd grown up next door to each other – she was Fiona McLaverty then, her family every bit as poor as the Carneys. Old Nellie McLaverty, Fiona's grandmother, had been the first to arrive once the word got out that his father had done a runner.

She'd arrived at the back door of their house, mostly unseen by any of them, with various small bits and pieces from the vegetable patch she tended in their small back garden.

There was never a word said, and maybe Kip would have been none the wiser, but he caught her, early one morning leaving a fresh baked loaf of brown bread and a brace of scallions, lettuces and a bunch of wildflowers for his mother.

Even though he was almost twelve years old, Kip thought he'd never loved anyone more than old Mrs McLaverty that morning.

Fiona was the same, even though she was a lot younger than Kip. No one dared say a word to any of the Carneys when Fiona was about – she was mostly like that annoying younger sister, until push came to shove and they needed her, she was always on their side.

Time was a funny thing.

Fiona was unrecognisable now from that skinny kid. These days she drove around town in a huge white Mercedes. She paraded around done-up as if she was a Christmas tree, in Kip's opinion. Blythe said she was always immaculately put-together; Kip reckoned she didn't so much as lift a finger at home.

But she still had, unknown to most people in the village, a kindness in her heart – some things are ingrained in you, probably. Despite all appearances, she never forgot where she came from, even if she'd never admit that to the likes of Blythe who, by comparison to both Kip and Fiona, had grown up with a silver spoon in her mouth.

Fiona had called him the previous evening, looking to meet up.

'I think Blythe is...' she said when she'd barely sat into his van. She'd never been one to tittle-tattle, not to make trouble for him and Blythe at least. Oh, he knew well enough she loved to gossip with the rest of the women in the village, but she'd always looked out for the people who meant something to her.

'Blythe is her own woman,' Kip said.

'Listen.' Fiona had a way of saying things sometimes, so you knew there was something you needed to hear. 'It's that boy, Danial.'

'Ah, the Vals,' Kip had really warmed to Melissa Val, he'd only called to her because Fiona said she needed some help. The woman had arrived from the other side of the world, on her own, to a cottage that hadn't been lived in for over a year, it was the least he could do as a welcome to the island. After hanging some shelves, he'd returned and painted the scraggy old back door for her. Lovely woman, she'd made him a spicy stew for dinner and talked to him about her life before she came to Muffeen Mòr. She was good company, easy to talk to; there had been seconds of the stew and pudding to finish.

'Blythe is telling people that Danial is behind the break-ins,' Fiona said.

'Danial, no, he's a good kid.' Kip knew a good kid when he saw one and it was shining out of that boy.

'I'm not sure she fully believes it either, but I think...'

'Go on.' Kip felt a thin film of sweat break out along his spine.

'I think that Danial and Siggy might have a bit of a thing going...'

'Ah, I see now, what you're getting at...'

'Exactly.' She rooted in her huge handbag and fished out a pair of reading glasses, handed them to him. 'Look.' She opened her phone and pointed towards the screen with her crimson nails.

'What's this?'

'It's our book club group. She's all but said she's seen him jump through the windows with the loot under his arm...'

'Oh, Blythe.' And Kip felt his heart turn over in his chest with disappointment in his wife. 'Please, Fiona, don't...'

'Do you think I'm mad? I'm not going to call her out on it, but Kip, you know how things are on the island, let the wrong crowd in on a rumour and it can become a witch hunt before dinner time.'

'And you think…'

'Well, apparently, she has Mae English in her ear more often than any of our usual gang.'

'Mae English? What in God's name is she doing hanging about with that bitter old crow?'

'Your guess is as good as mine. There may be nothing to it, but if she goes saying that to Mae, well, it's only a matter of time until there's a lynch mob after Danial and his grandmother.'

'She doesn't mean anything by it, you know that yourself.' Kip looked at Fiona now, but she didn't agree or make any sort of nod to say he was right, which only added to his worries.

'You needed to know. If she's not careful, this sort of stuff could lead to big trouble.'

'Bloody hell.'

'I'm so sorry,' Fiona said. 'I just had to tell you, I couldn't not…'

'I know.' He understood, he'd have done the same for her.

Kip watched as Fiona got out of his van and into her own Mercedes with a heavy heart. What was he to do?

This wasn't a physical thing he could pick up and move aside. This was something far beyond his area of expertise, which would always be more practical than cerebral.

Oh, Blythe, he thought, *what have you become?* And suddenly, he felt as if they'd spun so far away from each other, there may as well have been the Grand Canyon separating them.

32

Blythe

Present

Shell-shocked. Those were the two words that Blythe thought best described how she felt in the aftermath of Rae's bombshell about the hotel. They rolled around in her brain, as if they might make sense of the fact that she felt as if the only way to move forward was on some sort of automation.

Rae had broken down and cried when she told her, but what good were tears? The Hope Square Hotel – on its knees, worse, in pieces. It was unthinkable.

She'd even had that squirmy Cathal Regan in to value the place. Photographs of the hotel were splashed all over his social media accounts. Price on Application, indeed. Oh, Blythe knew his game well enough. Hadn't he come up here, a few years earlier? He'd had the nerve to ask if she'd sell Still Water to someone who'd dropped in to his office to see if there were any *doer-uppers* around the village they could buy. A *doer-upper* – that's what he'd called Still Water House! Well, she'd given him his marching orders and he had the good sense to give her a wide berth for a long time afterwards.

Her stomach churned when she pictured him, parading around the hotel, measuring tape in hand, a greedy look in his eye. Oh, God. She couldn't bear it.

Kip had tried to make light of it when she told him. But what did he know? It was all very well saying the hotel would still be there, but this was her heritage. It was Siggy's future.

Blythe made no secret of the fact that she had always dreamed of Siggy one day stepping up to run the hotel. Who else was there? They all knew, the hotel was always meant to be Blythe's. Rae may never have said it, but the fact was, Blythe was the rightful owner of the place, if it hadn't been for one stupid weekend, she would have inherited the hotel. Rae should have gone to college, trained as a vet perhaps or at the very least, found work in some shelter or animal practice. Would Marcus have wanted to marry Rae without the hotel? Maybe not, as the years had rolled on, Blythe had often wondered if they'd even been happy in the end.

And now this; if the hotel had been left to her, as it should have been, they would not be in this position today.

'No good crying over spilled milk,' Kip said when she told him. 'Maybe it's for the best, that place is far too big for Rae to manage on her own.'

'She has Siggy to help.'

'Has she?' He stopped, as if choosing his next words carefully. 'Siggy won't be here forever, this time next year…'

'Oh, for goodness' sake, Kip, you're like a broken record. Siggy will run that hotel and she'd be happy to do it. What kid wouldn't want to walk into not one, but two, family businesses, rather than struggle in the rat race on the mainland?'

'I can't have this conversation with you now.'

'So, that's it, you're just going to walk away?'

'No, I'm going out to the workshop to clean out the lawnmower.' He sighed like a man twice his age. 'Face it, Blythe. It's Rae's hotel, hers to do with as she chooses. There's nothing to be done about it.'

'You're wrong.' Blythe railed. 'That's the difference between us, Kip, I believe there's always something you can do about things.' She watched him shake his head and disappear out the back door. He really had no idea – not when it came to things like this. His family had never owned anything more than a plot in the local cemetery. Even their little cottage was rented from the council, how could he understand what it was to have your heart sewn into a place from the day you were born?

It was all too much. The hotel. This unevenness with Kip that seemed to expand with every unfinished sentence. And Siggy – she couldn't even begin to think about Siggy and that awful boy.

Instead of charging out and making a stab at fixing everything back to the way it should be, Blythe found herself immobilised. She was, she could admit it to herself, absolutely gutted, by the accumulation of everything.

More than any of them, though, more than anything else in the whole village, more than Rae employing that kid when she could have given a job to a local, more than knowing Siggy was falling in love with the last person in the village Blythe would want for her – more than that even. More than Mae English sneering at her as if she knew Blythe was finally getting her comeuppance. It was the idea that she was completely and utterly powerless when it came to Rae's decision around selling off a third of the hotel.

Kip was right.

There wasn't a damned thing she could do about it.

The hotel had been left to Rae. It was all down to her what became of it.

Blythe found herself tossing and turning during the night. She'd hardly eaten all day, left half-finished mugs of tea all over the house, somehow even tea didn't taste right now.

'You okay?' Kip whispered groggily next to her.

'Yeah, I'm fine. Just a bad dream,' she answered and pulled the covers back to let the air at her legs. She couldn't sleep. She shivered; padded her way as quietly as she could across the floor and opened the door with a slow groan. She crept downstairs, the house creaking and yawning awake with her. It was four-thirty in the morning. Bright outside, considering the hour. The moon was full and milky in the sky, the clouds swept back to let it glisten when nobody should be watching. Navy blue light flooded in through the windows in the rooms at the front of the house. She turned into the drawing room. This was her mother's room, in Blythe's mind at least, there was a comfort to sitting here, a feeling that her mother was close by.

It was as Blythe was sitting there, trying to straighten thoughts that raced too fast to catch up, that she spotted the lights left on in Kip's van. He was always bloody doing that and then complaining because the battery was flat the following morning. Blythe went in search of his keys. She shuffled into his huge old work shoes and tripped across the yard to where it was parked up. In the beam of the full headlights, she watched as moths and midges swarmed in circles enjoying the glow. How on earth had Kip not spotted the lights were still on when he'd come into the house in near darkness earlier? She pulled open the door quickly, already the cool night air was biting into her fading drowsiness far more than any camomile tea could have a hope of rescuing.

And then she smelled it.

Intense and familiar, oppressive on the frigid air around her. It was coming from the inside of the van. Unmistakable. Fiona Dixon. She'd recognise that cloying heavy scent anywhere. Blythe had never been able to wear a scent, couldn't bear any sort of perfume near her.

'NO.' She screamed and then, horrified, her hand flew up to cover her mouth, fearing her shriek might have wakened Kip and Siggy. She took a deep intoxicating breath. Toxic. That was the only word that lingered on the air around her. She backed slowly away from the van. All thoughts of switching off the lights, of saving the battery, of reminding Kip the following morning. All of it gone.

And then, as she stood there shivering in the dark, she realised. It really was all gone. Everything she held dear was slipping away from her. Her marriage. Her daughter. Her hotel. And standing there, in the flaccid night air, shivering as the icy dew crept around her bare legs, she knew, it was all spinning far too fast to do anything about any of it.

She was, in that instant, paralysed with fear. She moved, like a woman possessed, towards the open back door. Shrugged out of the jacket she'd been wearing and tossed aside Kip's boots. Then, she walked over to the old kitchen chair that her mother had always sat in and allowed the tears to flow down her cheeks until she heard the stirrings of her daughter over her head and she knew, it was time to get ready to start another day.

33

Rae

Eighteen Years Earlier

Sometimes, Rae thought, it was as if Marcus had been in Hope Square his whole life. Thank God things had worked out as they had because with Blythe struggling some days to stand without staggering lightheadedness, they'd be lost without him.

Especially Pappy.

Marcus was doing far more than any hotel manager would do, he worked long days, up before any of them making sure that everything was set out perfectly for the day. Most nights, after Rae went back to Still Water, he sat up with Pappy until late, playing chess and sipping brandy before linking the old man upstairs and making sure he was safely in bed.

It was funny, but Pappy would never have accepted help from Rae or Blythe. It was as if, he always wanted them to think he was there for them, rather than the other way round.

Marcus was wonderful with the guests too, everyone that met him simply adored him. Rae couldn't make sense of this growing unease she picked up between him and her sister.

What was that?

'Don't worry about it,' Marcus told her one morning as they walked along the pier, checking out the fishing boats for the best catch to put on the evening menu at the hotel.

'I want you both to get along, Marcus, I do worry about it.'

'Once Blythe has her baby, everything will be fine.'

'I'm not so sure,' Rae murmured because she knew that as much as Blythe resented Marcus taking over her position in the hotel, it would only get worse once she got back to work. Pappy was talking as if Marcus would stay on, keep the place running, simply because Blythe had a baby. Of course, on the surface, that idea made sense, except Blythe had no intention of allowing motherhood to slow her down. Blythe had big plans for the hotel. Rae knew, with each day she was away from it, her hunger to make it into the best hotel west of the Shannon was only eating deeper into her.

'Rae, you're overthinking this. Blythe's life has taken an unexpected turn; she'll have to learn to live with it and set her course appropriately.' Marcus picked up a couple of large crabs and placed them in a plastic container, nodding at the fisherman to let him know they'd be taking those for the hotel.

'What's that supposed to mean?'

'It means, we can't live our lives forever moulding ourselves around what your sister wants.'

'She doesn't just *want* the hotel – it's her whole life, Marcus, she's going to own it one day, no matter how many children she has with Kip.'

'We'll see.' He pointed across the deck of one of the boats to where they had landed a huge catch of mackerel. And then he smiled at her, as if they were talking about the weather and not the thing her sister's future happiness depended upon.

'There is nothing to see, Marcus, it's already agreed.'

'Listen to me now, I'm looking out for you, for us, here,' he spun round to look at her, placing his hands on her shoulders and squeezing just a little too tightly, so she wanted to wriggle from under his grasp. 'Rae, have you thought what's going to be yours out of all this? A huge house that is worth nothing at the end of the day, because without a good income, you'll never be able to maintain it.' He had moved them both away from the boats. 'And what about us? Does that mean that we go our separate ways?'

'Marcus, I don't want to work in the hotel forever, I've told you, I want to work with animals and...'

'And you will, of course you will. But sometimes, I look at you and I think, you don't realise your real worth in that family. It's as if everyone has already discounted you, Rae, except for me.'

'I don't think...' she said, but then, maybe he was right. She did just go along with things too often, just because it made life easier.

'Trust me, okay, it'll all be fine. You'll have a house full of cats and dogs and babies one day, just as you've always hoped for, but... first we must support your grandfather in the hotel, then after that, you'll see, everything will work out for the best.' He took her hand, placed it against his lips and kissed it lightly.

'Okay, but as long as we're clear, the hotel isn't part of my future.' Rae hated that she sounded so weak. God, she should have made this clear months ago. She should have been honest with him and cut through any notions he had of her being some sort of heiress, with a share in the hotel and a desire to live the rest of her days cleaning out rooms and booking in guests.

'So, that's that?' he said coldly then. 'We go our separate ways, we call it all off now, because, what's the point if...' He dropped her hand, stepped back from her.

'NO!' It sounded like a panicked scream to Rae, but it had come from a place of pure terror. She loved Marcus, she couldn't lose him, not over a silly row. 'Let's not talk about it now, okay?' She reached out to place her hand on his arm, tried to move closer to him, but he shrugged her off.

'Maybe I was wrong about you, Rae,' he said, and it felt as if there was a thousand miles between them, rather than just half a foot.

'Marcus, what are you saying, I love you, we love each other.' Suddenly, she couldn't catch her breath, terror raced through her veins. This couldn't be all there was, she had to make him see, she'd do anything to make him happy.

'If you really love someone, Rae... well, what would you know about it anyway?' He began to walk away, and she felt as if her whole world was being dragged from the canvas of her heart. She ran to catch up with him, she couldn't let him go like this. It was unthinkable, she couldn't lose him, she couldn't live without him.

'Marcus, please,' she was pleading with him now, but he kept walking. Tears were streaming down her face, she wiped them away, snot and spittle with them. 'Marcus, please, don't leave me, not like this.' She didn't care that people were watching her, she didn't care that they might think she'd lost all self-respect. 'I'll do anything, anything you want, just please...'

'Anything?' He turned and looked at her now and she couldn't make out what it was that had changed behind his eyes, but she recoiled, couldn't help herself, was she really willing to do anything to hold onto him?

'Yes. Anything,' she said as clearly as if she was in full command of whatever price he exacted.

'Oh, Rae,' he said, his whole expression softening back to his familiar self. 'What a lot of nonsense, it's just a silly argument, come here.' And he pulled her close and she just wanted to melt into him, because she needed him, she needed him to love her.

After that day on the pier, Rae felt increasingly as if she might be out of her depth with Marcus. It wasn't that she was afraid of him, exactly, more that he made her feel as if she was on a fragile probation of some sort. So, he read the Sunday broadsheets and handed her the fashion supplements. If she asked for the main sections of the paper, he'd hand them to her and scoff that really, he'd already read them and there wasn't much there to interest her. Actually, she felt that it annoyed him, when she took the larger paper, rustled it, and never quite got the hang of putting it all back together just the way he liked it.

After a while, she stopped asking for the papers and contented herself with the home and garden supplements or the fashion pages, if she was very bored.

'What's going on in the hotel today?' Blythe asked her one day when she got back particularly late. Marcus had insisted on a stock take. He had set up an inventory of every sheet and pillowcase, every scrap of food in the cupboards and freezers, even estimating how much time was left on the buffing matt of the old floor polisher. He suspected that they were being robbed blind by some of the ladies who came in and helped with the busy breakfast hour.

'Nothing, business as usual.' Rae was too tired to go into it. She couldn't face talking about one more nitty gritty thing to do with the hotel.

'It's obviously not nothing,' Blythe said sarcastically. Pappy and Marcus had agreed that it would be better if Blythe was allowed to rest, no point her getting stressed out with anything to do with the hotel. 'Maybe I'll call down tomorrow for a look,' she said then and Rae felt sorry for her, because she was stuck here, not allowed to put a foot on the floor for the foreseeable because she was in danger of losing the baby. Kip spent most of his days here, flapping about, making unwanted cups of tea and having his head snapped off if he said one wrong word.

'I'm tired, Blythe, I just want to go to bed.'

'I know what you're up to, don't think I don't...' Blythe said then and Rae could hear her voice, just that notch higher, the way it got these days when her blood pressure was raised.

'Honestly, Blythe, I'm not up to anything.' Rae held out both her hands, as if to show, there was no hidden agenda here.

'Oh, please. You and Marcus, cosying up to Pappy, every night, you come back here, too late to tell me what's going on and Marcus in Pappy's ear.'

'That's not the way it is at all.' Rae flew immediately to Marcus's defence.

'Oh, really, so he doesn't want to take over the hotel permanently?'

'Blythe, please, he's just helping out...' She said it so quickly, she almost believed it to be true.

'Hah! Marcus Johnson really fell on his feet when he tipped his cap in your direction,' Blythe said snidely.

'It's late, let's not argue.' Rae was too exhausted for this, and it wouldn't do the baby any good either.

'Ah, yes, you must have been like putty in his hands,' Blythe said softly now.

'I know you don't mean that, Blythe, so I'm just not going to argue with you,' Rae said, because if she didn't take the high ground, she was too afraid of where this might lead.

'Oh, I mean it alright. Here's the thing Rae, what you don't see, but you will...' Blythe was flushed now, her face almost exploding with rage. Rae was scared that she'd have some sort of attack with all the stress this was putting on her. 'He's always been after a hotel of his own. He knew exactly what he was getting into when he came here. He probably sounded Pappy out before he ever even asked you on a date, because that's the way he is, calculating. You...' She raised her finger and pointed at Rae with a shaking hand. 'And you fell for it, every single word from his mouth and now look at you, working yourself to the bone, throwing away your own dreams and doing your best to become what he expects you to be...'

'That's not true.' Rae heard the uncertainty in her own voice and she knew, from the way Blythe's expression changed, that her sister had heard it too.

'It's not too late, you know, you could call it a day now, go and start a new life, pretend you'd never met him, and everything could work out as it was always meant to.'

'Don't you realise, Blythe? Things are working out as they were always meant to,' that's what Marcus told her, every single day, 'they're just not working out the way you wanted them to.'

Rae ran to the door and flung herself through it, raced upstairs and threw herself onto her bed, then she cried until eventually, exhaustion finally took over and she slept – dead to the world.

Everything, it turned out, was in her grandfather's name. There had never been a will made to transfer the hotel to his son. 'Ah, there was never time, sure back then, getting to a solicitor on the mainland was a job in itself.' He was telling Marcus one night when Rae was getting ready to head back to Still Water House.

'Wouldn't it make more sense if Rae stayed here, once Blythe and Kip get married?' Marcus said then as if the idea had only just entered his head.

'I suppose, but what about...' Of course, her grandfather was thinking of what the neighbours would say, one Scott girl pregnant before she got married, the other living under the same roof as her boyfriend.

'Well, I mean, nothing would happen, I can give you my word on that,' Marcus said then and looked Pappy straight in the eye.

'I know that. She's a good girl and you're...' He raised his hand as if it went without saying that he would trust Marcus with his life, with all their lives, probably.

'But when the baby comes, Blythe will need me and anyway, if either of us was going to move into the hotel, I know for a fact, Blythe would much prefer it was her,' Rae put in between them.

'Ah, Blythe doesn't know what she wants until that baby arrives,' Pappy said then. 'You're right Marcus, better if Rae moves in here,' he looked at Rae then, 'sure, you'll be the odd one out there, in the middle of a newly married couple and a young family, you don't want that, do you?'

'But Pappy, really...' she said, but he'd already made his mind up. Blythe would not be coming to live in the hotel, rather, Marcus would be staying on to run the place and they both seemed to think that Rae would also.

The conversation unsettled her. But it was just a conversation, nothing would come of it, she tried to convince herself. After all, Marcus knew that she had plans of her own, he'd promised her that it would all work out for the best and she had to believe him.

34

Blythe

Seventeen Years Earlier

Nothing could have prepared Blythe for what she felt when Siggy was born. The birth had been much easier than she'd expected, but then, the midwife told her, it was often the way. She'd done her suffering before the labour ward; everything should go smoothly from here.

She'd been right.

Siggy was a perfect baby. Blythe knew she was biased, but truly, what newborn baby can make wind look good? Within a week of arriving home from the hospital, Siggy was sleeping most of the night, she was feeding well, and she was generally, the most agreeable baby anyone had ever clapped their eyes on.

Blythe was captivated by her.

The fact was, she could lose hours each day, just holding her, watching her, hanging off her every breath. She had fallen madly, deeply in love with the child from the moment she was born.

Kip, too.

He balanced Siggy in his huge hands, so she looked even smaller than she was and the tenderness in his eyes when he looked at her, almost made Blythe cry with love for both of them.

How could that be? She wondered, when her whole life had been spent with only one true love, how could it be that suddenly, a person so small, so tiny, could push everything aside.

Hormones.

That's what the district nurse said, and she warned against the tide turning and detailed the various things to watch out for if she found herself succumbing to the baby blues.

Not a chance.

Blythe was high on life. High on motherhood.

All thoughts of the hotel and Marcus Johnson swept aside, none of it mattered. Even when she thought of Rae, living in the hotel, taking up the space that was always meant to be hers. Somehow, it didn't make her blood boil over in the same way as it had before.

Blythe supposed it was mother nature's way of taking care of her young. All notions of going back to work in the hotel had suddenly fallen from the table of her mind. She was content to stay in Still Water House and take care of her baby, while Kip cooked for them, and his mother visited and kept the laundry piles moving through the washer and dryer.

Rae was smitten too, of course, no great surprise there. Blythe felt a swell of happiness in her, when she saw that the baby seemed to settle in Rae's arms, but when Marcus had held her, Siggy railed.

Good girl, Blythe thought to herself, *good girl Siggy*.

The name had been Blythe's choice. She called her after her grandmother. She knew on some level it would give Pappy great joy to think his beloved Gisela's name was living on, long after his dear wife had died. She promised Kip, the next one would be named for his mother.

It took all of three weeks of this domesticated harmony before Blythe began to feel as if she was somehow being trapped by it all. She woke up with a start one morning and knew, she was ready to go back to the hotel.

So, as soon as she and Siggy were fed and presentable, she set off for Hope Square. Her grandfather was of course thrilled to see the baby. Despite his reluctance to join in any baby excitement before Siggy arrived, he was completely hooked from the moment he set eyes on her three weeks earlier.

'Don't be ridiculous, you can't come back to work now,' Pappy almost choked on his tea when she mentioned that she was ready.

'Why not?' She was ready for his resistance. After all, hadn't he basically replaced her as soon as Marcus turned up on the doorstep?

'Because you have a baby, that's why not...' He shook his head as if it was obvious.

'Pappy, women go back to work every other day of the week after giving birth.' She stopped, lowered her voice. They were sitting in the lounge, Pappy had, for the last few weeks, commandeered a spot next to the fireplace, from where he could watch the comings and goings and still direct everything – without having to leave his chair. 'Seriously, if I was in a third world country, I'd have been out picking crops an hour after she arrived.'

'Well, fortunately for all of us, you're in Ireland and in the relatively comfortable position of being able to take your time.'

'Pappy, I need to get back to work.' Blythe bit down on the anger that was rising in her. 'Aside from anything else, I need to start earning wages again and...'

'And what about Kip, doesn't he have money?' Pappy said now. 'Really, Blythe, you have a lovely baby and a beautiful home. You have an able-bodied husband who needs to find himself a proper job.'

'He's actually coaching with the Connaught Rovers,' she said quietly, although of course, that was paying peanuts, barely enough to cover his ferry and car costs to and from training sessions.

'Well, then, there you go...' he said as if that was everything.

'I don't understand, Pappy, why can't I just come back to work, nothing has changed, I'm as committed to the hotel as I ever was, and I have big plans for the season.'

'Ah, but Blythe, that's the thing. Marcus has big plans too and we've already agreed to put some of them in place. He's on top of all the bookings and they are well up on previous years, so... really, I need to keep him on board until the end of the year, at least.'

'At least?' She whispered, hardly able to push the words through her lungs. This could not be happening. Was her grandfather telling her that she no longer had a job in their family hotel? Was he throwing her over for Marcus bloody Johnson? 'You can't do this...'

'Do what?'

'Pappy, I know you think you're acting in my best interests, but this isn't fair, I've given years of my life to making this place into what it is today.' She looked around her, tears threatening on the very edges of her eyes. She began slowly to take in the lobby around her, noticing little things at first, how had she not seen it before? Marcus Johnson, aided and abetted by her own sister and Pappy too, had come in here and systematically undone every single improvement she had made. From the white linen throws that she'd had some of the local women run up on their sewing machines, which he'd changed to a blue and white-striped material, to replacing the single lit candle on each table with tiny, but elaborate, floral and driftwood arrangements, giving the whole place a Nantucket vibe that would be lost on most of their regulars. Oh, the place looked fantastic, undoubtedly, but Marcus had only upgraded what she'd already made. The fact was, whether Pappy could see it or not, the original template had been hers alone. 'You can't just get rid of me,' she said flatly.

'It's not like that, Blythe, but we've all moved on. You have a new baby, you are a mother now, you'll have more children, and you won't have time for this place.'

'Who says?' She snapped at him.

'No one says, but that's life. And the hotel will go on, regardless. We're lucky to have Marcus, he's agreed to stay, when anyone half-decent would be gone again after the one season...'

'Lucky, hah!' She wanted to wring Marcus Johnson's neck right now.

'Look, you know, he could pick up a job anywhere in the world and in a year or two, probably name his price.' Pappy stopped and she thought for a moment, maybe he was going to give her some hope, say something that would put a timeline on this nightmare. 'The fact is, Blythe, the only reason he's here is because he's in love with Rae... and he's been good for her. She's a completely different person to the wild thing she was before she met him.'

'Oh, Pappy, you think it's a good thing that she seems to have put all her own dreams on hold? That she's dressing like the old ladies in the church choir and hasn't time for anything other than making *him* happy?'

'I think, it's settled her down and the way things were going… well, she was out of control. Marcus has been a good influence on her.'

'You're wrong,' she said then and she knew, she sounded like a stubborn child. 'You're wrong about everything,' she said, getting up and placing the baby in her pram. 'And most of all, Pappy, you're wrong about Marcus Johnson.'

There was no moving Pappy. He had made up his mind. For the next few weeks, Blythe managed to live on her state maternity payment, because certainly what Kip earned wouldn't keep a cat and kittens.

But, as summer faded into autumn and Still Water House grew colder, the bills seemed to come more quickly and more often through the letter box. It seemed every job Kip applied for was already given to some other man, more qualified or under the good fortune of nepotism.

It was one afternoon, sitting in the kitchen with his mother that set Blythe thinking.

'Seems a shame to have this big empty house and no money coming in. Could you not rent out some rooms?' Kip's mother was talking about taking in some of the students who came across to the island each year to help on the national park's survey work.

'That's seasonal and I'd hardly cover the electricity bill with the amount they can afford to pay,' Blythe said, and she cut another slice of rhubarb cake for them. Siggy was fast asleep in her cot next to the Aga, blissfully unaware of her parents fast approaching financial ruin.

'Well, then, why not do it properly… you know, make it into a guest house?' She was looking at Blythe now as if this was a no-brainer.

'A guest house? Here at Still Water?'

'Why not?'

'Well, it's not really set up for it, for a start, I mean... I'd need ensuites and a proper kitchen and...' The truth was, they hadn't lived in almost three-quarters of the house in decades.

'So, why not get to work on doing one room at a time. Take the winter months, let Kip do the donkey work and you be in charge.' She stopped and smiled. 'He might not be qualified, but he's very tasty at odd jobs. He did a whole big job on Mrs O'Flaherty's bathroom when she had her leg amputated, pulled out everything and made it all workable for her. He did most of the plumbing and all the painting too.'

'I didn't know that.'

'Oh, it was years ago, you were probably off in college, but there's no better man to put up wallpaper or paint to the tip of a hair. I swear, I often wonder, if he'd had a chance, he might have single-handedly had a go at the Sistine chapel, if that other buck didn't get in there before him.' She laughed at that, and Blythe found herself laughing too. She had grown to love this simple, kind-hearted woman and she could see why Kip adored her.

'I'll think about it.' But even sitting there at the kitchen table, with a washing machine full of baby clothes, Blythe felt that familiar surge of ambition rise within her. Her own business, right here under her nose. It sounded perfect.

'I'll just say this, Blythe, you could have your own boat built and seaworthy a long time before your old grandfather's ship steers into your port.'

'I suspect that ship is sailing towards the horizon without me.' Blythe confessed the fact that even to herself she'd found hard to admit.

*

That very evening, after she'd eaten dinner with Kip and they'd settled Siggy in her cot for the night, they took themselves off to the first floor of the house and the bedrooms that looked out across the island. These rooms hadn't been slept in for years, not in Blythe's memory. There were six on this hallway alone, but probably only four, if you factored in the renovation work to make them what she needed.

'We could easily keep guests here and it would all be separate from our own room and the baby's,' she said to Kip; they'd walked through the rooms so many times and now she was brimming with ideas.

'Are you sure you want to do this?'

'I do, if you'll help me,' she said then, because it would not be possible without a lot of cosmetic work and some reconfiguration.

'Blythe, you know I'd do anything for you, but when it comes to keeping guests, I'm not sure how much help I'll be at that. I mean, you've seen how I can't boil an egg without some calamity.' He laughed then.

'Don't worry, that part, I can do standing on my head, and if it really takes off, I can always get people in to help at busy times.'

'You think it could be that busy?' He was dubious, even though he was trying to hide it.

'I think it could be,' she said softly, but in her heart she had already decided, she was going to make Still Water House into THE place to stay on Pin Hill Island. She'd show Marcus Johnson a thing or two, and her grandfather would see what a huge mistake he'd made.

35

Rae

Present

It felt as if they'd hardly pinned up the for-sale sign, when already there was interest from buyers in looking at number three. Cathal rang up the morning after he'd put the details up on the estate agency website to ask if there was a good time for him to show the place to potential buyers.

'Actually, it's exceeded my expectations,' Cathal said.

'Any idea if people are interested in it for residential or for commercial reasons?' Rae asked.

'No idea. So far, it's been mostly online enquiries, so I haven't been able to get a sense of who we're dealing with, but it's the hottest property we've had on the books for quite a while, if that makes you feel better.' He laughed.

'Who'd have thought it?' Rae said almost to herself.

'Oh, these old buildings, people go mad for them – and the photographs didn't do any harm either. I mean, a view of the sea and all those original features, it's hard to get a package like that all wrapped up together. The only thing is…'

'What?'

'Well, the bank next door, that could potentially put off some of the buyers. For others, it mightn't matter so much, but people can be funny about having empty buildings nearby and things like that – who the neighbours are likely to be, if it was sold and what have you...'

'If that's going to put them off, we're probably better off without them on the square anyway,' Rae said.

'No. No. The more, the merrier, that's what we want, a frenzy of interest for when the offers start to roll in.'

Rae was worried about Siggy. It seemed as if she wasn't really herself these days. She had a feeling that her niece might have a little crush on Danial, which would be no bad thing. Poor Blythe, it would be like Rae and Johnno all over again for her.

It wasn't that though. Rae was pretty sure. It was something else. Something that Siggy was carrying closer to her heart than a simple crush.

'You're sure there's nothing wrong?' Rae asked Siggy again.

'Sure, I'm sure Rae, what could be wrong?' Siggy said then, before going to wipe down a table after a few of the church cleaning ladies had finished up their weekly tea and nattering in the window seat.

'Maybe Blythe was right,' Rae said then. It was pure impulse, but suddenly it felt like a good idea. 'Maybe we should go and get our hair done together.'

'Really? Would you really get some mad colour in your hair?'

'No. But the fact is, it's high time I started to take care of myself again,' Rae said and that was half the truth. The other half, which she could hardly admit to herself, was that it was high time she became part of the community again.

Oh, she had people drop in here for coffee and she kept her Soroptimists meetings over the years, but she had a shortage of real friends. Marcus had cut her off, one outlet at a time. The biggest loss was Blythe and Siggy, of course, but there were so many other casualties along the way that she hadn't realised until it was too late.

'It really is.' Siggy dropped the cloth from her hand and pulled out her phone.

'What?'

'Well, no time like the present. The place is empty,' she was dialling a number. 'Let's do it now?' she said. 'Hi Dawn, can you fit Rae and me in for an appointment...' Rae stood, a little dumbstruck watching her. They were really doing this. Fifteen years since she'd crossed Dawn Doherty's threshold to have her hair cut – or more importantly, to sit there and have a long natter about everything and anything under the sun, while they sipped coffee and munched on biscuits or flicked through gossipy magazines. 'Yes, of course, my aunt Rae, here in the hotel.' Siggy giggled at whatever Dawn said next and Rae winced. It'd be the talk of the town, if she even turned up for a wash and set. Damn it, anyway, she had to start somewhere. She walked over to the cash register behind the counter, took out enough to pay for both of them. 'Right away,' Siggy was saying.

'Right away it is,' Rae said and it felt like another delicious act of rebellion that would intensely irritate Marcus if he could see her now.

They walked up the street to Dawn's place, arm in arm and even though, she planned nothing more than a trim and a wash it was a step in the right direction. She might have lost interest in how she looked years earlier, but she'd missed the camaraderie of her visits to Dawn's and the connections with other women that she'd always enjoyed there.

The following day, Hugh Gilmore called in to Rae. Just checking in. He did a double take when he looked at her. Her hair didn't look all that different, what can you do with a boyish crop, but somehow Dawn had made it look more sophisticated, cared for; softer. Maybe next time, she would do something a little more drastic!

Rae had just got back from the bakery the following morning when her phone rang. This time, it was Cathal Regan.

'Good morning.' He sounded chipper.

'Good morning to you, too.' And she supposed it was, because it looked as if the sky was about to crack open with a huge downpour, which meant that there was a good chance, no one would come near the place all day long.

'I have news. We have a concrete offer on the property.' He stopped, and Rae wondered if perhaps he was going to follow that up with a drum roll. He needn't have bothered, suddenly her heart was racing.

'But nobody has come to view it yet.' She wanted to argue with him, even though she knew it was utterly illogical to feel as if her back had been put up in some way.

'Apparently, he doesn't need to. There are conditions. It's a one-time offer. They are leaving it on the table for a week. It's for the whole of number three – ground floor included. They are happy to put in a dividing wall along the original line of the building plans, and they've agreed to do that before taking possession of the building, to avoid any inconvenience to you.'

'There's a but…' she said because of course, if things seem too good to be true, then in her opinion they usually were.

'Hear me out, okay?' Cathal stopped and she heard a noise, like tapping, perhaps on a computer or a laptop. 'It's well over the asking price...'

'How much over it?'

'Two hundred thousand.'

'Wow – somebody's flush,' she said, and she wondered who had that sort of money. 'You're sure it's not some criminal gang looking for somewhere to hide their ill-gotten gains?' She laughed a little nervously. She was only half serious because she'd seen a programme on it recently, vacant properties picked up all over the place and left to rot – without a lot of awkward questions from the tax man.

'I'm as sure as I can be,' he said. She noticed he didn't give her an outright no. 'We have a few options.'

'Okay, what are they?'

'You can, of course, refuse the offer straight off. I can tell them that you want to take it to market and take your chances. If they want the place, they can fight it out with whoever else is in the ring. Of course, it's unlikely you'll make the same price.' He stopped. 'You can accept the offer as is, we take the sign down and push through with the sale. Or, I can contact the other people interested in the property and move the viewing forward, letting them know that there is a firm offer on the table and that will let us check the temperature of the market.'

'I'm presuming you would suggest I do that last one?'

'Of course, when would suit you to move it forward to?'

'Today? Tomorrow?' she said because she couldn't shake the feeling that the offer on the table was forcing her hand, and she wasn't sure she was ready to be rushed into this. It was much too big and really, whether it was true on paper or not, deep down, she knew, it affected Blythe every bit as much as it affected her.

36

Blythe

Present

Still Water House had never looked better. Blythe had worked like a mad thing to make sure there wasn't so much as a speck of dust to be seen, anywhere. Today was the day.

She checked with Finbar Lavin again. Finbar was the only man who could predict the tides with almost perfect accuracy. Even though there was meant to be a rhythm to them, island people knew, it took only an unexpected swell or a mist driving in from a storm far out to sea, to change everything without any warning.

'Everything looks good,' Finbar said, and he sounded as if he was standing at the edge of the world, drinking his cup of morning tea. There was no better viewing point, probably, on the island than the old Macken place. 'Is it today you have your big reviewer guest coming?' he asked then.

'No, no, I really don't know what you mean, Finbar. Every guest at Still Water is as important as the next,' she said, because the last thing she wanted was Morwenna Whythe, whom Blythe was convinced was Maura Whither, to twig that she suspected her of coming to review the guest house.

The booking had been very specific: a room with easy access, so Blythe had her on the ground floor with two rooms to choose from. She'd even turned down a two-week booking, just to accommodate her. And she was absolutely set on making sure that everything went smoothly.

Still Water House deserved to be included in the White Book, more so than many of those other draughty old places on the mainland, and she fully intended to make it shine to its very best. She had a good two hours to wait until the ferry arrived.

She was primed and ready. Siggy had made fruit scones, and they were baking in the oven, the aroma permeating the entrance hall from the kitchen. The main reception room was fit to receive royalty, with cushions plumped, flowers freshened, and the radiators turned on low, despite the pristine nets billowing ever so slightly at the open windows. She'd placed three cds in the old player on low repeat, Grieg, Mendelssohn and her personal favourite – the soundtrack from *Out of Africa*. At the huge open hearth, she'd lit a thick white candle in the storm lamp. Everything was perfect.

She was about to double check the front door again, to walk through it, see it as if from a newcomer's eyes when she spotted a familiar car on the avenue.

Rae.

What now? she thought, because Rae would not come out here to tell her good news. This was, she decided before Rae even turned off her engine, an irritation she was in no humour for today.

There was an offer on the hotel. Rae told her as she waited for the coffee to brew and suddenly, Blythe felt lightheaded, as if even standing there, her hand on the coffee pot, was too much. Somehow, she kept her balance, swung from the kitchen island to the table – one flagrant, out of control movement, thankfully, the pot landed safely and in the same motion, by some miracle, Blythe dropped into the chair opposite her sister.

'Are you alright?' Rae asked, because Blythe knew the blood had drained from her head, it was rushing to her feet, pulsing at an alarming rate through her body, so it felt as if her whole nervous system had taken off somewhere without her.

'I'm perfectly fine.' She managed, but she could feel her mouth twitching, her whole face felt as if it was suddenly, like everything else, just beyond her reach. Opposite her, unaware of her sister's discomfort, Rae was babbling on with details that floated in the air around Blythe's head.

Later she would hunger for these details, now, they felt like overload, as if another word could crash her newly fragile spirit.

It was a generous offer, well above asking price or anything you could reasonably expect to get in today's market. The reality of it was there – like something she could reach out and touch and yet, Blythe felt as if she'd been tasered. The idea that she had no control over the sale of part of the hotel.

'Do you know who wants to buy it?' she asked.

'No and it doesn't really matter at this point, because there may be further offers and even if there aren't, I have a few more days to decide if I'm going to accept it or not.'

'You wouldn't sell it to a stranger.' As she said it, she knew it didn't make any difference who bought it. The reality was, it wouldn't be any easier to take it, if it was someone they knew, or someone they didn't know. Blythe didn't want anyone else owning a part of the Hope Square Hotel. It was her family legacy. Things should never have come to this.

'I know you're upset,' Rae said gently.

'And how can you not be?'

'It's emotional,' Rae conceded. 'But it's for the best, the hotel can't go on as it is, this is just a decision to ensure its survival.'

'And will it survive?' Blythe asked. 'After you've sent a chunk of it to the guillotine, are you quite sure that it will survive then?'

'Honestly?' Rae looked at her now and the heaviest silence Blythe ever experienced dangled on the air between them. 'I don't know.'

'Hmph.' There was so much she wanted to say, but what was the point. She didn't have a casting vote. She didn't have any vote – Pappy had taken care of that years ago. 'Well, I hope it makes you happy,' she settled on.

'How can you say something like that? None of this is making me happy. You know, more than anyone, this was never what I wanted.' Rae hung her head now.

'Yes, well, you got it anyway, so here we are after all that.'

'I wish...'

'What?' Blythe's voice was shrill. 'What is it you wish, Rae? That our grandfather had left his will the way it was meant to be, is that what you wish?' Because wishing got you nowhere, Blythe knew that from bitter experience.

'I wish I could afford to hand the place over to you. That there wasn't any debt and there was some way I could...' She sighed.

'That's such a cruel thing to say.' Blythe got up. She didn't have time for talking nonsense and she didn't want to talk about this any longer. She couldn't, because if Rae stayed here for another minute, Blythe really wasn't sure that she wouldn't say something that there was no coming back from, that or burst into tears and rage at the unfairness of it all.

Blythe was sitting in her opulent drawing room when the doorbell sounded in the hall. She'd come in here to try and make sense of Rae's news. To settle her nerves, if she was honest. Now, she had to pull herself together and become the perfect hostess if she wanted to wow Maura Whither or Morwenna Whythe as she had called herself in the booking. Blythe took a deep breath; she could do this. She had to do this; she would not let the hotel come between her and the White Book. She took one deep breath, looked back at the room she had spent so long making just right, threw her shoulders back and walked with as much confidence as she could muster to the front door.

'Hello, you're very welcome, Morwenna?' She greeted the squat, angry-looking woman standing on her doorstep.

'Hmph. It's Miss Whythe. You never said on the booking site that this place was so far away from the village…' the woman said, and she glanced back at her bags which had been deposited by old Donnacha O'Neill on the gravel behind her. Donnacha was renowned for his bad temper, which only grew worse if it looked like his passenger was not going to tip. Blythe could hear his ancient Citroen roar down the avenue, he was long gone at this point.

'I'm sorry, I must check that they haven't changed around the details again,' Blythe said, feeling a sudden desire to run down the avenue after the old codger.

'Is my room ready?' the woman snapped.

'Of course, you asked for an accessible room, and we have two, so if you'd like to choose the one that suits you best,' Blythe said sweetly, thinking of the lucrative booking she'd turned down for this woman. She'd better be who she thought she was, although, looking at her now, she looked nothing like the woman in Blythe's mind's eye.

'I just want a room that's easy to get to, show me into the best one and let's have done with it. If I wanted an exercise in decision making, I'd have gone to one of those horrid coffee shops where they can't even make a cup of tea without giving you a hundred choices.' She was just testing her, or perhaps she was tired, Blythe decided, she would be nicer when she had a chance to rest.

Blythe showed her into the first room, mainly because she wanted to get away from her. Nobody in their right mind would fault it, it was a fabulous room with access to the garden beyond. There wasn't a four-poster bed, but the bathroom was generous and very accessible with discreet handrails and enough space to turn even the largest wheelchair. The bedroom was large enough to accommodate a small chaise longue and decent-sized dressing area behind a Chinese screen she had picked up for half nothing when other people thought they were going out of fashion.

'Here we are,' she said, and she picked up the room key and held it aloft as she went through the room and opened the French doors so Morwenna could appreciate the garden outside. 'If there's anything you need, just knock on the kitchen door. My daughter baked fresh scones that are cooling,' she had completely forgotten about the first batch in the upset of earlier. They were burned beyond words. 'But, if you're peckish now, I have homemade brown bread, local cheese and fresh coffee if you'd like some.' She smiled at the woman, who remained determinedly sour faced.

'No, thank you. Actually, I forgot to mention, I'm lactose intolerant,' she pinned Blythe with her eyes, 'violently so. In fact, if there's as much as a drop of milk in the vicinity of any of my food, I'll know about it.' She snatched the keys from Blythe's hands before going to the French doors and pulling them closed with a bang loud enough to rattle the panes. 'The pollen sets off my allergies,' she said then and Blythe felt her heart sink. This was not going to be an easy sell.

'No problem, the other room is...' She was going to say sea-facing, not taking in quite so much of the garden, but Morwenna shook her head with the look of someone who couldn't suffer another word.

'That'll be all,' she said then, dismissing Blythe as if she was a servant of the lowest standing in her personal employ. Just as Blythe was about to leave, she heard the woman's finger click behind her back. She turned to see Morwenna Whythe standing a little away from the fresh flower arrangement she'd spent almost half an hour putting together especially earlier.

'Take these away, will you? I can't stand flowers in a room. That unpleasant scent of them makes me feel like vomiting if I'm near them.'

'Oh, right, sorry about that. I didn't realise, most of our guests love them, not to worry,' Blythe said and somehow, she managed to keep smiling through gritted teeth as she carried them out of the room and into the kitchen instead.

After that, Blythe felt more like having a good double whiskey, rather than the strongest coffee she could make, but she wasn't sure her nerves would survive alcohol on top of all the stress. She'd barely sat down, having scraped the burned crust from one of Siggy's scones, when she thought she heard a bell tinkling somewhere in the distance. She walked out into the hall. Yes, she absolutely heard a distinct ringing sound, and it was coming from Morwenna Whythe's room.

She stood for a moment, not quite sure what she should do, but then, in case the woman was in some sort of peril, she knocked on the door.

'Come,' was the imperious response from inside. Blythe poked her head into the room, to see Morwenna, stretched out on the chaise longue, the covers had been thrown from the bed onto the floor and Morwenna was reclining with a long cigarette in the air, smoking and tipping the ash into one of the pricy pottery dishes that had come from an auction at Ashford castle a few years earlier. That bloody dish had cost her twenty-five euros and now, it was balanced precariously on the back of the chaise longue.

'I'm sorry, but this is a non-smoking home,' she said calmly, because this could just as easily be another test and Blythe knew that she needed to stick to her rules for the sake of other guests. 'Of course, you can smoke on the terrace, I'm happy to put a proper ash tray outside if you need it.'

'Oh, pooey, it's a world gone mad on political correctness, if you ask me. What harm has an occasional puff of smoke ever done anyone in a public place?'

'This is not a public place; it's a family home.' Blythe stopped; she could not afford to argue with this woman.

'Pah, well really.' Morwenna stubbed out her cigarette with an exasperated sigh.

'Can I get you anything?' She looked at the small brass bell which rested against the woman's leg. 'You rang?'

'I did. I find travelling with your own bell makes everything so much easier for everyone.' She reached out and gave the thing a second shake. 'I think I'd like to have some tea now. Obviously, Assam, two sugars. And something on the side, light, restorative.' She flicked her hand again to dismiss Blythe.

Breathe. Just breathe, Blythe told herself.

Within two hours of the woman arriving, Blythe was run ragged. After the tea, there was a bath, which had to be run by Blythe, because the old bat couldn't possibly do it for herself. Then, there were cards to be sent. The bed had to be remade. She objected to the down pillows and quilt. She objected to the Corrigan Mills woollen blanket. She didn't like the selection of books in the bookcase. She couldn't read with that lamp way over there. It was too noisy. It was too cold. It was too stuffy. Could Blythe possibly do something about the sound of the sea birds in the distance, apparently, Morwenna couldn't hear herself think from all that squawking.

Blythe wanted to wring the old witch's bloody neck before she even thought about how she'd prepare a beef stroganoff without any cream. This was an island, for heaven's sake. She was dependent on the local supermarket which had a tiny four-shelf section for all intolerances. As far as anyone knew in Muffeen Mòr, the only one who ever looked for dairy alternatives was a kid who'd moved into that commune arrangement on the far side of the island.

Blythe felt as if her head was fit to explode by the time Kip came back to pick up something or other from his shed and disappear again, leaving her there to mull over the news from Rae and the unrelenting demands of the woman she was certain held in her hands the power to count her in or out of the prestigious guide book she'd set her heart on having Still Water House in.

It would all be worth it, she told herself as she heard that infernal bell tinkling for what felt like the thousandth time that afternoon. When she opened that first edition, with a photograph of Still Water House inside it, it would all be worth it then. It was a terrible thing to admit, but when her brother-in-law died, she had found herself wishing that he'd lived, just long enough to see her final triumph.

What was wrong with her? The man was dead. Let him rest in peace.

Her life, if she was completely honest, felt empty for his loss – she hadn't liked him, she was not enough of a hypocrite to pretend otherwise, but knowing he was in the hotel had driven her on in a way that she lacked since he'd died. If she achieved White Book status for Still Water House – what then? She had no idea. It was so much easier when they'd been trying to make the place up. She'd been busy every hour of the day, with a young daughter and making ends meet, that she didn't have time to think about what next.

Now, it felt as if there was no more what next. Still Water House was as good as she could make it. Welcoming guests and hearing them compliment her and her home had lost its sheen. She was bored of her committee work. Over the years she'd been on the parish council, the school board, a serving Brown Owl with the girl guides and numerous other committees that she'd whipped into shape. But now, most recently, with the pedestrian crossing granted, there seemed to be nothing more she had the interest to do or to join. Siggy was almost grown up. Grown up and despite her best efforts to keep her near – growing away from her. Blythe was holding on for dear life, but Siggy would outgrow her. It was the same for her marriage. Was it too, pulling away from her? The dinner table that had once been a place of lively discussion was now, Blythe felt, the loneliest place in the world. Kip hardly spoke to her and she knew that beneath that silence there was a simmering resentment because he felt emasculated – he couldn't even have the last say on his daughter's camping trip.

The sale of the hotel was the tin hat on it all. Blythe just didn't want it sold.

There was nothing she could do about it. She couldn't afford to buy it, certainly not at the price currently being offered.

Did she want that badly enough to let go of Still Water House?

That night, she lay awake for hours, chasing sleep seemed futile when she saw that it was four-thirty and she still hadn't slept a wink. She padded downstairs, as silently as she could past Morwenna's door. If she heard that bell one more time, there was a good chance she'd take one of those bloody pillows and… She shook her head, firmly pushing from her mind visions of what she'd do to that awful woman. Instead, she turned towards the kitchen, headed for the back door, and slipped her feet into Kip's too-large work boots in the porch. The night air was cool, but not unpleasantly so. She was approaching that age where she valued a crisp night far more than a boiling heat.

In Kip's van, she noticed he'd left the keys in the ignition. One of those habits she'd given up trying to break years ago, it was as futile as trying to force down the cow's lick over his right eyebrow. She sat into the van, turned over the engine. Before she knew it, she was driving out the gate, towards Muffeen Mòr. It was a quiet road at this hour, a four-mile journey that she could do with her eyes closed, but somehow, there was an unfamiliar bleakness to everything tonight.

Cassidy's abandoned cottage, the overgrown hedgerows all along the road, waiting for the council to come out and tidy things up a little later in the year, the silence of the van. Kip never listened to the radio, unless it was a live match. Tonight, it all felt otherworldly.

The village was the same; deserted, dark, somehow hostile, as if even the old houses and roads knew her intentions were not good. She drove up towards the village square, pulled in across the road from the hotel. Sat there, with the van idling for a few moments before turning off the engine.

She had no idea why she'd come here. To take a mental snapshot of the place before it was changed forever, perhaps? Or maybe she was attempting to drill the reality of what was to come into her brain once and for all. Who knew how the mind works when you're up to ninety and you haven't slept a wink?

And then it hit her, a bolt that had been buried deep inside her for as long as she'd been able to say her own name. If she couldn't have the hotel – she couldn't bear to see anyone else have it.

37

Siggy

Present

The morning had been a bloody nightmare.
Siggy had woken to the sound of that irritating bell being rung by Morwenna Whythe. Her mother was convinced that the awful woman was in fact an undercover agent for the White Book brigade.

'She's just testing us,' her mother said.

'Testing is one word for it,' her father shook his head, and he left them to it, the first time she'd ever seen him leave the house without a hearty breakfast.

'I'll go.' Her mother disappeared down the hall, only to return half an hour later panting loudly, with sweat dripping from her brow. 'She only wanted the chaise longue moved to the other side of the room.' She collapsed into a chair in the kitchen.

'You didn't lift that thing on your own?' Siggy knew the weight of it well enough. It was Victorian, stuffed out with horse hair and it felt like the weight of a small car. 'You'll give yourself a hernia carrying on like that.'

'I'm alright,' but she looked flaked. 'It'll be worth it.'

'It better be,' Siggy said, and she turned over the bacon she was frying for the Buckleys who'd been booked into room nine. 'I've nearly done these breakfasts now, only that couple who booked into room four last night, the...' She couldn't remember their names. 'No sign of them yet, do they know we finish breakfasts in half an hour?'

'Not today we don't,' Blythe said.

'But Mum, I have to...' She had agreed to meet Rae for a walk on the beach.

'Listen, Siggy, I know, you have more important things to do than help me out here on a Saturday morning...' Her mother's voice had taken on that dangerous, slightly higher pitch that normally led to a lecture of some sort.

'Mum, I'm doing my fair share here. I've done four cooked breakfasts while you...' She stopped because she knew that old girl in number three was driving her mother insane with unreasonable demands.

'While I what, exactly?'

'Sorry, I know you're under pressure, but I promised Rae...'

'Oh, well, excuse me, a promise to my sister must take precedence over anything I might need.' She got up, moved towards the hob where Siggy was just removing the bacon for the Buckleys. 'I'll take over here, will I? After all, we wouldn't want to keep you from having fun.'

'That's not fair, Mum. I'm only here because you asked me to be here, most of my friends don't get out of bed until the afternoon on the weekends.'

'So that's it, is it?' Blythe shook her head and Siggy could feel the judgement being layered on her. 'You want to laze the day away while the rest of us get on with it, is that it? I'm doing this for you, you know. Think about it, Siggy, one day, all of this will be yours...'

'Dear Lord, Mother, will you listen to yourself?' The words were out before Siggy could stop them. 'You're not doing this for anyone but yourself, or maybe you're still doing it to somehow get the last laugh on Marcus and Rae, because, it's fairly obvious to everyone all of this,' she looked around the kitchen, 'all of it, was never about making a life for us, it was about something far beyond either Dad or I.' The words were out, there was no stopping the flow now.

'Siggy!' Her mother looked as if she'd been slapped hard across her face. 'How dare you? What do you know about anything, beyond this cosseted life I've made for you?' Her mother was screaming now, hysterical.

'I...' Siggy wanted to come back at her, to say, that was exactly the problem, she knew nothing of life beyond these four walls worth talking about.

'I've done my best to keep you safe from harm. Everything, every single thing has been about saving you from the mistakes I made...'

'Oh, getting pregnant with me, wasn't that the greatest mistake,' Siggy spat at her. 'After all, it cost you way more than you expected, didn't it?' She stopped to catch her breath, only barely registering her mother's shocked expression. 'Yes, Mum, of course I know, you probably spent years regretting me, wishing that you could have the hotel back again, be a Hope Square Girl? Isn't that what they called you and Rae? The Hope Square Sisters? Back when the Scotts were somebodies in this backward, bigoted place.'

'Siggy, no...' Her mother looked as if she might cry. But Blythe Carney never cried. It was the worst-kept secret never kept.

Somewhere beyond the kitchen door, a tinkling sound broke through the fetid stalemate.

'Well, aren't you going to get that?' Siggy watched as her mother's eyes darted desperately between the food cooling on the plates nearby, her daughter's tear-streaked face and that irritating bell ringing endlessly.

'We're not finished here,' Blythe said as she backed away from Siggy.

'Oh, but we are, mother, we really are,' Siggy said and she watched as her mother paused, her hand just touching the doorknob, about to race off to take care of Morwenna Whythe. Then, in a movement quicker than Siggy ever saw her make, she spun round. Stalked across the kitchen so she was right up in front of Siggy.

'Listen to me, if you ever speak to me like that again, I'll…' With that the door burst open.

'Didn't you hear me? Are you all deaf here?' Morwenna stood in the doorway, and never in Siggy's life had she wanted more to punch someone right smack in the centre of their face. 'I need a glass of water, I'm going to dehydrate in that room, hasn't anyone here ever thought of putting AC into the rooms?' She turned and walked from the kitchen, completely unaware of what she had interrupted.

'I'm out of here,' Siggy said then, pulling off the apron she'd been wearing earlier.

'Oh, off to your delinquent boyfriend, I suppose?' It was a taunt and if she wasn't so shocked that her mother knew about Danial, Siggy would never have risen to it.

'He's not a delinquent, he has far more principles than you have, with your talking about people behind their backs and judging everyone before you even give them a chance.' Siggy was crying now, she was too upset, she couldn't stop.

'I have it on good authority that…'

'If you're talking about that vile text that's doing the rounds, I've seen it, and I know for a fact that it's not true.' She watched as her mother's complexion drained, and she wondered if perhaps it hadn't yet reached her circle of friends.

'The text?' she said, stepping backwards and dropping into the chair.

'Yes. Oh, haven't you received it yet? I thought all you snobs stuck together, I can send it to you, if you'd like...' She whipped out her phone. But of course, she had deleted the vile thing. Even knowing it was on her phone made her feel as if she was somehow sullied by it.

'I know the text,' her mother said slowly. Her words were so measured, they sent a chill right into Siggy's heart. 'But what it doesn't say is that someone saw him do it. Did he tell you that when he was whispering in your ear and turning you against your own mother?'

'Oh, you're completely paranoid and – and...' Siggy stopped, because she knew she shouldn't say what she was thinking.

'Go on, you can't stop there, can you?'

'You're truly vile, do you know that?' Siggy screamed and then she threw the apron on the floor and made for the back door. She needed to get out of there, because honestly, if she had to listen to another word, she wasn't sure she wouldn't be the one causing bodily harm.

After she had walked to the village, it felt as if she had completely run out of steam. She dragged herself down towards the pier where a low wall ran the length of the road opposite the old fishermen's cottages. She decided to sit for a minute, just to get her bearings again. Really, she could hardly think. She'd never fought with her mother like that before, instead, she'd always tried to button up her emotions, tack them down to avoid conflict.

'Hey,' a friendly voice pulled her from her thoughts and she looked around to see Danial's grandmother standing at her back. 'Oh, no, you're crying, what's the matter?' she bent down but the wall was too low for her to sit on.

'It's...' but the concern in Melissa Val's eyes only opened the flood gates further and Siggy began to wail.

'Come on, come with me. Let's have some tea. Everything is better when you taste my tea.' And she held out her hand to lead her to the old McDaid cottage.

It took a few minutes to properly orient herself once Melissa showed her into the tiny sitting room. It was dark, in a comforting way, with walls the colour of African sun, thick tapestries and beautiful urns. The sofa, a two seater, was covered with a throw that looked as if it had been spun from precious stones, but felt as soft as mohair. Siggy sat there, while Melissa moved around the kitchen, boiling the kettle and making sounds with cupboard doors, cups and cutlery.

'Please don't go to any trouble,' she called. 'I'm fine, really, just...'

'It's no trouble, we'll just sit and take a minute and if you want to tell me what's upset you, fine, but if you just want to pull yourself together, well...' she placed a tray on the ottoman.

Of course, it all spilled out of Siggy. The argument with her mother. The things they said to each other and now, the guilt she felt for all of it.

'I think that's the thing about working in a family business and living at home with your parents, it's hard to keep perspective on things. You love your mother very much and I'm sure she loves you, but it's hard enough to keep things straight when it's just family. Throw in a business too and...' Melissa shrugged as if to say, no one could possibly handle it. 'You are very lucky to have such a great support system around you.'

'I know that, and I have Rae as well, which is great – she's more like a best friend than an aunt most of the time...'

'But?'

'I feel as if I'm suffocating here; trapped on Pin Hill Island for the rest of my days.' She stopped, she hadn't said it before, but now she knew, for a long time, it had been a background noise in her growing discontent. 'It sounds crazy, it feels like desertion to want to leave. You know, as if I'm letting everyone down and throwing away my future without really appreciating what I've got.' And there was a lot now, Danial too, was another thing to consider.

'Is that the plan? That you will take over both places one day?'

'There is no one else,' Siggy said. 'I think,' she said then, because this had always been what she believed even if it wasn't put into words. 'I think Rae would just like to see me being happy. You know, if the hotel wasn't going to do that, or if I decided to do something else instead, she'd understand. She'd be okay with it; she'd probably help me in any way she could if I asked for her help.'

'She is a good person to have on your side,' Melissa said. Siggy knew Melissa had already experienced Rae's kindness. Rae had arrived down here one evening with dishes and cutlery and other odds and ends all beautifully matched up and presented as a gift to Melissa. Siggy only knew it because Danial told her about it the following day when they were walking on the beach together. Rae would never breathe a word about it.

'And your parents?'

'My dad would be fine. I mean, he'd worry about me, probably. He'd text me every day, with all the worst emojis!' She made a face.

'You're their only child, of course, they are going to be more...' She waved her hands as if the explanation lay on the air itself.

'But my mother, she's a whole different story.'

'Blythe?' She said the name as if trying it on for size.

'She'd go mad if she thought I was even thinking of leaving.'

'I've heard lots of good things about your mother,' Melissa said carefully because Siggy suspected, she hadn't experienced the kind and good person Blythe could be when she was on your side. 'Perhaps you need to talk to Rae and your dad first and then maybe...'

'I don't think I can talk to my dad at the moment,' Siggy said. She couldn't tell Melissa that she thought he was having an affair; bad enough she'd told Danial, anything more would be a betrayal of both her parents.

'I know everyone has a lot on their plates, but Siggy, time moves on quickly, one week into the next and soon it's another year and then suddenly before you know it,' she stopped and made a puffing sound with her lips. 'It's too late.'

'And you don't think I'm being selfish?'

'Oh, dear girl, you're being the very opposite, you need to follow your heart, we only have one life.'

Melissa's words stayed with her. Galvanised her in a way that gave her a sort of quiet serenity. She was going to follow her heart, somehow it would all work out.

The following day, if there was even one occasion to sit and chat to Rae about what was going through her mind Siggy would have snapped it up, but her aunt was as busy as she'd ever been. Before they opened for the morning there was a meeting with a surveyor who was working on behalf of the buyer interested in number three. Rae spent almost two hours going through the place, answering questions, talking about various ways the building could be separated and what would and would not be acceptable to her in terms of disruption.

When the hotel did open, there was a sudden rush, as if word had filtered into the village that they were already busy and so people turned up to add to the workload.

By mid-afternoon, the rush seemed to have abated, and Siggy sat down with Danial for their lunch. She'd made a fresh vegetable soup which had quickly run out earlier, so she'd made a second and third batch which had just about stretched to lunch for them both. There was just one bowl left over for Rae whenever she got back from her appointment with the solicitor to work out details around the property deeds in preparation for sale.

It was nice, sitting here, pleasantly tired after the busy morning with Danial – who was good company.

'You're in a good mood,' he said, cutting into her thoughts.

'Am I?'

'Yes, it feels as if you know something that no one else does,' he smiled. 'You have a secret?'

'Maybe I do,' Siggy said lightly, 'maybe I do.'

That evening, when she got home, she downloaded a heap of prospectuses for the following academic year. Then she made a list of her top six favourites and exactly what sort of points she'd need to get entry into them.

For a few days, she was positively buoyed up on the dream of leaving the island the following year, although she told no one. What was the point?

Her mistake was leaving the notebook lying open on her bed when she went into school the following Friday.

Her mother was the shade of an overripe tomato by the time she got home.

'What on earth? When were you going to tell me? What sort of girl does this to her mother, just when everything is so...' she'd never seen her mother so upset, so devastated.

'Mum. I'm a grown woman. The idea of running the hotel, it's not my dream.'

'It's a wonderful opportunity for anyone your age. Have you any notion how many people would give their eye teeth to have a place like that just handed to them?'

'No, Mum, the only one who'd want to spend their life locked into a dying business in the middle of Muffeen Mòr is you – there's nothing here for me now. My friends are all going to be heading off to college and I want to go too...' She stopped because she didn't want to blurt out something that would do far more damage than anything she could say about her own dreams.

'You're not going, I'm telling you now, I absolutely forbid it.'

'I'll be an adult, Mum, you can't stop me. You can either give me your blessing and wish me well or I'll just go...'

'Give you my blessing,' her voice had risen to the level of soprano. 'Over my dead body will I be giving you my blessing to go living in some filthy flat on the other side of the country – you know those places students stay? Full of germs and serial killers, you know that?'

'Oh, Mum,' Siggy said before whipping her notebook out of her mother's hands and racing downstairs and out the front door.

Once outside, Siggy suddenly realised, she had no idea what to do next. There was a cold breeze starting up and it looked as if the sky might open with rain. She'd walked out in little more than a T-shirt and a pair of shorts. Well, she couldn't go back. There was no point. Whatever chance she had of keeping things on an even keel, she knew that arguing with her mother would only drive a deeper rift between them.

She set off walking towards the village, perhaps she could stay in the hotel for a few nights. Rae wouldn't mind.

The hotel was closed when she arrived in the village. She pushed her key through the front door, hoping not to scare the living daylights out of Rae. She checked in the little flat, but there was no sign of her aunt. She went to the bar, poured herself a large glass of wine. Rae wouldn't mind, it was for medicinal purposes – then she went upstairs to one of the rooms they'd aired in case they got last-minute bookings. On a whim, she wasn't sure why, she turned right instead of left. They had no plans to let out the rooms in the part of the building that was to be sold, but the rooms had been aired for the viewing earlier in the day. She chose one of the top-floor rooms with a view of the sea and guaranteed not to disturb Rae when she got back. No one would be booking in here this year. She could stay for as long as she needed and really, not put anyone out – that would suit her perfectly.

Tomorrow, they had a party of six arriving. For now, Siggy thought, the best thing she could do was just turn in for the night and put the argument with her mother. The glass of wine would knock her out. She wasn't a drinker, generally, one large glass would put her to sleep within half an hour. And she needed to sleep. For all her bravado, she was upset. She hated fighting with her mother and hated even more this secret she was carrying about her father.

Soon her eyes began to feel heavy. She would think about it tomorrow, for now, she needed to rest.

38

Blythe

Seventeen Years Earlier

Blythe and Kip worked so hard that winter. But somehow, it hardly felt like work at all. The trick was, she knew, to bring each room up to its highest standard, so basically, she decided to do just one room at a time because there was simply no budget to do any more. With a lifetime in the hotel business, she was savvy enough to repurpose all that she could and pick up whatever was needed as cheaply as possible. Second hand was always best, since the house was so old, and she wanted to retain that original character.

Kip, too, proved to be not only talented and hardworking when given an opportunity and some praise, but also very savvy at picking up materials from odd jobs where there were bits and pieces left over. By the time spring came round, they had two charming rooms, with ensuites, and the large sitting room to welcome guests on arrival. Blythe set to sprucing up the family dining room which they'd only ever used at Christmas, because the table sat twenty and in winter, it took blazing fires in both hearths to keep the chills at bay.

The best part, as far as Blythe was concerned, was that they managed to make their plans and carry out the work without anyone beyond themselves and Kip's mother having any idea of what they were up to.

On the morning that she received a letter from the tourism board telling her that they'd been accepted onto the books as a listed guest house, it all felt surreal. Blythe's hands shook as she read the letter out to Kip. She was strangely nervous, with butterflies playing around her insides, but then Kip had shot up from the table, taken her in his arms and she'd known, this was really happening. They had done it, together, this was their real beginning.

'You'll have to tell your grandfather now,' Kip said later.

'I know.' She was in part dreading it and a little part of her had looked forward to this day for months now. She had not accepted what fate, and her grandfather, had allotted to her, instead she had gone out and taken her destiny into her own hands. He would be proud of her. Maybe not today, but someday soon, Pappy would come and ask her to take over the hotel again. She was quite certain of it.

The hotel was quiet when she dropped by later that afternoon.

She hadn't called in for weeks, she hadn't had time, although, she didn't tell Rae or her grandfather what had kept her so busy, until now.

'Pappy?' She called out, surprised to see he was not ensconced in his usual spot.

'He's out in the garden.' A woman she didn't recognise came out from the room behind the reception desk.

'Thanks, I'm Blythe by the way, who are you?'

'Hello Blythe, Rae has told me all about you. I'm Rosa, I'm here to help for the summer.'

'I see,' Blythe said, and she couldn't help but feel hurt that no one had come and asked her, if she'd like to lend a hand.

'Ah, Enkelin, there you are, and you've brought precious little Gisela.' Her grandfather waved at her from the midst of a plot of waist-high sunflowers. 'Look, your sister has me driven demented with flowers,' he laughed then as if he'd never imagined anything so crazy.

'It's nice to see you out and about,' she leant in and kissed his cheek.

'Look at her, more like her grandmother every single day,' Pappy said, leaning over to plant a kiss on the baby's head and Blythe could have sworn she saw a tear glisten in his eye.

'I wanted to talk to you, Pappy,' she said and she saw his shoulders hunch and she knew, he expected her to come grovelling for work in the hotel. 'I have news,' she said simply.

'Oh, that's marvellous, another baby, now, there you go, what did I tell you...' He was about to go on down that wrong road until Blythe interrupted him.

'It's not that, Pappy, I'm not pregnant, but I'm really excited about this, and I wanted you to be the first to know.' She began to lead him towards the small garden bench that sat against the wall of the old stables.

'Well, I'm intrigued, if it's not a baby...' He lowered himself gingerly onto the bench.

'No, far more exciting.' She stopped. Nothing could compare to having Siggy, but she was so exhilarated with the challenge of getting her own business up and running, well, she was carried on a wave of enthusiasm. 'I'm opening my own guest house...'

'You're what?' Her grandfather's expression had completely changed. 'What do you mean, you're opening your own guest house?'

'At Still Water House, I just got the listing this morning with the tourism board, we're officially open for business – I'm your new competition.' She laughed, because she was only joking, really, two rooms were hardly on the same scale as the Hope Square Hotel.

'I don't know what you think you're playing at, but I won't allow it.' Her grandfather's voice had changed to thunder. 'You're meant to be taking care of that baby, making a proper family with Kip, what on earth do you think you're playing at? Bothering the tourism board, probably bandying about my good name to get you on the books too, no doubt?'

'Actually, Pappy, I didn't have to bandy anyone's good name. There is a process, they came and looked at where I propose to take guests, they checked out the whole house and of course, my background in catering college helped. Kip and I have got this up and running between us, and I intend to make a great success of it, so unless you're going to wish me luck, then, I'm not sure there's much more to be said about it,' she said and with that, she hoisted the baby up on her hip and stalked towards the open door of the hotel.

On her way past, she spotted Marcus, lurking in the conservatory – her conservatory, which only fired her up further.

'I suppose you heard all that.'

'I did actually,' he was gloating, enjoying the fact that not only had he swiped the hotel from under her nose, but also the fact that he was splintering a family that had once been as close as could be.

'Well, in case you missed anything Marcus, I intend to give you a run for your money with this place. I'm going to make a great success of it. One day, Still Water House will be in the best guide books in the world, and this place will be nothing more than a three-star hotel.'

'Blythe, you can talk all you want, but at the end of the day, you're going to be running a two-bit bed and breakfast in a house that needs a new roof and probably rewiring and plumbing. Let's see how you get through this season before we start awarding any Michelin stars for the greasy fry-ups?'

'We'll see, Marcus, we'll see.' She pushed past him, but as she did so, she was jubilant to see a flash of cold fear in his eyes. He knew she could make Still Water House into anything she wanted, and at this moment, much and all she had always loved this place, she wanted more than anything to make her guest house into something ten times better than the Hope Square Hotel.

39

Rae

Seventeen Years Earlier

Marcus was fuming. Rae had never seen him in such a state. He paced up and down the conservatory, cursed under his breath, and smashed the teacup he was drinking when he left it down so hard on the marble wash table.

'What's wrong?' Rae said softly from the doorway. She began to wipe up the mess with a cloth from the bucket she was carrying. It was all over his trousers and when she started to pat the wet from his shoes, he kicked forward to shunt her off, his foot only missing her face by a hair's margin. She almost lost her balance.

'Oh, for goodness' sake, now look at what you made me do, will you stop that fussing about,' he barked.

'I'm sorry, I didn't mean to upset you.' But she was in shock, trying to steady herself on her feet, trying to make sense of what could be wrong.

'Well, you did,' he thumped his fist into his open palm. 'That bloody sister of yours.'

'Blythe, oh no, what has she done? Did she say something to you? Or?' Rae's mind raced with terrible scenarios.

'I suppose you're in on it too?' He rounded on her now. It was something that always bothered him, the idea that Rae was too close to Blythe, that she told her sister far too much. Marcus always sulked when she went to visit Still Water House, she had a feeling the only reason he thawed was to interrogate her for every word that had been uttered by Blythe.

'In on what? I've no idea what you're talking about,' she said now.

'Oh, please, you've probably known all along.'

'Marcus, you're not making any sense, known what?'

'This guest house she's opening, of course?' He moved right up before her, so she had to take a step backwards, but now, she was pinned against one of the tables and it was bruising into her legs. 'It's all just a game to both of you, isn't it? You have no idea what it's like to start out with nothing.' She watched as a thin film of sweat seeped from his upper lip, his breathing suddenly heavy. His asthma. An upset like this, a few months earlier had led to a full attack. It was horrible. Honestly Rae thought he would die. And for what, he'd nearly collapsed over table settings in the dining room.

'Blythe is opening a guest house? Where?' Rae stopped, but of course, there was only one place she could open it. 'At Still Water House?' she said. It made perfect sense. Of course, Blythe should make something of the place. 'But isn't that good news? I mean, if you want to stay on here, doesn't that make things easier?'

'Are you mad?' He was fuming, his whole body had turned to the colour of wet cement. She realised that he had no idea how close he was standing to her, pinning her there, his body throbbing with anger, his breath coming now in ragged bursts. She had to do something. She reached into his pocket. Pulled out the inhaler he always carried and held it up for him to take it.

'Marcus, please, it isn't good for you to get so upset.' She tried to move away from him. He stepped back then, just a little, took two puffs, but still it seemed, he couldn't quite keep up with his short breaths.

'Do you think?' He was so angry, she wasn't even sure she recognised him anymore.

'Please,' she begged. And maybe it was the terror in her voice, but he stood back another fraction, puffed the inhaler once more. They stood there, for a long while, staring at each other. One trying to breathe, the other willing him to.

'You really don't get it, do you?' he said, wiping the sweat from his face with a fresh napkin he picked up from the table.

'I don't, I really don't. We should be happy for Blythe and Kip, they'll have their own business. They'll be able to maintain Still Water House and what a wonderful place to have a family...'

'Can't you see, I'm looking at my future being flushed down the toilet here.'

'How can you say that?'

'Rae. Really?' He ran his hands through his hair; she wondered if he was about to have another attack, but he took his inhaler again and this time she knew he was stronger. 'It's an island – there are only so many visitors every year.'

'It's not just visitors, we have weddings and funeral lunches and a good passing trade all the year through, really, the hotel has always been busy enough to make a good profit.'

'That's all well and good when you own the place, but what about me?'

'What about you?'

'Rae, honestly, your head is so stuck in the clouds, you have no clue.'

'You're overthinking this.'

'Of course you don't understand?' he rolled his eyes. 'You wouldn't know what a balance sheet was if it hit you on the head, but turnover and growth is a reflection of a manager's dynamism – and there can't be growth if you're halving the market.'

'Bloody hell, Marcus, Blythe can't possibly cut into our profits in any real way. She won't have more than a couple of rooms and even then, there are no ensuites in Still Water House. The hotel is in the middle of the village, the ferry docks just a couple of hundred yards away.'

'And yet, for all of that, she's managed to get into the tourism guide for this year, so she'll be booking in people just as readily as we are...' He drawled as if he was talking to someone with no understanding of any of it.

'Seriously?' Rae was impressed, but she always knew Blythe could do anything she set her mind to. In that moment, Rae felt so happy and proud for her sister, but she bit down the words, because that was the last thing Marcus would want to hear.

The next few days, Rae found herself desperately wanting to go and visit Blythe. She yearned to hold the baby in her arms, sit by the old Aga in the kitchen in Still Water House and feel as if the world was still safe and open-hearted.

But the fact was, she was reluctant to tell either Marcus or Pappy that she was going to visit Blythe. She wasn't even sure Blythe would want to see her. She had heard Pappy and Marcus talk about the Still Water House listing. It had been chosen as the cover image for this year's tourism board brochure. Pappy, she could tell, was just a little proud of Blythe's achievement, but he was worried too. It was all wrapped up in the idea that she had married Kip so quickly. He still didn't like Kip, it was as if he expected the worst from him.

Rae felt torn between the two sides, but she missed Blythe desperately.

Sometimes, she'd go down to the old broken-down tree house at the end of the garden and sit beneath it, remembering when they were girls – not all that long ago, really and she would cry, for the way things had turned out between them.

40

Rae

Sixteen Years Earlier

Rae ran to the back door of the hotel to find Rosa screaming as if she'd seen a vision of the devil himself culling the strawberries, but in fact, when Rae pushed past her, she realised it was her grandfather, stretched out, face down across the ridges he'd been digging the previous day.

'NO!' the scream that rose up inside her never made it to her lips. Old Packie, the night porter who'd been having breakfast in the kitchen, managed to grab her shoulders, holding her in place for a moment so she could pull herself together. When she wriggled free and knelt beside Pappy, she knew it was bad. He was broiled in sweat, his eyes staring vacant, as if he was ready to leave them. In that moment, she thought about something Blythe had said years earlier.

When their mother died, Blythe said, it felt as if she was still with them. Apparently, when no one was looking, Blythe slipped back into her mother's room to see if she could wake her up, really, her passing had been so peaceful, it seemed as if she hadn't fully left.

This time, they were lucky.

'You were lucky,' the doctor told him the following day as Blythe and Rae sat there, taking it all in. 'So, no more missing your medication, no big shocks or...' And he looked to the two women who sat silently, next to each other. 'I mean, obviously, your grandfather has to enjoy life, but for a while, until everything settles down, nothing that will aggravate him, it's all about treading water until he is stronger.'

'What about our wedding?' Marcus stood at the door and honestly, Rae was so dazed, she wondered what he was doing there.

'A wedding is always something to look forward to,' the doctor smiled, 'yes, a wedding could be just the thing, so long as there's no stress around it.'

'But...' Rae said softly, and all eyes turned on her, she felt Blythe's gaze more than any other. She couldn't do or say anything to upset her grandfather now. They hadn't planned to get married as such, nothing official at any rate. She was twenty-one years old, even if she absolutely adored Marcus, couldn't imagine life without him, she was only twenty-one. She still harboured the dream of training to be a veterinary nurse, of seeing life beyond the island, maybe even travelling the world for a few years.

'Of course you can still do all those things, darling,' Marcus promised her when they were alone together later. 'We'll do them together, this way, they'll be part of our adventure. We are going to have such an amazing life, I've always known it.'

'And babies?' Because she definitely wanted children, but not while she was backpacking around Asia or visiting the Empire State building.

'As many as you want!' He pulled her close and kissed her, long and hard, and it felt like some time since he'd done that, but it didn't matter. Everything about him just filled her with desire.

Marcus told Pappy, they didn't want a circus for a wedding. It felt surreal to Rae. So many times, she wanted to say, *it's too soon. I'm not ready*. Of course, Marcus said, that was just nerves – everyone had them. Then, she would look at Marcus, and she knew she couldn't live without him. He was her rock. These days, he was her only rock. Blythe was hardly talking to her, and Pappy's health was deteriorating with every passing day. Marcus said it would kill him if they created too much of a fuss. She needed Marcus. Or at least, it felt that way, as if, without him, all oxygen would be snuffed out. He had built her up from a fragile girl to the woman she had become, and when he wrapped her up in that familiar warmth, it was still easy to dampen down her fears.

Without telling her, he went to the mainland and bought her the most beautiful engagement ring. Edwardian. Delicate. Simple. When he slipped it on her finger, she never wanted to take it off. She told herself; it was fine that they hadn't even booked a honeymoon. That could wait, until later. There were guests arriving in the hotel the following morning and it went without saying, Marcus simply had to be there to welcome them.

The night before her wedding, Blythe invited her to stay in Still Water House, to avoid any bad luck of seeing the groom before the ceremony. Rae didn't need luck, she and Marcus were meant for each other, but she relished the thought of staying with Blythe and getting time with Siggy.

It was strange being back at Still Water House. This had been her home. A happy home for many years, until it was tinged by tragedy. Somehow, in a few short years, Blythe and Kip had managed to strip, sand and rag roll it into a very comfortable and contented home again. It felt, as she sat in the generous drawing room, that anywhere her eyes rested, Blythe had worked to update, save and restore. It was truly a testament to hard work, a great eye and an ability to re-purpose so skilfully that it was only on second or third glances that Rae saw where her enterprising sister had cut corners and somehow made gilt.

'Oh, you haven't seen the half of it. There are rooms upstairs that look like they're straight out of *The Haunting of Hill House*.'

'Except we don't have any ghosts, do we?' Kip laughed then.

'If we ever did, they are long gone with all the pulling apart we've done this last year or two.' Blythe laughed then and Rae thought, she couldn't remember the last time she'd seen her sister so content. The three of them sat there, talking long into the night, when probably Rae should have gone to bed, but it felt emotional, the idea that in a few hours' time, she would be a married woman, and she had some inkling that would change things forever between them.

Kip told her about his own father.

'My old man was no prince.' They'd been drinking beers, watching a match on the television in Still Water House.

'I don't remember him at all,' she said.

'You must remember him,' Blythe shouted from the kitchen. 'He was the man in the rose garden...'

'The man in the rose garden,' Rae felt as if she'd just been doused in a bucket of icy water. 'Of course, I'd completely forgotten that day.' And she had, the main thing she remembered was Blythe's arm around her, protecting her and somehow making her feel safe, when she was probably just as scared herself by all the commotion.

'I don't think Pappy ever forgot it.'

'You think that...' Rae stopped, because she didn't want to hurt Kip's feelings.

'Well, it's the only thing that makes sense,' Blythe came and sat on the arm of the sofa next to Kip, leaning into him. For a moment, she kissed him in such an automatic way, Rae thought, she probably didn't even realise she'd done it. Then, he handed her his bottle of beer and she sipped from it.

'Where did he go, that day?' Rae had been much too young to think about such things at the time.

'Ran off with another woman... some poor eejit who left her kids behind for him and believed his big talk about a new life. She was back again within a month, begging her husband to take her back.'

'That's terribly sad.'

'I think we were better off without him. My Ma certainly was...'

'Is that why...' She stopped. It was the worst-kept secret in the village, how Kip had a soft heart for families in dire circumstances. Rae knew he'd spent two weeks sorting out Maureen O'Heir's kitchen after her husband smashed the place up on one of his drunken binges. Maureen told her, one day in the post office, that Kip refused to take one penny for all the work he'd carried out for her. He'd even managed to call in a few favours and pick up materials for half nothing from some mate who was emigrating and wanted to clear out his workshop. 'Sorry.'

'No, you don't have to be Sigmund Freud to figure it out. Any analyst worth his salt would probably say I was making up for my father's sins.' He laughed at that.

'You're a good man, Kip Carney.' Rae smiled at him fondly.

'Well don't go telling Blythe that, will you, it'll shatter the whole allure I have going on with her.' He laughed and raised his can of beer in salute, then pulled Blythe in for a very long and rather embarrassing kiss.

Rae woke up the following morning to sunshine, which was a nice surprise, because these last few weeks the weather had been as unpredictable as she ever remembered. It was a sign, a good sign.

Even so, there was a nervous lisp in her voice when she finally said, 'I do.' She'd had the strangest dream that Marcus might have second thoughts. Which was ridiculous of course, because he adored her. When he looked into her eyes that day, as she walked up the aisle to marry him, she fell in love with him all over again. If that was even possible. It was that feeling, as she concentrated on putting one foot before the other, that with his eyes alone, he could undo her, and it made her want to lose herself in him even more. She was so happy when they kissed to seal the deal. She just knew that they would have something just like Blythe and Kip, maybe even better one day.

That summer, the days ran into each other more quickly than ever before, so quickly in fact, that they hadn't time to breathe after their wedding. Rae was delighted when she checked the guest book and saw there was a full week free in September. It felt to her, as if it was written in the stars, the perfect week for their honeymoon.

'Honeymoon?' Marcus had been distracted ever since the wedding. It was as though, after they signed the marriage register, he had assumed some great responsibility and instead of bringing them closer, it moved him further away. 'Rae, we're in peak season, we can't just up and leave your grandfather...' He didn't even lift his head from the crossword.

'I *know* that, Marcus,' she wanted to remind him, that he had promised they would go before the end of the month. Mrs Daly could easily and quite happily cut through the work if they took a day or two away. It wasn't much to ask. 'But maybe we could book something for later.' It was a compromise, he'd set his jaw in that way, that she knew, there was no point trying to wheedle him, it never worked with Marcus, it just irritated him. 'It would be something to look forward to,' she said then and she walked across and leant over his shoulder, draping herself as she would have done when they first started dating.

'Oh, for goodness' sake, Rae, you're going to make me spill my tea.' He shrugged away from beneath her. 'Anyway, I'll have enough to look forward to if we make a profit at the end of this year, between all the shenanigans with your sister opening her guest house and then the weeks of bad weather just when you'd be hoping to get the early school holiday crowds in.'

'What's this?' Pappy said then. The doctor had insisted he use a walking aid for moving around the hotel, although it frustrated him no end.

'Marcus says we must put the honeymoon on hold,' Rae said, slumping back to her seat. She knew it was immature, but she felt so disappointed, she had hoped they'd get to stay in a hotel and be pampered for a change.

'I've never heard such nonsense.' Pappy shook his head. 'Marcus, I insist you take a honeymoon with Rae.' Pappy shook his head and navigated himself gingerly into the carver chair that Rae had placed at the head of the table for him. 'My treat. Where would you like to go, Rae?'

'Hang on, Jack, we can't just walk out the door and leave the hotel?' Marcus stopped a moment. 'I mean, how would you cope? If anything happened, well, I'd never live with myself.' He threw a side-eye towards Rae as if she was no better than Nurse Mildred Ratched.

'Ah, whist now, stop with that nonsense. Amn't I better checked out than any of you after my last visit to the hospital. I know my limits, but I don't need babysitting, thank you very much.' He turned to Rae. 'So, where is it going to be, Meine Liebling? Timbuktu or Shangri-La? Which will it be?' He was making fun of her now.

'I think, Timbuktu?' she said, biting off the corner of her slice of toast and they both laughed at that.

'Seriously, though, book when you want, where you want and it's my treat,' the old man said and he winked at Rae, while Marcus concentrated on his crossword.

It was later that day, when Rae was putting some of the bedrooms back to rights that Marcus marched in and closed the door with a firm click, turning the key so they would not be disturbed. For a moment, from behind, she thought he was being romantic, that perhaps... but when he turned, her heart sank. His face was grey. His skin had that filmy sheen to it.

'What the hell?' he said, gasping for air.

'Here.' Rae patted his pockets, found his inhaler in the waistcoat he'd taken to wearing recently. 'Take it,' she said quietly and she tried to pull him down to sit on the bed next to her so he could catch his breath. Two puffs and his whole posture changed quite rapidly. 'Are you okay?'

'Am I okay?' He spat at her. 'What do you think?'

'Did something happen?' She had noticed that his asthma attacks were always triggered by something. There was either great stress, excitement or anxiety before they hijacked his breathing. Sometimes, she worried that if he was alone and he didn't have his inhaler, well... it didn't bear thinking about.

'Did something happen?' He had squeezed up his voice to sound like hers but ugly.

'I'm sorry, I don't understand.' It must be his asthma, she thought, she didn't know much about the condition, but perhaps he was still only coming out of the attack.

'I'll tell you what happened – this morning, that's what happened.' He turned now to look at her and she tried to slide away from him on the bed. There was a violence about him that was completely unfamiliar, for a moment, she thought he might strike her. 'I don't appreciate being made to look a fool by my own wife, that's what's wrong with me.'

'I don't understand,' she said then and she hated that her voice was simpering. 'I'd never...'

'Oh, please. Miss Perfect. Always so good. Don't think I can't see right through that goody two shoes act. Your grandfather paying for a honeymoon. Well, I'm not having it. I'm not leaving this hotel until the season is well and truly over, do you hear me? The last thing I need now is leaving here and that sister of yours getting her feet under the table as soon as my back is turned.'

'It's not like that at all, Marcus, don't you see?'

'I see, well enough.' He grabbed her arm as she was just moving out of his reach.

'Please, Marcus, you're hurting me.' But she was too shocked to make much more than a whimper and he pulled her harder, so hard she thought he might yank her arm from its socket.

'There'll be no more talk of honeymoons. That's a man's place to organise, do you hear? If I hear mention of it again, so help me,' he twisted her arm back, just enough to make her gasp. 'I'll bloody break it next time.' And then he let her go, with a flick that felt as if he was casting off something that truly disgusted him.

When he left the bedroom, Rae ran to the door and locked it after him. Then she fell to the floor behind it, too shocked to cry, too numb to know that she couldn't. Tears streamed down her face, but she felt nothing, it was as if he had emptied out some integral part of her. And suddenly she realised, that maybe this is what Blythe feared would happen and that alone confirmed, she could never admit to anyone that she had made a terrible, terrible mistake in marrying Marcus.

41

Rae

Present

Of course there was no problem with the deeds. Rae hadn't expected there to be, Pappy had sewn up every part of his granddaughters' inheritances as tightly as if he was expecting someone to pull them apart.

She'd met with the solicitor two hours ago. Now she felt stuck. The offer on the table was miles beyond what she could have hoped for, certainly enough to pay off the outstanding loans on the hotel and take care of any upgrades needed. But still, it felt as if something was holding her back. Blythe? She wasn't sure.

Suddenly, she craved Pappy's advice. She needed him to tell her this was the right thing to do – or it wasn't. To show her, if there was some other option that would put things right. Of course, she couldn't ask Pappy, but she could go and sit at his grave and maybe that would settle her mind.

The sun was sinking slowly on the horizon opposite, but there was no closing time on the island cemetery. She could park outside and slip through the old-fashioned turnstile gate.

As she picked up speed heading out of the village, she spotted Blythe's familiar old Land Rover coming towards her. Rae slowed down as it approached, thinking perhaps Blythe was headed for the hotel, maybe she was ready to call a truce? But instead, the Land Rover picked up speed. Her sister glanced at her as she passed, but she didn't wave. Her expression was set in such a determined frown, it was with a sense of relief that Rae knew she wouldn't have to spend time with her this evening.

At this hour, the cemetery was empty of visitors, no sounds here other than the creaking branches of yew trees swaying in the quiet graveyard. Marcus's grave was in a newer section of the cemetery, opened only a year before he died. She took a left turn, hardly glancing at his grave. The path towards where her grandparents and her parents lay was narrow, shoots of daisies and buttercups forcing their way through, but only just.

Her grandfather had chosen this headstone with great care and love for his wife Gisela, when she had passed years before him. He had purchased a large plot at the time. Rae knelt across the marble plinth as she always did and began to pull any stray weeds. At the headstone, she had planted a basket of simple summer flowers. Every colour she could get her hands on flooded across the surface of the planter and trailed down along the sides where she'd trimmed them back only a week before. She looked at the headstone, even now, years after he'd died, it felt like a wrench to her stomach to see his name engraved there. When he died, her safe port had been stolen from her in an increasingly stormy sea.

Pappy had chosen a headstone of mottled grey marble with a black font when her grandmother died. That first day, when she'd come here and seen the stone engraved with his name, it had taken her by surprise. It was quite beautiful, straightforward, sturdy – just like Pappy.

'Oh, Pappy.' It was all she could manage tonight. These days when she came here it was just to spend time, but in the beginning, she'd cried rivers here at all hours of the day and night.

'What should I do…' she let the words hang on the cool evening air.

The darkening sky overhead brought with it a lowering of the temperatures and she shivered, pulled her jacket closer around her shoulders. She would sit for a while, 'for as long as it takes,' she told him, as she rubbed the cool marble of the headstone gently. 'Until I know what to do for the very best.'

She must have been there well over an hour when she heard the whimpering sound. At first, she hardly noticed it, the silence was so rich here, her thoughts so tangled that it skirted about the edges of her consciousness. But then the flight of crows back across the village from their day time watching points, brought her senses back to the present moment.

It sounded like a puppy. Or two puppies. They were crying, hungry perhaps. She looked around the graveyard and that's when she spotted a cardboard box, resting up against the tap that people used for watering flowers during the summer months. Rae walked across to it. And she was right, the sound of soft crying and pawing nails, was coming from inside. Above it, the tap had dripped down and made the cover a soft, sodding sponge. She lifted it open carefully, just in case it wasn't a puppy, it could be anything, she realised as she raised the cover gently. A nest of rats? Did rats live in nests? She really wasn't sure. She dropped the cover again, a tint of fear at what might be inside. Her car was a good distance away if she wanted to race back to it. She looked around, spotted a discarded half a pair of shears poking from the top of a bin.

She pulled it out and used it to lever up the cover of the box, peered in to see three tiny puppies squirming about. White and black and brown, it was hard to know what breed they might be, if they were any breed at all. She picked them up, one by one.

She'd never been able to have a dog in the hotel, another thing she'd sacrificed, because she'd yearned for one for years, especially when Marcus ruled out the hope of any babies for them. That had made her virtual estrangement from Siggy even harder to bear. No good thinking of that now. She waited for a beat, the pain always lessened if she pushed it hard from her mind.

As to a pet, she knew that if she brought one to the hotel, he was capable of doing anything to it, just because he could, it would be another way of hurting her; she couldn't do that to a defenceless animal.

These poor little things, so small and soft. So pathetic and vulnerable. There was no way she was leaving them here, although she had no idea what she could do with them at this hour of the night. They'd need to be fed and kept warm. Instinctively, she pulled them into her. They were shivering, their eyes closed. They had no idea what sort of world they'd been abandoned to, she held them close to her face. They weren't exactly fragrant, but somehow, they made Rae's heart crack open with an unexpected rush of warmth. She looked across at her grandparents' grave, the dying sun just now moving down the headstone, across the surface and then, for a little while it lingered on the frame.

And that's when she noticed it.

A triskelion: it was carved into the stone, more visible now with the sun gleaming across the light gold paint. She knew what it meant, and she knew too that Pappy would have put it there for a reason.

It was her answer.

The triskelion, or the spiral, in Irish mythology symbolised new beginnings. It was a sign of hope.

'Oh, Pappy.' She knew exactly what his answer was; this was a time for new beginnings and maybe she already had the first of those in her arms. 'Oh, thank you, thank you.' She nuzzled the puppies closer to her face again and now, she hardly noticed the pong, because the tears that were racing down her face were such a mixture of happiness and relief. 'Thank you, Pappy,' she said, blowing him a kiss and then she headed towards her car in the last rays of dusky light.

42

Blythe

Present

When that annoying little bell rang for the umpteenth time that morning, Blythe didn't move. She was past breaking point. Morwenna Whythe had been here three days at this stage. Three long and horrible days and Blythe was at breaking point.

A second tinkling sound propelled Blythe from her chair. What could that awful woman want now?

She had turned Blythe's whole house upside down since she arrived. She had complained about absolutely everything. From the cats in the garden, to the unscented candles in the empty fireplace grates. There wasn't one kind word from her in the time she'd been here. And she never left. Not once. She didn't so much as stroll past the front door. Instead, she moved from her bedroom to the dining room and from there to the sitting room. She ran every other guest out of the house with her rudeness. And this morning, as Blythe had been preparing breakfasts for the sixteen other guests who were due to leave on the early ferry, she had rung that infernal bell constantly. Blythe was run ragged, fetching and carrying. The final straw was when she asked for a change of sheets, because she had managed to spill the whole cafetiere of expensive French coffee across Blythe's lovely Belfast Linens.

It was too much.

Blythe felt her feet begin to pick up pace.

She didn't care at this point if the woman was the queen of Sheba. She didn't give two flying bananas if she was a reviewer sent down from St Paul's pearly-gated mansion in the sky. Blythe couldn't take one more ring of that irritating bell.

'That's it.' She screamed as she flung open the door. 'That's it.' She hardly even registered the shocked expression of the woman stretched out on the chaise longue. 'Let's be having you. I'm not taking another moment of this, I don't care if you're Satan's sister, which I suspect, you probably are, but I'm not putting up with another moment of this.' She was beside herself with fury at this point.

Blythe dived at the bed. Pulled the woman's belongings that were strewn there, off it. Blitzed the entire room like a demon, gathering up various clothes and shoes and anything that didn't look as if it belonged to the room. She was stuffing them into a bag, shoving them in, no care as to whether they creased, curled or rotted. In her fury, she noticed that there was a dollop of the soy yogurt on a cream cardigan, and she found herself stuffing that even more solidly, hoping it would make an even bigger mess.

'You can't do that,' Morwenna had taken herself off the narrow couch now and she was lumbering around the room, flapping her arms as if she was some sort of annoying fly who might put Blythe off if she kept moving and wittering in her ear.

'I can do this, and I am doing it. I'm throwing you out.'

'I'll...' Morwenna had suddenly lost some of her imperiousness. 'I'll report you to...' She stopped. 'I'll put up a stinker of a review on all the websites.'

'Morwenna,' Blythe turned on her quickly and the woman, who'd been supposedly unsure on her feet, stepped swiftly back from her. The movement gave Blythe a measure of malicious joy. 'We both know you're the sort of mean-spirited woman who would give a stinking review anyway. I've bent over backwards for you. I've welcomed you into my home and you've been insufferable from the moment you arrived.' She folded over the lid of the wheelie case she had stuffed almost beyond capacity and began to zip it closed with all her strength. 'So, you can put up whatever reviews you want, but if you don't want to walk the two mile journey from here to the ferry, I suggest you come now, because my offer to get you there runs out in the next thirty seconds and you were right by the way – it's a very, very long walk.' Blythe turned on her heels and dragged the suitcase out the door. 'I'll be leaving your case on the pier for the next ferry, if you want to come with it, you'd better come now.'

Blythe never made a journey like that journey. Not one word was spoken between the two women. At the pier, Blythe walked to the back of the car, took out Morwenna's case and threw it on the ground. By the time she sat back into the jeep, her passenger had already fled.

There would be no White Book entry now, it seemed. But at that moment, Blythe felt as if she was so stupid to have ever believed it mattered anyway. She hardly remembered driving back to Still Water House that day. The front door had been left wide open; such was the haste with which she had left it earlier. As she passed by the room that had been Morwenna's, she pulled shut the door. She would clean it when she was ready. Not now. Not today.

Today, she was too depressed to do anything more than curl up at the end of the garden in one of the old blankets that she kept outside for visitors to use in the summer. She watched as the tides changed in the distance, thinking about everything her life had become and what frightened her most was that she could see nothing ahead. For the first time in her life, her plans were dashed aside, she had no idea what she wanted from the rest of her life. She had no idea where this life was leading and most terrifying of all, she wasn't sure she wanted to go forward anyway.

It was late when she realised there was only one thing she could do now. Suddenly filled with pangs of loneliness for the hotel, she unfurled herself from the blanket she'd been wrapped up in and headed towards her jeep.

Later, as she drove into Muffeen Mòr, she knew it was irrational to feel this way about bricks and mortar, but she needed to run her hand along the gable, look up in the immense size of the place, remember the happy times there with Pappy. She had no other agenda, just to sit close to the hotel while it remained everything it had always been to her.

On the floor of the jeep, in the passenger footwell, a can of kerosene sloshed its contents noisily on the uneven roads. She hadn't noticed it earlier, perhaps Kip had left it there. Funny how she could hear the kerosene this evening; normally, you couldn't hear yourself think over the noisy old engine. On the passenger seat, a box of fireside matches glared up at her. She had not put them there, had she?

Was she finally losing her mind?

Not until she met Rae on the road did the thought occur to her that somehow, she was moving to the beat of someone else's drum this evening. Had she slowed down? Blythe wasn't sure, but once she knew the hotel was empty, it was like a sign.

Not that Blythe was a believer in signs. She left all that crazy mumbo jumbo to people like Rae, but still, if she'd ever been driven to do something crazy, there had always been the failsafe – she simply couldn't if Rae was in the hotel.

Now, driving into the village, she knew for sure. The hotel was empty. Siggy had mentioned earlier in the week that their first guests of the season were arriving tomorrow.

It was, as Rae might say, another *Sign*.

The square was eerily silent when she pulled up in the Land Rover. She sat there for a while, staring up at the hotel. How much of her life was given over in the service of it? She'd spent her youth working here and far too much of her life thinking about the place. If it was possible to love a building with the very bones of you, Blythe loved the hotel.

She loved it too much, probably, she realised now. She took a deep breath. Grabbed the can of kerosene and stalked over towards the end of the building.

She walked along the side in the dusky light. It was only this end she needed to set alight. Just enough to put a spanner in the works of the proposed sale. The insurance would cover any damage.

No one would want to buy a torched building.

Out of sight of any passers-by, she broke the glass window in the small anteroom that had been cut out of the lobby years earlier. This had been a side door once and fed directly from a servants' staircase, which was only open now as an emergency exit.

Blythe knew nothing of setting fires, but she needed enough to alert a passer-by that something was up, but not so much to do a huge amount of damage. She doused the stairway with the fuel, ran a trail of it towards the doorway leading into the lobby and then pulled the door out firmly. Just as she struck the match, in the distance she heard the wails of the fire brigade. It jolted her and she let the match drop before she was ready.

Instantly she was surrounded by the flames racing along the trail of kerosene. She dived out of the way of the hungry blaze, and by some miracle managed to land on her feet on the path next to the hotel.

The sirens now, she could hear, were fading into the distance.

The flames swished higher. Shit.

There was only one fire brigade unit on the island. What now?

She would have to alert them. But how?

She stumbled away from the hotel.

What had she done? What on earth had she done?

Blythe ran towards the jeep now, tears beginning to fall down her cheeks. She had to get help. She couldn't let the place burn down.

'Mrs Carney, is everything alright?' It was that boy, Danial.

'I'm fine,' she snapped. Except she wasn't. Suddenly, she didn't know if she was coming or going. She had no idea where her mobile phone was, had she even brought it with her?

'You look as if you're not fine at all. Shall I call my grandmother? Were you looking for Siggy?'

'Siggy?' She felt completely bewildered. What on earth was he talking about?

'She's in the hotel. I saw her go in earlier,' he said and he pointed to a seat beneath one of the huge chestnut trees on the square.

'Siggy is in the hotel? Now?' Oh God. What had she done?

'She went in about an hour ago. I'm sure she's still there, I would have seen her come out, so... you could knock on the door...' He was still talking but she couldn't hear him.

'Have they given you a key?' she shrieked.

'No. Why would I have a key?' And then, suddenly, his expression changed. 'The hotel,' he pointed across, his extended arm shaking. 'Fire. There's a fire in the hotel,' he said, but his voice was hardly more than a whisper. 'Siggy...' And then he was running towards the front door without a backward glance at Blythe.

43

Siggy

Present

In room number twenty-two, Siggy snored softly. Her dreams were filled of Danial and a vision of a future she couldn't quite pin down, but left a sweet taste in her mouth.

The remains of a glass of white wine sat on the bedside table next to her. She'd drunk half of it, but she was so tired, and it was a long day. The argument with her mother and the walk back into the village had left her feeling drained. When she sank down into the bed and her head touched the pillow, she experienced that most delightful feeling of utter exhaustion rewarded with crisp cotton sheets and a pitch-black room – thanks to the blackout curtains and total silence. For one delicious moment it felt as if she was the only person in the whole universe.

And of course, it was made even more soothing because no one knew she was here. She sighed with a measure of deep contentment. She'd made up her mind. Her mother couldn't keep her a prisoner here forever, the worst was over, it was out in the open. She just wanted to drift off into a deep, deep sleep and tomorrow she could send her mother a text and tell her that she was staying here in the hotel.

For now, she was happy not one person had any idea she was here.

Perfect.

44

Rae

Twelve Years Earlier

'Siggy?' Rae wasn't sure if it was her or not. 'Siggy?' but she was such a surprising blend, not only of Blythe and Kip, but instead, it was like looking at herself. Yes, there was Kip's chin and something in the set of her that was all Carney, but the rest of her was Rae. Still, here in the county hospital, it was the last place she expected to run into her own family.

'Hey,' the child said, she pulled up to a halt, her trainers pinching a squeak on the shiny floor which seemed to delight her.

'Where's your mum?' It was all Rae could manage. And then, walking down the corridor, she saw Blythe, talking on her phone, yanking her handbag up to find something to write on, eyes pinned on her daughter ahead; because as always, Blythe never did one thing at a time and Rae felt a rush of love for the sister she hadn't seen in months.

'Rae,' Blythe dropped the phone, then seemed to remember that she'd been amid what had looked like a business conversation, something to do with insurance, from what Rae could gather as Blythe smiled, put her finger up, to indicate she'd be just a minute.

'Aunty Rae?' Siggy said then, and she threw herself against Rae's legs and Rae felt her heart melt. She picked the child up, hugged her tight. Rae felt sure she would dissolve with love for the child. Oh, God, how had it come to this? That her time managed to become so filled up with the hotel and Marcus. No. She knew that wasn't true. The fact was, Marcus made sure the hotel stood as a barrier to her getting any time to call out to Still Water House. 'We're going to the... the...' She scrunched up her adorable little face. 'The *eternity* ward.' Siggy was at that adorable age, where she mightn't know the meaning of a word, but she was going to make a stab at pronouncing it anyway.

'What on earth?' Blythe put her arms around Rae. 'What are you doing here? Is everything alright?' Blythe stood back from her now, examining her with critical eyes, which just made Rae's hackles rise.

'I'm fine.'

'You're obviously not fine when you're sitting in a waiting room in the hospital,' Blythe said and they both dropped into the chairs set out for patients to queue until they were called for an appointment.

'It's nothing. My eye ducts are blocked and they think I might have to have a small operation to open them up, or maybe replace them...'

'Urgh.' Blythe shivered.

'It sounds ickier than it is,' Rae laughed. There would be anaesthetic, but the recovery would be worse than the procedure. 'Anyway, never mind all that, what about you two?'

'We were visiting the maternity ward, Kip's sister-in-law has just had a baby.'

'Of course, I had forgotten.' New babies were always a big deal on the island, that and deaths. Hatching and despatching were favourite conversation topics of the ladies who lunched in the hotel on Thursday afternoons.

'So, you're going back this evening?'

'Yes, I'm taking the bus, because…' Marcus complained so much about her driving, she'd all but given up taking the car out. It seemed every other time she went anywhere he managed to find a bump or scrape or some switch that she had broken, even though she never remembered causing any damage. Once, he spent a whole week complaining because a stray leaf had been left in the footwell after she'd used it.

'Bus? You'll come with us; I've brought the jeep.'

'Yaay, Aunty Rae is coming in the jeep.' Siggy jumped up and down with excitement.

'But, we'll go for lunch first,' Blythe said with authority.

'Oh, I can't, Marcus is expecting me back.'

'For goodness' sake, Rae, he can't spare you for five minutes to come and visit your own sister?' Talk about hitting the nail on the head. It had begun shortly after they were married, there was always some last-minute thing thrown in her way, so she had to cancel any plans to drop into Still Water House. And then, even if she did manage to escape the hotel for an hour or two, he sulked and argued with her for days afterwards, seething because he saw her visit as an act of disloyalty to him and the hotel and their marriage. It was as if he would always believe Blythe was plotting against him and Rae was so weak willed, she would fall in with some dire plan to take him down.

Nothing could be further from the truth.

All Rae wanted was to spend time with Blythe and Siggy. So many times, she longed to sink into the big old sofa in the drawing room and curl up next to Blythe to feel the comfort of her older sister next to her. It was such a strong physical ache sometimes, just thinking of Still Water House and her family, who she knew she was becoming more estranged from with every passing day, thanks to Marcus.

'Oh, come on, it's just lunch,' Blythe said. 'My treat.'

'Okay,' Rae said. 'I'd love to, if you're sure…' Not that she could offer to buy dinner for Blythe, well not unless Blythe fancied sharing fish and chips, because she hadn't much more than the bus fare in her pocket. Marcus controlled all the money in the hotel. He was meticulous about every little detail from the food stocks in the kitchen to the kilowatts it took to heat the place in every season.

'So, how are things?' Blythe asked when they were settled into a booth in what had once been their mother's favourite restaurant. It was dated now, of course, but miles from the beaten track. They were unlikely to bump into anyone here who would tell tales from school to Marcus. Silently, Rae was thankful to Blythe; perhaps her sister had picked this place for that very reason.

'Ah, you know, same as always.'

'You've lost weight,' Blythe was examining her now and the look of sadness in her eyes almost broke Rae. 'You know you could leave…'

'Don't.' Rae put up her hand and shook her head. Only Blythe would talk like this. Her sister had never been shy about saying what she thought needed to be said.

'He doesn't own you, Rae.' She shook her head, laughed a cruel, sardonic sound. 'He doesn't even own half the hotel, but he'd likely want to take it if you left.' The hotel still cut to the bone of the contention between Blythe and Marcus.

'That's not going to happen.' Rae said softly. She had ordered the salmon. Now, she wondered if she could face it. She dearly loved her sister, there were times when the physical yearning to see her niece almost made her feel ill, but the fact was, Blythe had a way of turning her inside out. Maybe because she could see right through her. Worse, she could see right through Marcus.

'Is that a bruise?' Blythe had spotted the purple mark on her arm. It was only visible because this blouse had become so loose, it slid up when Rae was reaching for the tartar sauce.

'No.' Rae pulled her arm back, covered it over with her sleeve again.

'Oh, Rae. You could stay with us, you don't have to…'

'Yaay, Rae is coming to our house!' Siggy was jumping up and down on the chair next to them and suddenly, the intensity of their conversation seemed to burst, 'can she stay in my room?' Siggy was singing now, so thrilled at this novelty event.

'Shh, Siggy, for heaven's sake, sit on your seat.' Blythe rolled her eyes, but she couldn't hide her smile. Siggy was adorable, you couldn't help but be joyful in her presence.

'Let's change the subject, shall we? I hear, someone is getting ready to start school this year?' Rae leant down towards Siggy and blew in her ear.

'Me. Me. Me.' The child made a sing-song out of the sentence.

'Well, I'll have to see you in your new uniform…' Rae smiled then. She looked at Blythe. 'Can you believe she's…' And then she felt the loosening of a tear in her eyes. She'd missed so much. 'It's only my tear ducts,' she said, dabbing her eyes.

'If you say so,' Blythe said, but she reached out and took Rae's hand across the table, squeezing it hard. 'Don't forget us, Rae, we're still here for you,' Blythe whispered as the waitress came and refilled their glasses of white wine.

Rae arrived back at the hotel, feeling both lighter after the time spent with Blythe and heavier at the thought of having to be back on Hope Square. She tried to push the feeling of unhappiness down in her, but it was a constant these days. She felt it as a sort of emptying of her spirit, as if life had pulled out a stopper and it was flowing down the drain.

By the time Rae realised, after they were married, what *having a bit of a temper* really meant, it was too late to end things. Of course, back then, she was young and in love and she couldn't see what had been right under her nose all along. Even if she had, what did she know of living with someone who made you feel you had to walk around them on your tippy toes, so as not to step on the shards of glass they scattered wilfully at your feet without warning.

Sometimes, she would look back and wonder, if things had worked out differently, would they all have been happier if she hadn't married Marcus? Or would it just be Rae who would have been happier, because there was no question now, she knew marrying Marcus had been the worst decision she'd ever made.

Blythe had been right all those years ago. Marcus had chosen her because he saw in her a slip of a girl who was weak. Someone who would bend to his will and God help her, but apologise, because she couldn't make two or three of herself to please him.

And there were no children. There never would be. Marcus made that quite clear a year into their marriage. Perhaps it was kinder than a someday approach, but Rae still looked in the mirror some days and thought – it's still not too late.

But then, the idea of going against Marcus – well, Blythe had said it once, years earlier – she was trapped.

'How come you're so late? I had to do six rooms out and the breakfasts and…'

'One of the machines was being serviced. The waiting room was full. Actually, I was lucky to make the last bus at all,' Rae lied. She'd never been good at lying, but she'd practised this, silently in the jeep while Blythe and Siggy sang 'The Wheels on the Bus' and she'd closed her eyes and tried her best not to sob.

'Hmph,' he said then, satisfied that maybe there wasn't much he could do about it. 'Anyway, what did they say?' He hardly looked at her. Honestly, sometimes she wondered if he even liked her anymore.

'I'll have to have the operation, but it'll be in a few weeks.'

'You did tell them it can't be in peak time?'

'I did.' She sighed and she wondered if she dropped down dead in the dining room, would he walk over her to deliver a scrambled egg breakfast to the paying guests. 'Anyway, it's been a long day. I'm tired.'

'Well, I don't know how you could be tired, I'm the one keeping the show on the road,' he said then and she wondered if he'd have a list of jobs for her to do before she turned in for the night. She hoped not. She hoped that she could just go to bed, lose herself in a book and close her eyes before he joined her in their uncomfortable marital bed.

'Did you pick up my inhaler?' he asked, because of course, there was a football match at the weekend and these days, that was his only real passion outside the hotel. He would sit in one of the bedrooms, lock the door, pull down the blinds and turn the TV on loud. In the early years of their marriage, it had frightened her, how involved he got in a match. The worst of his asthma attacks happened when he watched the county team – especially if they were taking a beating.

'Of course.' She handed him the pharmacy package from her handbag.

'Good.' He grunted, snatching it from her. He never said thanks. She'd stopped expecting it at this point.

45

Rae

Present

Rae stopped at the supermarket just as Mr Singh was closing for the evening. She had no idea what to feed puppies whose eyes had not yet opened, but she settled with Mrs Singh's approval on baby formula which appeared to have every added vitamin under the sun listed on the back of the pack.

She knew instantly as she turned into the square that something was wrong. Hugh Gilmore's garda-marked car was parked opposite the hotel with the blue light flashing.

'What's happened?' She screamed, leaping from the car and racing towards him.

'I'm sorry Rae.' He pointed towards the hotel. Now she could see it for herself. The ground floor, on one end of the building, was on fire. Through the windows, she could see flames licking up the curtains, smoke billowing out through the cracked open window.

'Oh, God.' She looked back at the car. Strangely, before even thinking of the damage to the hotel, she thought about the puppies. She had planned to go inside immediately and make up the formula for them. Now what?

'Rae, Rae, oh, God…' Blythe came running towards her. 'I had no idea.' She looked devastated, bereft, but Rae couldn't fully take in what she was saying because Blythe wasn't making any sense. 'My Siggy. My poor, poor Siggy. I'll never forgive myself. I can't take it. I really can't.'

'Rae.' Danial stood next to Blythe for a moment, he took her arm, pulled her slightly aside. 'I think Siggy is inside.' It was a whisper and yet, Rae felt as if it was so loud it shook her to the core.

'She can't be, she went home earlier…'

'Maybe, but I saw her come back,' he said then.

'Hugh. Did you tell Hugh?'

'He says we must wait for the fire engine. Have you got your keys?' he asked, but he didn't wait for her to answer. Instead, she watched as his eyes darted to her abandoned car and then, before she could say another word, he sprinted towards it. In grim fascination, she watched him, not quite sure what he was doing and at the same time, on some level, knowing she should stop him. He pulled the keys from the ignition. Sorted through them in an instant and then he was racing towards the front door of the hotel. He was like lightning. She never knew anyone to move so fast.

'Here son, come back, you can't do that, there's a protocol…' Hugh was labouring after him. 'What's his name again?' He looked back between Rae and Blythe.

'Danial. He's Danial,' Rae said softly. *Oh God.* What was happening?

'He's going into the hotel?' Blythe turned towards Rae as if somehow one of them might make more sense of what was happening, than the other.

'What happened?' Rae looked at Blythe now. 'No. Don't tell me. It doesn't matter, none of it matters anymore,'

Rae said and she knew it was the truth. If the whole place burned to the ground, it would be a relief at this point. She started to cry.

'It's alright, it'll be alright.' Hugh put his arm around her and said softly, 'The insurance will cover any damage and...' Then Hugh's radio blared, and he pulled away from her.

Rae could hear it, voices muffled across the static. The fire brigade was on their way. They would be here in less than fifteen minutes.

A lot could happen in fifteen minutes.

'Rachel.' It was Mrs Singh from the shop. She was probably the only person in the whole village who called Rae by her proper name. 'I...' She smiled sadly and then Rae saw, she was holding the puppies. 'I can take them back to the shop, look after them for you, until you're...' Her words trailed off.

'Oh, Mrs Singh, thank you so much.' Rae put her face down to the little pups again. They were sleeping now.

'It's the least I can do, I'm not going to be much help here standing about like...' She looked around and then Rae noticed that half the village had turned out and were standing in the square, staring fixedly at the hotel, their expressions horrified.

'You're welcome to stay with us, also, you know when...' she said kindly. Rae thought for a moment, it was a strange thing how in the very worst of times, you only then saw the very best of people.

'Thank you, Mrs Singh,' Rae said, although she wasn't even sure if the woman heard her above all the noise around them as the fire brigade had just arrived on the square and now there was so much rushing about that it was hard to focus on what you were thinking, much less saying.

'Did a kid run inside?' one of the firemen asked her.

'Yes. Danial. He went in through the front door. He's looking for my niece... I...' She could hardly speak.

'Siggy? Kip's kid?' he said, and she nodded then, because it was as much as she could manage. With that, he took off and Rae watched as they set to work unwinding hoses and getting to grips with putting out the flames.

Out of the corner of her eye, Rae spotted Melissa Val and Kip standing on the edge of the green. She walked over to them, her legs so shaky she wasn't sure how she was managing to put one in front of the other.

'You heard?' she said when she reached them.

'I'm so sorry, your lovely hotel.' Melissa stuck out her arms and pulled Rae towards her.

'No. No, Melissa, not that...' She mumbled, pulling away from her new friend. She looked into Kip's eyes and from there into Melissa's. 'It's Danial and Siggy...'

'God no, no, no,' Kip said, and she watched as he seemed to crumble into half his usual size before her eyes.

'What my Danial and Siggy, what is it?'

'Danial went inside to save Siggy, Melissa, I'm so sorry. I should have stopped him, but he was so fast, he just ran...' She couldn't of course, because she'd been reeling. Everything about this was wrong. And now, she watched as Kip scooped up Melissa as she seemed to lose her balance.

'I'm fine,' Melissa said, although she clearly was not fine. Kip held onto her because it looked as if she'd completely lost her balance. 'Oh, God, my head is swimming.' She staggered backwards again in shock.

'It's going to be okay,' Kip said and somehow, Rae knew, they had to believe him.

'I'll be fine in a minute. It's my blood pressure, the shock…' Melissa was saying, but her eyes had flooded with tears. And Rae couldn't help but think, this was all wrong, standing here with Kip, supporting Melissa while Blythe stood a little away, a spectral version of her usual self, grimly mesmerised by the flames engulfing the hotel.

46

Blythe

Present

The smoke was choking, filling her lungs and churning up her stomach. Blythe heard the front door of the hotel blast open. Even from here, standing across the street where they'd been pushed back to by the fire service, she could feel the flash of heat pouring out. The crowd around her surged forward and for a moment, it felt as if she was going to drown between or beneath them, but somehow, she kept herself upright, pushed through to the very front.

'Siggy?' Her voice was more like a keening moan than her own. 'Is that my Siggy?' She wiped the tears from her eyes, she could hardly see, not that she'd noticed that a moment ago.

'Danial, thank God, you are alive.' Melissa Val pressed past Blythe, elegant even in these circumstances, then she noticed Kip following the woman, his arm steadying her, being the strength he had always been quietly in the background for Blythe.

'Kip?' To Blythe, suddenly the word sounded so small, as if it no longer fitted in with her voice. Perhaps it never had. 'Siggy.' Because then, she saw the boy was carrying something. Something heavy, covered over in what looked like a sheet. Wet and clinging. Siggy? Blythe ducked under the cordon that had been set up to keep people back.

'Mrs Carney, no.' The local police sergeant tried to hold her back.

'Siggy,' she cried and she pushed past him. The boy had fallen on the road, dropped first to his knees to leave the sodden sheet and its contents safely on the ground. Then, he'd collapsed next to it.

It was Rae who moved the sheet back from Siggy's face. Blythe falling clumsily to her knees; it felt as if she'd been poured from a sack into a useless heap of insignificance on the road. She reached out, touched her daughter's face. It felt waxy and warm; cold and dead all at once. Next to them, the boy's grandmother was bent over Danial, rubbing his arms, folding him over to get fresh air into his lungs, and he seemed to be reviving with the effort of it.

But Siggy was quite still.

Blythe was vaguely aware of others around her, Kip and Rae and a man who was carrying out a first aid scan of her daughter's body, checking her breathing, checking her pulse. It was all happening in a confused blur around Blythe, who just sat there, emitting a gentle moan that frightened her. She couldn't stop the sound coming from her, would she be stuck like this forever – suspended in something worse than purgatory.

The man, she recognised him now, another of Kip's many friends. He was setting Siggy's head at an angle, preparing, Blythe knew, to do CPR.

She had stopped breathing.

The knowledge of it came to Blythe just as the man began the first set of compressions on Siggy's chest.

Another round.

Blythe had to remind herself to breathe, perhaps she could breathe for both herself and her daughter.

Another round of deep breaths. Again, a sequence of crushing compressions.

With each hammering, Blythe felt herself drown a little deeper.

This was her fault. All of it. Siggy lying in the street – half-alive, maybe already mostly dead. Danial, a young man who should have his life before him – a brave and good young man, as it turned out. Braver than any of the local boys, that was for sure. The hotel, probably destroyed beyond saving. And Rae.

Blythe looked around her. Rae was knelt next to her. Her eyes pinned to Siggy's face. If it was possible to love a child more than Blythe loved Siggy, she suspected that was what Rae felt for her niece.

'I'm so sorry.' Blythe whispered, but of course, no one heard her amid the chaos surrounding them. 'I'm so sorry.' She couldn't live with herself if Siggy didn't make it through this, Blythe knew that without any question.

And then, as if the whole world stood still, for one precious eternal and at the same time fleeting moment, she saw her daughter's chest rise.

She's breathing.

Someone said it. Blythe heard it like an extended sigh of relief. She's breathing.

Thank God.

She's breathing.

The district nurse, who must have just arrived, took over, working quickly, taking Siggy's pulse, her blood pressure, placing an oxygen mask on her face. She too, examined her for broken bones and other injuries, because then she was being slid onto a stretcher, by the local Order of Malta crew and swept up into the back of their ambulance.

Kip at her side, Blythe following.

'I'm sorry. There's only room for one person to travel with us,' the driver said and Blythe tried to speak, but she knew she had no right to say a word.

'I'm going.' Kip said and for once, she couldn't push him aside and have her own way. She had done this. All of it. She knew Kip knew it too.

Blythe backed away from the ambulance. Not sure what to do next, her heart breaking at the sound of the doors being banged shut. It was driving off, into the night, towards the air ambulance she could hear in the distance, her daughter being moved away from her.

She'd already lost her, though, Blythe knew that.

It was too late to undo the damage she had done.

'Blythe, come on.' It was Fiona, standing next to her now. How long had she been here? 'I'll take you to the hospital…' she said, and she was dragging her across the square to where her car was parked and ready.

'Why?'

'Why?' Fiona looked at her with a perplexed expression. 'I'll take you to the hospital, I've called Finbar, he'll meet us on the pier,' she said slowly as if Blythe had some sort of hearing problem. 'To be there when Siggy wakes up…'

'But,' Blythe had a feeling no one else would offer. Why would they? At this moment, her legs were too jittery to even get her car into gear, much less organise a boat to take her across to the mainland and travel from there to the hospital thirty-odd miles beyond. 'Fine,' she said and then she looked back at the hotel. It was ruined. The whole place was going to be destroyed at this point. The fire had taken over; the first floor was completely alight. The flames had risen, so now, she could see the upstairs rooms' window drapes were already dancing with fire. She stood for a moment, wrapped up in an eerie silence of her own making – watching as the Hope Square Hotel disappeared before her eyes.

47

Rae

Present

Rae had been completely honest when she told the fire officer at this point she didn't give a fig if there was nothing but the foundations left of the building by the time the fire was put out.

It was the truth. All she cared about was that Siggy and Danial were safe.

It felt like forever, but in fact, it was only hours.

She'd made her way to the hospital. Melissa was travelling with her grandson, but she'd need a lift home and some support while she waited to speak to the doctors.

By the time Rae found them in the A&E department, she was relieved to learn he was already sitting up and even if he was bruised and burned, his prognosis was good enough that he would be released from hospital within twenty-four hours.

'It's a precaution, if I insisted on taking him home, I think they'd let me, but it's better to stay, make sure that there is no concussion,' Melissa said, looking at her grandson with unmistakable love in her eyes.

For his part, Danial couldn't say very much, his face still covered over in an oxygen mask. He was hooked up to a drip for fluids.

'Have you heard if Siggy is...' Rae asked because she was sure Blythe wouldn't want her anywhere near her family at this point. All of this, she had a feeling was her fault – Blythe would blame her. She should never have put part of the hotel up for sale. At this moment, Rae felt as guilty as if she'd lit that damn fire herself.

'She is going to be fine,' Melissa said. 'One of the ambulance men came in to let us know. Danial managed to save her from any burns by wrapping her in the soaking sheet, but her lungs are going to take some time to recover.'

'Thank God for that.' Rae felt as if a huge weight had been lifted from her chest.

'I think she's in ICU, but you'll have to check.'

'I don't think I'll be very welcome.' Rae began to cry. It was probably relief. Danial and Siggy were both going to be okay. Thank God.

'None of this is your fault, Rae.' It was Jay Larkin. He too must have dodged past the busy nurses outside to check that Danial was okay. 'Now, you need to pull yourself together.' He put his arm around Rae, which only made her cry more.

'Look,' he said when the tears subsided. 'This young man is a hero. Siggy is going to be fine, alright, so it may take a few days for her to get back on her feet, but maybe, all of this...' Jay stopped for a moment as if he was going to say the most difficult thing that he'd ever had to say. 'Well, it can be surprising how a near disaster can put things into perspective. I'd say even Blythe might look at things differently after tonight.'

'She was there, too,' Danial whispered as he tugged at the oxygen mask to move it from his mouth.

'What's that, darling?' Melissa leant in more closely to hear her grandson speak.

'I saw her, walking around the hotel, she had...' His breath was still ragged, his voice thin, shaking and hardly more than a whisper.

'Don't strain yourself son, there'll be plenty of time later, you can tell us all about it,' Jay said softly.

'No. No. I think Mrs Carney did this, I think she set the hotel on fire...' He stopped, looked from one of them to the other.

'Blythe?' Rae felt as if she'd been pushed backwards, right off her feet, as if the ground beneath her had turned to something malleable and maybe she would never feel what it was to stand on solid earth again. 'Blythe torched the hotel?' she repeated, because there had to be some mistake, surely? Blythe loved the hotel, far more than Rae did, that was for sure. 'No. Blythe would never...'

'If it wasn't going to be the Hope Square Hotel anymore, maybe...' Jay said gently.

'Oh, my God. She could have killed all of us.' And then, Rae remembered seeing her on the road earlier. Blythe knew she wasn't there. She mustn't have realised that Siggy had returned to the hotel later. 'Oh, my God.' She felt herself fall backwards. Melissa stepped forward, grabbed her around her waist, guided her to the only available chair in the cubicle. 'Blythe did this? All of this, oh no. Oh, no. Blythe – how could you?'

Blythe may have set fire to the hotel, or she may not, but ultimately, the blame for everything as far as Rae was concerned lay firmly at her own door. This was the train of thought careering around Rae's mind as she tried to push open the door of the intensive care unit. Of course, it was locked. She noticed then a keypad on the side and a serious-looking sign that said, *Immediate family only. One visitor per patient permitted.*

So, that was that. She pressed her face up against the glass panel in the door, on the off chance that Siggy was in one of the open-fronted cubicles opposite. No such luck. She dropped down onto a faux leather bench, completely and utterly emptied out by it all. She started to cry again – was this it?

Was this her life now? No family. Nowhere to call her own either, because let's face it, if the hotel was at this point burned to the ground, she no longer had a home, much less a business.

'Oh.' It was an exclamation more than a greeting but when Rae looked up, she saw Blythe standing across from her.

'How is she?' Rae dried her eyes roughly. Her voice wobbled, unsure if she was being confronted by a friend or foe.

'She's going to be fine,' Blythe said, and even she sounded different to her usual no-nonsense self. 'By some miracle, she's going to be fine.'

'Thank God for that.' It was the confirmation that Rae needed. She'd already heard, but she needed to see for herself, just to be sure, because at this point, it felt as if nothing could be depended on.

'Kip is with her now, but if you want to go in next…' Blythe said, and she dropped to the bench on the opposite side of the corridor.

'What about you?' Rae asked because after all, Blythe was Siggy's mother, Rae was only an aunt.

'I…' Then the strangest thing happened.

Blythe began to cry.

Blythe, who she'd known all her life, had never cried before anyone. Even when their parents died, she had kept her grief to herself. Rae had never once seen her drop a tear, although she remembered a time when Blythe had cried herself to sleep every night, that had been behind a closed door in a dark room where she believed she could not be heard.

'Oh, Blythe, I'm so sorry for what I've done. Putting the hotel up for sale....' Rae said then and she moved to the bench next to her sister and put her arms around her.

'You're sorry? What on earth have you to be sorry for? You've done nothing, your whole life, you've just tried to keep the peace and make everyone happy, you've...'

'You make me sound like a saint and I'm a long, long way off that...' Rae said, because even if Blythe didn't know it, Rae knew now that she was going to sell the hotel, if she could, if anyone would buy what remained of it from her. She would sell it and she would start again.

'I started the fire, Rae.'

'I know,' Rae said simply and then Blythe looked at her as if to check she'd heard what she'd said.

'And I almost killed Siggy. And that boy...' Blythe started to cry again. 'I got it all so wrong, didn't I?'

'How were you to know?'

'Oh Rae, seriously?' Blythe shook her head, moved out of Rae's embrace. 'I can't face Siggy now.'

'Blythe, we're sisters. No matter what happened, no matter what you've done, we'll always be the Hope Square sisters, and I will stand by you through this.' She pulled Blythe to her once more and this time, they fell against each, clinging desperately, and they both cried, but there was comfort at least, in being together.

48

Rae

Eighteen Months Earlier

The Americans may have been celebrating the Superbowl that day, but in Ireland, all anyone could talk about was the Six Nations, Ireland versus Italy match. Rae had little or no interest in it, which was just as well. The hotel was empty. They'd had a wedding, a lovely couple, Tony and Mark – they'd come down with a bunch of friends and family and stayed for three days with their ceremony celebrated in the conservatory at the back of the hotel. Rae had watched as the two men exchanged vows. They were so in love, it made her heart crack. This, she thought, not for the first time over the years, is exactly how Blythe had planned to use this space. Blythe. She'd worked so hard to bring the conservatory back to life. She'd done all the hard work herself. Pappy had been dubious about it. He really should have known better. Blythe's instincts were never wrong.

Rae planned to spend the day clearing away the remains of the weekend. There were several loads of table linen washing, before she even got to the beds.

She had switched on the washing machine with the second load when she realised her mistake. There, resting against the glass was Marcus's brand new inhaler. It must have been on one of the tables and folded in with the cloths without her noticing it. Already, the machine was filled up with water, there was no stopping it until the cycle ended. It was too late.

Rae felt the blood rush from her head. If Marcus saw what she'd done, there'd be hell to pay. The last time she'd washed one with their own laundry, he had hit her so hard, she'd been knocked against the staircase, and she'd fallen, bruising her back and neck so badly it had winded her for several days. She could have broken a rib, for all she knew, but there was no point telling Marcus she needed to go to a doctor.

Hugh, the local garda sergeant, had spotted the bruising when she bent to take glasses from the washer at the bar. He had not asked her what had happened, but when they were away from other ears, he touched her arm. 'You don't have to stay with him, you know? You just say the word and half this island would be lining up to help you...'

'Oh, Hugh, I just fell, that's all.'

'Yeah, right.' He stood back a little, because Marcus had walked into the bar.

'What?' Marcus said, but Rae could see, he was not his usual confident self.

'I'm just saying, it's good we live on a small island, we can all look out for each other. For our own, at any rate.' Hugh said, keeping his eyes on Marcus, and Rae thought she'd faint with the discomfort of just standing there between them. Then he looked at Rae. 'You know where I am, Rae.' He said then before turning and walking out the door.

That was a year ago.

Rae tried to think. Was there a second inhaler in the hotel? Marcus would come looking for this one before the match. She needed to find one and replace it for him. She ran to the flat, rifled with shaking hands through the drawers in the locker by their bed. Nothing. Then the bathroom cabinet. Again, no luck. Perhaps there was a puff or two left in one of the older ones she thought. She raced down to the recycling. The game was starting in half an hour. Not long. Certainly not long enough to make it to the mainland, even if there was a chemist shop open on a Sunday, which there definitely wasn't.

In the shed she found the small container where Marcus stored old batteries, aerosols and yes, inhalers for recycling. She pulled the only one that was there out. It'll be fine she told herself. She held it up to the window, checking the date. Took off the cap, squeezed the end. It made a sound, but it was all but empty.

She checked her watch again. Went back to the container, even though she knew that she had the only one in her hand. It would be okay. Maybe he wouldn't need it.

As she raced up the path to the back door of the hotel, the inhaler in her hand, she wondered, should she just tell him her mistake?

It could happen to anyone, couldn't it? I mean, he must have left it on one of the tables to begin with, it was hardly entirely her fault. No. She knew Marcus; he wasn't rational about these things. He would fly into a rage. There would be no watching the football, not without an inhaler. He got too caught up in the action. He nearly always ended up having an asthma attack. She tucked the inhaler in her pocket, surely, just this once it would be fine.

She spotted him in the flat, searching through the same drawers she'd searched through a few minutes earlier. Already, he was becoming irritated. He hated losing things.

'Okay?' she asked, although a part of her wanted to run to the furthest part of the hotel, maybe to the tree house as she would have as a girl with Blythe, to escape his anger.

'No. Not okay. What did you do with my inhaler?' he said angrily.

'Me?' Rae said and for a moment, she teetered between two worlds. One, a familiar place, full of resentment and bitterness and loneliness; another an escape. She felt the inhaler in her pocket..

'Who else? Aren't you always putting things in strange places?' He shook his head as if he had completely run out of patience. 'I don't know, some of these days, you'll put yourself away and no one will question what's happened to you,' he said softly and she knew it was a threat. He'd been making them for years. Usually, they centred around falling down the stairs or being electrocuted in the bath. For years, she'd had nightmares thinking of what he might do to her. She always took extra care to lock the bathroom door and move the laundry basket behind it, just in case.

'Is it this?' she said then and her voice felt as if it came from very far away as she produced the inhaler from her pocket.

'I might have known.' He snatched it from her hand and stalked past her, so close he almost sent her spinning off her feet.

It was a funny thing, walking the beach later that afternoon. Knowing he was sitting there, watching the match, probably drinking a beer, maybe reaching for his inhaler.

Rae felt as if the world had stilled. She felt calm, almost serene.

When she returned to the hotel, a good hour after the match was over, the linens drying slowly in the stables, there was no sign of him. She walked upstairs quietly, so quietly it was as if she was afraid to wake the dead.

Because the hotel was empty of guests, he had left the door unlocked. When she pushed it open, somehow, she wasn't shocked. She wasn't even sad. She noticed the half-drunk glass of beer on the table next to him. The inhaler on the floor. She didn't cross the room to close his eyes or check if he was breathing. Taking a deep breath, she pulled out her phone to call the ambulance.

49

Siggy

Present

Siggy came round gradually. She'd been aware for a time, before she realised where she was, that there was an ache in her body that felt as if she'd been crushed beneath a herd of elephants. When she tried to move, she realised, the pain was worse in her chest, as if the heaviest elephant had sat there for the longest time.

'Siggy.' Her father was holding her hand. His expression was creased into a million lines of worry. Her eyes bounced around the ward. She was in hospital. But it was so quiet, nothing but beeps and hushed noises, as if someone had padded the place out with cotton wool to soundproof it from reality.

'What happened?' she whispered. It was only now she realised her throat felt as if it had been sandpapered dry. 'Can I...' She looked towards the small paper cup in his hand.

'Ice, I'm afraid that's your lot for now.' He smiled at her, relief flooding his features. He was crying, but she had a feeling these were tears of joy.

'What… how did I get here?' she croaked.

'Long story.' He shook his head. 'The hotel went on fire. We were lucky young Danial Val spotted you going into the place. He ran in, risked his life to get you out of it, darling girl, you're lucky to be alive.' He started to cry again, big silent tears racing down his cheeks.

'The hotel caught fire? How? I mean…'

'I don't think they properly know, but it was… The guards will be looking into it, but none of that is important. All that matters is you are okay. The doctors say, a little rest and you'll be fine.'

'So… I don't understand, I mean…'

'Little girl, there isn't a mark on you, we are so lucky, it could have been a very different story.'

'Where's Mum?' Because suddenly, Siggy had the most terrible fear creep over her. Her mother should be here. Had she gone into the fire too?

'Don't worry. She's here. She's fine. She went to get a cup of coffee. Only one of us can be here at a time and so…' His voice trailed off; there was something he wasn't telling her. That was the thing about her dad, he didn't know how to make a poker face – so much so, he never bothered trying.

'I'll get her, if you want…' He started to get up.

'Hang on, what about Rae? And Danial, are they alright?'

'They're fine. Rae wasn't even in the hotel when it went up. And Danial – well, I'd say he's the village hero after this. He's got a few bruises and some burns, but nothing that's going to keep him down for very long. He'll be out of here by tomorrow morning.'

'That's good.' A good measure of tension seeped from her body with that. Everyone was okay. 'And the hotel? What's that like now?'

'Honestly, I don't know, but I'd say it's a goner.'

'That bad?'

'Siggy, when something like this happens and you realise what you have to lose, it's amazing how your perspective changes. Your mother would have knocked that place to the ground to get you out of it safe and sound,' he said sadly.

'What about Rae? What will she do now?' Because the hotel wasn't just her aunt's job, it was her home too. It was all she had, really, apart from walking on the beach and going to her Soroptimists' meetings.

'Rae is going to be fine. She always had her priorities in the right order; she knows that life doesn't begin or end just because of bricks and mortar. She's not as sentimental about the place as you might think.'

'But where will she live?'

'Anywhere she wants to, I suppose. There'll be insurance. She can live with us, if she fancies it – Rae will be fine, don't you worry. Now, I'm going to get your mother, she needs to see for herself that you're alright.' He bent down and kissed the top of her head and all the worries she'd had about him and Fiona seemed suddenly to amount to nothing. He was her dad and now, in this moment, that was all that mattered.

'Oh, darling Siggy.' Her mother looked a lot worse than Siggy felt. 'I thought... I really thought...' She dropped down on the chair next to Siggy's bed. 'Thank God, you're okay, I can face anything so long as you're alright.'

'Mum, what on earth?' Siggy had never seen her mother so diminished. It was as if she had somehow contracted by a good sixty per cent, so now, she was a watered-down version of her usual self. 'I'm alright, come on, it's grand.' Although the more she spoke and tried to pull herself up on the pillow, the more it felt as if gravity had multiplied and it was dragging her back down. 'Really, there's no need to be upset.'

'Didn't your father tell you?' She was as pale as the moon.

'Tell me what?' Siggy felt her heart dropping like a stone in her chest. 'What else? Someone didn't make it? Who?'

'No. Not that. It's me.'

'I don't understand.' Siggy tried to reach out to take her mother's hand, but there was no reaching it, and her mother didn't move to bridge the gap.

'I did it. I set the hotel on fire. This is all my fault. I almost killed my own child – I don't deserve to be here. I don't deserve you. I never did, nor Kip neither, although I'm only realising it when it's too late.'

'Mum, seriously, you did not set the hotel on fire. You wouldn't, you just wouldn't.' Siggy was almost laughing, but she knew even as she said the words, all she felt was a growing hysteria working its way through her brain, into her body, along her nerve endings. 'You're wrong. You love the hotel. You're in shock. That's it. You're just in shock.'

'No. Siggy. No. I know what I did and now...' She hung her head and everything about her spoke of a deep shame.

'Why on earth would you do something like that?' But maybe Siggy already knew. It would be about letting the place go. She wouldn't be able to stomach someone else owning even a square foot of the Hope Square Hotel.

'You know.' Her mother looked at her now.

'Better to burn the place to the ground than let anyone else have it?' Siggy said and her voice was dry, but this time, not just because it felt as if she'd been dehydrated on industrial levels.

'I'm such a terrible person. That's exactly how I felt.'

'And now?'

'I'm so sorry. I've been wrong about everything.'

'Oh Mum, don't say that.' She was talking about that terrible fight they'd had. 'I said awful things to you, things I didn't mean...'

'But you were right, you were right about it all. I have no place telling you that you should stay or go and...' She looked so miserable. 'The thing is, Siggy, I thought by keeping you on the island, I could keep you safe, but look at what happened, you almost died, right there on Hope Square.' Then she sat a little taller, firming up that backbone everyone knew her for. 'You were right. Danial Val is worth ten times any of us. He saved your life when I might have been responsible for...' She stopped. 'And the worst thing is, it was me.'

'Shush, Mum, you didn't mean it. You were just stressed, I mean, look at the last few weeks.'

'No, Siggy. Not that.' She shook her head, looked down at the floor as if she wanted it to swallow her up. 'I sent that vile text. I put the rumour out around the village that Danial was a wrong one. I wanted to split you two up, to get rid of him, because I...' She stopped. 'Well, before any of this meant anything to me, I had a... an experience. And it scared me and since then, I've judged everyone that isn't... like us,' she looked at Siggy now, to see if she understood. 'That isn't,' she sighed, 'one of us. I'm sorry. I've judged them all, simply because of one terrible thing. I'm so, so sorry, my darling. For everything.'

Outside the cubicle, the nurses had begun to flap about and Siggy tried but failed to see what was happening.

'I'm sorry,' a nurse poked her head around the door, 'but the police are here to arrest you,' she stopped, suddenly embarrassed, looking from one to the other of them.

'It's probably nothing,' she smiled unevenly at Siggy. 'Just a chat. Right?'

'It's okay,' her mother said then. She bent down and kissed Siggy's head, stayed close to her, for just a second longer. 'I have to go now, but I love you, Siggy, don't forget that, no matter what happens, yes?' she said and then she rose from the chair, stood for a moment as if she was taking in everything about her now completely shell-shocked daughter for the final time and then she turned towards the door and walked out of the ward.

'I love you too, Mum,' she whispered when she caught sight of a young guard stepping forward to read her mum her rights, before leading her off down the corridor and away from Siggy. And that was when it hit her, exactly how much trouble her mother could really be in for setting fire to the hotel.

50

Kip

Fifteen Months Later

It was a week after the trial before it all felt real to Kip. Siggy too, seemed to move through the house like a ghost, as if she was almost afraid to believe that it was over. Blythe had been lucky. Well, if you could call a five-year suspended sentence good luck.

'It's beyond lucky. It's far more lenient than I deserve,' she said as they sat on the rug before the fire in the drawing room. The old sheep dog was snoring and on the sofa two cats were wrapped up in each other, they were all just comforted to be cosy inside Still Water House, while a storm raged in the chimney. They had shut the doors of the guest house, for now at any rate. Blythe needed a break, maybe they all did; everyone deserved to take a little holiday now and again. They had no plans to reopen the place. Kip was enjoying having his home to himself and his family, being able to wander about in his bare feet with a mug of tea in his hand, without bumping into some stranger on the stairs. It was, he realised, the most splendid luxury.

'Don't say that, Mum.'

'It's true.'

'It's what *you* think, but there isn't a living soul on Pin Hill that agrees with you, and there's no denying that.' Kip pulled her close to him. They were drinking mulled cider. The apples were picked from the garden – the end of this year's crop, not nearly so abundant as last year's, but Blythe had steeped them in cloves, star of anise and a cocktail of spices that had been lying about in the larder.

'Everyone was very kind. It was far more than I deserve,' Blythe said then. But she was wrong, because just a week earlier, the courthouse on the mainland was packed to standing room only. Half the island residents had travelled across to support her. Instead of a victim impact statement, one after the other, so many of their neighbours and friends had stood up and spoken of the good things that Blythe had done for them over the years.

'People just told the truth, that's all,' Rae said. She was curled up with her three dogs on the deepest and oldest sofa nearest the fireplace. 'Blythe, you've gone out of your way to help so many islanders over the years, people don't just forget that sort of kindness.' Their solicitor said it was the first time she'd ever seen a judge cry on the bench. Even Danial Val had stood up and told the court, he held no ill will towards her. He, above anyone, persuaded the judge that Blythe's actions were a moment of madness, regretted as quickly as they were done. You would have to be made of stone not to be moved by it all. The end result was when her sentence – suspended – had been handed down, Blythe had stood in the open court and sobbed like a baby. First time ever, but it had unlocked something further in her. Rather than diminishing her, Kip felt as if it had set her free, allowing herself to be so vulnerable in such a public way proved liberating in a different way to avoiding a jail term.

Rae sipped her apple cider. 'This is delicious,' she made a point of sniffing it deeply. 'I feel as if I've landed in heaven,' she said, nestling further beneath the dogs.

'I'm so glad you came to stay here in the end,' Blythe reached up and squeezed her hand gently.

'Yeah, it's great having you here,' Siggy said, because of course, Rae seemed to be as much like Siggy's sister as she was Blythe's.

'I thought it would be strange, you know coming back here after all these years, but it really does feel like coming home.' Rae stopped. Kip marvelled at how the sisters skirted around any mention of how things had ended up. Although, one evening, after quite an amount of sloe gin, Rae admitted that she too had felt robbed of the life she'd always dreamed of, but the moment passed and Kip was glad to see that for the first time in years, Blythe really seemed to have let the whole thing go.

'It's bloody good to have you both here, though,' Kip said for the umpteenth time and pulled Blythe close to him. And, then, as had happened so many times over the last week, Siggy and Rae threw themselves on the pair of them and they all began to cry, until they started to laugh. It really felt as if they were getting a second shot, at everything.

Kip fully expected Blythe to kick up a fuss when he suggested they have a celebratory dinner to mark Siggy starting college. The idea of their daughter taking off for Dublin was the one thing Blythe had always banked against, but with everything that had happened, now it seemed as if all bets were off.'

The one thing that hadn't changed was that Kip loved Blythe as much now as he ever had, maybe seeing her so vulnerable these past few months had made him love her even more, if that was possible. Whatever crazy notions his wife had about something going on between himself and Fiona had been as ridiculous as snow in the Sahara. Thank goodness Blythe finally managed to come to her senses. The gulf between them had been all about letting Siggy grow up and become independent. There had only, ever, been one woman for Kip.

A few days later, they were in the kitchen, putting away some groceries. Siggy and Rae had gone out walking the dogs across the fields. They probably wouldn't be back for hours yet.

'A party?' she'd repeated after he mooted the idea first. 'To celebrate?' And for a moment, he worried that maybe it was a step too far.

'It's just, it's a big moment for her, you know, going to college, a new phase in her life and...' He stopped, because they both knew in many ways, it was a bigger step for Blythe.

'I think it's a marvellous idea,' she said, gripping a jar of coffee to her chest as if it was the holy Bible. Her eyes brightened up in a way he couldn't remember in years. 'Something simple, a dinner, here at the house, her favourite – roast lamb, all the trimmings, I'll organise everything,' she said then.

'Really, Blythe, there's no need to take it all on yourself, I'm happy to...'

'Oh, Kip, it's the least I can do,' she said, although she'd been working like a demon in the garden all summer. 'I need her to know that she has my blessing.'

'If the weather is nice, maybe we could have it outside,' he said because, thanks to Blythe's work, the grounds were particularly spectacular now.

'Sure, we could take a table outside and...' She stopped. 'Kip?' She stood up, she'd begun cleaning out an already pristine cupboard beneath the sink.

'Yep?' he turned to look at her; there was something slightly off in the way she said his name.

'Do you think we could ask the Vals to come as well?'

'To our little celebration?' He thought about it for a moment. They'd always marked every occasion just among themselves – family-only affairs to celebrate birthdays, communion, confirmation – they'd invited Rae and Marcus, of course, and his own family, but outside of that, never anyone who was not related. 'I suppose we can ask.' As far as he knew, Melissa Val bore Blythe no ill will. Like everyone else in the village, she just felt sorry for her by the time her case went to trial.

'It's just that since they are going away together and...' She stopped and for a moment, he thought she might cry once again. 'I'm not trying to make things better with them, I just...' She'd already apologised, and he knew it was with genuine remorse. He had a feeling that Melissa and Danial knew it too. Even though Siggy and Danial would be staying in digs very close to each other near the university, it still didn't mean they'd want to spend an evening in Blythe's company any time soon.

'I know...' His heart ached to see the reduction in someone who had been such a force of nature and now was condensed to little more than the rest of them. Sometimes, he thought, it was like watching a god become mortal. 'Do you want me to ask them?' he said, because he could put it in a way that they didn't have to feel obliged to say yes.

'Would you?' And again, he thought, how pathetic she seemed in herself, and it made his heart twist with a sadness like he'd never felt before. 'And of course, we'll have Rae too...'

The weather Gods were shining down on them on the evening of the celebratory dinner. All week, the sun had shone, warming up the ground and the walls of the old orchard where in the end, they had decided would be best to sit, to avoid any stray westerly winds. He helped Blythe drag out an old table from his workshop.

Tonight, Blythe had covered it with a blue and white gingham tablecloth. She had gone searching in the old stables and found a selection of brass lamps, which she'd cleaned and shined and put candles inside. These were set on the orchard walls and along the path around the table. From the kitchen, there was an aroma of cooking lamb, fresh mint and roasting buttered potatoes – she really had gone all out.

Their guests were due to arrive at seven – a reasonable hour, too late and the evening chill would have set in, despite the warm weather.

With twenty minutes to go, Blythe walked from the kitchen, down the path towards Kip. He was kneeling beneath the table, trying hard to even things out, fixing the wobble that was as much down to the age of the table as it was to the uneven paving beneath it.

'Here,' she said, and she bent down next to him, tucking her head beneath the tablecloth. 'Have some...' She held out her glass of wine to him.

'I can't quite...' He couldn't fix the blessed thing, and he knew how much something like a wonky table could really annoy her.

'Don't worry about it, no one will notice,' she smiled at him, and he almost lost his breath – something about the proximity of her, the smell of freshly-washed hair and the twinkle that seemed to just about have made it back into her eyes, disconcerted him.

'Are you sure?' he said a little hoarsely.

'I'm sure.' They walked across to the old swinging bench where she had unfolded a woollen blanket earlier. 'Let's sit for a minute before they arrive,' she said and she handed him the glass.

Upstairs, through the open window, he could hear Siggy humming as she got ready for the evening. Blythe hadn't allowed her to do one thing in preparation, only get herself ready. She sounded happy, their little girl was suddenly all grown up.

'Ah, so this is where you're hiding,' Rae came into the orchard.

'You're back!' Blythe said as if Rae had been gone for a week.

'I got delayed, sorry.' Rae made a face. 'The whole village is talking about Shakira English.' Rae was never one to gossip.

'Let me guess...'

'You know what I'm going to say already.' Rae shook her head sadly. 'She and her boyfriend were arrested for those robberies, so that's that.'

'That's that,' Kip said and he couldn't help but feel sad that it came as no surprise, but at least, any lingering whispers about Danial would be put to bed.

'Oh, Blythe, it's beautiful.' Rae nodded towards the table, and she sat down next to Kip on the swing.

'Oh, it's nothing.' Blythe stood up and walked across to the table, filling a glass of wine for Rae.

'Liar, you've been flat out all week getting this ready,' Rae giggled.

'Shush, don't let me down,' Blythe laughed then too. 'Actually, I've enjoyed it. It's sort of got me thinking.' She turned now to look at Kip.

'Here we go,' he could feel a rush of that familiar old excitement in the air.

'I've been thinking about the hotel... I'd like to rebuild it.' She looked from him to Rae.

'You and Kip?' Rae's eyes danced with excitement. 'You'd do that, start again...'

'If Kip was up for it, yes, and of course, if you didn't mind...'

'Mind? I think it would be the most wonderful thing.'

'A whole new adventure?' Kip said thoughtfully, then he linked his fingers through Blythe's, squeezed her hand in his. 'I'm up for it, if you are...' Because of course, they were too young to retire and settle for clearing back the garden or mending the occasional broken fence.

'To our next adventure...' Blythe said, and she wrapped his fingers around hers on the stem of the glass and then held it up to toast a new beginning for all of them.

'And I could stay on here?' Rae said softly. The dogs were racing around the orchard, picking up fallen apples, and dropping them again. This place suited her, it always had, she'd never wanted any other life.

'Of course, this has always been your home, Rae...' Blythe said softly.

And in that moment, sitting here, watching the sky turn orange and pink, Kip felt happy too. Happy that his wife and sister were as close again as they had been as the young Hope Square girls, happy to be sitting next to Blythe, ready to begin the next chapter of their lives together. This, he thought as he handed her back the glass to sip from too, this is how I always dreamed our family would be – simple and perfect, together.

The End.

Acknowledgements

THIS BOOK is dedicated to Bernadine Cafferkey-Barrett. Sister, best friend, fashion inspiration and saver of bacon many times over. Thanks for putting up with me xx

Big confession – this book was not written in one sitting, rather, it's been on my desk top for over a year, being picked apart and put together thanks to a fantastic team of lovely people. I am very grateful to have had Vicki Mellor at my side; a publishing director who really is so much more. I'm so glad we're working together on another Pin Hill story, Vicki, this book would not be what it is without your brilliant insights and dedication to getting it just right.

Team Aria once again have been truly superb to work with, there are so many names and hopefully, I'll get everyone in but here goes....

Huge thanks are due to Holly Humphreys, Jo Liddiard, Shannon Hewitt, Nikky Ward, Lydia Forbes, Charlie Hiscox, Zoe Giles, Yasmeen Doogue-Kahn, Sophie Dawson, Rhian McKay, Nicola Bigwood, Jessie Price, Gemma Gorton, Leah Jacobs-Gordon, Wilhelmena Asaam and here in Ireland – Lorraine Levis, Lana Morrison, Hannah Cronin and Cormac Kinsella.

My thanks to Super-Agent – Judith Murdoch, I count myself very lucky to be a J girl. Thanks are also due to Rebecca and Nick and all at David Luxton and Associates who handle film and foreign rights.

Thank you to all those who champion my books near and far, booksellers, bloggers, reviewers and booklovers.

I am grateful to you, the reader, for picking up my book. I hope you really enjoy spending time with the Sisters of Hope Square and the rest of the islanders on Pin Hill.

In the real world of writing and editing this book there was family Hogan, Seán, Roisín, Tomás, Cristín and Granny Christine – for whom I am grateful every single day.

A special thank you to James, for not alone sharing this journey with me, but very often, making it possible.

About the Author

FAITH HOGAN is an award-winning, million copy bestselling author. She is a *USA Today* Bestseller, *Irish Times* Top Three and an Amazon UK Number 1 Best Selling writer of twelve contemporary fiction novels. Her books have featured as Book Club Favorites, Netgalley Hot Reads and Summer Must Reads; *The Bookshop Ladies* was shortlisted for an An Post Book Award in 2024. She writes grown up women's fiction which is unashamedly uplifting, feel-good and inspiring, and she writes twisty contemporary crime fiction as Geraldine Hogan.

She lives in the west of Ireland with her family and their Labrador named Penny. She's a writer, reader, enthusiastic dog walker and reluctant jogger – except of course when it is raining!

You can find her on Instagram @faithhoganauthor.